Collateral

Also by De'nesha Diamond

The Parker Crime Chronicles
Conspiracy
Collusion
Collateral

The Diva Series
Hustlin' Divas
Street Divas
Gangsta Divas
Boss Divas
King Divas
Queen Divas

Anthologies
Heartbreaker (with Eric S. Gray and Nichelle Walker)
Heist and *Heist 2* (with Kiki Swinson)
A Gangster and a Gentleman (with Kiki Swinson)
Fistful of Benjamins (with Kiki Swinson)
No Loyalty (with A'zayler)

Collateral

DE'NESHA DIAMOND

KENSINGTON BOOKS
www.kensingtonbooks.com

KENSINGTON BOOKS are published by

Kensington Publishing Corp.
119 West 40th Street
New York, NY 10018

All Kensington titles, imprints, and distributed lines are available at special quantity discounts for bulk purchases for sales promotion, premiums, fund-raising, and educational or institutional use.

Special book excerpts or customized printings can also be created to fit specific needs. For details, write or phone the office of the Kensington Sales Manager: Kensington Publishing Corp., 119 West 40th Street, New York, NY 10018. Attn. Sales Department. Phone: 1-800-221-2647.

Dafina and the Dafina logo Reg. U.S. Pat. & TM Off.

ISBN-13: 978-1-4967-0588-4
ISBN-10: 1-4967-0588-2
First Kensington Trade Paperback Printing: December 2020

ISBN-13: 978-1-4967-0590-7 (ebook)
ISBN-10: 1-4967-0590-4 (ebook)
First Kensington Electronic Edition: December 2020

10 9 8 7 6 5 4 3 2 1

Printed in the United States of America

Prologue

Just do it. Jump.

Shalisa Young stood on top of the St. Elizabeth Hospital building, in the dead of night, while the rain plastered her thin gown to her body. Numb, she felt neither the rain's growing intensity nor the icy wind. All she cared about was ending it.

The needles.

The buzzing voices.

The pain.

Life.

The moon glimmered off the Potomac, transforming it into black glass. It was beautiful. The view of the city was also beautiful. Maybe she'd miss it.

"Ms. Young," a nurse screamed from behind her. "You don't want to do this!"

Shalisa let the words wash over her. The woman didn't know what the hell Shalisa wanted. *They* just wanted to keep pumping her with drugs. Drugs that made it difficult for her to think.

"Shalisa, sweetheart. Talk to me. You don't want to do this. Please." The nurse crept forward. She wasn't alone. Shalisa heard the soft shoes of the orderlies steadily approaching. No doubt they thought that they could snatch her back from the edge before she leaped.

Like the last time.

But last time she'd been weak. A small part of her had still believed that there had been a mistake, believed that she hadn't done what everyone said she had. She hoped—prayed—for the day when her mother would walk into her bedroom and say that it had been a horrible nightmare.

Shalisa now understood that day was never going to come. She'd *killed* her mother.

Tears splashed her face and mingled with the rain. She hadn't meant to do it. She had been angry with people constantly hounding her about when she was going to get better. The doctors. The pills. The disappointment.

No one understood why she couldn't get better like Tomi Lehane had. She'd breezed through college and now worked at the *Washington Post*. How come she was able to put everything behind her? How was it that she was happy and successful?

"Shalisa, please," the nurse pleaded. "Back away, and let's go inside!"

My mother. My sweet mother. The one who'd turned the city upside down looking for her when Craig Avery kidnapped her. The one who'd held prayer vigils and tacked posters in every neighborhood. Shalisa couldn't understand how she could've done such a thing. She'd just wanted her mother to leave her alone for a little while.

She hadn't wanted to hurt her.

She hadn't wanted to kill her.

But somehow she had—just by *thinking* about it one night.

The orderlies closed in.

Shalisa tugged in a deep breath and stepped off the ledge.

———

Dr. Zacher arrived at the city morgue clutching a black lion's-head walking cane. The chief medical examiner, Paul Mitchell, had been roused out of bed to meet the doctor and his assistant there personally. Security cameras monitoring the property outside and inside the facility had been shut down. The doctor signed no visitors' logbook and moved about the place as if he owned it. Other than the customary greeting of "Good evening," Mitchell and the mysterious doctor sidelined small talk.

Upon entering the sterile room, Mitchell led Dr. Z and his assistant to the morgue's cold chamber. There, he pulled out a center drawer to display Shalisa Young's dead body.

Dr. Z sighed wearily.

"You are, of course, welcome to take all the time that you need," Mitchell said.

"Thank you."

Mitchell turned and strolled out. Once alone with his assistant, Ned, Dr. Z spoke. "It's a damn shame, isn't it?"

"Yes, sir," Ned responded robotically.

"When I think of how close Dr. Avery came to a breakthrough, it breaks my heart." He shook his gray head. "Sure, he lost his mind toward the end, but he was still brilliant in a lot of ways. A man ahead of his time, really. While he was given free rein with his experiments, even the government gets a little nervous when the body count gets too high. So he was fired, but he kept claiming that he was just on the verge of success.

"But the government's loss was to be T4S's gain. The new arms race was in creating the perfect soldier—or rather, super soldier. Drones are great. You can kill the enemy from great distances without putting boots on the ground. But it's a messy business. High civilian casualties. And, unfortunately, killing the innocent tends to create more pissed-off terrorists. So what has become clear is that even a great superpower country like the United States can never fully eliminate the option of boots on the ground. In these times, Uncle Sam would rather turn to security firms like ours than risk the political backlash of sending more soldiers to die in hostile territory.

"It's better to run a war off the books and preferably with an army of elite super soldiers. Ones who are stronger than the average man or woman. Soldiers who won't need to rely on . . . robotics, for example. Which is a great concept, but what happens when the enemy can hack into the system or it parts break down on the battlefield? You'd need an army of repairmen on the field as well then."

Dr. Z leaned in closer, marveling how both serene and amazingly preserved the body looked for someone who had plunged to her death. In fact, Shalisa didn't look broken at all. One could easily believe that the young blonde had simply died in her sleep.

"Extraordinary." The doctor's curious gaze swept the entire length of the deceased's body several times, and his fascination grew.

"Dr. Avery had no problem delivering enhanced strength, but he wanted to go after the great golden goose."

"I'm sorry, sir. But what is that?"

Dr. Z turned a wide smile toward Ned. "Psychokinesis."

"Sir?"

"The psychic ability to influence a physical system *without* physical interaction."

Ned frowned. "Is that real, sir?"

"Depends on who you ask. There has never been any really convincing evidence, but the theory persists even among the naysayers."

"Do *you* believe it exists?"

Dr. Z chuckled. "My working scientific philosophy is: *Anything* is possible. One thing for sure, it's a compelling theory. There are some who believe the ability was once very common in ancient civilizations. They believe it as a working theory of how things like Stonehenge or the Egyptian pyramids were built. The ability to read minds, move objects just by thinking of it? Who wouldn't want to be able to do all of that?"

Ned nodded.

"Unfortunately, most of Avery's subjects died excruciating deaths during his home experiments. Except the three women—now two—the police rescued from his basement. Even I had thought that Dr. Avery died a complete failure until Ms. Young here killed her mother. She kept repeating that she'd only *thought* about it. Of course, the courts found her insane, and then we were free to experiment with her at St. Elizabeth. I believe the tests aggravated her state of mind, and things went very wrong. Now here we stand."

"What will happen to her now?" Ned inquired.

"Now we'll have her transferred to our lab for a more extensive examination." He sighed and rubbed his tired eyes. "Fortunately for us, she has no living relatives to claim her body, so instead of being buried in a potter's field, she will be donated to science."

Ned absorbed the doctor's words. "But what about the other two?"

"Ah. *That* is the trillion-dollar question."

Twenty-four hours later . . .

"Dr. Z, there's has been a change in plans," Ned announced rushing into the lab.

Dr. Z looked up from his notes and speared his assistant with a tired look. "What is it now?"

A relative has stepped forward and claimed Shalisa Young's body from the morgue."

"A relative?" Dr. Z frowned. "I wasn't aware that Ms. Young had any more relatives."

"Apparently, she does—an aunt out of Oregon. She showed up unexpectedly with all the right documentation. The morgue had no choice but to turn the body over to her."

Zacher stormed away from his table. "And who is this supposed aunt? Where has she been all this time?"

"I've already checked her out, sir," Ned said, following his boss out of the lab and into his office. "She's legit. Apparently,

Ms. Young's aunt had a falling out with the family decades ago, got married and changed her last name, and sort of fell off the radar."

"Great." Zacher dropped into the chair behind his desk and braided his hands together.

Ned stood, waiting for an order. When none came, he asked, "Sir, what would you like to do?"

Dr. Z weighed his options when a trickle of compassion made its way to his heart. "Nothing." He sighed. "These girls have been through a lot—maybe it's only fair they should be allowed to rest in peace. Let her go."

Ned nodded. "Yes, sir."

1

Office of the Washington Post

Reporter Tomi Lehane slammed the phone down and raked her fingers through her jet-black hair. "Abrianna hates me."

Photographer and colleague Jayson Brigham rolled his chair into her cubicle and cocked his head with a lazy smile. "I doubt that."

"Then why isn't she answering my calls? It's been days since I ran that last article about her parents."

"Her mother did commit suicide while she was in jail after it ran," he answered honestly. At Tomi's sharp look, he added, "That doesn't mean that she hates you. Those two didn't get along anyway, right? If anything, you guys need a break from each other. Give Abrianna some time."

Tomi dismissed Jayson's advice. "I *had* to print the story. It's news. Cargill Parker is the second biggest story in the country—next to her."

"Yeah, bringing down a presidency is sort of a tough act to follow, but running a child sex-trafficking ring out of a D.C. country club is as close as anyone is going to get."

"I never expected Marion would hang herself in that cell. I thought . . . Who am I kidding? The only thing I was thinking was beating everyone to the punch before Cargill Parker tossed my ass out of here. Now that he owns the damn paper, I'm sure that pink slip will arrive any day now."

Jayson didn't respond, and that was more damning.

Tomi swiped away a tear and bolted to her feet. "I better get home. It's late."

Jayson stood while she gathered her things. "You all right?"

"I've been through worse shit than this. But maybe I had hoped that Abrianna and I could be . . . I don't know."

"Friends?" he asked.

She shrugged. Being rejected by the cool kids stung.

"You guys will always have a bond. You survived some shit that most couldn't wrap their heads around."

"Being kidnapped and tortured in the basement of a murderous mad scientist is hardly reminiscing material." Tomi sighed. "Sorry. I don't mean to turn you into my therapist."

"No. It's okay."

"I'm going." She patted him on the shoulder as she exited her small space. "I'll see you tomorrow."

An exhausted Tomi arrived home to an excited and *hungry* Doberman shepherd dancing by the door. The doggy door in the laundry room saved her from returning to ruined carpets and floors. However, her long work hours at the paper made Rocky aggressive whenever he did see her. But it couldn't be helped. Ever since Abrianna Parker blew back into her life, nothing had been the same. First, Abrianna had been framed for murdering the speaker of the House by none other than the new chief justice of the Supreme Court *and* the president of the United States. Shortly after, news of Abrianna's billionaire father running a child-sex trafficking ring out of a famous D.C. country club hit the media circuit, and things got crazier, leaving a trail of dead bodies everywhere.

When Abrianna brought Tomi the whole story on a silver platter, it made her the hottest reporter on Capitol Hill. Not only was she was a rising star in print, but she was fast becoming a regular on the cable news circuit. However, chasing the story about Abrianna's father may have cost her Abrianna's trust. That saddened her. She and Abrianna shared a horrific past. When they were teenagers, they'd been kidnapped and tortured by D.C.'s serial killer Craig Avery—however, recently, they had discovered that Avery was more of a mad scientist who once worked for some quasi-paramilitary firm. And the crazy concoctions Avery used to inject them with killed all but three girls: Tomi, Abrianna, and Shalisa Young. After Shalisa took a headlong dive off the building of a government psychiatric hospital, Tomi and Abrianna were the only survivors.

At home, Tomi took a couple of steps into the house before her big baby knocked her down.

"Okay, boy. Get off of me." She laughed.

Rocky ignored her. Instead, he slobbered and licked her face.

Tomi sat up. "Aww. Did you miss momma, huh?" She scratched behind his ears the way he liked it and was rewarded with more kisses.

Thump!

Tomi and Rocky froze.

"What was that?" she asked.

Rocky's ears pointed up as he cocked his head from side to side.

Tomi pushed her hundred-pound baby off of her and climbed to her feet. Had the sound come from upstairs or the basement? She looked to Rocky, but he just stared back. "You're a lot of help, you know that?"

Leaving her bag and purse on the floor, Tomi went for the .38 holstered at her back. "C'mon, boy." She and the dog crept to the basement door.

Heart pounding, Tomi turned the knob and then cringed when

the rusted hinges announced to the whole world that she was opening the door. She hit the light switch, but it lit only the top of the stairs and not the basement.

She stood there, cringing. In the three years that she'd lived in the townhouse, she'd only been in the basement three times before. A psychiatrist wasn't needed to tell her why. Of the three Avery survivors, Tomi had been huddled in the mad scientist's basement the longest. Ten months. Ten months of hellish torture, watching other teenage girls die around her and scared every second that she would be next.

He's not down there. It was silly that she had to say that as she coached herself down each step, determined to conquer her fear. At some point, she'd stopped breathing. She was sure of it. However, her heart sounded like an African drum in her ears as she crept along. At the bottom of the stairs, she hit the second switch and flooded the room with light.

Nothing.

Other than boxed summer clothes and home tools, the coast was clear.

Relieved, Tomi sighed and lowered her weapon. "I'm going crazy." She rolled her eyes and marched back up the staircase.

Rocky sat on his haunches at the top of the stairs, panting happily at her return. She closed the basement door.

"Thanks for having my back."

Rocky barked.

"Yeah, yeah. I'm going. I'm going." She holstered her weapon and headed to the kitchen. As she crossed the living room, she noticed the lace curtains billowing, the sliding glass door open. "What in the hell?" She shifted direction from the kitchen to the dining room.

A disappointed Rocky whined.

Tomi palmed her weapon again and performed another slow creep. The closer she got to the open door, the louder Rocky whined. When she reached the door and glanced out into the backyard, again she didn't see anything. She relaxed, but then her entire scalp tingled. Instinct made her duck. The sliding door exploded and became a cascade of shattered glass. Rocky barked wildly. Tomi quickly crawled out of the dining room.

However, her shooter wasn't outside. He was in the house.

She heard another suppressed gunshot.

Rocky cried out and then hit the floor, hard.

Tomi's scream died in her throat when a hand gripped the back of her head and snatched her to her feet. A needle was jammed into her neck. Her eyes widened as the plunger emptied a drug into her bloodstream. A poisonous fireball roared through her veins, closing off her throat and shutting off her oxygen. She dropped her weapon and slumped into a man's arms, but before she blacked out, she heard more gunfire. Her attacker released her to return fire.

She hit the floor with a *thump!* Eyes still wide open, Tomi had an unobstructed view of Rocky's still body. Her big baby. Were they now going to watch each other die? Tears swelled and blurred her vision. Smoke. Fire. Her townhouse was going up in flames.

Just before losing consciousness, she was picked up and carried out of her townhouse and into a waiting van. The last faces she saw were Dr. Zacher and Jayson Brigham.

The Bunker . . .

In the bowels of Washington, D.C., Douglas "Ghost" Jenkins, a lifelong hacktivist, paced inside his underground bunker while he replayed a news clip for Kadir and Abrianna.

> *"D.C. fire investigators are trying to determine what caused the fire that tore through a northeast side home in a Grant Park neighborhood.*
> *The fire broke out late Friday night and likely originated*

on the main level of the house, but currently remains under investigation. One firefighter was taken to the hospital for respiratory distress, officials said. That firefighter has since been released, according to D.C. fire spokesman Vito Alfonsi.

The home is owned by Washington Post *reporter Tomi Lehane. As most people know, Ms. Lehane broke the national news story about the murder of former House Speaker Kenneth Reynolds that had led to the White House, which led President Daniel Walker to step down. She had also become a staple on several political cable talk shows. Ms. Walker has not been located in the home, and, so far, no one has been able to reach her for comment.*

Ghost shut off the television and swung his gaze toward Abrianna and Kadir. "So, what do you guys want to do?"

Abrianna broke eye contact. "I'm not sure there is anything we can do."

Ghost's brows rose—then he took in her body language. The stiff back, crossed arms with her hands gripping her biceps, and the stiff jaw. He stepped back while his eyes narrowed. "What did I miss?"

"What do you mean?" she asked.

"*What do I mean?* A month ago you were down my ass about how we needed to protect this chick from these T4S assholes, and now you're acting like you couldn't care less if the bitch lives or dies."

"That's not true." Abrianna stood but turned her back.

Ghost's gaze shifted to Kadir. "You want to give it another try to sound more convincing?"

Kadir pulled a deep breath. "I'm not exactly sure what the hell it is you think we should do, either. T4S is a heavily armed paramilitary mammoth. If we storm that place like a Z-list A-Team, it would be suicide."

"So, tough shit for Ms. Lehane. Is that it?"

"*Nobody* said that," Kadir responded defensively. "First of all, we don't know for sure that they have her."

Ghost opened his mouth.

"I admit there's a good chance that they do have her," Kadir cut him off. "But Lehane is a reporter. She could be out of town or on assignment. We don't know yet. And if they *do* have her, they could have shipped her to any one of the facilities around the *world*."

"I'm still hearing '*fuck that bitch*,'" Ghost said. "And nobody is telling me why. I thought this chick was one of the good guys. Has that changed?"

Silence.

"Ah, I see." Ghost sighed. "This has something to do with that last article she wrote about your parents." He nodded to Abrianna.

"My *adopted* parents."

Ghost's brows inched toward to the center of his forehead. "Okay, Team Petty. Enough. You're pissed off. I get it. But you guys gotta put that shit to the side. A woman's life is at stake. That used to mean something to you."

"It still does," Abrianna snapped. "But Kadir is right. We don't know for sure what happened. If T4S did pull this off, we need a real plan on how to get her out. You have guns; well, they have *more* guns. *And* they have powerful friends and the protection of the government. Whatever we do decide to do to get her out of there, it has to be smart."

"What if they kill her?" Ghost asked.

"They won't," Abrianna assured. "I don't know what they want with her—"

"Or you," Ghost countered. "They put out an extraction order for you, too. Remember? If these motherfuckers are bold enough to take out a famous reporter like Lehane, they will be just as bold coming after you, too—again."

Abrianna and Kadir shared a look.

"Ah, *now* I have your attention."

Someone hammered on the bunker's front door.

Ghost swung his AR-15 toward the door. "Who the fuck is that?"

No one had a clue.

Randall, one of Ghost's hacktivist/militiamen, punched up the digital feed from the security camera.

At the familiar sight of Abrianna's three best friends, Julian, Draya, and Shawn White, Ghost groaned, "I gotta find another spot. This place gets more foot traffic than a gay club's bathroom."

"Sorry about that," Abrianna apologized. "I sent out a 911 text on our way over here."

Ghost rolled his eyes and then opened the large metal door.

"Is everything all right?" Draya rushed inside. "We came as fast as we could." She rushed over and wrapped an arm around Abrianna and then checked her over. "You good?"

"Yeah, *I'm* fine."

"It's her reporter friend who is in trouble," Ghost filled them in, closing the door. "T4S snatched her up and set her place on fire as a cover-up."

Draya's eyes grew large. "What? Tomi Lehane?"

"At least that's Ghost's hypothesis," Abrianna corrected, not convinced.

"What are we going to do?" Julian asked. "You guys have a plan?"

"Yes," Ghost said.

"No," Kadir and Abrianna barked at the same time.

Shawn chuckled. "Glad you guys cleared that up." He folded his arms and swung his gaze around the room. "Did we interrupt a cat fight?"

"No fight." Abrianna forced a smile. "A disagreement on tactics." She found Ghost's gaze again. "If we go in after her, we'll only get one shot at it. We need to be smart, not reckless. That's all I'm saying."

Ghost thrust up his chin and re-evaluated her. "Fine. We'll do this your way. After all, it's your neck on the line."

2

Dr. Charles Zacher was dying—and he knew it.

At last check, he had three tumors growing in his head, which were responsible for his crippling headaches, endless puking, and sporadic nosebleeds, which always happened at inopportune times. The worse part was he had no one to blame but himself. He'd spent years trying to replicate Dr. Craig Avery's human experiments. He had no choice. His professional neck was still stretched beneath a corporate guillotine.

T4S wanted and expected results. After all, they'd poured billions into his research and development department.

Zacher doubled over his office's bathroom and retched more blood than food into the toilet. Once he started, it was impossible to stop. After an eternity, his stomach muscles cramped into a large charley horse and made it impossible for him to stand back up. The madness continued until he passed out. When he woke, his head was pressed against the bowl's cold porcelain, his neck had a crick in it, and his stomach was empty.

Bang! Bang! Bang!

"Dr. Z," Ned queried from the other side of the door. "Are you in there?"

Dr. Z clutched his head.

Bang! Bang! Bang!

"Dr. Z?"

"Stop hammering on the damn door. I'll be out in a minute."

The banging stopped, but Ned lingered at the door. Zacher could hear his thoughts humming through the door. "Get me a coffee," he barked.

"Yes, sir. Right away."

Zacher rolled his eyes and peeled himself off of the floor. He took one look inside the bowl and frowned in disgust before flushing the toilet. After he shuffled over to the sink and braced his weight against the counter, he looked in the mirror and didn't recognize the man staring back at him. At least, not at first. Years were stripped off his sixty-five-year-old face. His once gray hair was now a rich black with springy, coiled curls not seen on his head in almost three decades. But his eyes were bloodshot, and his nose was swollen like he'd done enough coke to knock out a horse. There were also dried blood and vomit caked on his face.

This is going to take more than a minute.

It took twenty. But Zacher was refreshed after a shower.

"Your coffee, sir." Ned thrust Zacher's favorite mug toward him. Zacher touched the cup. "It's cold."

"Um, yes, sir. Sorry about that, sir."

"Get me another cup." Zacher dismissed him with a wave.

"Right away, sir." Ned jetted out of Zacher's office.

Zacher returned to his desk and saw he'd left his latest blood test results exposed. Quickly, he shoved the new reports into his personal file and crammed it back into his desk before Ned blew back into the office.

"Here you go, Dr. Z. Nice and hot." Ned set down the mug and beamed at his boss.

"Thanks."

"My pleasure, sir."

Zacher pulled out another stack of test results. "How is our test subject doing?"

Ned coughed and cleared his throat. "She is still stable, sir."

"Still hasn't woken up yet?"

"No, sir."

Zacher shook his head. "All right . . . keep me posted."

"Yes, sir." Ned lingered.

Zacher sighed. He was befuddled by this latest turn of events. The propofol injected into Ms. Lehane during the extraction should have long worn off and evaporated out of her system by now. It was only a sleeping agent, commonly used by millions of anesthesiologist across the country. It was meant to put her in a deep sleep, not make the woman comatose. But Tomi Lehane wasn't the typical patient, and the general anesthetic had a different effect.

In the meantime, it didn't stop Zacher from running tests. He needed to break the code to what was happening with Tomi Lehane's DNA. If he could do that, he could advance T4S's interest—and save his own life.

3

Abrianna and Kadir rode home in a cocoon of silence, but at the same time, the air between them was filled with the things they couldn't say. No matter how many times Abrianna shrugged off any guilt for Tomi's situation, it crept back onto her shoulders and weighed her down. "I made the right call," she blurted out.

Kadir nodded but kept his hands on the wheel at ten and two and his eyes on the road.

"Don't tell me you think we should've blasted our way onto the T4S compound to rescue Tomi?"

"Nah. You made the right call," he admitted.

"Then why the hard face and the silent treatment?"

Kadir sighed and weighed his words. He cast a look at Abrianna, but her face was an unreadable mask. "Aren't you the least bit worried about her?"

Her features pinched together. "Why wouldn't I worry? What kind of question is that?"

His gaze returned to the road while tension layered the space between them. Abrianna seethed. She shouldn't have to explain anything to anyone. Her relationship with Tomi was . . . complicated—and not the social media kind. It was a real-life, multilayered, 3D jigsaw puzzle. The months that she, Tomi, and Shalisa were huddled in Dr. Craig Avery's basement weren't building blocks for some long-lasting sisterhood—far from it. It was months of listening to each other's harrowing screams and watching other teenage girls die on tables or sitting in their own sick.

Dr. Avery stripped away their femininity and their humanity. They were treated like lab rats. They endured poison after poison being injected into their veins, while wondering and praying for death to save them. And like an evil bitch, death would never come.

When Lieutenant Gizella Castillo and her men charged into that basement to rescue them, it had been a miracle—the first one Abrianna had ever experienced. She came close to believing in some higher power, but the universe was only playing with her. The police were going to hand her back over to her parents.

Abrianna landing in the clutches of Dr. Avery in the first place had been a cruel twist of fate. She was fourteen years old and had gathered the courage to run away from her evil adoptive father. Cargill Parker was a sick fuck who had raped her and her brother, Samuel, almost nightly. Cargill was rich and powerful. He controlled everyone around him, including Marion, her adoptive mother. For years, Abrianna had dreamed of running away. Then one day, the opportunity presented itself, and she ran—only to land in Avery's clutches.

"I need some air." She hit the automatic button and rolled down the window. The night's cold air nearly froze the tears on her face.

Kadir placed a hand over hers and squeezed. "I'm sorry," he said. "The question was out of line."

"No." She shook her head. "It wasn't."

"I'm worried about you."

"I'm mad, *and* I'm worried about Tomi. That's okay, isn't it?"

"Yeah. Sure."

Abrianna sucked in a breath. "I want to go and see her place."

Kadir frowned. "Do you think that's wise? What if those guys from T4S have the place staked out?"

"Yeah, you're right." She powered up the window.

Kadir sighed. "I guess it wouldn't hurt to swing by." He glanced at her. "You'll go all tingling and shit if you sense danger, right?"

"Let's hope."

After looking at reports of Tomi's home fire on her phone, Abrianna and Kadir drove to the reported address.

"I believe that this is it," Kadir said after being lucky enough to find a parking space across from the burned-out townhouse.

"Oh my God." Abrianna stared up at it in horror. She took in the total destruction that included the two townhouses next to the charred and hollowed-out place. She reached for the door handle.

"Where are you going?" Kadir asked.

"I want to get a better look." Abrianna climbed out of the car.

"I don't think that's a good—"

Slam!

"—idea," Kadir grumbled as he climbed out of the car. While Abrianna jogged halfway across the street, he grabbed a flashlight from the trunk. When he caught up to her, he took her by the elbow. "I have a bad feeling about this."

"Chill out. It'll only take a few minutes." She broke free from his grip and then ducked underneath the yellow crime tape and jogged up the stone staircase to a ruined townhouse.

Kadir swept a bright light across the charred structure. "This was some intense heat. Are we sure that someone didn't drop a bomb on this place?"

"I was thinking the same thing." Abrianna glanced around.

"Are you looking for something in particular?"

Abrianna hesitated because she was looking for something—only she didn't know what. "I'm trying to figure out how it started."

"The papers said the fire marshal hasn't figured that out yet. At least, the marshal hasn't released it to the press."

"Yeah." She looked around again.

They lingered a while longer—long enough to make Kadir uncomfortable.

"Have you seen enough?" he asked.

Abrianna hesitated again before admitting, "Yeah, I guess."

"Then we should get out of here. I don't like being out in the open like this."

Abrianna hitched up a smile and almost laughed at him when the back of her head tingled. "Yeah, you're right. We better go." She tried to keep the alarm out of her voice, but Kadir picked up on it.

"What? Are we being watched?"

"I'm not sure."

"Come on."

He reached for her hand just as the entire back of her head went from a tingle to a burning sensation. "Duck!"

Kadir trusted her and did as she commanded, no questions asked. A bullet whizzed by his head, clipping his right earlobe. "Fuck!"

"Are you all right?" she asked.

There was no time to answer. Another bullet zoomed past, and then in the next second, a hailstorm of lead flew in their direction.

Abrianna went for the Tiffany-blue Glock .45 tucked at the back of her black jeans and wildly returned fire. She had no confidence she aimed in the right direction.

"Keep moving," Kadir shouted. It was his turn to bark the orders. They rushed toward the back of the burned-out structure and down another flight of steps into the backyard. From there, they ran blindly, unsure of where to go.

House lights turned on up and down the residential street, and the gunfire stopped.

"Bree, hold up," Kadir shouted.

Abrianna kept running like a human cheetah with her scalp still tingling.

"Bree!"

She turned to shout back, but then something slammed into her neck. Her legs tripped over air as she fell forward.

"Abrianna!" Kadir launched forward and caught her before she cracked her head open on the street's pavement. Tires screeched, and Kadir glanced up in time to see a black van charging toward him.

"Shit!" Kadir tossed Abrianna over his shoulder and was prepared to take off running when the van's door jerked open, and Ghost and Roger shouted, "Get in!"

Relief swept through Kadir. Ghost had a knack for showing up at the right moment. He raced and dove into the van while the damn thing was still in motion. When he and Abrianna landed on the carpeted floor, he heard another series of bullets slam into the van's windows. Glass cascaded over him, but Ghost floored it, and they rocketed out of danger.

Ghost swore. "I swear you two can't follow simple directions like: 'Go somewhere safe.'"

Kadir hung his head while Ghost continued, "I swear people think I talk for my health."

"Let it go, Ghost."

Ghost rolled his eyes. "Letting it go."

Roger crouched over Kadir and Abrianna. "Is she going to be all right?"

"When isn't she?" Ghost barked from behind the wheel. "That girl can take a licking and keep on ticking."

Kadir's jaws clenched as he struggled to squash his annoyance. Yes, Abrianna tended to heal quickly, but there was always the possibility of the one time that she wouldn't.

"Is there something sticking out her neck?" Roger asked.

"What? Where?" Kadir brushed his fingers along the column of Abrianna's neck.

"Right side. Near the back."

Kadir felt it. "What the fuck?" He yanked the object out and held it up. "Ghost, hit the light."

Ghost grumbled but turned on the interior light.

"It's some kind of dart," Roger marveled.

"Tranquilizer gun," Kadir and Ghost said at the same time, but Kadir added a stream of expletives.

"You know what this means?"

"The extraction order is still in effect," Kadir answered.

Ghost nodded. "Can I say it now?"

Kadir sighed. "Make it quick."

"I told you so."

"Feel better?" Kadir asked.

"You have no idea. What now?"

It was on the tip of Kadir's lips to say that they needed a doctor. However, Abrianna had made it clear during several previous life-or-death incidents that she was never to be taken to a doctor. "What about your off-the-grid warehouse pad?"

Ghost rolled his eyes. "Why not? You guys have practically turned the place into a bed and breakfast anyway."

Kadir smirked. "Thanks, buddy."

Ghost grumbled.

Kadir leaned over Abrianna's still form and brushed a kiss against her lips. "Hang in there, baby. I'm going to get you somewhere safe."

4

Abrianna heard Kadir's voice, but it was faint and sounded far away. She tried to run toward him, but instead, she tumbled into the past and into Dr. Craig Avery's basement of horror where she begged for death.

She tossed and turned throughout her fevered nightmare. Everywhere she turned, evil's razor-sharp claws slashed across her body. She screamed, terrified. Visions of being strapped to a pole and then spun over a fiery pit filled her head. In the distance, she could hear maniacal laughter, but she couldn't make out where it came from.

"Please! Let me go," she shouted and begged. Hot tears scalded while they streaked across her face. The more tears she shed, the louder the laughter grew. Her pain had never meant anything to anyone. Hadn't she learned that lesson already?

The pole turned, spinning her over a growing pit of fire. The closer the flames came toward her face, the louder she screamed and fought to get loose. Somewhere in the recesses of her mind, she knew this torture wasn't real. She'd been here before. If she could wake up, she would be able to prove it.

But no matter how loud she got, the torture went on forever.

"Wake up! Please!"

The fire singed every hair on her body while her skin blistered and curdled. Surely, she was cooking from the inside out. Her grip on reality waned. Maybe this horror was really happening. She would die roasting over this pit, and there was nothing she could do about it.

"Pleeeaassee wake up," she sobbed.

"There, there. Everything is going to be fine," Kadir soothed from the great beyond.

For a brief, miraculous moment, something cool pressed against her forehead. She attempted to lean into it, but the coolness disappeared as fast as it came. The fire below resumed its endless torture.

"No, please," she cried.

Kadir's cool touch returned. "It's all right."

She sighed, too exhausted to build up hope. Then the fire retreated until it crackled so far below her that she could no longer see it. The tears blanketing her face cooled. At long last, Abrianna tumbled into a deep sleep where she thought of nothing and no one.

5

Fears Mount for Missing Reporter

At BridgePoint Hospital, private detective Gizella Castillo re-read the *Washington Post*'s article, detailing the search for her friend, their missing investigative reporter Tomi Lehane. A strange consensus, despite it being highly unlikely, was that the reporter had vanished into thin air. Castillo couldn't judge from the reporting how vigorously her former police department was searching for Lehane. Like most police departments across the country, resources were limited and triaged. If Tomi had anything working in her favor, it would be her recent meteoric rise with the historic newspaper. Her explosive exposé linking former president Walker and Supreme Court chief justice Katherine Sanders to the murder of the United States House speaker Kenneth Reynolds had many in the industry fast-tracking her for a Pulitzer Prize. Celebrity in and of itself is a superpower.

Castillo lowered the paper and turned her head to glance out of the window. The day was still gray with thick, menacing clouds threatening to burst at any second. The scenery matched her mood. Too much has happened and in such a short period of time. Processing it all had been difficult—until now . . . while she sat next to a hospital bed, waiting for the love of her life to re-cover from a gunshot to the head. It was a miracle he'd survived.

He wouldn't have, had she not arrived at his place when she did. Castillo's heart tripped inside of her chest while images flashed in her head. She played defense, blocking them as fast as she could, but the one of her discovering Dennis, lying in a pool of blood, kept sneaking past her defenses. Occasionally, Castillo's vision blurred, but she'd pull herself together before her tear ducts flooded.

Dennis is going to pull through this, and everything will go back to normal. It was meant to be a confirmation, but it came out sounding like a prayer. The first few raindrops from the brewing storm splashed against the window, and Castillo's mind veered from Dennis back to Tomi. She shouldn't feel responsible for Tomi's disappearance or believe she could have done something to prevent it—but she did.

Castillo's bond with both Tomi Lehane and Abrianna Parker was as strong as it had been nearly seven years ago when she, as a police lieutenant, had rescued the girls from a crazy serial killer—or mad scientist, she'd come to learn lately. Getting those girls out of Avery's clutches had been the highlight of her career. Unfortunately, she'd broken a lot of rules and laws to get it done, but it had been worth it. Eventually, her inability to do everything by the book forced her to retire early, but it didn't stop her from fighting for the most vulnerable in the nation: missing children.

Now, Castillo ran a private detective firm called the Agency. It had been a one-woman operation until Abrianna Parker had brought her boyfriend and friends over to help bring down her father and his sex-trafficking ring. It worked—but going after Cargill Parker may have blown back on Dennis. It was the only thing that made sense.

Castillo and Abrianna were able to get eight-year-old Lovely Belfleur to identify Cargill Parker as her abuser, and days later, Castillo was in a gun battle outside of the child's house with a group of hired thugs sent to kill the girl. Shortly before they'd arrived, a patrol car showed up at her stakeout. The officers told her their chief had sent them to take over the stakeout. She left, but her gut told her something wasn't right and she returned to the Belfleurs' house. The patrol car was nowhere in sight. Minutes later, all hell broke loose.

Once she and her small stakeout crew took out the hit men, Castillo had rushed to Dennis's place and . . . the bloody images flashed again. Castillo had to shake her head this time to dislodge them from her mind. But they would be back.

"Water."

Castillo tossed the paper aside and sprang up from her chair. "What was that, baby?"

Police Chief Dennis Holder smacked his dry lips as he rotated his head toward her. "Water," he croaked again.

"Sure thing." Castillo turned toward the tray table next to the bed and poured ice water into a plastic cup. When she returned to his side, she elevated the hospital bed and placed the cup to his lips. "Here you go, baby."

A smile fluttered at the corner of his lips before he took a sip. "What?"

Dennis ignored the question and greedily drank from the cup. Once it was empty, he leaned back while his smile ballooned wider.

"Are you going to tell me why you're grinning like that, or are you going to make me play twenty questions?"

"You called me *baby*," he boasted.

Castillo rolled her eyes. "Don't let it go to what's left of your head."

"Ah, is that any way to talk to a man recovering from being shot in the head? I could have been killed—then you would've regretted never having called me *baby* when you had the chance."

She groaned and returned the cup to the tray. "You're going to milk this for all it's worth, aren't you?"

"Every. Second. Of. It."

Castillo sighed and pretended to be annoyed. Until she almost lost him, she hadn't realized how much she loved him. *If he asks me to marry him again, this time I'll say yes.*

Dennis's smile softened. "You know, you don't have to spend every minute of the day here. I know you have tons to do at your office."

"Are you kidding me? There's no other place I'd rather be than right here."

He smiled expanded again. "You're such a beautiful liar."

Castillo chuckled and hung her head.

"It's okay." He opened his hand, and she placed hers in his. "I know that corkboard in your office is calling your name. All those lost children . . . and lost friends."

She sighed and shook her head.

"I know you," Dennis insisted. "It's killing you not to be out there looking for Tomi. I'm fine now. The worst part is over, and they have some pretty good drugs in this place. So, go. Find your friend. I'm not going anywhere."

———◦◦◦———

"Why can't we find this bitch?" President Washington snapped, slapping the morning paper down on her desk in the Oval Office. "Every day Lehane remains MIA, I take another hit in the polls."

"It's been a week," Sean Haverty, Kate's chief of staff, said. "There's a good chance she might not be found alive. That's not going to improve your numbers, either. The conspiracy theorists are still having a field day with this one. Half of the country believes the administration had something to do with the fire and her disappearance."

Kate rolled her eyes. "I'm more interested in winning over the thinking public—not the loons."

"The loons vote in larger numbers," Haverty reminded her.

"We have to change that—somehow."

Alan Gohl, the senior advisor to the president, injected his two cents. "Since we don't know what happened, our only choice is to take the hit, and hope the narrative dies out."

"Ha! In an election year? You have to be joking."

"Is there another option I'm missing?" he challenged.

"That's what you're supposed to be telling me," Kate snapped. "You're the fucking advisor. Advise. And give me a better option than me falling on a sword and hoping no one notices I'm bleeding out."

Gohl blanched from the reprimand and cast a nervous look around the room. "You need a straw man," he offered. "Someone else who had an ax to grind with Ms. Lehane."

It took Kate two seconds to follow his train of thought and also to dismiss it with a wave of her hand. "Forget it."

"Why?" Gohl sat up in his chair. "She's perfect."

"Yeah. The bitch also has nine lives," Kate tossed back. "Walker used Abrianna Parker as a hail Mary, too, and look how that turned out. The public loves that hooker-with-a-heart-of-gold bullshit too much. She already brought down a chief justice, a president, and her own billionaire father." She shook her head. "Nah, I prefer to stay far away from the bitch."

"Who else could it be?" Gohl questioned. "Lehane exposed an awful lot of family secrets, which resulted in Marion Parker killing herself in a jail cell. There are already a few talk radio hosts floating the idea that Parker may have had a hand in her disappearance. I'm sure with the right investment, we can get them to jam the accelerator on this."

Kate paused, hating that she was already reconsidering this option.

Seeing his argument was making headway with the president, Gohl pressed, "We don't go after her directly. We get the foot soldiers to do it. We keep our fingerprints off it. That's it. Social media will take care of the rest."

The Oval Office went silent while Kate resumed her pacing. She weighed the risk. What she'd said about Abrianna Parker was true. Thus far, the woman had proven to be bulletproof in the political arena. The camera loved her, and she always pulled off the impossible. However, Kate's back was against the wall, and she had to do something.

"Let's do it," she instructed Haverty, "but make sure we have deniability, or the race will be over before we're even at the starting line."

6

Fear exhausted the body.

In the past decade, Kadir learned this lesson firsthand—and life wasn't through with him yet. While he sat at Abrianna's bedside, stroking her limp hand, he recalled how many times in the past year they had been on the run for their lives. The volume of bullets they'd ducked and dodged from street thugs, political thugs, and now paramilitary thugs rivaled anything Hollywood released as a summer blockbuster.

They'd survived it all—so far.

This last brush with death scared him more than the previous times. Whatever poison or drug laced that dart, it had dropped Abrianna like he'd never seen. In the past, Kadir had witnessed Abrianna's breathing stop in her sleep, but in the last three days, as she'd lain in Ghost's apartment, she looked more like a corpse.

Kadir broke down. No amount of reasoning or reassurance from Abrianna's friends consoled him. She was dead, and *they* were in denial. The heart, the brain—the body—all needed oxygen to survive. He'd wept endlessly with his head placed against her chest and heard no heartbeat. She was gone.

It wasn't the first time Kadir had loved and lost. He'd honestly thought he could never go through that type of pain again. But there he was, begging Allah to spare Abrianna's life and not receiving an answer. Maybe it was because he wasn't a devout Muslim. His prayers were at the back of the line. He couldn't eat. He couldn't sleep. By the third day, Kadir's fear had morphed into anger. He wanted to raid Ghost's cache of military weapons and go at T4S head-on. They were responsible for this. They'd destroyed his life before and now they were doing it again.

Kadir had grown up in Washington, D.C. He'd programmed video games at nine and built databases when he was a teenager. In high school, he'd placed first in a statewide competition for a computer program that he'd designed. Scholarships to MIT and Stanford followed, but he'd elected to go to Georgetown University. However, the scholarship had been revoked when he'd exploited a security flaw in their computer science department.

After that, Kadir took his talents to the military. There, he'd transformed into a lean, mean, fighting machine and a sniper shooter. He'd also met Ghost in the armed forces. They had saved each other's lives on the battlefield more than once. However, it had also been a critical time that tested his Muslim faith. Sometime during his three tours to the Middle East, he found he no longer felt like he fought for America's freedom.

To him, something far uglier lay beneath the surface.

That had been confirmed when his military stint ended, and his work for a private security firm started. The money had been better, but his conscience took another hit. Corruption was everywhere.

Once stateside, Ghost convinced him to join an electronic civil disobedience group dedicated to exposing the truth about growing, unregulated shadow governments. This led Kadir straight to T4S, where he hacked into the private security firm.

T4S provided services for a variety of intelligence agencies, from the Marine Corps to the Pentagon, the Department of Defense, and major corporations. Kadir's hack had netted more than three million emails, which he'd turned over to *Rolling Stone* and WikiLeaks. The hack had exposed that there was no division between government and corporate spying. It also revealed the federal government's hatchet job of falsely linking nonviolent activist groups to known terrorist groups. The government would then prosecute activists under terrorism laws—just as they had done to Kadir. Seven years ago, he landed before Judge Katherine Sanders—future chief justice of the Supreme Court.

While he sat in jail, Kadir's high-school sweetheart and fiancée, Malala, died in a car accident. It was karma that he would go on to play such a pivotal role in bringing Judge Sanders down for murder and conspiracy with the president of the United States.

Now, it was time to seek justice for Abrianna.

"I'm not going to let them get away with this," Kadir promised while tears poured down his face. He lovingly brushed Abrianna's hair back. She had the face of an angel—a tough angel, but an angel still.

The first night he'd seen her step out onto the stage at the Stallion's Gentlemen's Club was still seared in his brain. From the first roll of her hips, he'd been hypnotized. Her long legs and steep curves were cherries on top. He'd fallen in love right there on the spot. Days later, she was running for her life when she dove into the backseat of his car, dodging bullets.

They had been together ever since.

"Wait!" Ghost pleaded with him, blocking his exit from his apartment. "I'm telling you to wait, man. Abrianna is going to pull out of this. I know it sounds crazy. But trust me."

Ghost wasn't making any sense.

"A couple of days ago you were ready to go head-to-head with these assholes. Now, you wanna pump the brakes? What the fuck?"

"A couple of days ago, you guys were talking more sense than I was. Now, you done flipped the script. This is your grief talking because you think your girl is gone. I get it. And I've been where you are right now, thinking Bree was gone and everyone else had lost their marbles believing the chick was going to rise from the dead. Guess what? They were right, and I was wrong. I'm telling you. You're going to have to trust me on this. She's going to pull through."

Before Kadir could snap back, a soft moan drifted over to them. Kadir's heart stopped. Slowly, he twisted his neck toward the bed.

Abrianna's head moved, and then it thrashed among the pillows while a long, suffering whine filled the room.

Kadir raced to her side. "Bree, baby. I'm here." He grabbed her hand. She was burning up. "I need towels and cold water," he barked to the crowd of friends who gathered at the door.

"We're on it," Shawn and Draya shouted in unison and scrambled off.

"There, there. Everything is going to be fine," Kadir soothed.

"Here you go." Shawn carried in a steel bowl of ice water, and Draya handed Kadir a stack of clean towels.

Kadir dipped one towel into the water, wrung it out, and then placed it over Abrianna's forehead. He watched as her body visibly slumped in relief.

"No, please," she cried.

Kadir's cool touch returned. "It's all right."

Seconds later, she drifted off to sleep, but this time her chest rose and fell.

Ghost placed a hand on Kadir's shoulder. "See, bruh? I told you she was going to be copacetic."

Kadir hung his head. He was grateful to have been wrong. He closed his eyes, thanked Allah, and then resumed cooling Abrianna down. Everything would be all right.

⇒●⇐

Abrianna opened her eyes—but nothing looked familiar.

When she moved, she regretted it. The motion in her head spun clockwise while her stomach acid went counterclockwise. The combination made her collapse back down. "Oh."

"Try to relax." Kadir's voice reached her ears before he hovered over her.

Abrianna squinted until her triple vision focused and there was only one unshaven Kadir smiling at her. "You look like shit," she croaked.

He chuckled. "Well, you look like heaven to me, but I'm biased."

She laughed and then stopped. "Ow, don't make me laugh."

"Brace yourself for a stupid question. How do you feel?"

"Like shit."

"So, you're saying we make a pretty good couple?"

"Ha, ha. Ow, ow."

"My bad. Sorry about that. I'll try not to make you laugh." Kadir brushed her hair and kissed her forehead. "I'm just happy to have you back. You scared me."

Abrianna frowned while she attempted to part the clouds in her head. "What happened?"

"What is the last thing that you remember?"

She opened her mouth but drew a blank. "I, um . . . nothing."

Kadir squeezed her hand. "It'll come back to you. No need to stress yourself."

"How long was I out?"

He hesitated. "A few days."

Three, she knew. It had happened before—several times.

"Here. Drink this." Kadir pressed a cup of cold water to her lips.

Abrianna drained the cup in one long gulp, but remained thirsty. "More."

"No problem." Kadir poured her another cup.

It went down as quickly as the last, but, at least, the spinning slowed down—enough for her to attempt to move her head again. "Ghost's apartment?"

"It's almost like a second home, huh?" Kadir joked.

"Good. You leeching muthafuckas can chip in on the rent and

groceries," Ghost grumbled, entering the room. "Welcome back to the land of the living, Bree."

"Missed me?" she tested.

Ghost shrugged. "You grow on people."

She smiled.

"Kinda like toe fungus."

Her smile stretched wider. "Aw, you love me."

Kadir jerked. "What?"

Ghost slapped his hand on Kadir's shoulder. "Relax, I wouldn't do you like that—besides, I make it a rule never to date chicks who are stronger than me."

Kadir frowned. "Thanks for the reassurance."

"Don't mention it." He delivered another slap.

"Do I have a say in any of this?" Abrianna asked, enjoying the joke.

Ghost rolled his eyes. "Baby girl, when I turn the charm to one hundred, there's no resisting this." He struck a couple of poses.

"Don't hurt me now." She laughed. "Ow, ow."

"Okay, that's enough." Kadir spun his boy around and then pushed him toward the door. "She needs to rest." Before he shoved Ghost out, Shawn, Draya, and Julian suddenly clogged the doorway.

"Is she up?" Shawn asked, but didn't wait for an answer. He and the other two misfits shoved Ghost and Kadir back. "Bree!"

Abrianna's smile grew wide enough to show every single tooth in her head. "Hey, guys." In a flash, three sets of arms wrapped around her and nearly squeezed the life back out of her before they unleashed a torrent of questions at her. She bore the pain of their tight hugs, but she couldn't answer their questions. They would be patient with her—like always. They had been through a lot together, especially her and Shawn. When they were teenagers, Shawn had been the one who'd encouraged her to run away from home. He'd been tossed out on the streets after he'd come out of the closet. On his own, Shawn had bragged about his newfound freedom, and Abrianna had been desperate to escape her home.

Within hours of running away, Abrianna landed in Craig Avery's evil clutches, but it was Shawn, Draya, Tivonte, and Julian who doggedly searched and rode the police's ass to find her. After that, they were as thick as thieves—literally, because they'd had to become thieves, drug dealers, and everything else to survive. She couldn't imagine life without any of them.

Kadir gave the friends space to hug it out and surround Bree with love. It was hard hanging back. He wanted this moment to be private. He didn't care if it was selfish. The heart wants what it wants.

Ghost slapped Kadir's shoulder again. "Now that your girl is back, what do you say to you reacquainting yourself to some soap and water?"

Kadir cut a sharp side-eye to Ghost, who tossed up his hands. "I'm just saying. I can only burn so many incense and candles before risking a three-alarm fire. And I would like to keep this place off the grid."

"Enough. I get the picture." Kadir laughed.

"Yeah? Because I was going to say that your girl smells like fresh lavender and she's been dead for three days."

"Fuck you, Ghost." He kept walking.

"That's it?" Ghost frowned. "I have a few more jokes."

"Nah, I got it." He headed out of the room and made a beeline toward the bathroom. Minutes later, he'd lathered up and stood beneath a showerhead powerful enough to strip three days of sweat and worries off of his body. After the stress swirled down the drain, Kadir tackled his fast-growing beard until his face was as smooth as a baby's bottom and he could recognize himself in the mirror again. "There we go." He winked at his reflection. Abrianna wasn't the only one returning from the dead.

When he went back to the guestroom that he and Abrianna shared, her friends buzzed around, removing empty plates and helping her out of bed. "Where are you going?"

Abrianna glanced up. "Hey. I, um, was headed to the other bathroom. My bladder is threatening to humiliate me in a few seconds."

"Here. Let me help." He rushed to her side, sideswiping Julian out of the way and sweeping Bree into his arms.

"Hercules, Hercules," Julian joked.

Bree wrapped her arms around Kadir's neck. "You know, I'm capable of walking."

"What a coincidence. I am, too." He hauled her off before she could utter another protest. After transporting her to the bathroom, Kadir scrubbed down the tub and ran her a hot bubble bath.

"I know that you're already clean, but care to join me?" Abrianna slumped beneath the water and then lifted one leg so he could watch the bubbles race down it. "There's plenty of room."

Kadir cocked a smile and dropped his towel. "I thought you'd never ask."

7

President Kate Washington spent two hours rehearsing a speech to give to her party's leadership before deciding to ditch it and wing it. Still, she drew a blank when she entered the Cabinet Room, and everyone turned toward her with sly smiles, shifty eyes, and forked tongues. She coasted farther into the room. She would have to get through this night, relying on her charm and gut instincts—pretty much how anyone survived Capitol Hill.

"Thank you for coming tonight." She made a beeline to Senate minority leader Scott Presley and shook his hand.

"It's an honor to be invited to the White House, Madame President—especially without the insufferable company of our friends across the aisle. I'm sure our Republican colleagues are bitching up a storm into the nearest CNN camera as we speak," Presley joked.

Kate expanded her own calculated smile. "I don't know if that's true—but it *feels* true."

Everyone joined in with fake laughter before cramming into the limited seating the room provided.

"I hope you've called this meeting to tell us that you've come to your senses and you have decided, for the good of our party, not to run to hold this office in the next election," Presley said with a pointed look.

"Oh, I'm always level-headed when it comes to these matters."
Kate's smile grew as she folded her arms.

The room fell silent as a palpable fear thickened the air.

Presley's face flushed an angry red. "With all due respect,
Madame President, if you're about to tell us what I think you are,
I beg you to reconsider. Your candidacy would tear the party in
half. Whether it's fair or not, you're a symbol or a reminder of
President Walker's corrupt administration. The party deserves a
fresh start."

"And I've decided that *I am* that fresh start already in progress.
Walker's sex and murder scandals are in the past. They, like him,
are dead and buried. My poll numbers have leveled off."

"They are in the tank at thirty-three percent."

"And they have nowhere to go but up," Kate reasoned.

Presley shook his head and scanned the room. Not a single senator looked happy about any of this.

Senator Janet Bell from New York spoke up. "You're making a
big mistake. You will cause more damage to the party simply because of your pride. You must put aside your personal ambitions
and think of the country and what's best for the nation. We have
a long way to go to repair our image around the world."

"And my administration has been working around the clock to
do that," Kate volleyed back. "I am the first female president of
the United States—the dream of our progressive base. Do you
really want to challenge that by running another Wonder bread
white guy?"

The white men—which was most of them—grumbled.

"The base is stable. Going forward, I promise you I will work
relentlessly to win the public's trust back for our party. My policies are aligned with what the American people want: better
healthcare, livable wages, and criminal justice reform. I can unite
and right this ship, and I want to make sure that the party has my
back."

Everyone grumbled to one another. She hadn't won over the room.

"And what if we say no?" Senator Mark Rhodes of California asked.

Kate's smile vanished when she looked Rhodes in the eye. "Then I will take it as a declaration of war and torpedo whoever you run against me. I'll destroy the party limb from limb if need be. You will *not* fuck me over."

———•◦•———

At the top of the hour, cable news host Greg Wallace looked straight into camera A and welcomed his audience to the show. Over his left shoulder, a digital placard with the words *All the President's Killers* guaranteed the channel surfers would stop and turn into the program.

"First up, the *Washington Post* is out with an explosive headline tonight that's rocking Capitol Hill: 'All the President's Killers.' The *Post* is not pulling any punches with this one. They are gunning for this administration's jugular in their quest to get answers about their missing hotshot reporter, Tomi Lehane. As of this viewing, it's been seven whole days since the young reporter's townhouse went up in flames. However, fire investigators have yet to discover the cause of the fire or find any proof that Ms. Lehane was even in the home when it burned to the ground.

"This story has enough intriguing elements to spin the conspiracy theorists among us into a tizzy—and I find myself among them. Joining us tonight is former lieutenant governor of Maryland and current MSNBC political analyst Michael Townsend and senior reporter for the *New York Daily News* Aaron Cornell. Thank you two for joining us tonight. Let's start with you, Michael. Did the president kill Tomi Lehane?"

"Whoa." The older African-American statesman held up his

hands to chest level and shook his head. "Talk about a loaded question."

"It's what the people want to know," Wallace countered, "especially with rumors swirling around this town that President Washington intends to run to hold the White House. Anyone could easily make the case that this messy business with the missing reporter is just Washington's way to tidy up a few loose ends from the previous administration."

Cornell nodded. "If that's the case, it was a *miscalculation* on the president's part. If Ms. Lehane doesn't turn up, this case is going to be an anchor around Washington's neck the whole campaign. It's a nightmare scenario for the Democratic party and a gift to the Republican front-runner and favorite, Governor Bo Hardy."

"A gift indeed! I love gifts!" Texas governor Beauregard Hardy barked and then muted the television in the center of his campaign headquarters. "This is going to be a walk in the park." He laughed, shaking his entire six-foot-four frame.

A dozen advisors and campaign volunteers burst into spontaneous laughter.

"Hot damn." Hardy plopped a fat cigar into his mouth. "That little piece of *hot tail* won't know what hit her when we're through with her." His laughter deepened while the others around him sounded as fake as their smiles looked.

Dr. Zacher was no different. He watched the wealthy tycoon finish holding court with his young, bright-eyed minions while disgust curdled in his gut. But, as the research and development director, hobnobbing with the political and military elite was a part of his job description. It kept government security contracts flowing T4S's way.

This time, Zacher wasn't schmoozing alone.

"Pierce." Hardy's voice boomed across the room before he stomped over and whacked Pierce Spalding solidly on the back.

Spalding's eyes bulged, no doubt wondering whether the giant Texan had snapped his back in half. The look on the boss's face was the highlight of Zacher's night.

"Come on into my office," the governor invited them with a championship smile. "I always do my best thinking over a nice brandy."

"By all means," Spalding said, gesturing. "Lead the way."

The governor escorted his potential donors to the back office of his headquarters.

When Zacher entered the room, Hardy's gaze landed on him. "And what is it that you do, *boy?*"

Charles's back stiffened, but he kept his expression neutral. "The name is *Dr. Charles Zacher.* And I'm the head of research and development. I'm the one who brought your campaign to the attention of Mr. Spalding. I believe you're the perfect candidate to advance our mutual . . . *interest.*"

The corners of Hardy's lips twitched, but his pale blue eyes remained flat. "Given the amount of money T4S is considering donating to my PAC, your interests are *my* interests." He expanded his cheesy smile before launching the same bullshit alpha whack to Zacher's back—but this time he got a surprise. "Whoa, *boy.*" Hardy shook his hand. "What are you made out of—steel?"

Zacher smirked. "I've been known to put in a good workout every now and then."

Hardy's smile turned plastic as he re-evaluated Zacher. Afterward, he chuckled and headed to the bar. "Three brandies, coming right up. Have a seat."

Zacher and Spalding glanced at each other and ignored the offer to waltz around the room. Zacher took in all the campaign paraphernalia and the jubilant all-American photos that screamed *family values.* There were no photos of the trail of strippers and porno stars the good governor saw on a regular basis—the ones whom T4S had already signed to ironclad nondisclosure agreements and had written fat checks to silence them.

"Here we go." Hardy handed out the brandies while still wearing his plastic smile. "What do you say we make a toast?"

"In due time." Spalding shut him down and then moved to one of the empty chairs. "First, we should hammer out what our company's expectations are after you win the next election."

"Careful." Hardy wagged a finger. "That sounds a lot like quid pro quo language. I can't have anything to do with such illegal activity."

The room fell silent.

Hardy threw his head back and laughed. "I'm just fucking with you." He strolled over and leaned against his desk. "You should see the look on you guys' faces." He chuckled and chugged his brandy down in one gulp. "Now, why don't we cut through the bullshit and you two tell me how ol' Bo Hardy can be of service to T4S once I'm sitting in the Oval Office?"

8

Liberated from hospital duty, Castillo returned to the Agency—to her real life. When she strolled through the door, she was surprised to see her new employees Draya and Julian there, manning the phones. They were ringing off the hook. A first.

"Oh thank God, you're back." Draya hung up from a call. "How is Dennis?"

"Um, good." Castillo looked around. "What's going on?"

"What does it look like? We're hot." Julian laughed. "Turns out when you crack a child sex-trafficking ring and help bring down a presidency, it's good for business. Your schedule is crammed, packed for the next three months."

"No. That's not what I meant," Castillo said. "Did you guys clean up in here?"

Draya brightened. "I straightened up and organized a few things. You like it?"

She hated it. "Um, well. See . . . I kind of . . . have a system."

Draya's smile dimmed. "Does your system include a Magic 8-Ball? Because that's the only way you'd find anything in here."

"Funny." Castillo marched over to a row of file cabinets, only something was missing. "Where is the coffee machine?"

"Where it's supposed to be: in the kitchen."

"There's a kitchen?"

Draya slapped her hand onto her hip. "Please tell me you're joking."

Castillo shrugged. "Only slightly. Can you point me in the direction of this rumored kitchen?"

Draya took her by the shoulders, spun her around, and shoved her forward.

"Thanks."

"Uh-huh." Draya picked up a notebook and followed her boss into the kitchen.

Ding-dong.

Castillo jumped and spun around. "What in the hell was that?"

"Oh, we installed a digital bell. You like it? We can now hear someone when they come through the door."

"A what? For what? What was wrong with the old system?"

"What old system?"

"The one when someone walked into the office, and I look up and say, 'Hi, may I help you?'"

"I don't know. It's so . . . regressive."

"And a digital bell makes us the Jetsons?"

Julian rushed into the kitchen "There is a Mr. Trey Garrett here, wanting to speak to you."

Castillo shrugged. "Am I supposed to know who that is?"

Julian handed over a business card. "He says he's Kadir's parole officer." He stepped forward and lowered his voice. "Kadir might have missed a check-in appointment."

"That's not good." She pocketed the card and poured herself a cup of coffee. However, after a sip, she spat it back into her cup. "Aarrgh. What is this?"

The color zapped out of Draya's face. "Um. It's . . . coffee."

Castillo sniffed the pot and then spotted the coffee can next to the machine. "Decaf? Are you shitting me? This is just brown water." She clunked her mug down on the counter and abandoned it.

"I can make you some regular coffee." Draya rushed to dump the coffee into the sink. "Just give me a few minutes."

"Don't bother. My taste buds are ruined." Castillo stormed back into the office.

A chubby, slovenly dressed black man looked up with an unreadable expression. "You must be the famous Gizella Castillo." He extended his hand.

Castillo's brows sprang high up her forehead. "And you must be the one with the fancy business card. What can I do for you?"

"I'm looking for one of your employees: Kadir Kahlifa. Is he around?"

"Not at the moment. I sent him on an errand."

"To?"

"It's top secret . . . a private errand. I run a *private* investigation firm. Sometimes things have to be kept secret for our clients' protection. You understand?"

A corner of the parole officer's mouth sloped unevenly. "You understand that Kadir missing his appointment with me makes him in violation of his parole, and I can have him arrested and sent back to jail, right?"

Castillo's patience was strained.

"There must've been some kind of mix-up." Julian jumped into the conversation. "Kadir mentioned to me that his appointment was tomorrow. He must've gotten the dates mixed up," Julian lied and picked up his jacket. "I'll go and replace him on his . . . errand and, um, send him over to your office now."

The other corner of Garrett's lips lifted, but his smile missed his eyes. "I see. Then, why don't you do that, son? I need to lay eyes on him before five o'clock." He turned and headed toward the door. "This is strike one, and unlike baseball, he's out on the second strike. Do I make myself clear?"

Castillo folded her arms across her body. "Crystal."

"Good." Garrett opened the door, and that ridiculous digital

bell chimed. "By the way, nice place you have here. It's . . . cozy."
He winked. "Later."

Once he exited the office, Draya handed Castillo her fresh cup
of coffee. "Wow. What an asshole."

Castillo accepted the mug. "Nah. He's just doing his job." She
turned toward Julian. "You told me you didn't know where
Kadir was."

Julian smiled sheepishly as he slid on his jacket. "Yeah, um,
sorry about that. It's sort of a secret. We're not allowed to tell
anyone."

"We?" Castillo glanced at Draya. "You knew, too?"

Draya shrank beneath Castillo's disappointed gaze. "Sorry. We
were sworn to secrecy."

Castillo nodded. "I thought that I, um . . . never mind." She
headed to her desk. She wasn't about to whine about being kept
out of the loop. However, she had thought that she was a part of
their tight inner circle. How many times did she have to prove she
could be trusted?

"I better get going," Julian said.

"Yeah, sure." She waved Julian off. When the bell chimed as
he exited, Castillo snapped, "Disable that damn thing! It's already driving me nuts."

"Yes, ma'am." Draya rushed to take care of it.

Castillo pulled herself together. It was silly for her to feel hurt.
They don't owe her anything.

Draya returned to her desk and the ringing phones. However,
there was no way to ignore the palpable tension layering the
room.

"I assume that Kadir is with Abrianna?" Castillo asked.

Draya hesitated. "Yeah."

Castillo nodded and took another sip of coffee. "Are they all
right?"

Draya hesitated again.

"You would tell me if they got themselves tangled up in something again, right? If they were in trouble?"

Draya nodded and then burst into tears. "Oh my God. It's awful."

Castillo jumped out of her chair and rushed to Draya's side. "What's so awful? Something has happened, hasn't it? You can tell me. What is it?"

"We didn't want to burden you. You already have a lot on your plate. You know, with Dennis and all."

Castillo's heart sank. "How bad is it? Tell me."

"It's Bree. She was shot."

"What?"

"It's okay now," Draya reassured quickly. "She's awake, but . . . this shit can't keep happening. It's exhausting."

"Draya, who shot her?"

"That's just it. We don't know. We think it might be the same people who're behind Tomi Lehane's disappearance—but we don't have any proof."

Castillo grabbed Draya's hand and snatched her out of her seat. "Take me to her."

———————

After a night of making love, Kadir woke up hard and ready for another round. Abrianna submitted with a smile despite not being fully awake. These tender moments were too few and far between with them, but were treasured when they came around.

An hour later, they emerged from underneath the sheets, giggling, panting, and sweaty.

"We're going to have to get out of this bed sooner or later." Abrianna curled underneath his arm.

"I vote for later," he murmured, capturing her lower lip. "Much later."

"How about never?" she suggested.

"Sounds good to me." When she laughed, the sunlight streaming through the slats of the Venetian blinds splashed across her face in a way that stole his breath. His angel. "What do you say to us waking up like this for the rest of our lives?"

Abrianna's laughter faded even though her smile remained. She searched his face. "Are you . . . asking me something?"

Kadir froze as he replayed his own words in his head. He *was* asking her something. His heart skipped around in his chest. *What if she says no?* Why wouldn't she reject him? What did he have to offer? He was an ex-con with a federal noose ready to lynch him at any second. His current employment was at a small, private investigation firm, which paid barely above minimum wage. They had been able to stack some cash from a handful of political shows to whom they had granted exclusive interviews regarding how they, along with Tomi Lehane, had taken down a presidency, but what could he offer her for the future? All of this raced through his mind while Abrianna stared expectantly up at him.

Fuck it. "Will you marry me?" Kadir asked.

Abrianna lit up. "Yes!" She threw her arms around his neck and choked off his air supply. "Yes! Yes! Yes!"

He laughed until he had to tap out with a croak, "Air."

"Huh? Oh." She released him with a harder chuckle. "Sorry." Abrianna sat up in bed and had to do a double-check. "You are serious, right?"

"Absolutely," he assured her. "I know I'm supposed to have a ring and all but—"

"That's okay. We can shop for one later. I can't believe it." She gasped. "I gotta tell Shawn and Draya." She bolted out of bed, taking the top sheet with her.

"Wait. Where are you going?"

"I'll be right back." She raced out of the room, squealing.

—→•←—

Ghost opened the front door to his off-the-grid warehouse apartment to see Gizella Castillo standing next to a red-faced

Draya. "You've got to be shitting me. A cop? You brought a cop to my pad?"

"Where is she?" Castillo shoved the door open and pushed her way inside.

"Come the fuck on in then," Ghost offered. "Make yourself at home while you're at it."

"Sorry," Draya apologized to Ghost's towering size. "But she has a right to know."

"*Nobody* has a right to know about *this* place," Ghost countered. "That's the whole point of being off the grid. Can we try and wrap our minds around that concept?" He swung his gaze to Julian, who'd beat the women to the apartment by two minutes.

"Don't look at me. I didn't bring her here," Julian said.

Castillo had had enough. "Stop bitching and tell me where she is."

"I'll take you up to their room," Draya said.

"Of course, you will." Ghost rolled his eyes and then kicked the front door shut with the back of his heel.

Draya stopped and turned on Ghost. "There's no reason to be rude. Gizella is one of us."

"Correction: She's one of you all. She's not a part of *my* team. She's a cop."

"Ex-cop," Castillo amended.

"*And* you're also dating a cop—which makes you a double threat to my safety and liberty."

Castillo laughed. "Paranoid much?"

"You have no idea," Draya grumbled.

"Only around those who help prop up this unconstitutional police state the American people are held hostage to," Ghost ranted.

"Again. I'm not a cop." Castillo stepped forward.

Ghost also took a step forward. "You may as well be one."

A loud squeal filled the entire apartment. Castillo and Draya jumped while Ghost's hand automatically landed on the gun holstered to his hip.

"Draya, Draya, guess what?" Abrianna raced toward them.

Castillo took in Abrianna's wild hair, glowing face, and the sheet wrapped around her body. She felt foolish for having been worried.

Abrianna skidded to a stop and then threw her arms around both Draya and Castillo. "I'm getting married! I'm getting married!"

Draya and Castillo couldn't respond even if they tried. Abrianna's tight squeeze choked off their air. The women tugged on Abrianna's arms.

"Oops. Sorry about that. But can you believe it? Kadir just proposed. Where is Shawn?"

"He did what?" Ghost blinked and swiveled his gaze to his best buddy as he joined the crowd.

"Don't look so surprised." Kadir chuckled. "You had to have seen it coming."

Abrianna rushed back to his side where his long arms enveloped her, and he planted a kiss on her upturned face.

Their audience looked neither happy nor saddened by the news. They looked . . . shocked. It took a few seconds before the newly engaged couple noticed their lack of enthusiasm.

"What's the matter? Aren't you guys happy for us?" Abrianna asked.

"Huh? Yeah, of course." Draya plastered on a smile. "I'm . . . *thrilled* for you two."

"Congratulations," Castillo added.

"Yeah, congrats," Julian tossed in with a butterfly smile. "I'm happy for you, Bree."

"Thanks," Abrianna cheesed. "But, do me a favor and don't tell Shawn. I want to be the one to tell him. He'll kill me if he hears it from someone else."

"Sure, no problem," Draya agreed, and then cast a look at Julian.

Ghost folded his arms and shook his head.

Kadir sighed and met his buddy's gaze head-on. "I take it that you don't approve, Ghost?"

"You don't need any approval from me—to screw up your life. The man upstairs gave you free will for that shit."

"Thanks, Ghost. I knew I could depend on you for your support." Kadir's smile tightened.

"Uh-huh."

Julian snapped out of his shock. "Unless you're planning to have a jailhouse wedding, you might want to throw some clothes on and go see your parole officer. He came by the office looking for you. You missed a check-in appointment."

"Fuck!" Kadir spun on his heel and took off toward the bedroom. "Give me five minutes. I have to get dressed."

"No problem, man," Julian called out. "I'll just wait out here."

"He's not in a lot of trouble, is he?" Abrianna fretted.

"A little," Castillo said. "His PO is a prick, but if he wanted to play hardball, he would have called the cops already." She looked Abrianna over. "Care to fill me in on this whole getting shot business?"

"What? Oh." Abrianna waved off her concern. "It was nothing."

"Nothing?" Draya, Ghost, and Julian thundered.

"You were literally a corpse for three days," Ghost reminded her. "Again."

Castillo's confusion deepened. "Again?"

"Yeah. It's a nice parlor trick Bree pulls off every time she ODs or gets shot. The shit is creepy as hell."

Abrianna rolled her eyes. "Anyway, as you can see, I'm fine." She winced. "I have a bit of a headache, but other than that." She shrugged.

"Where were you shot?" Castillo stepped forward, ready to give a personal examination if need be.

"Um . . ."

"In the neck," Draya filled in for her.

Abrianna looked surprised. "My neck?" She reached up to touch it for herself.

"On the other side," her friends pointed out.

"Wait. You don't know where you were shot?" Castillo pulled Abrianna's hand down and inspected the whole area.

"I, um . . ."

"I don't see anything," Castillo said.

Ghost laughed. "Of course not. She's a freak of nature."

Castillo touched and felt around Abrianna's neck. "Amazing. What caliber?"

"It wasn't a bullet," Ghost informed her. "It was some type of poisonous dart. It dropped your girl like a stone."

"But who?"

"Going off a strong hunch, it had to be the same people behind Tomi's disappearance. I had Kadir take me over to her townhouse, and within minutes we were attacked."

"T4S?" Castillo asked, wanting to make sure that they were all on the same page.

"Who else?"

Kadir blew back into the room, pulling on a T-shirt and wiggling one foot into a shoe. "I'll be back as soon as I can. We have to celebrate tonight." He kissed Abrianna. "Make sure you get some rest, and I'll see you later."

Before Abrianna could say a word, Kadir and Julian raced out of the front door.

"Are you sure that he's not in any trouble?" she asked Castillo.

"We'll find out soon enough."

Abrianna looked panicked.

"I'm pretty sure he's going to be okay." Castillo folded her arms. "But back to you. What are you going to do? You can't just sit back and wait for those assholes to take you out again. And what about Tomi? What the hell are they doing to her? Is she still alive? Can we even rescue her? That place has got to be like Fort Knox."

"I don't want to sit on my hands and wait for them to take another swipe at me."

"Then let's call them out," Draya said.

"What do you mean?" Abrianna asked.

"Clearly, they're coming after you and Tomi because they want their secrets to remain hidden. I say we expose them. Put their business on Front Street. All of it."

A smile bloomed across Ghost's face. "I take all that shit I said earlier back. I liked you the moment I laid eyes on you."

Draya grinned. "To know me is to love me." She turned her attention back to Abrianna. "If you ask me, you don't have a choice."

Abrianna took two seconds to think it over. "You're right. I'll do it."

Ghost blinked. "You will?"

She nodded. "Yep. Something has got to give. And the best way to get anyone's attention in this town is in front of the cameras—on cable news."

"Another exclusive interview?" Ghost asked, following her thinking.

"You got it."

9

Sana'a, Yemen . . .

"It's not safe to travel to the funeral." Baasim Kahlifa pleaded, following his father around the room while he rushed to get dressed. "Please, stay home."

Muaadh Kahlifa shook his head. "Nonsense, son. They would not be so foolish as to bomb the funeral of such a prominent diplomat—especially one who has fought diligently to broker their peace deal. No, Baasim. You're letting the rebels' foolish talk get the best of you. Even war has morals."

"Maybe once upon a time, father. But we are not up against people who believe in rules, honor, or even morals. Look around." Baasim stepped forward. "Millions have fled the country. Too many are starving in the streets, and Allah only knows how many others are in desperate need of medical care. The Saudis and their coalition of murderers are not interested in peace. They are intent on destroying this country. They will not stop until they've destroyed every Shia-armed militia. They've declared them all part of al-Qaeda or ISIL—whatever it takes to get the west to stream an endless supply of weapons and launch indiscriminant air attacks. This is a proxy war against Iran—you know this!"

"Are you going to preach to me that Iran's hands are clean in this?"

Baasim sucked in a huge breath.

"I didn't think so." Muaadh smiled. "Look. I know a great many things—even the things you think I do not know." He pulled a deep, patient breath and then gazed into his son's eyes. "Now, stop this. You're worrying for nothing. It's only proper that I pay my respects to the Ruwayshan family. You could come with me or stay here with your mother. Either way, I am going." He patted Baasim's shoulder and then turned and wrapped his head in a white scarf.

"Foolish, foolish man." His mother burst into tears and raced from the door.

"Daishan," Muaadh called out, but when his wife failed to return, he shook his head. "Women."

"I can't blame her for being upset, father. We're living in difficult times. People are dying all around us."

Muaadh sighed. "You're not going to start that nonsense about our returning to the States again, are you?"

"I can't believe I'm about to say this, but it's safer."

"Ha! Who are you—Kadir or Baasim? I can't tell you two apart anymore."

Baasim ground his teeth and counted to ten before trying again. "Kadir and I don't agree on a lot of things—"

"You don't agree on anything, the last time I checked. But now you keep coming to me with talk about returning to America— the land of double talk, immorality, and corruption. No, I won't hear of it. They already stole one son from me. I won't have them take another person or anything from me. No."

"And how much has this country taken? Can we even call it a country anymore? It's infested by infidels and extremists."

"But it is *our* land!" Muaadh jabbed Baasim's chest with his finger. "It is in *our* blood! We fight for what belongs to us! We fight for our people!"

Baasim hung his head. There was no point in arguing with his father. Once his mind was made up there was no changing it. "I will go and pay respects with you."

A smile bloomed across Muaadh's face. "Ah, there's my good son."

The White House . . .

At five a.m., President Kate Washington marched into the Situation Room. Her secretary of state, Raymond Ford, generals from the Pentagon, and her national security team were already seated around the table. In five minutes, the team reviewed the plans for a risky attack on a heavily guarded home of a senior al-Qaeda collaborator. However, it wasn't the who that was the problem, but the where. The house was smack-dab in the middle of a mountainous village in the remote part of central Yemen.

The mission had once been rejected by the previous administration. Former President Walker had believed that the commando raid was too risky for the American Special Operations forces and foreign civilians alike.

However, Kate was desperate for a win—actually, she needed several of them. She needed wins in her foreign policy. She had to prove that a woman could protect the nation. She needed to display strength and show no mercy to America's enemies.

In the months since Walker's decision, the US military had intercepted arms shipments from Iran to Yemen—more specifically to the Houthis. The Houthis began as a theological movement, preaching peace, but now they were at the center of an international conflict. The rise of the Shia rebels picked up momentum when thousands of supporters of the movement protested in the streets of the Yemeni capital Sana'a, urging the government to step down. Since the government was indeed propped up by the west, that was never going to happen.

The Houthis' rise in power sparked fears of Iranian expansionism along the porous border Saudi Arabia shared with Yemen. The Arab Gulf States charged that Iran controlled four Arab capitals: Baghdad, Damascus, Beirut, *and* Sana'a.

The two missions presented to Kate addressed former president Walker's previous concerns and were now described as low-risk. A simple smash and grab for intelligence. At present, SEAL Team 6 rotated into the region every six months, and the national mission force required presidential approval to attack. Their team working with the United Arab Emirates concluded that suspicious activity was happening in the small village. A raid for electronics and documents would reveal al-Qaeda membership and concentrations. The official mission was to then exploit the stolen material and stage rapid follow-up airstrikes. The *unofficial* mission was to kill or capture Qasim al-Rimi and suspected al-Qaeda leaders hiding in the area.

Kate salivated at the chance to hang two al-Qaeda leaders on her mission-accomplished wall. No matter what happened, it was going to be a game changer. If the leaders were present, it would be a big win. If not, then the fruitful site exploitation would lead to successful follow-up raids. Her mind was made up long before her Joint Special Operations Command finished their brief on it and a second target within the same area. With a smile, Kate signed her name across the executive order. "Time to make America proud."

Sana'a, Yemen . . .

It was early in the afternoon when the Al-Sala Al-Kubra Community Hall filled up with men wearing white scarves and carrying traditional *jambiyas* in their belts. Thousands crowded the Great Hall among rumors that the former president, a Houthi ally, would also be in attendance. That got the room buzzing and served as further proof that there would be no strike on the funeral's proceeding.

Baasim remained unconvinced and stuck to his father's side like glue. The services started, and the Great Hall filled with music—and something else.

A few people were suddenly on the move.

Baasim's head sprang up, and he cast a worried look around the room.

At his side, his father continued chanting and appeared utterly unbothered.

"Is that a jet?" someone murmured.

More heads sprung up with panicked looks.

A loud rumble drowned out the music. The sound was unmistakable. An aircraft—flying low.

Baasim tugged his father's arm and hissed. "We have to leave."

Muaadh sighed. His entire body crumbled. "You can go, son. I'm not leaving.

"What?"

The hall shook for the third time, followed by a loud whistling.

Baasim hopped to his feet and, again, attempted to pull his father up. "It's a missile!"

Everyone scattered, except for Muaadh.

"Father!"

BOOM!

10

Scott Wolf jutted his head into the Oval Office. "Madam President?"

Kate straightened with the phone tucked beneath her chin. "Yes. What is it?"

"You're needed in the Situation Room."

One look and she knew it was more bad news. "On my way." She returned her attention to her call. "I'm sorry, but duty calls. We'll continue this conversation at another time, Prime Minister Trudeau. Yes. It's been a pleasure." Kate hung up the phone and jumped out of her chair.

"Should I come with you?" Haverty asked, standing from the chair before her desk.

"Sure, come along."

Once she and Haverty joined Wolf in the hall, she asked, "So, what's the emergency?"

"I'll let the generals fill you in," Wolf said.

"That bad, huh." Kate and Wolf finished their march to the Situation Room.

Once Kate took her seat, Secretary of Defense Robert Easton launched into his briefing. "SEAL Team Six landed five miles downhill from the objective. Our SEALs hiked to the village in silence to surprise the AQAP operatives. But as the SEALs neared the village's outskirts, there was trouble. Overhead, drones and spy planes detected unusual activity."

"The mission was compromised?"

"We have reason to believe that may have been the case. Overhead surveillance of the targeted area revealed fighters moving into position ahead of our arrival."

"You knew you'd lost the element of surprise and you went ahead anyway? Why wasn't I informed?"

The generals cast looks among themselves.

Easton cleared his throat. "We assessed that it didn't change our objective, Madam President. We did review the risk versus the payoff and decided to proceed."

Kate read the room. "I take it that things didn't go according to plan?"

Easton drew a deep breath. "That is correct, Madam President."

"Figures." Kate sighed. "Give me the bad news. What happened?"

"Entering the village, the SEALs met fierce and unexpected resistance. Landmines and defensive positions were prepared. Even women took up arms. Within the first five minutes of the firefight, a SEAL was mortally wounded, hit with a bullet above his armored breastplate. A MEDEVAC was deployed. On the ground, the SEALs continued to battle. Twenty-six AQAP fighters were killed, including two leaders. However, al-Rimi was not at the target. In addition to the SEAL's death and multiple American injuries, the unraveling of the mission also resulted in the death of at least thirty civilians, according to our sources. Half of those civilians were children. All in all, within fifty minutes it was over. We lost one SEAL. At least ten additional American servicemen were injured. The site exploitation was also compromised. Because of the injuries, the destruction, and the quick exit, we did not have enough time to collect documents and electronics."

Kate took in all of the information. "So, it was one big cluster-fuck, that's what you're telling me? We killed all those people, lost an eighty-million-dollar plane, gathered *no* intelligence, and captured *no* terrorist leaders," she concluded, feeling her blood pressure rise.

"I can tell you . . . that we did everything in our power to prevent loss of life for innocent civilians," said Easton. "But combat is a dirty business, especially up close and personal on missions like these."

Kate saw his mouth moving, but she only heard the possible spin from her political enemies playing across every cable and talk radio station once word of these missions leaked to the press.

They would all have a field day.

"We also have a bit of further bad news."

"What a shock."

Easton continued, "Our second airstrikes hit their target in Sana'a. However, we've since learned that the intelligence was faulty. We struck a funeral ceremony."

"A funeral?" Kate echoed.

"How in the hell did command fuck that up?"

"We don't believe the intelligence failure was on our end."

"What the hell is that supposed to mean? The Saudis lied to us?"

"That or they were simply . . . wrong."

An instant headache exploded against Kate's temples. "So, we just murdered how many more people?"

"We're still accessing the numbers, but thousands were attending the services."

"Fuck. Of course there were." Kate sighed. "I should have known this shit was too good to be true," she swore, shaking her head.

The room fell silent while the president processed what this all meant to her political career. Then, Kate's gaze sliced toward Easton. "You work at the pleasure of the president, right?"

Easton cast another look around the Situation Room table. "That is correct, Madam President."

"That's unfortunate—because I'm *not* pleased."

"Yes, Madam President."

She stood from the table. "You're relieved of duty, general. Enjoy civilian life."

11

A determined Dr. Charles Zacher marched into his large lab at T4S to check on his test subject, Tomi Lehane. "How is she doing?" he asked, stopping before the floor-to-ceiling Plexiglas dividing the room.

His assistant, Ned, rushed to his side. "We still have brain activity."

Zacher nodded, satisfied. Monitoring the young reporter was tricky. Since she'd been under his care, she has been in a coma-like state—with no pulse. The extraction team believed she was dead, but Zacher remembered an incident in Lehane's file when an old boyfriend had believed she'd died in her sleep and made a 911 call only to see his girlfriend rise from the dead on the paramedic's gurney. Needless to say, that was the end of that relationship.

He was close. He could feel it. After years of trying to replicate Dr. Craig Avery's experiments to create the perfect super soldier for T4S, he was on the verge of a breakthrough. The best part for Zacher was that he hadn't stacked up anywhere near the number of dead bodies as the late genius or thrown the city into another panic by snatching teenagers off the streets. He did kidnap one *former* teenage test subject, but that was fudging the margins a bit.

Ned fidgeted at his side.

Zacher reeled in his annoyance. "What is it?"

"It's, um. Have you given it any more thought as to how she started that fire?"

Zacher had thought of little else. He'd known about the mind reading, telekinesis, self-healing, and their extraordinary strength— but the ability to set fires? That possibility—that kind of power— made his dick hard.

"Sir?"

"One puzzle at a time." Zacher stared at his test subject with a tinge of regret. She looked nothing like the feisty reporter who'd monopolized the cable news circuit a few weeks ago. Gone were her long, dark locks. Zacher had shaved them off. The once rosy tint to her cheeks and lips was gone. Now she was the unattractive color of paste and bordering on white marble.

No matter.

She was still alive—which meant she was useful to him.

The back of Dr. Z's head tingled. "Spalding is here."

"Sir?"

The metal door slid open behind them, and Pierce Spalding stepped into the lab.

"How did you—?"

"Dr. Zacher," Spalding's hard baritone rumbled across the cold room. "You're a difficult man to get a hold of."

Zacher plastered on his professional smile, spun on his heel and greeted his boss. "Spalding, to what do I owe this pleasure?"

The men clasped hands and shook.

"I think you know. I've been waiting for a status report on our . . . guest here for over a month." Spalding move to stand in front of the Plexiglas to gaze at Lehane strapped down by reinforced restraints.

"I'm still working on it." Zacher returned his attention to Lehane.

"That's it? I've traveled all this way for nothing? What about the blood? Your last report said you were running tests."

Zacher sighed. He didn't like discussing an incomplete report, but Spalding's hovering made it clear that he had no choice.

"Oh, the blood tests are fascinating," Ned piped up.

Zacher cut Ned a murderous look.

"Is that right, now?" Spalding inquired, crossing his arms. "I'd love to hear about it."

"Ned, why don't you go and get us some coffee," Zacher suggested through clenched teeth.

"Uh, yes, sir."

"I take mine black," Spalding told Ned.

"Sir. Right, sir." Ned tripped over air, scrambling to get out of the lab.

The men watched him.

Zacher was annoyed—and Spalding amused.

"It's hard to get good help these days," Spalding joked.

"You have no idea."

Spalding slapped Zacher's back. "Now, what about those test results? What's so fascinating about them?"

Zacher turned away from the Plexiglas and walked over to his cluttered desk. "I'm still working on the way to best describe it. The white blood cells are off the chart. As you know, the normal leukocyte count for a healthy individual is usually between forty-three hundred and ten thousand eight hundred cells per cubic millimeter of blood."

"Yeah."

"Lehane is testing at nearly three times that. It's far higher than anything we had on Shalisa White at St. Elizabeth's. I believe that it may be because of time. It's been seven years since Avery injected them with his serum, and it has matured into something . . . fascinating—to borrow Ned's word."

"High white cell count indicates inflammation. Is it in the subject's urine, too?"

"No. Not a trace."

Spalding frowned.

"The samples I drew on Monday were different than the one I drew on Wednesday. And those were different from the sample I drew on Friday."

"I don't follow. How is that possible?"

"It's another mystery. It's almost as if . . ." Zacher struggled for an explanation.

Spalding grew frustrated when Zacher's mental computer remained frozen. "Don't hurt yourself. You need to figure this out and replicate it."

I'm trying.

"Any idea how long that will take?"

"It's a bit premature for me to give you an ETA on this. What's amazing is how her white cells demolish everything I throw at them: bacteria, viral and infectious agents. It doesn't matter. Malaria, hepatitis-C—"

"Cancer?"

"Obliterate cancer cells—within *hours.*" Zacher exhaled. "We've known about the self-healing mechanism—broken bones, gunshots—but this is something different altogether."

"The burns?"

Zacher nodded. "When they brought her in, she had burns over sixty percent of her body; as you can see there isn't a mark on her."

A smile eased across Spalding's face. "She's the real deal."

"Not only that . . . Follow me." Zacher led Spalding to the metal door next to the Plexiglas and slid his identity card and pressed his thumb against the security pad. The metal lock disengaged and allowed both him and Spalding into Lehane's chamber. The second they crossed the threshold, static charged in the air.

Spalding watched the hair on his arm stand up.

Zacher smiled. "It takes a while to get used to that."

"Amazing. This is coming from her?"

Dr. Z nodded and walked over to his subject, still strapped down. From a metal tray next to the bed, Zacher grabbed a pair of rubber gloves from a box and put them on. Next, he stripped a new syringe out of its package. "The first three times I drew Ms. Lehane's blood, I had no trouble." He uncapped the needle. "Now, it's a different story." He went to prick her arm, but instead of puncturing her skin, the needle bent.

"What the—"

Zacher added more pressure until the needle snapped.

"Holy shit."

"Exactly. I've tried several different instruments with the same results. My hypothesis is that the subject is not in a coma but is in a sort of . . . chrysalis. Out of three samples we obtained, the leukocyte is only a fraction of what's going on. Her cellular structure is in a constant state of change—like it's trying to perfect her DNA. The only question is: What is she transforming into?"

"Fascinating. We can reap the rewards for Avery's expensive experiments—finally. You have to figure out a workaround to start dissecting."

"Dissecting?"

Spalding's brows dipped together. "We have to get under the hood and find out exactly how *everything* works."

"But then she would die."

"An unfortunate side effect."

Zacher remained confused.

Spalding patted Zacher's arm. "Don't worry. We still have Abrianna Parker for backup."

12

"Mr. Kahlifa, I'm glad to see that you could squeeze me into your busy schedule." Trey Garrett leaned back in his chair and evaluated his parolee after he bolted through the door.

Kadir rushed to explain. "I'm sorry about that, Mr. Garrett. I'm not sure how I got the date screwed up, but I promise you that I'll take extra precautions from here on out to make sure that it will never happen again."

A silence grew thick and heavy between them.

Kadir came close to beseeching the man with prayer hands when Garrett sighed and set his front chair legs back down solidly on the floor. "See to it that it doesn't." He gestured to the empty chair in front of his desk. "Have a seat."

Relief flooded Kadir's body before he jetted to the chair. Once seated, he was handed a clipboard with a questionnaire.

"You moved," Garrett said. "You don't think that I should have known that?"

"Um, I'd planned to tell you that on my next appointment."

"You mean the one appointment that you missed?"

Kadir grimaced.

"I take it that you're living with the girlfriend whose face is plastered all over the place?"

"Yes. We're, um . . ." Kadir's smile grew. "We're engaged."

Garrett's eyebrows jumped and crashed into his hairline. "Congratulations. You two are barreling full steam ahead, huh? How long have you known each other?"

Kadir stiffened.

"I don't mean to pry," Garrett added.

Kadir chuckled and met Garrett's gaze head-on. "That's not true."

A real smile laced Garrett's face. "You're right. I'm prying—especially since you're not following the rules. If I were a hardass, you'd be on your way back to prison right now. You've broken enough rules."

"Like I said, it won't happen again."

"I believe you." Garret set a plastic cup on the desk.

Kadir sighed.

Garrett cocked his head. "Is there a problem?"

"Huh? No." Kadir forced a smile. "No problem. You, um, got a pen?"

"Always." Garrett snatched a pen from his desk and handed it over.

Kadir rushed through the questionnaire as fast as he could, feeling Garrett's eyes on him the whole time. He suppressed the urge to ask the man to stop staring. After he begged for a second chance, he couldn't then flip the script and come off hostile or confrontational. He finished the questionnaire and handed it back.

"You know what comes next," Garrett said, nodding to the cup.

Kadir hung onto his smile as he stood and picked up the cup. And as he strolled to the bathroom, Garrett climbed out of his chair and followed.

At Kadir's deep sigh, his PO laughed. "C'mon. This isn't exactly pleasant for me either, you know. It's standard practice to make sure your piss actually comes out of your dick."

"Yeah, I get it." Kadir pushed through the bathroom door and unbuttoned himself at the urinal.

And then nothing.

After a full minute, Garrett asked. "Are you dehydrated or something?"

No. I just don't like another man looking at my dick. "Can you, um, turn around or something? A little bit?"

Garrett laughed. "Really? How in the hell did you make it in prison?"

"One day at a time."

"Fine. I'll turn one shoulder."

"Thanks, I appreciate that."

As soon as Garrett turned, Kadir's bladder gave up the ghost and unleashed more than enough to fill up the small sample cup. Once it was capped and sealed, Garrett produced a brown paper bag and exited the bathroom. "See, that wasn't so bad, was it?"

Kadir didn't respond.

When they returned to the main office, a young woman waited.

Garrett handed over Kadir's sample like he was handing over a takeout order. "Barb, please take this next door to the lab."

"Yes, sir, Mr. Garrett." Barb took the bag, flashed the men a smile, and then rushed out of the office.

"Now if I can get your fifty-dollar fee, then you can be on your way."

"Fee?" Kadir patted his back pocket for his wallet—the wallet he'd forgotten. *Shit.*

"Is there a problem?"

"No, um. Could you give me a second? I think I left my wallet out in the car."

Garrett lifted a brow but then gestured for him to go on.

"Thanks." Kadir jogged out to the car, where Julian waited for him. "Can you do me a favor and loan me fifty dollars? I forgot my wallet."

Julian laughed. "Damn, man. You're having quite a day."

"I'm batting about a five hundred. I still got engaged this morning."

Julian's smile tightened. "True that."

Kadir cocked his head. "Do you have a problem with Abrianna and me getting married?"

"Nah." Julian's gaze fell while he dug out his wallet and then fished out fifty dollars. "Here you go."

Kadir accepted the money and then wondered whether he should push for an honest answer. "Thanks, I'll get this back to you when you drop me back off at the house."

"No problem."

Kadir turned and marched back into the office. The whole way, Julian's gaze burned a hole into his back.

Garrett took Kadir's payment and jotted out a receipt.

Kadir glanced at the television suspended in the corner of the office. CNN's red banner said "Breaking News" in bold letters. He turned away, but then his gaze snagged on the words "Sana'a, Yemen." "Hey, can you turn that up?"

Garrett looked up to see what had caught Kadir's attention, and then he reached for the remote on his desk.

"At least twenty-three civilians, including women and children, were killed in a Yemen raid on an al-Qaeda target according to sources. Questions mount over the botched raid approved by President Washington."

Kadir moved away from Garrett's desk and walked toward the screen, hypnotized.

On screen, the images cut from piles of rubble to the White House Press Room.

The White House press secretary, Sam Murphy, marched into the pressroom and straight over to the podium. *"Afternoon, everyone,"* he greeted. *"I want to inform you that the president got off the phone just a short time ago with Canadian Prime Minister Trudeau, discussing an attack on a Quebec City mosque last night. She offered her thoughts and prayers to the victims and families as well to all Canadians."*

Kadir sucked in an impatient breath. "C'mon, get back to what's going on at Sana'a."

"That's right. You have family over there," Garrett said, moving to stand next to him.

Murphy continued, *"Also we carried out a successful raid against al-Qaeda in the Arabian Peninsula, which resulted in the death of an estimate twenty-six AQAP members and the capture of important intelligence that will better enable us to counter and prevent future terrorist plots."* Murphy cleared his throat. *"Tragically, during this raid, the life of a brave service member, Alex Jamison, was taken, and ten were wounded. Our thoughts and prayers are with the family of this fallen American hero, and we also pray for a speedy and complete recovery of those service members who sustained injuries.*

"President Washington traveled today to Dover Air Force Base to join the Jamison family as his remains were returned to the US. Amid new reports raising questions about the operation, I want to make clear that the detailed, public accounting of the decision-making process began during the Walker administration. I'll open the floor up for questions."

Immediately, the crowd of press reporters shouted out questions. Kadir spun on his heel. "I have to go."

Garrett turned with him. "Hey, is everything all right?"

"I don't know yet." Kadir marched out of the door.

Garrett watched as Kadir jumped into the passenger side of Julian's SUV. "See you next month," he shouted. "On time!"

Julian disconnected his call and started the vehicle. "You good?"

"Yeah. Can you get me back to Ghost's crib?"

"Sure thing." Julian backed out of the parking space and then pulled off. "Are you sure you're all right?"

"I will be. As soon as I get a hold of my parents."

The president took a deep breath and then watched her press secretary get slaughtered by the press. Despite the White House calling the Yemen disaster an unmitigated success, every reporter and political enemy knew otherwise. More blood was in the water and the sharks were circling. "Just fuck me."

"I don't know. Murphy is holding up well," Wolf said, nodding toward the screen.

Kate took another look and watched Murphy swipe back sweat, stumble through explanations, and promise to get back with them at a later date on questions he didn't know the answers to. "Are we watching the same program?"

"It's going to be fine. We'll get our operatives out on the cable shows and push our talking points. This is a two-day news story—tops."

13

Kadir believed the worst.

All hope had twisted into a giant knot and settled at the bottom of his gut. He'd known since his release from prison how bad the civil war in Yemen had gotten. He'd even talked until he was blue in the face trying to convince his father that he should return to the United States. His parents held dual citizenship. They could return at any time. But his father refused.

America had changed since 9/11. Tolerance for Muslims disappeared the moment those planes crashed into those buildings in New York. At first political leaders preached tolerance, but a decade later, they saw that there was more power in stoking fear than tolerance. After Kadir, a military veteran, was thrown in jail for what his father called a political witch hunt, his parents declared the American dream a giant illusion and opted to return to their homeland. Two years later, the country was plunged into a civil war between the Houthi rebels and supporters of Yemen's internationally recognized government.

The Houthi and the Yemeni government had battled on and off since 2004, but much of the fighting had been confined to the Houthis' stronghold, northern Yemen's impoverished Saada province

A decade later, the Houthis controlled Yemen's capital, Sana'a, and proceeded to push southward toward the country's second-biggest city, Aden. Alarmed by the rise of a group they believed to be backed militarily by Iran, the regional Shia power, Saudi Arabia and eight other mostly Sunni Arab states began an air campaign aimed at restoring Yemen's government. The coalition received logistical and intelligence support from the United States, United Kingdom, and France.

They have been fighting ever since.

Julian and Kadir rode back to Ghost's place in a tomb of silence, which to Kadir took forever. Kadir's entire life passed before his eyes several times during the trip. His mind had focused on all the times he'd disappointed his parents, whether they were real or imagined. However, that wasn't the case for his twin brother.

Baasim was the golden child, Muaadh reincarnated. They shared the same beliefs and ideals. Kadir envied his twin for that. Envy was tricky. It wasn't jealousy, but it was in the general area. Kadir never doubted that his father loved him—even now. But nothing he could ever do would get him closer than Baasim in his father's heart. And then there was his mother, Daishan. She was the epitome of femininity and motherhood. The sun rose and set on her boys. Their happiness fulfilled her, and it took so little to either put a smile on her lips or bring a tear to her eyes.

Kadir drew in a ragged breath. Suddenly, he missed them so much that his entire body ached.

Julian had barely rolled to a stop in front of Ghost's place before Kadir hopped out of the vehicle and rushed into the building.

Clustered among her friends, Abrianna jumped up from the couch when Kadir stormed into the apartment. "Baby, you're back."

Kadir said nothing as he blew past the living room and headed straight to the guest room.

Julian entered the apartment, and everyone's gaze swung in his direction.

"What's going on?" Abrianna asked.

"I'm not sure, but I think it has something to do with his parents."

"What?" Abrianna broke free from her circle and rushed after Kadir to the bedroom. "Kadir?" She entered the room to find him placing the SIM card back into his cell phone—a big no-no at Ghost's place. "What are you doing? What's going on?"

"I got to get in contact with my parents. Something is going on in Sana'a."

"What?"

"It's all over the news—some sort of coalition attack that went to shit. They're reporting civilian causalities—both women and children."

"Oh baby. I'm sorry." She waltzed over to him and attempted to draw him into her arms, but he turned away and pressed call on his cell phone.

We're sorry. You've reached a number that is no longer in service.

"The fuck?" He hung up and then tried the number again.

Torn between wanting to be there for him and giving him his space, Abrianna sat on the edge of the bed and watched him pace while he tried one number after another. Then, finally . . .

"It's ringing," he said. Hope transformed his entire body.

Abrianna smiled and crossed her fingers. Despite getting through a few miraculous events in her life, she still wasn't buying into the notion of an invisible, let alone merciful, God granting wishes if you prayed to him in the right way.

"Hello, Baasim," Kadir said. "It's Kadir. I'm, um, hearing some disturbing news out of Sana'a. I'm concerned about Ummi and Baba . . . and, of course, you. I can't get either one of them on the phone. I'm hoping that you get this message and will call me back—as soon as you can. Please. All right, then. I'll talk to you soon." He wanted to say more, but words failed him, and Kadir ended with an awkward "Bye." He disconnected the call and then just stared at the phone.

"He'll call back," Abrianna said.

Kadir nodded. "If he's alive."

"Of course he's alive." She sprang up from the bed. "You mustn't think like that." Again, she attempted to wrap her arms around him, but he shied away. "I'm sorry—but are you mad at me?"

"What?" Kadir met her gaze. "No."

She fluttered on a smile and tried not to feel ridiculous. This time when she took Kadir's hand and braided it together with hers, he didn't pull away. "I just . . . don't know what I'd do if . . ."

"Don't do that." She pressed close to him. "We'll hope for the best and deal with whatever comes our way . . . *together*. We're a unit now."

A corner of his lips curled upward. "Together. Yeah. I like that."

———❖———

"Amateur hour is over," Bo Hardy declared to a crowd of 40,000 beneath the political banner reading "Rise Up." "It's time for the little lady in the White House to admit that she's way over her head. We have Navy SEALs dying left and right—innocent civilians being *murdered* in their own beds. And President Washington has the nerve to look the American public in the eye and call that hot mess in Yemen a success."

The Texas crowd booed and jeered.

"Humph." Hardy shook his head. "If that's what the government calls a success, then I'd hate to see what failure looks like."

The jeers turned into cheers.

Hardy's lips stretched across his face. He had his fans in the palm of his hand, and he reveled in it like a king before his court.

"The American people need to send a man to do a man's job. What? What? Somebody has got to say it, right?"

The crowd went wild.

———————

The president muted the television and then sliced an angry glare toward Wolf. "A two-day story, huh?"

He sucked in a breath and looked around the room, but no one was going to take a verbal bullet for him.

"I don't know why the fuck I even listened to you. You told me that raid was a win-win. Does this look like we're winning to you? Huh?"

Wolf hung his head so low that it was almost at the center of his chest.

"Here I am, the most powerful woman in the world, and I can't get shit done. Everywhere I look I got Parker and Hardy two-tagging my ass all over cable news. I'm living inside the fucking Twilight Zone. I can't shake either one of these muthafuckas off."

The office remained quiet.

"Right. Nobody has shit to say." Kate sighed. "Get out!"

"Madam President—"

"Get. The. Fuck. Out! Or does no one understand English anymore? Do I need to get an interpreter or something?"

The platoon of political ass-kissers filed out of her office. All except Don Davidson, who lingered by the door.

"Let's have it," Kate barked. "I know you have plenty to say."

"Don't you think that you may be overreacting?"

"I have a lot at stake." She thrust up her chin. "I sacrificed a lot to get in this office. I've made history as the first female president."

"But you weren't elected—not to mention, you have blood on your hands."

Kate's eyes narrowed. "Why do you keep bringing that up?"

Davidson pulled her into his arms and pinched her ass. "Maybe I like getting a rise out of you. Your angry face gets my dick hard."

Kate shoved him back and then slapped the hell out of him. "The fuck is wrong with you?"

"Whoa-ho." Davidson cupped his face where her handprint glowed. "The president has a temper." He grabbed her again, this time by her hair, and yanked her flush against his body. When she struggled to squirm out of his embrace, he tightened his grip. "That's right, Katie. Fight me." He backed her up to the office's desk. "I like it when you fight."

"Get off of me before I scream."

Davidson shoved his hand in between Kate's legs. "Just what I thought: nice and wet." He slipped two fingers in between her pussy's lips and twirled them around while he nibbled on her earlobe. "I know what you want." He laughed.

Kate lifted her chin in defiance, but the act only exposed her long neck for him to devour. Her pulse raced at the sound of his zipper zipping down and then he entered her with one powerful thrust. They yanked, pulled, and clawed at each other until they were sweaty and well satisfied.

"Damn, woman. If you weren't married, I might've been persuaded to put a ring on your fine ass." He slapped her ass for emphasis and then tucked his wet dick back into his boxers.

The president pushed off of her office desk, straightened her panties and clothes, and then slapped the taste out of Davidson's mouth. "You do that shit again, and I'll have your ass thrown into Gitmo. Do you understand me?"

Davidson's other cheek now glowed red. "Yes, Madam President." With a wink, he turned to walk out of the Oval Office.

14

Abrianna lay in bed next to her fiancé, craving a fix.

It had been two months since her last hit. Actually, sixty-four days, but she swore that she wasn't counting. She was past the physical withdrawal, but the mental ones were a son of a bitch. The constant negotiating to go five, ten minutes—or even another night—longer exhausted her.

"Are you all right?" Kadir brushed a kiss against the top of her head.

"Hmm?"

"You seem . . . tense," he said. "I hope it isn't because of me."

She seized on the excuse. "What? Are you the only one allowed to worry?"

"No, but—"

"But nothing. Your family is *my* family now. I'm sure everything is going to be fine. For once, I'm going to be the optimist. Like Ghost said, we'll get up in the morning and go to the state department and see if we can get hold of someone at the embassy in Yemen. We'll find out the truth—at the very least about your brother. He's a natural-born American citizen. Right?"

Kadir nodded, but he didn't meet her gaze in the moonlight.

Abrianna noticed something. "How come you never talk about your brother?"

"Baasim?"

"Uh-huh." She propped herself up on her side and started playing with the hairs on his chest. "I always thought that twins were like inseparable or something."

"What? Did you read that off the internet?"

"Where else? Everything is on the internet these days." She leaned over and kissed him. "Mmm." She loved the way he tasted.

"I love it when you do that." Kadir pulled her down and slid his finger through the back of her hair. "I bet I can make you moan even louder than that."

"Oh, that's easy money. What will you give me if I make *you* moan? Hmm?" She straddled his hips.

Kadir's brows rose up to meet his hairline. "Everything I have is yours."

"Is that right?" She reached in between her legs and positioned his cock so she could ease him all the way in.

Kadir hissed. She was as tight as a virgin. Surely, her body's natural healing ability had something to do with that. He struggled to control and pace himself. It was either that or embarrass himself by coming within a couple strokes. When he bit his lower lip, the jig was up. Abrianna laughed. "Are you holding out on me?" She rotated her hips. "Hmm? Is that what you're doing?"

Kadir squeezed his eyes tight, but the moan was out of his mouth before he could stop it. The next twenty minutes was nothing but sheer bliss—two souls becoming one. Kadir had to have been a wish her heart made when she wasn't looking. He was perfect for her. They were perfect together.

Sated, Abrianna rolled over. "You did it again."

Kadir snuggled into a spoon. "Did what again?"

She turned in his arms to look up at him. "Avoided telling me about your brother."

Kadir drew a deep breath. "There's not much to tell. He's my other half in a way. He looks like me and talks like my father."

"Were you two close?"

"We were, and we weren't. I think our Facebook status would be: it's complicated." He curled a lock of her hair around his finger. "I wish that we were closer. When we were kids, we were. We did everything together—all the annoying things like dressing alike and finishing each other sentences."

"What happened?"

Kadir shrugged. "We grew up."

The silence that followed was different, so Abrianna waited. There was something that he wasn't telling her. Then, she took a guess. "Was it a girl?"

He stiffened.

"Malala," she said, uneasy about bringing up Kadir's first fiancée.

Kadir stopped playing with her hair and drew a deep breath.

"So you both liked the same girl? Is that it?"

"Baasim . . . noticed Malala first. He used to write reams of poetry about her. I even teased him about it, never letting on that I liked her, too."

"And then?"

"And then . . . one day I stole one of Baasim's poems, and I gave it to her—only she thought it was from me."

"Oh you slick dog." She playfully popped him on the shoulder. "You stole your brother's girl."

Kadir sat up in bed and hung his head. "Technically, she wasn't his girl. He never made a move. Hell, he wasn't even planning to."

"So, you stepped up?"

"Something like that." He shook his head. "I wish that I could say that I'm sorry about it, but . . . I'm not. I'm sorry I hurt my brother. What I did wasn't honorable or anything. But what Malala and I had . . . we were . . ."

Soul mates.

He didn't say it, but the word lingered between them just the same.

Abrianna recalled the broken picture frame in Kadir's old apartment and understood perfectly why the brothers fell for the girl. Judging from their prom picture, she was a burgeoning beauty who could've had any man she wanted.

"Eventually, Baasim got over it—even claimed that he'd forgiven me—but things were never the same."

A question started needling Abrianna at the back of her head, but she just didn't know how to ask it. "So, he never made a move on her while . . . you were on tour or . . . when you got locked up?"

Kadir's head snapped up. "What?"

She shrugged and didn't back down. "Baasim *never* made a move to win Malala back? Ever?"

"No. Of course not. He would never do something like that." He flipped the top sheet off of his body and stood.

"Wait. Where are you going?" She clutched his arm.

"I'm just, um, going to take a shower."

She cocked her head and held on. "But I like you hot and sweaty." She pulled him back down to the bed.

He complied.

"I didn't mean to upset you."

"I'm not upset," he lied, lying on top of her.

Abrianna cupped his face while tears brimmed in her eyes. "It's okay to admit you still have feelings for her. I understand. Malala is a part of your past. She's still a part of you. And you know what? It's also okay for me to be jealous of her."

"There is no need for you—"

"Shh." She placed her finger against his lips. "It's normal. You were engaged to her. I'm going to be jealous of every woman you ever loved, dead or alive, except for your mother."

Sadness rippled across Kadir's face.

"It's going to be all right. We're going to find them."

"Still being the optimist?"

"Absolutely."

"Good. One of us needs to be."

Abrianna and Kadir rushed into the Harry S. Truman Building a few blocks away from the White House and headed straight to the Department of State. The calm inside the large office was the polar opposite of what they were both feeling inside. An attractive redhead approached them, wearing a red lipstick smile and gazing up at Kadir like he was a god descended from heaven.

"Can I help you?"

"Yes, I'm looking to get in contact with someone at the Yemen Embassy. I'm looking for my parents."

The woman's stenciled brow lifted. "Are they Americans?"

"I . . . believe so."

"It's kind of a yes or no question." The woman's smile grew.

"Yes . . . they were granted citizenship about thirty years ago, but I don't know whether they've renounced their citizenship since they returned home seven years ago."

"Oh I see."

Abrianna stepped in, "But his brother is a natural-born citizen. If we can find him, then we can find his parents, right?"

"I'll tell you what, wait right here and let me get you the necessary forms and the right officer to help you with your inquiry. Just have a seat. Mr., um . . ."

"Kahlifa."

"Mr. Kahlifa." She shook his hand. "I'll be right back."

"Thank you." Kadir glanced around and found the chairs the woman gestured to and sat, but he couldn't keep still.

"It's going to be okay." Abrianna grabbed hold of his hands and squeezed them.

He nodded with a weak smile but still bounced his legs and rocked in his chair for a full ten minutes before Ms. Redhead came back with a one-page form and a pen. By the time Kadir had filled in the information, another woman appeared—this one much older and more handsome than pretty.

"Mr. Kahlifa?"

"Yes?" Kadir sprang to his feet.

"Hello. I'm Mrs. Georgia Harrington."

They shook hands, and then Kadir handed over the one-page questionnaire.

"Come with me." She turned and led the way.

Abrianna and Kadir fell in step behind the foreign service officer and followed her to a small office that could've doubled for a closet.

"Anything?" Harrington asked the redhead, sitting behind the desk.

"We're still on hold," the redhead said, getting up from behind the desk.

"Thanks."

Everyone maneuvered around one another in the small space until the redhead exited the office, but not before giving Kadir a lingering parting look.

Annoyed, Abrianna glanced down at the redhead's blue pumps and snapped one of the heels in half. She tumbled and hit the floor hard.

"Oh my." Harrington glanced as she leaned over her desk. "Are you all right?"

The redhead quickly got back to her feet, but when she did, her face nearly matched the color of her hair. "Yes. I'm fine." She removed her shoe and picked up the broken heel before hobbling off.

Abrianna snickered, and when she turned around, Kadir glared at her. "What?"

"Behave," he hissed.

On the speakerphone, someone picked up the line. "Thomas Crane."

"Hey, Thomas. Georgia here. I know things are pretty hectic out there, so I'm not going to take up too much of your time." She picked up the questionnaire. "I'm looking for three civilians in Sana'a. Um, the Kahlifa family. A Muaadh and Daishan Kahlifa— they are in their fifties. I have an address."

Crane sucked in a sharp breath after Harrington gave him the address.

Kadir tensed. "What? Is there a problem?"

"No, um. Hold on for a second."

Soft Muzak played over the speaker again.

Kadir shot another nervous look at Abrianna, and she applied more pressure to his hand.

"It's going to be all right," she whispered.

Mrs. Harrington also shared a patient but awkward smile with them. Five minutes later, Crane came back on the line. "I don't have a Muaadh or a Daishan Kahlifa on the list, but the list is still a work in progress."

"What about a Baasim Kahlifa?" Harrington asked. "Their son?"

"Baasim Kahlifa?"

"Yeah. You know him?"

"No, um. I don't have anyone by the name—but it doesn't mean that we won't. It's been less than forty-eight hours since the two strikes."

"Two?" Kadir pulled away from Abrianna and braced himself on the officer's desk. "There were two strikes?"

"Please, stay calm, Mr. Kahlifa. It doesn't do anyone any good to get yourself worked up until we know all the facts on the ground. We have your contact info here on the questionnaire, and I promise you as soon as I know anything, I *will* get back with you."

Kadir kept staring at her like he suddenly didn't understand English.

"Okay. We'll go now." Abrianna touched Kadir's arm and brought him out of his reverie.

"Yeah, sure. Okay." Kadir drew himself up and backed away from the desk.

"I don't want you to think that no news is bad news," Harrington said. "It really does take some time to compile these lists. Not everyone thinks to check in with the embassies. I say that to say, don't give up hope."

"We won't." Abrianna tugged Kadir. "Thank you for all your help."

"It's my pleasure." Harrington stood and offered her hand.

Once the formalities were exchanged, Kadir and Abrianna exited the small office. More people buzzed about, more people filling out questionnaires as they headed out of the State Department.

"Hey, will you slow down?" Abrianna asked, struggling to keep up with his long strides.

"This was a complete waste of time," Kadir complained. "They don't know jack shit."

"It's still early," she parroted. "Give them some more time."

Kadir shook his head and kept moving, trying to outpace bad news.

Abrianna forced herself to let him—let him do what he had to do. She feared she was on the borderline of nagging him to death. Once they pushed through the glass doors and into some fresh air, Kadir slowed down, stopped, and then sucked in a deep breath. She took his hand and waited him out.

"What if they're gone?" he seemed to ask the universe. "I'll have no one. I'll be alone."

"How can you say that?" She leaned against him and stared up into his eyes. "We have each other. And I'm going to keep reminding you of that until it sinks in."

Kadir sighed.

Abrianna cupped his chin and forced him to look at her. "You got that?"

A smile eased across Kadir's lips. "Got it."

15

Dinah Lehane sat in front of CNN's camera with her hands clutched in her lap. Her red, tear-rimmed eyes beseeched the nation instantly as she appealed to the people who held her daughter captive. "Please. I'm begging you as a mother. Let my child go."

News host Rory Shields lowered his voice. "Have you or the police been contacted by anyone demanding money or anything for her safe return?"

Mrs. Lehane unclutched her hands and swiped beneath her swollen nose. "No. Her father and I have heard nothing. It's like we're reliving a nightmare."

"You're talking about when your daughter was kidnapped by Dr. Craig Avery when she was a teenager."

Dinah nodded. "It seems like it was yesterday. And now . . . I don't understand why this is happening to us again. My daughter is a good person. She performed a service to this country by exposing a corrupt government, and I can't help but feel . . . believe that she's being punished for that. I just want my baby to come home. Please."

"To be clear," Shields said, "is it your belief that the government has something to do with your daughter's disappearance?"

"Who else could it be?" She sniffed. "The chances of it being yet *another* mad scientist has to be like a trillion to one. No. Her father and I believe wholeheartedly that some powerful people are extracting some type revenge out on my daughter. Now, I don't know if it goes all the way to the current president or the people who were attached to the previous administration. But I believe it has everything to do with those articles she wrote about President Walker and Chief Justice Katherine Sanders. I just know it."

Air Force One

The president shut off the television in her sky office and cast a withering look at Elias McMullan, her campaign manager. "I can't win for losing. Next, they'll be telling the American people that I eat puppies for breakfast, too."

"Maybe you should reach out to the Lehanes and assure them that the administration is doing all it can to look into her daughter's disappearance."

"Tempting. But it could backfire. The mother seems pretty set on blaming her daughter's disappearance on me. Hardy is already whipping up his crowd to have me locked up. This bullshit will have my party primarying my ass."

McMullan chuckled and shook his head. "It's much too late for that. They'll have to grin and bear it. Still. It would look better to be seen reaching out to her than not," McMullan reasoned.

"Fine. Make it happen."

———※◆☽———

At the MSNBC studios, Abrianna's heart broke watching Dinah Lehane on CNN in the green room. "We should reach out to her."

"And tell her what?" Kadir asked.

"The truth," Abrianna said. "T4S is the real culprit."

"We don't know that they aren't acting under the president's orders. Or have you not been paying attention to what Ghost and

I have been telling you for the past year? There's no division between government and private companies anymore. For all we know, they can be one and the same in this case."

He has a point. Abrianna braided her fingers together.

Kadir paced inside a room the size of a closet. "Are you sure you want to do this?"

"No, I don't want to do this. I have to do it. There is a big difference." Abrianna waved off the makeup artist. "Can you please give us a few minutes?"

"Sure." The woman gave them a tight smile before leaving.

Once they were alone, Abrianna confessed, "Look, I'm already nervous enough. I wish you wouldn't hover and pace like that."

"I'm sorry, but I'm not sure that this is the right thing to do. If anything, going on national television and telling them that you and the other girls were science experiments for that evil company isn't going to do anything other than piss them off."

"Yeah, it might piss them off, but they won't be able to do anything about it. If I turn up missing after this broadcast, the spotlight will be centered on T4S."

"Doesn't mean they won't try and kill you."

Abrianna smirked. "They've been trying. So far, I've been indestructible."

"Key phrase: so far. It doesn't mean that they haven't been trying to figure out a way to take you down. Don't forget, we still don't know what was in that dart that dropped you like a stone."

"Bullets drop me, too. It's just that I always self-heal."

Kadir stopped. "What are you saying? That I have to keep watching you die and come back to life?"

Her smirk morphed into a full smile. "It's better than the alternative."

Kadir looked ready to argue the point but instead acknowledged, "You're right."

"Of course I'm right." She pushed up from the chair and then wrapped her arms around Kadir's waist and pulled him flush against her. "One thing you're going to have to get used to the fact that I'm *always* right."

"Always?" He laughed.

"That's right. Always." She snaked her arms around Kadir's head and drew him down for a kiss. From the moment their lips connected, his body relaxed against hers. She liked to believe that she had the power to vanquish all the stress and worries that plagued him. It wasn't true—even with her . . . gifts. But she wanted to believe it anyway.

A knock sounded on the open door, and Abrianna and Kadir regretfully ended their kiss and pulled apart.

———➤◆◀———

"Welcome back to the show." Joy Walton greeted Abrianna and Kadir with a hug while they were still in the makeup chair. "I have to tell you, my team was surprised when you called. Happy—but surprised."

"I have to do what I can to help Tomi."

Joy nodded and stared into Abrianna's eyes as if she had her own bullshit detector. "You really believe you know what happened to her?"

"Absolutely."

Joy nodded. "Great, let's get you in front of the camera." She patted Abrianna on the shoulder. "See you in five."

Abrianna nodded and cut a look over to Kadir, who kept checking his phone every few seconds. She grabbed his free hand to get his attention—bring him back to the here and now. "It's okay. He's going to call."

Kadir smiled, but his eyes didn't.

The Filibuster with Joy Walton was an old-school, hard-hitting journalism show. The hostess regularly made news by pinning politicians down and knocking them off talking points. People either loved or hated her, which suited Joy fine.

"Welcome to the show," Joy told her audience. "We have a

special guest joining us this evening. I'm sure many of you recognize Abrianna Parker. She has been the talk of Washington for months. She, as well as Tomi Lehane, a reporter for the *Washington Post*, broke the story behind the murder of the House speaker, Kenneth Reynolds. The story brought down a president as well as the chief justice of the Supreme Court. More recently, the same reporter brought down a sex trafficking ring that involved Ms. Parker's adopted father, Cargill Parker."

Abrianna shifted in her chair.

It was Kadir's turn to take her hand and braid their hands together.

Joy leveled her gaze and smiled at the couple. "Welcome to the show."

"It's our pleasure to return."

"Before we came on the air, I asked you whether you knew what had happened to your friend and reporter Tomi Lehane, and you said that you did. Do you care to expand on that?"

Abrianna took another deep breath as she watched from the corner of her eye camera two with its bright red light focused on her. "It's a complicated story, but I know who has Tomi because . . . the same people have tried to grab me as well. Last week they were almost successful again."

Joy sat straighter in her chair. "So, you are saying that she was taken—kidnapped, if you will?"

"Yes."

Joy looked stunned and happy to be breaking this news on her show. "And who are the people you believe to have taken the reporter?"

"The private paramilitary firm T4S. They have been monitoring Tomi and me since we were rescued from Dr. Craig Avery's basement. And I'd recently learned that Dr. Avery was a former employee of the firm . . ."

Ned burst into the lab. "Dr. Zacher, there's something that you gotta see."

"Not now. I'm in the middle of something." He peered back into the microscope.

"Yes, um. But I'm pretty sure that you want to see this," Ned persisted. "Like, I'm positive that you want to see this."

Zacher looked up and noted Ned's anxiety. "All right." He stood from his stool and abandoned his work. "This better be good."

"Yes, sir." Ned motioned his boss to follow him to the break room, where a television hung suspended in the corner above the water cooler. On screen sat a smiling Abrianna.

Zacher automatically smiled back before his ears tuned in to what she was saying.

"*Dr. Avery worked under the tutelage of Dr. Charles Zacher—who still works as head of research and development for the firm to this day. What happened to me and the other teenagers in Avery's basement was no act of a random madman, but was, in fact, a controlled scientific experiment from a leading private contract firm.*"

Joy Walton shifted and leaned closer in her seat. "*Controlled experiments? What kind of experiments?*"

Abrianna sucked in a deep breath. "*We were injected with all kind of concoctions. They were painful and torturous. A lot of the girls died screaming while still chained to the wall. He got off on it. But he always saw getting rid of the bodies as an imposition.*"

"*And what was the purpose of these experiments?*"

Abrianna shook her head. "*For years, I didn't know. I, like many, had believed that Avery was just crazy. I begged for death plenty of times. We all did. But, in the last few months, pieces of the puzzle had fallen into place. Tomi brought me an article about Dr. Zacher. I recognized him immediately.*"

"*You did?*"

Abrianna nodded. "*Yes. You see, I met him the night Avery kidnapped me—at the Union Central Station. For years, while I was living underground, I saw him regularly. He'd disguised himself as a homeless old man and we would talk regularly in Stanton Park—up until speaker Kenneth Reynolds's death. It was a ruse. Dr. Zacher is far from homeless."*

"But why the ruse?" Joy asked.

"I can only assume that he was continuing Dr. Avery's work—monitoring his subjects. Since the Walker conspiracy story broke, Tomi and I have been under the spotlight. I imagine that T4S hasn't been too happy about that. About two months ago, I was snatched off the street in broad daylight. Had it not been for a group of friends, I might be behind T4S's impenetrable walls . . . just like Tomi is—right now."

Zacher's smile had melted, and horror washed over him. "Holy shit."

16

"What the hell is she talking about?" Kate pulled her attention away from the television.

Davidson and Wolf looked lost while Haverty pressed his lips together.

"What the hell am I thinking? How silly of me to think that anyone knows anything about anything around here."

"I know who T4S are, Madam President," Haverty said. "I just don't understand what Parker is alleging they have done."

Davidson stretched back in his chair and laid his left ankle across his right knee. "It seems pretty clear to me: Parker is giving you a lifeline."

Kate's gaze zoomed back to the television.

"*What were these experiments about?*" Joy Walton asked.

"*From what Tomi shared with me in the article, and what is searchable on the internet, T4S is in a global race to develop faster and stronger soldiers.*"

"*We have the video cued up. And this can be found on YouTube,*" Joy informed the television audience. On screen, Dr. Charles Zacher took to the stage before members of the Defense Advanced Research Projects Agency and grabbed them with his opening: "*Imagine a soldier who can outrun any animal on the planet, carry hundreds of pounds with ease, communicate telepathically with his squadron, go weeks without eating or sleeping, or regenerate lost limbs on the battlefield, and be completely controlled, mind and body, by military technicians thousands of miles away. Does this sound like science fiction to you? If so, you're not living in the real world.*

"We are in a twenty-first-century arms race among a vast array of covert technologies that are presently under development. There will be a new kind of soldier, a genetically modified and artificially enhanced superhuman fighting machine that dominates the battlefields of the future. The engineering of these super soldiers is not only a top priority for the Pentagon, with black budget projects with classifications so high that not even the president of the United States has the clearance to access."

The president muted the television again. "What the fuck is *he* talking about, Wolf?"

Wolf shrugged again. "I—I . . ."

"Don't tell me that you don't know. Find out!" She stomped her foot.

"Yes, Madam President." Wolf scrambled toward the door.

"And don't come back in here until you have some real answers," she shouted at Wolf's back.

Davidson remained parked on the couch before the television, grinning.

"You find this funny?"

"Just the part of you losing your cool instead of seeing this as the gift it is. The bitch could have sat there on camera and concocted any story she wanted, and the media would have eaten it up."

Kate stood from her chair and waltzed around to the front of her desk. "You don't believe her?"

Davidson pushed himself up from the couch. "It doesn't matter what I believe. All that matters is that bitch cleared you from Lehane's disappearance. She shut down the conspiracy theorists from pinning the one murder you didn't commit on you. If you ask me that's a reason to celebrate." In two quick strides, Davidson swept the president into his arms and spun her around.

"Let go of me, you idiot. Are you crazy?" She attempted to weasel out of his arms.

Davidson rolled his eyes and released her. "I wish that you would relax. This is good news."

Kate's phone chirped.

The president gave Davidson her back as she turned and punched the button for her secretary. "What is it, Diana?"

"Elias McMullan is here for your four-thirty appointment."

Kate sighed. "Send him in." She massaged her temples before addressing Davidson. "You better go."

He sighed at the casual dismissal. "You know, I miss when you were just the *vice* president. You had more time on your hands." He reached for her hand, but she pulled away.

"Madam President, are you watching Joy Walton's show?" McMullan, Kate's campaign manager, stormed into the Oval Office. "Abrianna Parker is on."

Kate reached for the remote again. "Yes, Davidson and I were talking about it." She turned the volume back up.

"Talk about a hail Mary. Am I right?"

The president's gaze swung between the two men while she remained cautious. "You think so?"

"Absolutely. What do you know about T4S?"

"Only that they are a private security firm and tend to be loyal Republican donors. Um . . ." She struggled to shake a few more cobwebs off of a few memories. "They lobbied Walker a couple of years ago to, um, use private paramilitary forces in Afghanistan to replace professional soldiers with what are essentially mercenaries. Walker wasn't too opposed to it if I remember correctly." She shrugged. "I wasn't, either, if you want to know the truth. Our current military involvement in Afghanistan is too costly and inefficient."

"And what about all this human experimental stuff?" McMullan asked.

Kate shook her head. "I know nothing about it, but I put Wolf on the case to dig up everything he can find."

"Good, good." McMullan clapped his hands together. "It may not matter anyway. We can still use them as a straw man for a lot of the headaches facing your candidacy."

"Really?"

McMullan's smile doubled in size. "Why the hell not? Better yet, if you go on record backing Abrianna Parker's conspiracy theory, you can win over at least half of her supporters, and then you'll be in like Flynn."

"Back her?"

"C'mon, you've complained at least a thousand times about how the public loves her. If you two are fighting on the same side, it's like killing two birds with one stone. Issue a pardon for that hacker boyfriend of hers and give them some kind of medal. The media will eat it up."

Kate glanced over at Davidson, who opened up his arms with a smile. "Now, can we celebrate?"

<hr />

Dr. Zacher's phone trilled inside of his pocket. He didn't have to retrieve the sucker to know that it was Spalding, ready to lose his shit. Zacher let the phone ring. He didn't have anything to say anyway.

Ned fretted by his side. "Is this as serious as I think it is, sir?"

Zacher nodded as he watched Joy Walton sign off. Next to her, Abrianna and her companion smiled proudly into the camera.

"Well played, Bree." The corners of Zacher's mouth curled upward. "Well played."

"What are we going to do now, sir? This could be a media nightmare."

"Could be? It's officially a major clusterfuck." Zacher pulled a deep breath. A media tour flashed in his head, and he felt sick. Spalding would serve him up to the masses without batting an eye. "We don't have much time," he said. "We need to complete the tests before hell opens up underneath this place and swallows us whole." He nodded, agreeing with his own assessment. "Back to work." He'd concentrate on one thing at a time.

Zacher spun on his heel.

Bang!

Zacher and Ned jumped as the entire place went dark.

"What the hell?" Zacher waited for a second, but the backup generator didn't kick in, and everything remained pitch black.

Zacher inched his way back into the hallway and glanced around. He saw nothing, but it wasn't necessary. He had practically lived in the underground lab long enough to know exactly where everything was located.

"Sir? Should I call upstairs to see what's going on?" Ned asked.

The red lights over the exit doors came on—but nothing else— no alarm, no sirens—nothing. "Yeah. Go ahead and give them a call."

Zacher's cell phone trilled. This time, he scooped it out of his pocket and read the caller ID screen.

Spalding.

Rolling his eyes, Zacher slipped the phone back into his pocket. He'd deal with that problem later. He turned and headed toward his lab. However, when he got to the door, his electronic key wouldn't work. "Fuck. I don't have time for this shit." He tried his key again.

Nothing.

"Ned, did you get them on the phone yet?"

Ned stepped out of the break room with his cell phone tucked beneath his chin. "I'm getting this weird fast-busy signal like their phones are off the hook or something."

"What?" Zacher tried his key again. "Goddamn it." He scooped his cell phone out again and placed a call himself to security and received the same fast-busy signal. "This shit doesn't make any sense." He dialed another number. This time, he went straight to voice mail. "Hey, Jessup. This is Dr. Zacher down in the research lab. I have a blackout down here, and my assistant and I can't get anyone on the phone. You included. I'd appreciate it if you'd give me a call back." Zacher ended the call and then waited. As he reviewed what was happening, a sick feeling churned in his gut. Maybe he should've taken the call from Spalding.

Nah.

Suddenly, something shifted. Static charged the air; the hairs on the back of his neck stood at attention—then it was the hair on his arms and chest.

BOOM!

Zacher was swept off of his feet and hurled into the wall behind him. The metallic taste of blood filled his mouth before he registered the pain in his head.

An army of boots pounded across the stone floor. He barely made them out beneath the ringing in his ears. Four figures, dressed in black, rushed past Zacher to the door of his lab.

"Wait. What are you doing?" Zacher pushed himself out of the wall. Chunks of plaster and debris rained down around him.

The men in black turned toward Zacher with guns pointed.

Zacher thrust out a hand. "No!"

The guns flew from the men's hands, startling them. However, Zacher's advantage was temporary. He was suddenly hit with an invisible and powerful force that sent him flying back into the wall.

Head ringing, Zacher tried to climb back out again.

BOOM!

A sweltering heat rolled into the place as glass shattered and flew everywhere. Zacher kept trying to get up, but his arms and legs wouldn't cooperate. It was as if something heavy sat on top of him. Zacher couldn't wrap his brain around what was happening, and soon the heat overtook him—but he couldn't tell where it was coming from. At one point, he thought maybe it was . . . internal.

The men darted into his lab.

Someone else is coming. A second later, he heard another set of boots slapping the floor. Whoever it was, they weren't in a hurry. Suddenly, fear slithered down Zacher's spine. It wasn't an emotion that he'd experienced often.

The boots drew near, now crushing glass underfoot. *Who the fuck is it?*

Zacher waited, unable to do anything other than peer out from the hole in the wall.

Crunch. Crunch. Crunch.

Zacher's heart hammered against his chest. At the same time, it pounded his eardrums.

Crunch. Crunch. Crunch.

Darkness encroached—tugging him as he waited for the figure to step into view.

What's the matter, Dr. Zacher? You're not feeling too well? A woman's voice filled Zacher's head.

Who the fuck are you?

The visitor, dressed head-to-toe in black, stepped into view. *What? Don't you remember me?*

Zacher drew a blank, but when the visitor pulled back the hoodie and a pile of blond hair spilled out, recognition hit Zacher like a ton of bricks. *It can't be.*

A smile curved the woman's lips. *Aww. You look like you've seen a ghost.*

Zacher fainted.

17

"And we're clear!" the producer said into everyone's earpieces the second the camera lights switched off.

Joy removed the earpiece from her ear and slumped back in her chair. "Wow. I don't want to toot our own horns, but that was a damn good show."

Abrianna smiled. "I just wanted to get the truth out there."

Kadir leaned forward. "And save Ms. Lehane's life before it's too late."

"Lofty goals." Joy removed her microphone pack. "It's a hell of a story. I'll give you that."

"It's the truth," Abrianna insisted.

Joy held up her hands. "Hey, I'm not here to judge. I want to get this information out there, help find a fellow journalist. Again, thanks for coming on the show. You're more than welcome back at any time." She offered her hand, but Abrianna hesitated.

Kadir accepted the offer first, giving Abrianna more time to regroup. By the time she took Joy's hand, Abrianna's plastic smile matched the host's.

They disconnected their microphone packs and exited the set.

"Are you all right?" Kadir struggled to keep up with Abrianna.

She didn't answer. Instead, she grabbed her purse and bottled water from the green room and hightailed it out of the building.

"Will you please slow down?" Kadir hissed.

Abrianna couldn't. She had to get out of the building before the one thing she couldn't control embarrassed her. Her tears.

Once they were outside on the sidewalk, Kadir grabbed her by the arm and spun her around.

"Will you please talk to me?" Kadir barked.

"What's there to talk about?" she shouted. "We failed! Can't you see that? We convinced no one! She might as well have patted me on the head before sending us on our way!" She snatched her arm free and spun away from him, but she remained in the center of the sidewalk, much to the other pedestrians' annoyance.

"What? What are you talking about? Were we in the same interview?"

"This was a mistake. I sounded like a lunatic in there—secret scientific experiments—kidnapping by private security firms." Abrianna shook her head harder. "The guys over at T4S are having a good laugh at my expense. If anything, all we did was piss them off."

"Good." Kadir won her full attention. "I want them to be pissed. Don't you?"

She blinked.

"I want to get under their skin—like they've gotten under ours. What you did in there was tell them that you're not afraid of them. And you exposed their dirty little secret. They are the ones on the defensive for once—not us. How is that a bad thing? How is that failing?"

Abrianna didn't have an answer, but the anxiety in her chest eased.

Kadir cocked his head and read Abrianna's expression. "Are you with me?"

She pulled a deep breath.

"Hmm?"

"You really think that it went okay in there?" she asked.

"It went more than okay." He slid his arm around her waist. "I'm proud of you."

Abrianna stared into his eyes for a few seconds and believed him. "Okay. Maybe I'm trippin'."

"Come on, let's get out of here."

"Ms. Parker?"

Abrianna spun around.

"Ms. Abrianna Parker?"

She blinked, surprised to see that such a deep baritone belonged to a five-foot-two white dude in a pinstripe suit. "That depends. Who is asking?"

The dude smiled and reached inside of his jacket and pulled out an envelope. "The name is Silvo Ricci. I worked with attorney Marcus Lautner."

Abrianna stiffened.

"Your father's personal attorney?" Silvo offered.

"Yes, I know who the asshole was."

"Right. Anyway, your parents had wills. Here are your copies."

"Wills?"

Silvo nodded. "Come to the office this Friday."

Abrianna shook her head and handed the envelope back. "No. No, thank you. I'm not interested."

Silvo held up his hands and refused to take the envelope back. "You should think about it some more. Besides, it's a will, not an ugly Christmas sweater you can return to the store." He tilted his head. "I'll see you Friday."

Tomi Lehane was placed in a new lab in a new facility while a new team of doctors stared on in awe. Her brown skin looked like shiny copper and was both cold and hard to the touch. No one knew what to do with her, but they were all excited to start running tests.

Only one set of eyes feared for the young reporter and what might happen to satisfy doctors' curiosity.

"Fascinating," Nate Hunter whispered under his breath as he stood above the lab, looking down at his new stolen treasure. "I have to hand it to those clowns over at T4S. They actually stumbled over the development of the century." He chuckled. "Amazing."

Cold green eyes turned toward Hunter. "You said she would be given a choice to work with us."

Hunter sighed. "And she will be—but I'm fairly confident that Ms. Lehane will come around if for no other reason than to seek revenge on the people who are responsible for her current state. Don't you agree?" When he didn't receive an answer, Hunter hitched up a smile. "Besides, I've been told a time or two that I'm very persuasive."

"Welcome to the first debate night of the Republican presidential campaign, live at the Xcel Energy Center in St. Paul, Minnesota. I'm Rebecca Turner, and my co-moderators are Tim Jacobs and Dave Clark." The audience's cheers were as loud as a Super Bowl crowd as the cameras zoomed around the vast arena.

The moderators' smiles stretched wide while they basked in the audience's exuberance and energy. No one enjoyed the moment more than Texas governor Bo Hardy. Judging from the size of his smile, he believed that everyone in the place had come to see him. The men and one woman standing at podiums next to him appeared small—nervous—unsure.

It took mere minutes before the moderator launched into the news of the week. The president's botched raids in Sana'a.

"It's like I've been saying." Hardy laughed. "You don't send a woman to do a man's job."

The crowd roared with laughter.

"It's true." He turned to the woman next to him. "No offense, little lady."

She looked offended.

Hardy continued, "The skirt in the White House is playing with our soldiers' lives. They and their families deserve real leadership. We're being mocked around the world. Our friends take advantage of us, and our enemies are making fun of us. I promise you that all of that changes when the American people put me in office."

Thunderous applause erupted.

A few rounds of foreign policy questions ensued before Tim Jacobs brought up the news of the day: Abrianna Parker's sensational interview on a competing network. When the cameras settled on Hardy, he looked dubious at best.

"I'd admit Ms. Parker has a hell of a story. One minute, she's a lady of the evening, and in the next, she's the daughter of a billionaire child-sex trafficker. It's hard to keep up. Now, this cockamamie story about T4S kidnapping and running experiments on teenage girls sounds like tinfoil nonsense to me. But I'm sure the president's liberal base will bite, because it takes the focus off this corrupt administration. Let me make it perfectly clear that I'm not biting. I know many guys over at T4S, and they have been doing a damn good job, providing services to the United States federal government. They guard officials and installations around the world. They are as patriotic and American as . . . hell, apple pie." Hardy shook his head. "I don't buy it. No. The real culprit behind Ms. Lehane's disappearance is clear to me, and it's the pretender in the White House."

<hr />

Zacher tossed and turned throughout a fevered nightmare. Everywhere he turned, razor-sharp claws slashed across his body. He screamed, terrified. Visions of being strapped and tied to a pole and spun over a fiery pit filled his head.

"Let me go," Zacher roared. Hot tears scalded as they streaked across his face. The pole turned, spinning him over a growing pit of fire. The closer the flames came toward his face, the louder he roared and fought to get loose. Somewhere in the recesses of his mind, he knew this torture wasn't real. It couldn't be. If he could wake up, he would be able to prove it.

But no matter how loud he screamed, the torture went on forever. "Wake up! Please!"

The fire singed every hair on his body while his skin blistered and curdled. He was cooking from the inside out. His grip on reality waned. He could die roasting on this pit, and there was nothing he could do about it.

After an eternity, he was pitched closer to insanity when he heard voices somewhere in the distance.

"How much longer is he going to be out?" a voice boomed. "I need him! Everything has gone to hell in a handbasket because of that Parker bitch."

The voices faded, and the fire below resumed its endless torture.

"You don't think we're sitting ducks here?" Abrianna asked. It was the first night back at their apartment, and neither one of them knew how to behave. Each was too busy trying to act normal, like they didn't expect T4S's armed private soldiers to charge in at any moment.

"We're safe," Kadir insisted before draining the pasta. "We calculated the risks and played the only card we have at the moment. T4S would be stupid to come after us after our placing such a hot spotlight on them."

"And once the spotlight goes away?"

Kadir sighed and then conceded, "*Then* we're sitting ducks."

Abrianna waltzed to the kitchen and watched Kadir toss the pasta in the lemon sauce. "So, we need to keep my interview in the news cycle."

"Which is Ghost's job. So stop worrying. Ghost is very good at what he does."

Abrianna nodded. Ghost had saved her ass many times. There was no reason to stop trusting him now.

"Dinner is ready."

"Mmm. It smells divine." She smiled and headed over to the wine refrigerator and picked out a Soave. When she returned to the table, her gaze fell onto the envelope Silvo Ricci had given her.

"Are you going to open it?" Kadir set their dinner on the table while she filled their wineglasses to the rim.

"No. Whatever it says, it's a bunch of bullshit anyway."

"Maybe." He grabbed the Parmesan cheese and the grater. "Tell me when." He grated the cheese while she sipped her wine and stared at the envelope. "Any second now."

Abrianna remained silent.

He cleared his throat and stopped grating. "Bree?"

"Huh?"

He chuckled. "Is that enough cheese?" He nodded to the white pile of cheese in her bowl.

"A tad bit more."

His eyebrows shot upward.

She smiled. "No. I'm good. Thanks."

Kadir grinned and took his seat across the table from her. Over his food, he said a quick prayer.

Abrianna drained the rest of her wine like it was water.

"More?" Kadir grabbed the Soave and refilled her glass without her acknowledging that he'd said a word. Now was his big moment to jar her out of her reverie. He drew a deep breath and reached into his pocket and removed a black velveteen box. He opened it, slid out of his chair onto bended knee.

"Kadir, what are you—"

"Let's make this official." He held up the ring. "Abrianna Elise Parker, will you marry me?

Abrianna's eyes rounded at the sight of the two-carat emerald-cut ring while she cupped her mouth to hold back an an unexpected squeal.

"Is that a yes?"

"Yes! Yes!" She held out her trembling left hand while Kadir removed the ring from the box and then slid it onto her finger. "Oh my God. It's so beautiful." Abrianna admired the ring on her hand for a few seconds and then threw her arms around his neck and squeezed.

Once again, Kadir had to tap out before he passed out.

Abrianna released him but then peppered his face with kisses.

"I take it that you like the ring?"

"Are you kidding me? I love it. I can't wait to show it off." She held out her hand again.

"I'm glad you like it." He tilted her chin toward him and kissed her solidly before returning to his chair. Abrianna admired the ring, but then her gaze drifted back to the envelope.

"You know that the offer still stands. I can open it and read it for you. If it's some bullshit, I'll tuck it back into the envelope, and we'll never talk about it. But somebody should read it."

Abrianna hedged.

Kadir picked up the envelope. "I'm dying to know what it says." Before she could stop him, he ripped it open.

"Kadir—"

"Shh. It's open. Now, let me read."

Abrianna slumped back into her chair and watched Kadir's expression as his gaze roamed over the first page. Five seconds in, she reached for her wineglass. "Well? What does it say?" She took a long sip and prepared for the worst.

"It's a bunch of legalese stuff so far." He turned the page.

Abrianna returned to nursing her wine.

"Eat something," Kadir told her without glancing up.

It was at the tip of her tongue to tell him that she wasn't hungry, but that would be rude. Abrianna grabbed her fork and for the first time noticed the amount of cheese sitting in her bowl.

"Bon appétit." She mixed the pasta and cheese together and took her first bite.

"Holy shit!"

"What is it?" Abrianna asked with a mouthful of pasta.

Kadir placed his finger on the center of the document and appeared to read the same line over and over again.

"What?" Abrianna quickly swallowed. "What is it?"

He pulled his gaze up from the document and looked her in her eyes. "It all goes to you."

"What all goes to me?" She dropped her fork and snatched the papers from Kadir's hands.

"Everything. The money, the property—you name it. You're rich."

"There's got to be some kind of mistake. Cargill *hated* me." Abrianna scanned the page until it snagged on the same line that had caught Kadir's attention.

"I, Cargill Lynwood Parker, of sound mind leave my entire estate: monies, properties, stocks, bonds to my daughter Abrianna Elise Parker if she's found within five years of my demise."

"He drew this up before this past year," she said.

"Yeah. About three years ago, I'd say."

She shook her head and tossed the pages away from her. "That's insane."

"We already knew that his head wasn't screwed on too tight."

Abrianna reread the words again.

And again.

"What about Samuel?"

"He thought Samuel was dead. And legally, he is dead—death certificate and all. He's a whole new person now."

"He still deserves a part of the estate."

Kadir shrugged. "He wasn't Cargill's biological son."

"I'm not his biological daughter."

"Okay. Give him a part of it if you feel that strongly about it."

"What about all his victims? Surely, they are going to come after the estate."

"It's kind of hard to go after criminal charges after someone is dead. Your stepdad was a billionaire several times over. I'm sure if you chose to settle the civil cases, you'd still have plenty of money left over."

"Still, I don't feel right about this."

"Then do something good with the money."

"So, you think I should take this?"

"What else are you going to do? Give it to the government—let them take it? What does that prove or solve?"

"I don't know."

"My two cents: Take the money. Right all the wrongs that Cargill did in his life—at least the best you can. After that, you're free to do whatever you want—to *go* wherever you want."

"Like the French Riviera," Abrianna whispered. She'd saved up her whole adult life to move to the European coast only to have her dirtbag of an ex-boyfriend Moses rob her blind. Abrianna struggled to process it all. Her dinner went cold as she flipped through the other pages and drained her wineglass.

Knock! Knock! Knock!

Abrianna and Kadir looked up.

"Are you expecting someone?" she asked.

Kadir shook his head, dabbed the corners of his mouth, and stood from the table.

Abrianna abandoned the will and stood. "Hold up." She raced to the closet and pulled out the Tiffany-blue .45 gun.

"What are you doing?" he hissed.

"You never know."

Knock! Knock! Knock!

Kadir approached the door and peered out of the peephole. He gasped.

"What is it?"

Kadir's hands fumbled over the locks. When he yanked the port open, he still couldn't believe his eyes. "Baasim?"

18

It was late when Castillo rolled up to Dennis's two-story home. After she parked, she reached over into the passenger's seat and removed bags of Chinese food from the local takeout. As she fast-walked to the front door, the smell of their dinner made her stomach growl. *Just a few more minutes*, she promised herself while fumbling to pull the house key from her jeans pocket. After she managed that one-handed trick, she slipped the key into the lock. However, she was surprised when the key wouldn't move. *What the hell?*

She tried again. The lock wouldn't budge.

Castillo withdrew the key from the lock and verified under the flickering porch light that it was indeed the right key. She tried it again, hoping that the third time was the charm. She got the same results. "Goddamn it."

Castillo knocked on the door and waited.

And waited.

After knocking several times, she peered through the glass side paneling but still couldn't see a damn thing. Her knocking transformed into a pounding. She heard someone approach. Yet, after another ten seconds, the door still hadn't opened. "C'mon, Denise. I know you see me standing out here!"

The door unlocked and jerked open.

Dennis's older sister, Denise, stood on the other side with her hands on her hips. "Do you have any idea what time it is?"

"Yes. Dinnertime." Castillo held up the bags and pushed her way inside.

"We had dinner three hours ago."

Castillo rolled her eyes and made a beeline to the kitchen.

"Did you hear me?" Denise asked, stomping behind Castillo.

"I'd be surprised if everyone in the tri-state area didn't hear you," Castillo volleyed back as she pulled out cartons of food from the bags. "I'm sure whatever you made for dinner was nice. But, as we always say, there's always room for Chinese."

Denise's thin lips flat-lined.

Castillo grabbed a dinner tray from beside the refrigerator, placed their meals on top of it, and opened the fridge. "Where's the beer?"

"There isn't any," Denise said. "I poured that devil's juice down the drain as soon as I moved in."

"What? That was *my* beer."

"My bad."

"Uh-huh. You owe me about twenty bucks. I take cash or a check." Castillo took another look inside of the refrigerator. "Water and *prune* juice?"

"To make sure that Dennis stays regular."

"By liquefying his colon? Sounds like you're making more work for yourself." Castillo shuddered and grabbed two bottled waters and added them to the tray and went to exit the kitchen, when Denise blocked her path.

"Where are you going?"

"Where do you think?"

"I've already bathed and put Dennis in his pajamas."

"Pajamas? Since when does Dennis wear pajamas to bed?"

"I bought them."

"Ah. You have thought of everything."

"It's now my job. I'm Dennis's caregiver for however long it takes for him to get back on his feet."

"That's great. I'm sure Dennis appreciates you for doing this for him. Now, if you'd excuse me, I'd still like to have dinner with my boyfriend. It won't be the first time we've eaten dinner in bed." Castillo pushed past Denise and jogged up the stairs. On the landing, she stopped as a sense of déjà vu overwhelmed her. The last time she'd been up there, she'd discovered Dennis in the bedroom lying in a pool of his own blood.

Castillo shook it off. "Dennis?" She rapped on the door and entered before he had a chance to answer. The first thing she noticed were the flickering lights from the television set. When she moved farther into the bedroom, she saw Dennis sitting straight up in bed. "I didn't think you were asleep."

"Hey." He beamed at her.

"I brought you some dinner."

"Chinese?"

"You know it."

"My girl. I knew you loved me."

Castillo rolled her eyes the way she always did whenever Dennis got too mushy on her. She moved over to the bed and handed him the dinner tray. "Hold this."

Dennis took the tray while Castillo stripped out of her jacket, toed off her boots, and climbed into bed with him. "Watching anything interesting?"

"Only the news. They are saying there was a second airstrike in Sana'a that happened shortly before the botched job that our government failed to mention. It was supposed to be another terrorist site, but surprise, surprise, it was a funeral ceremony."

"Ouch."

"Tell me about it. I don't see why we don't get out of the Middle East already. It's one giant mess over there."

"Where is it not a big mess?"

Castillo grabbed the sweet and sour chicken. "Do you know that your sister threw out all my beer?"

"I'm not surprised."

Castillo popped open the carton of white rice and mixed it in with her sweet and sour chicken. Belatedly, she noticed Dennis was having a hard time opening a container.

"Here. I can do that for you." She set her food aside and took the carton. "Do you want some rice with yours?"

"Sure. That'll be great."

Castillo fixed his plate and handed it back over.

"Thank you," he mumbled.

"Not a problem." She pecked his cheek. "Instead of watching this depressing stuff, why don't we Netflix and chill?"

"Sounds like a plan to me." He turned toward the nightstand, but he had a hard time gripping the remote control.

"I got it."

"*I* got it," he snapped.

Castillo backed off.

"Sorry." He grimaced. "I didn't mean to bite your head off. But if I'm going to get better, I have to do some things for myself. Between you and Denise, I feel like a giant baby."

Castillo tossed up her hands. "My bad."

"I'm sorry," Dennis apologized. "It's going to take me a while to . . . adjust."

Castillo smiled. "Of course it is. But . . ." She hesitated.

"But what?"

"I worry about you being too hard on yourself. You're driven and . . . I worry."

A smile flickered back onto his lips. "You might be right," he admitted. "I already wish rehab was over, and I was back at the department."

"You're going back?"

"Not immediately." He shrugged. "I know they're going to

have to replace me temporarily. But, yes. Returning to work is the goal."

"Oh." She picked up her meal again.

"What?" he challenged.

"Hmm? Nothing." She crammed food into her mouth in hopes of avoiding an argument about whether he was deluding himself. He took a bullet to the head. The department was likely to give him a gold watch and thank him for his service. He should thank his lucky stars he had benefits and a pension, but judging from the energy in the room, Dennis was *not* ready to hear it.

Dennis watched her chew her food for a full minute before he changed the channel to Netflix's interface.

Castillo frowned. "What am I sitting in?" She touched the mattress. "Why is the bed wet?"

Dennis glanced down. "Damn it!"

Castillo was slow, and by the time she put two and two together, Dennis was bellowing for his sister.

Denise blazed into the room like a fireman responding to a three-alarm fire. "What is it? What happened?"

"Help me to the bathroom," Dennis told his sister.

Castillo set her meal aside again. "I can help you." She reached for Dennis's arm, but he and Denise swatted her away.

"It's okay. *I* got him." Denise pulled her baby brother to his feet, locked an arm around his waist, and helped him walk to the bathroom. It wasn't until they'd slammed the door that Castillo climbed out of the wet bed. After that, she didn't know what to think. So, instead, she stripped the bed, flipped the mattress, and grabbed clean sheets from the hallway linen closet. When she returned to make the bed, Denise stood alone in the center of the bedroom with her fake, condescending smile in place.

"Dennis said he wants to call it a night."

"Call it a night? What the fuck does that mean?" She glanced at the bathroom door. "Dennis?"

Denise stepped closer and lowered her voice. "Can't you see he's embarrassed, Gigi? Leave him his pride."

The request was a gut punch. Castillo cast another long look at the door.

"Please?" Denise added.

"All right. I'll get my stuff," she said. Castillo inched around the large woman and grabbed her shoes, jacket, and dinner. Minutes later, she was back in her car with a wet ass and bruised feelings. "Well, that went well."

19

Abrianna lowered her gun and moved to stand next to Kadir at the doorway. The man on the other side was a replica of her fiancé—except for the long hair and beard.

"Hello, brother."

Kadir flew across the threshold and wrapped his arms around his brother. "My God! I've been so worried about you." Kadir stepped back so he could have another look at Baasim. "Thank God, you're all right."

However, Baasim's gaze shifted to her, and curiosity lit his eyes. "I'm sorry if we're interrupting anything." Baasim became more ruggedly handsome the moment he smiled.

"We?"

Baasim's smiled widened. He turned out of Kadir's arms and gestured for someone to come from around the corner.

Slowly, a petite, sun-kissed woman stepped into view. "Ummi!" Kadir bolted from Baasim's side to throw his arms around his mother.

"Kadir, my baby. Praise Allah. I thought I lost you."

Kadir squeezed her tight and lifted her up.

She squealed like a teenage girl.

When Kadir set her back down, it was so that they could rain kisses all over each other's faces. "I'm so happy to see you. Where's Baba?" He glanced up and looked around—neither his mother nor Baasim spoke. Instead, they hung their heads.

Abrianna experienced a quick kick to the gut.

When reality dawned on Kadir, he looked as though he was ready to fall over.

"Maybe you should come inside," Abrianna suggested.

Kadir's mother's gaze landed and sized Abrianna up in a nanosecond. What she thought of Abrianna remained hidden behind a mask.

"Yes, yes. Please come on inside," Kadir suggested, guiding his mother into the apartment.

Baasim's midnight gaze lingered on Abrianna. "Do you always answer the door armed?"

Abrianna blushed and then tucked the gun behind her back. "Only when I can't help it."

A smile twitched at Baasim's lips.

Once Kadir shut the front door, an awkward silence expanded between them while his mother and brother waited for a proper introduction.

"Um, Mom, Baasim, I'd like to introduce you to Abrianna Parker—my fiancée."

Surprise colored both of their faces.

"We just made it official tonight," Abrianna offered, flashing the ring. When they said nothing, she changed course. "Would you like something to drink?"

Silence.

"Coffee, tea, water?"

Kadir's mother came out of her shock and cleared her throat. "Tea would be lovely."

"Great. I'll go and put on some water. Excuse me." Abrianna first stopped by the closet to put away her gun and then smiled at the group before heading to the kitchen.

"Fiancée?" Kadir's mother repeated.

Kadir cleared his throat. "Please . . . sit down. Tell me about what happened to Baba."

His mother took a breath. "I'm afraid that your brother will have to tell you about that." She followed Kadir into the living room. "This is a nice place you have." She glanced around.

"Yeah. It's not bad for someone that last I checked didn't have a job," Baasim commented.

"A lot has changed since the last we spoke," Kadir said.

"You mean a lot has changed since you got out of prison."

"Yeah, that, too."

Baasim smiled. "I can't bust your balls too much. From what I read, you did help bring down an American president—that is one hell of an achievement. Pop was pretty proud."

"He was?"

"So, is your fiancée the woman who was in all the papers?" his mother asked. "The ex-prostitute?"

Kadir jerked and then struggled to find the right words. "Bree has lived a . . . *complicated* life."

His mother drew in a deep and indignant breath but remained silent as the grave.

Kadir reached for his mother's hand. "Please. Give her a chance. She means the world to me."

His mother's head came up almost proudly while she studied her son. After a few seconds of evaluation, she pushed up a smile. "I'm not closed-minded, you know. Of course, I'll give her a chance."

Kadir kissed her hand. "Thank you. That's all I ask."

"We only have black tea. I hope that's all right?" Abrianna announced, returning to the room.

"Here." Kadir turned. "Let me help you."

"It's okay. I got it."

Kadir took the tray from her hand anyway and set it on the coffee table.

Abrianna still handed out the cups and saucers. She didn't grow up under the perfect billionaire trophy wife without learning the basics of hosting.

Kadir's mother watched Abrianna's every move like a hawk. Regardless, Abrianna served everyone without spilling a drop.

"Thank you."

Abrianna smiled, feeling as though she'd passed a test.

Kadir turned his gaze toward his brother. "What happened to Baba?"

"What else? Your new president killed him."

Kadir heard the accusation. "Are you insinuating it's my fault?"

"I'm not insinuating anything. But your conscience may be. I'm simply stating facts."

"Baasim," their mother snapped. "Be nice to your brother."

"You know me, Mom. I just like to tease him from time to time. Keep him on his toes. Isn't that right, bro?"

Kadir's chin jutted upward.

The brothers looked ready to square off.

His mother sighed. "There will be no fighting. I won't have it."

Even Abrianna froze at Kadir's mother's sharp tone.

The brothers' hard gazes broke off.

Kadir pulled another deep breath. "Please, tell me what happened."

"We went to a funeral for a Supreme Political Council member." Baasim hung his head. "I told Father . . ." He looked to his mother "We tried to tell Baba that going to the funeral was dangerous, but he was adamant about enemy forces not daring to attack the proceedings of such a prominent figure. He was fighting a new war with an old mind-set. He was so convincing that . . . I went with him."

Kadir blinked. "You were at the funeral?"

Baasim nodded as his jawline hardened again. "I can still hear the jet's engines roaring overhead—and the pandemonium. I grabbed Baba's hand, but he refused to get up."

"Was he in shock?" Kadir asked.

"No." Baasim shook his head. "He was . . . resolute—defeated. I couldn't get him to get up—even when the missiles whistling toward us were unmistakable. I was tugging on him when the whole world flipped upside down and went black. I lost my grip in that darkness."

Kadir's hands balled at his sides.

Abrianna placed a hand against Kadir's shoulder, and he hung his head.

However, Baasim's gaze leveled back on his brother. "When they pulled Baba from the rumble, he was almost unrecognizable. I only got a few scratches."

"I wish I could have been there," Kadir murmured.

Relentless, Baasim cocked his head. "But you could've been, right?"

The brothers squared up again.

Baasim continued, "How many times did Baba beg you to come home?" He looked to Abrianna. "But you were too busy with more important things—or other people."

Abrianna's temper flared, and the coffee table shook the tea setting around.

Their mother gasped while Baasim took two steps back.

"Bree, it's all right." Kadir grabbed her hand before meeting Baasim's gaze again. "My brother often misdirects his anger. I'm used to it."

The table settled down. "Sorry." She turned, picked up the tea tray, and scrambled out of the living room.

Kadir was fast on her heels.

Abrianna shoved the tray onto the counter. "I can't believe I did that."

"Hey, hey, hey." Kadir turned her around and pulled her into his arms. "It's okay. You're fine."

"Right. Only now they think I'm some sort of freak."

"They don't—they won't. I'll talk to Baasim," Kadir assured Abrianna and kissed the top of her head. "But, fair warning. If you're going to be a part of my family, you're going to have to learn not to let Baasim get under your skin."

20

Bo Hardy was all smiles when he and the other Republican candidates exited the debate stage and passed reporters shouting out questions. Campaign manager Matthew Rowland caught up with Hardy and praised his performance.

"Get me Pierce Spalding pronto," Hardy hissed.

"Yes, sir." Rowland punched buttons on the cell phone that was always in his hand while they continued their march out of the arena among the controlled chaos.

By the time Hardy settled into the back of an SUV, Pierce Spalding was on the line.

"Spalding, buddy," Hardy boomed. "There seem to be a few details you left out during our last conversation. Were you trying to embarrass me on the national stage?"

"No, of course not. You got it all wrong." Spalding assured. "This whole conspiracy theory has taken us all off guard. We have no idea what this Parker chick is talking about. It's all bullshit."

"Yeah? Because she knows that brainy buck Zacher you got over there pretty well."

"Hardy, I'm telling you. It's all nonsense."

Hardy's patience waned. "It better be, because I took a bullet for you in front of the whole world. We may be new friends, but let me be clear"—he straightened in his seat—"I am not a man you fuck over. I take shit like that personally. If you are into some shady shit, it's best that you tell me now, so we can get our fucking stories straight. You make me look stupid out here, and I promise you, I'll burn you and your fake army to the ground. Do I make myself clear?"

Silence drifted over the phone.

"Spalding, buddy. Don't make me have to ask again. Is there something I need to know about T4S and Ms. Parker?"

Spalding cleared his throat. "Maybe we should schedule another meeting."

Hardy sighed. "Set it up."

President Washington channel surfed every cable news show, evaluating the political reaction to Parker's bombshell interview. Most of the pundits were like her, cramming information on who and what T4S was and did. In other words, everyone recited word for word from T4S's basic Wikipedia page—that it was a private paramilitary company founded by billionaire trust fund brat Pierce Spalding.

T4S provided for a variety of intelligence agencies, from the Marine Corps to the Pentagon and Department of Defense—as well as major corporations. The media had also linked Parker's boyfriend, Kadir Kahlifa, to Parker's latest wild conspiracy theory. The GOP pundits were too eager to remind the nation how, seven years ago, Kahlifa had hacked T4S and had stolen millions of emails, which he'd turned over to *Rolling Stone* and WikiLeaks and other dog-whistle syndicates. Kahlifa was an ex-con who had influenced his girlfriend into believing this cockamamie story.

Other pundits reminded everyone that the hack had exposed that there was no division between government and corporate spying—and how the Department of Justice often linked nonviolent activist groups to known terrorist groups so that they could prosecute under terrorism laws.

Kahlifa and his supporters exposed the growing authoritarian culture, and how the law was far too often used to protect those in power rather than to hold them accountable. It was up to people like him to fight for transparency in the shadowy world of national security. To many people, Kadir Kahlifa was a hero.

So far, the hero narrative looked more persuasive.

Kate's team dug up more information—and she was alarmed by just how intricate and vast T4S was. T4S had been awarded trillions in just the past two decades from the Central Intelligence Agency and the State Department to provide security details in some places and a private army in others. There was also a trail of accusations and charges from numerous Middle Eastern countries clamoring to bring members of T4S to justice. But nothing fascinated the president more than Dr. Charles Zacher. There was a copious amount of video on the web about the global race for producing the world's first super soldiers. From there, it wasn't hard for the average conspiracy theorist—or political operative—to connect the dots.

Abrianna Parker *could* be telling the truth.

The question: How much did Kate want to gamble? Last night, Bo Hardy had made his choice—but only because he wanted to hang Lehane's disappearance around her neck and sink her campaign.

Kate turned toward a smiling McMullan and slapped the folder down in front of him. "We need to capitalize on this. We need to get Parker to do more interviews—TV, radio, podcasts. All of it." She took a deep breath and actually smiled. It was the first time in months, because it was the first time the news cycle had taken its foot off her neck and didn't insinuate that she was the devil incarnate. Surely, that was worth a ten-second smile.

"I'm already on it." McMullan winked and pulled out his cell phone. "Abrianna Parker isn't listed anywhere, so I placed a call to Martin Bailey over at the *Washington Post*. He didn't have a contact number for Parker, *but* he put me in contact with an attorney who helped Parker's boyfriend out of jail and—"

"Get to the point." Kate rolled her hands.

"I found Kahlifa—the advantage of him being on parole." McMullan chuckled at his own joke. "Now, we can either send a letter or make an official call from the Oval Office and invite him and Parker to the White House. We take a few pictures, parade them in front of the media and voilà."

"Just like that?" Kate winced. "Shouldn't we feel them out first?"

"We're not asking them to be spokesmen. We just need them to be the bright shiny objects for the media on the Lehane case. That's it. Anything more than that will complicate your baggage with hers, and let's not forget, Parker still has plenty of baggage."

"You're right. Close but not too close."

"Of course I'm right. I've never lost a campaign." McMullan thrust out his chest and tossed her a wink. "Our major baggage is managing the Walker scandal. As long as your fingerprints aren't on any of that mess, everything the other side lobs our way is unsubstantiated bullshit and doesn't need to be dignified with a response."

"Right." Kate nodded.

"What do you want to do?" McMullan asked. "Write or call?"

21

The headaches were back. Abrianna woke with the back of her head humming like a loud generator. She needed something to quiet the noise, but that something meant her getting high. She couldn't go back down that road. She had made too many promises, and this time she intended on keeping them.

Carefully, she climbed out from underneath Kadir and then tiptoed away from the bed to their adjoining bathroom. After a steaming hot shower, she felt better, but the humming continued. She headed to the kitchen for some coffee, but the aroma was already wafting throughout the apartment.

When she reached the living room, Baasim was rolling up a rug, and his mother was in the kitchen cooking.

"Morning," Daishan greeted. "It's good to see that one of you likes to make use of the morning."

Abrianna pinned on a smile. "I was just coming to make some coffee."

"Ah. Let me get that for you." Daishan turned toward the coffeemaker. "Would you like cream or sugar?"

"Oh, that's not necessary. I can make it."

"No. I don't mind," Daishan insisted. She grabbed a coffee mug from the right cabinet and turned toward the coffeemaker.

Uncomfortable, Abrianna tightened her robe's belt and cast a look toward Baasim, who saddled up at the kitchen's island and returned her assessing stare. The buzzing in the back of Abrianna's scalp grew louder and then wrapped around her frontal lobe.

Baasim cocked his head. "Are you all right?"

Abrianna broke eye contact and fluttered a weak smile.

"Cream and sugar?" Daishan asked again.

"No cream, lots of sugar." Abrianna watched her future mother-in-law rush to fill her order. While she stood in the middle of the kitchen feeling useless, she scanned the amount of food Daishan had made. "This is quite a . . . feast."

"Breakfast is the most important meal of the day. I like my boys to start their day off right." Daishan handed Abrianna her coffee before she returned to her black tea.

"Thanks." Abrianna took a sip.

"Would you care for something to eat?"

"It smells great." Abrianna picked up a ladle and stirred what looked like soup. What is this?"

"It's called stew of fool. It has brown beans, tomato, onion, and chili. Then you have some fried eggs with onion, or you have it with liver and some spices. And we eat it with flatbread.

"Um, I'm sorry. I shouldn't. I'm having brunch with some friends of mine in an hour."

Daishan stiffened.

"But, you know what? I'll have a slice of this. What is it? It looks delicious."

"It's called m'shewsha, which is basically eggs, semolina, and flour and warm honey." Daishan made a small slice and placed it on a saucer.

Abrianna accepted it and grabbed a fork. "Mm. This is wonderful." She chewed and moaned. "I must get this recipe from you. This is delicious."

"I'm glad you like it." Daishan smiled and then asked, "Do you not know how to cook?"

Abrianna choked. "Excuse me?"

"I, um, noticed that Kadir cooked last night, and clearly, you two aren't big on breakfast."

"Or morning prayers." Baasim's dark gaze seared into Abrianna.

Sweat beaded Abrianna's hairline like she was under an interrogation spotlight. "No, I admit it. Cooking isn't exactly my thing."

Daishan's lips pressed into a firm line as she looked down her nose at her future daughter-in-law. "I see."

"But, you know, once Kadir and I are married, I intend to learn." She softened the blow with another fake smile.

"There's nothing like putting the cart before the horse." Baasim laughed. "How long have you two been living together?"

"Um . . ."

"How long has Kadir stopped doing his daily prayers? Does he attend a mosque regularly?" Daishan asked. "Do you have any plans to convert to our religion?"

"Um, er . . . I, um, haven't really given it any thought."

Baasim and Daishan looked at each other.

The buzzing in Abrianna's head grew to a deafening level. She set aside the rest of her m'shewsha and rubbed her temples.

"Haven't given it any thought?" Baasim inquired, cocking his head. "Doesn't exactly sound smart, does it? Do you have a habit of leaping before you look?"

Abrianna flinched.

"Or maybe you're just like Kadir—another hopeless romantic." She thrust up her chin. "What's wrong with that?"

"Nothing is wrong with love," Daishan cut in, giving Baasim a hard glare. "Baasim is just pointing out that marriage requires much more than strong emotions. Compatibility with *religion,* careers, children—the list is endless."

Baasim shook his head. "I give it six months—tops."

Abrianna cut a sharp look Baasim's way, and the barstool snapped, dropping him like a stone against the hardwood floor.

Daishan gasped. "Baasim! Are you all right?"

Abrianna took another sip of her coffee before she followed behind her future mother-in-law.

An embarrassed Baasim climbed to his feet, and after he assured his mother that he was all right, he picked up the broken stool.

"Oh." Abrianna winced. "I've meant to get that chair fixed." Abrianna shook her head. "But you're all right? No broken bones?"

Baasim's dark gaze smote Abrianna where she stood, and yet she kept smiling.

"I better get dressed. Enjoy your breakfast." Abrianna marched off, sipping her coffee.

<hr>

Since Abrianna's interview with Joy Walton, conspiracy theorists flooded the dark web. Ghost and his crew were in the zone, uploading some of the material they'd been leeching from T4S's mainframe. Finally, people were waking up and demanding answers. So far, T4S hadn't released a public statement, but it was clear this wasn't a one-day story, and their position wasn't sustainable.

The Revolution's message boards were on fire. People around the world connected T4S to everything from corruption to murder. The Middle Eastern citizens accused Americans of being willfully ignorant about things that were right in front of them, their taxes paying for things they had no clue about. The result was a secret and unaccountable government that could snatch teenage girls off the streets and experiment on them and then get away with it.

Ghost spoke before a green screen, excited that this week's broadcast was going to reach more viewers than ever before. He held back on the information about Dr. Zacher and his experiments on himself. That information he was going to keep in the tuck as his ace card—or until Abrianna ordered him to release the information. As soon as the broadcast was over, Wendell waved him over from the other side of the camera.

"Yeah. What is it?"

"I think you need to see this." Wendell led him over to his terminal. "Something weird has gone down over at T4S."

"Let me guess. They're purging records." He chuckled under his breath.

"I'm not showing any evidence of that just yet, but I think they were breached."

Ghost folded his arms. "Another hacker got in? I'm impressed. Any idea who it is?"

"No. No. You're not understanding me. Their headquarters was *physically* breached—somebody broke into that muthafucka."

"Say what?" Ghost swept Wendell out of his seat so he could read the screen and ghost around T4S's mainframe."

"See right here? Yesterday the whole system went down. The backup generator failed, and their network was down for a full twenty minutes. When they came up, several calls were placed to 911 for emergency services. Several ambulances were dispatched and took people to the hospital.

"Fuck. That's huge," Ghost said, impressed. "We definitely have to find out who has balls big enough to pull this shit off. I'd like to shake their hand. Was it just an attack or did they steal anything?"

"That's the million-dollar question. We're going to have to get out of here. They're running diagnostics on everything, and it's just a matter of time before they find our back door."

"They are checking to see if anything was stolen, too."

"Yeah, and we're the ones uploading stolen files."

"Then let's get out of there." Ghost tapped one key on the keyboard, and the system went haywire.

"What the fuck?" Wendell asked.

"They found us," Ghost growled, trying to escape out the mainframe backdoor they'd created. "Shit. Shit. They're running a tracer. Everybody unplug—right now!"

The whole team jumped to their feet and started ripping everything out of the sockets. They looked like mini-tornados spinning around the room. When they stopped, they were out of breath.

"Is that everything?" Ghost's paranoia kicked up a notch. The last thing he needed was for T4S to track him to his underground bunker. They would storm the place, and he and his crew would meet an untimely death—fuck a trial.

"We need to evacuate," Ghost decided. "And . . . kill the servers."

***

"Your mother doesn't like me," Abrianna informed Kadir the moment he stepped out of his morning shower.

"What?" He rubbed a towel through his wet hair. "She doesn't know you. Give her time."

"She knows that I don't cook, do morning prayers, and that I'm shamelessly living in sin with her son. All things that your brother doesn't apparently approve of, either."

Kadir stopped. "Did they say this?"

"They didn't have to." She cheesed broadly. "By the way, if you're hungry, your mother cooked enough to feed an army."

Kadir marched over to the bed and set next to her. "You two are going to love each other—in time." He brushed a kiss against her forehead. When that failed to put a smile on her face, he pressed a deeper, more meaningful kiss against her lips.

That worked.

"You feel better?" he asked.

"Yeah," Abrianna lied, not wanting to mention her throbbing

head. She set her coffee down and then braided her fingers with his. "How about you? I'm sorry about your father. I'd really hoped that—"

"It's okay." Kadir lowered his head. "I, um . . . have to believe that he's in a better place right now. And, judging from Baasim's account, Baba knew what he was doing—what he wanted. I have to respect that."

"Just like that?"

He looked back up. "What else can I do—other than to be grateful that I still have my brother and mother?"

Abrianna felt like an ass. "You're right. I'm sorry for what I said. I shouldn't have—"

"It's all right," he cut her off. "There's naturally going to be an adjustment period, but it's going to be all right." He kissed her again, pressing her back onto the bed.

Moaning, Abrianna broke the kiss. "We can't do this right now. I have to get dressed and go meet the guys."

Kadir's trailed kisses down her neck. "No. No. We've got plenty of time." He untied her robe's belt and then whipped the towel from around his waist.

Abrianna smiled. "I guess a few minutes won't hurt."

22

Breakfast was cold by the time Kadir joined his mother and brother in the dining room. However, the second he entered, his mother bounced up and started reheating everything.

"Kadir, baby. You're up. Let me fix you a plate."

"Oh, Mom. You don't have to put yourself out," Kadir said.

"Nonsense. It's been forever since I've been able to cook for you. Since *anyone* has cooked for you, apparently."

Abrianna caught the glib comment as she entered the room.

"Mom," Kadir hissed.

"What?" She blinked up at him with innocent eyes. "What did I say?"

Kadir cast an apologetic glance at Abrianna, who forced on a smile and headed to the door. "I gotta get going. I'll see you all later."

Kadir joined her at the door. "Be patient," he pleaded.

"I didn't say anything." Abrianna held onto her smile as she opened the coat closet and removed her gun and tucked it into her back holster.

Kadir tensed. "Maybe I should go with you."

"I'll be fine. Besides, don't you have to go back to work? I know Castillo is cool and all, but surely she still would like for you to clock in every once in a while."

"Yeah. I told her I would come in this afternoon, but . . ."

"Everything is going to be fine. We already agreed that T4S wouldn't dare come after me right now. And if they do, I got something for their asses."

Kadir looked uneasy but brushed another kiss against her cheek. "Tell Shawn and Tivonté I said hey."

"You got it." Abrianna glanced around Kadir. "You guys have a nice day." She turned and opened the door and nearly plowed straight into Roger.

"Hi. Are you ready to go?"

"Go?" Abrianna faced Kadir.

He shrugged. "You didn't think that I was just going to let you roam out in the open without some kind of backup, did you?"

"So, I get *Roger*?"

"Hey!"

Abrianna whipped around and flashed a fake smile. "No offense, Roger."

Roger shrugged it off. "None taken."

Kadir folded his arms. "It's either Roger, or *I* go with you."

Abrianna glanced over at Baasim and Daishan, who pretended they weren't ear-hustling in on their conversation.

Kadir leaned in close. "Please? Do this for me?"

Abrianna sighed. "Fine. I'll babysit Roger."

"Hey! I'm still standing right here," Roger complained.

"Thanks, baby." Kadir kissed Abrianna and added, "Be careful out there."

"There's nothing to be worried about. T4S may be evil, but they are not stupid." She gave him one last peck on the cheek and headed out the door again. "C'mon, Roger. If you're a good boy, maybe I'll buy you some ice cream when we're done."

Kadir chuckled as Abrianna marched out, and Roger followed like a puppy with a gun holstered on his hip. Once they drove off, Kadir shut the door and turned to face his family.

Baasim smirked. "I have so many questions."

"So do I." His mother placed a plate on the table and then grabbed the remote. "I've been watching the news all morning, and your fiancée is all over it. None of it makes any sense to me."

Kadir sighed. "I have a lot of explaining to do."

"Oh, this sounds like it's going to be a long story." Baasim rolled his eyes and then grabbed his jacket. "How about you leave me the CliffsNotes, and I'll take a look at it when I get back?"

"You're going somewhere?" Kadir asked.

"Yeah. I need to take care of a few things: swing by the DMV, the bank—you know, the usual so I can get out of your hair sooner rather than later."

"There's no rush," Kadir said. "You know you're more than welcome to stay here as long as you'd like."

Baasim curled a half smile. "That's very nice of you—but I'm still going to have to peruse the CliffsNotes later." He slapped Kadir's shoulder, tossed him a wink, and then left the apartment.

Then Kadir was alone—with his mother.

Daishan patted the back of the dining room chair. "Have a seat . . . and let's talk."

⋙•⋘

"We need to make a quick stop," Abrianna told Roger as soon as he started the car.

"A stop?"

"Is that going to be a problem?" she snapped. The pain in her head caused her right eye to twitch. "If it is, you get the hell out, and I can drive myself."

Roger sighed. "You're never going to forgive me for that one . . . indiscretion, are you?"

"Indiscretion? Is that what you're calling it?" Abrianna laughed. "You tried to cop a feel when I was out cold."

Roger nodded. "I was an asshole—and I've been apologizing for months."

"Yeah, but let's be honest. You only apologized because I placed a gun in your face." She rolled her eyes.

Tension layered the space between them before Roger muttered another apology.

"At the next light, hang a right," Abrianna instructed.

He followed orders. Five minutes later, Abrianna was in her old stomping grounds, searching for a familiar face. "I don't know about this," Roger worried as he drove past suspicious looking thugs eyeballing their vehicle. "Are you sure we're in the right area?"

Abrianna chuckled. "What's the matter, Roger? You scared?"

"Nah." He shrugged. "Just . . . concerned."

"I bet you are. You'll be all right." She slapped a hand on his shoulder. "Stop at the next brownstone on the right."

Roger's eyes widened. "We're stopping?"

"Just for a few minutes."

He swallowed so loud she heard his gulp.

"If you want, you can keep the doors locked."

He gulped again as he parked in front of the brownstone. "Nah. If I fuck up on this job, I'll never be able to show my face in the bunker again. I'm coming up with you."

Abrianna stopped with her hand on the door. "I admire this sudden burst of courage, but it's not necessary. Stay here."

"But—"

"Stay. Here."

Roger made another loud gulp. "Yes, ma'am."

"I'll be right back." She hopped out of the car, but then smiled when she heard Roger lock the SUV's door. When she approached the brownstone, two ten-year-olds on dirt bikes blocked her pathway to the door.

"You're not from around here." The tallest of the two sneered at her.

Abrianna stopped and folded her arms. "Not any more. I'm here to see a friend."

"Name?" the other one inquired.

She cocked her head with a bemused grin. "Duane."

The tall one jumped back in. "You mean D-Dawg?" He looked her over again. "You don't look like one of D-Dawg's hoes."

"That's because I'm not—and watch your mouth."

"Bitch, you ain't my momma," the boy snapped.

"Out of my way, kid." She pushed past them and entered the dank and musty building. She held her breath as she rushed up the stairs. On Duane's floor, four men in matching black jeans and leather jackets quickly towered over her.

"Can we help you?" a cornrowed brother with a baby face asked. "You look kind of lost."

"And you look like you should be in somebody's school somewhere. I'm here to see Duane or D-Dawg—or whatever the hell he is calling himself these days."

The men's gazes raked over her.

"Yeah, yeah. I don't look like one of his hoes. I've already been given the 411 on that. I still need to talk to Duane. Tell him Abrianna is here to see him."

They hesitated.

"Today."

Finally, one of them peeled off and walked down to Duane's apartment and knocked. When the door cracked open, Abrianna's message was given, but the door slammed shut.

The messenger turned away from the door with a smile. "Doesn't look like the boss-man wants to see you."

Abrianna sighed. "Well, I did ask nicely." She glanced at the two men in front of her and forced them to slam their heads together. They immediately dropped to the floor.

The dude at the door leaped backward. "What the fuck?"

"Sorry about this." Abrianna swept her arm to the side and sent baby-face crashing into the wall, knocking him out. She winced. "That did look like it hurt." She stepped over the two bodies sprawled out in the hallway in front of her. At Duane's door, she knocked.

The door was snatched open.

"I said I didn't . . ."

Abrianna rammed her shoulder into the door and knocked Duane, in his bathrobe, back five feet.

"Goddamn it," Duane grunted, picking himself off of the floor. "What the fuck—"

Recognition slammed into him, and he backed away. "It really is you."

"Surprise." She back-kicked the door shut. "I need to holler at you for a minute," Abrianna said.

"No, no, no." Duane turned and took off running.

Bree rolled her eyes. "Now, where are you going?" She rushed after him.

Duane made it to a .45, spun around.

The buzz at the back of Abrianna's head intensified, warning her to duck just as he fired. Now, she was pissed and launched into a full-body tackle, which ended with them both skidding across the apartment's carpet.

Duane dropped the gun and hit his head on a corner of the coffee table. "Ow, fuck!"

She rolled him over, straddled him, and raised her fist.

"Whoa, whoa. Don't hit me. I'm cool." Duane surrendered with his hands up.

"You shot at me."

"I'm sorry. I'm sorry." He scrambled to get away. "But you burst in here like the Terminator."

Abrianna expelled a long breath and rolled her eyes. "You always were such a pussy." She stood. "Get up."

Duane hesitated, but when she offered her hand, he accepted it. She pulled him to his feet as if he weighed nothing.

He eyed her wearily. "I haven't seen you since Moses disappeared—except on television."

"Yeah, I'm a real celebrity." She glanced around. "Are you holding?"

"What?"

"Are you fucking holding or not? I don't have all day."

A slow smile eased across Duane's lips. "So, you're still using, huh? Figures. Once a junkie, always a junkie." He laughed.

"Oh, you *do* want me to hit you?"

"No, no." Duane shielded his face.

"I'll take an eight-ball, and I'll get out of your hair," she said. "And don't you even think about charging me."

"Hey, I didn't steal those pink bricks from you and Moses, I swear. I lost money on that deal, too."

"Aw, it's not like I'm going to make you sell your ass to a madam and then get you swept up in a murder conspiracy with the most powerful people in the country to pay back a debt you don't owe."

"I didn't have anything to do with that."

"Yeah, I forgot. Moses played you, too. The drugs were never missing."

"That muthafucka."

"The eight-ball, *please*. It's the last time I'm going to ask."

23

Kadir finished relaying everything he and Abrianna had been through for the past year to his mother. Judging by the different expressions she made during the telling, he worried whether he was winning her over.

"And this is the woman you want to give our last name to? An ex-stripper and . . . a lady of the evening?"

Kadir drew a deep breath and then leaned back in his chair. "There's more to her than that."

"Yes. She's also the daughter of a billionaire," his mother added sarcastically. "Who, I might add, that according to you was also sick in the head. Her mother also committed suicide in jail—and she grew up thinking she killed her own brother. She's a drug addict—"

"*Was* an addict," he corrected.

His mother cocked her head and caressed the side of his face. "Kadir, sweetie. I may not be hip or a woman of the world, but even I know that once an addict, always an addict."

He paused. She voiced the one thing he knew deep down inside but had been refusing to confront. "Well, that may be the case, but right now, she is trying to get better—and I'm going to be here for her every step of the way."

Daishan shook her head. "I just don't understand why you would want someone so damaged."

"Is that why you don't like her—because she's damaged? Well, here's a news flash for you, Mom. I'm damaged, too. Or, did you forget that?"

"I didn't say I didn't *like* her." She shifted around in her seat. "I'm just pointing out that she has a lot of baggage. And yes, I get that you do, too, but that's part of my point. With so much *luggage* between you two, I don't see how you could possibly hope to build something *solid*."

"Like everybody else, one day at a time," Kadir reasoned. "I'd hoped when I told you all of this, you could understand her better."

"Oh, I understand her—I even feel sorry for her. She's a lovely girl." His mother grabbed his hand. "I just don't think she's the right woman for you. She's nothing like Malala."

Kadir stiffened.

Daishan hung her head. "I didn't mean—"

"Yes . . . you did." Kadir stood. "You know, I gotta get going. I may have a cool boss, but I still have a job I'm supposed to show up to every once in a while."

"Kadir, honey. I didn't mean to upset you."

"The sad part about that statement is it's probably true. Malala is gone, Mom. She was a wonderful woman and I loved her very much. It took me a long time to get over her. And now, I'm in love with another amazing woman—and just because she's damaged doesn't make her any less amazing. If you can't see that, I'm sorry. But I am going to marry her and I would love to have your blessing."

Daishan lifted her chin. "And if I don't?"

"It will make the holidays extremely awkward."

Their gazes locked together in an old-fashioned mother versus child stare-down.

The phone rang, saving Kadir from withering and having his bluff called.

"I'll get it," his mother said, reaching for the portable on the table next to her before Kadir could object. "Hello." Daishan listened and then frowned.

Kadir tensed and then reached for the phone. "Who is it?"

His mother pulled the phone away and then held it out to him. "It's the president of the United States."

Kadir took the phone from his mother. She had to be mistaken. "Hello."

"Yes, is this Mr. Kadir Kahlifa?" a woman asked.

He paused. "Yeah."

"Please hold for the president."

Kadir glanced at his mother. "It's the president."

"I know. I told you that." Daishan grabbed at the phone. "What is she saying?"

Kadir leaned to the side so his mother could listen to the call.

"Mr. Kahlifa, how are you?"

"Madam President?" Kadir double-checked.

"I hope I'm not calling you at a bad time?"

An awkward silence lapsed over the phone as emotions charged through him.

On the other side, Kate glanced over at McMullan, worried that she had made a mistake. "I, um, saw your and Abrianna Parker's interview, and I want to hear more about the charges she leveled at T4S. I'd like to get to the bottom of what's going on."

Another long pause.

"Mr. Kahlifa?"

"That's why you called?" Kadir asked.

Kate shot another look to McMullan and shook her head. "I was under the impression that we both want to help Ms. Lehane. I'm interested in learning whether there is any truth to whether T4S had anything to do with the reporter's disappearance as well what happened to her, Ms. Parker, and all those teenagers who were killed by Dr. Avery. I want to get justice for those girls."

Silence.

"*Plus* . . . you may be interested to know that I have been reviewing your criminal record, Mr. Kahlifa, and, working with my team, I believe that you're a good candidate for a presidential pardon—given your work in bringing justice for house speaker Reynolds's death."

"Justice," Kadir repeated with a laughed. "That's funny coming from *you*."

"Excuse me?"

"The airstrikes in Sana'a," he said. "They killed my father and very nearly killed my mother and twin brother. How do you suppose I get justice for them?"

The president stammered. "I, um . . ."

"Yeah. That's what I thought." Kadir cleared his throat.

"Mr. Kahlifa, I'm so sorry for your loss. I . . . had no idea."

"Of course not. How could you have? It's not like you have the world's best intelligence agencies at your disposal."

"You're upset, Mr. Kahlifa."

"You're perceptive, Madam President. However, I will tell my fiancée you phoned. She may have a different reception to your call."

"I see. Well, um, yes. I'd appreciate that." Kate's hand tightened on the phone. "I do want to extend my heartfelt condolence for your loss. My thoughts and prayers are with you and your family."

"I can't tell you how much that doesn't help," Kadir said smoothly.

The president drew a breath. "I made the call for the strikes. The buck stops with me."

"Trust me. I know." Kadir disconnected the call.

———————

At La Plume, Abrianna made a beeline to the bathroom. After locking herself in a stall, she sat on the toilet and removed a compact mirror and her pink eight-ball. Her hands shook as she sprinkled the pink power out of the plastic bag. "I just need a little bit," she whispered to herself.

You have a problem, Shawn's voice floated inside her head.

Guilt settled on Abrianna's shoulders while she made her perfect pink lines. Then the thousands of times she'd promised her friends that she'd get help echoed in her head. No one understood. The constant buzzing at the back of her head chipped away at her sanity. Drugs were her only relief. She wasn't about to give them up.

Abrianna inhaled the two pink lines and then twitched her nose while the powder burned her nasal cavity. She rocked backward, gasping, and then had to remind herself to breathe.

Someone walked into the bathroom, and Abrianna scrambled to put everything away. When she exited the stall, she washed up at the sink and avoided her reflection. By the time she joined her friends at their table, she was all smiles, and her head was in the clouds.

"What's with this *Driving Miss Daisy* thing you got going on?" Shawn thumbed toward Roger sitting alone across the restaurant at a table near the door.

Abrianna chuckled. "Believe it or not, he's my bodyguard."

Shawn and Tivonté sputtered out a laugh.

"I know, right?" Abrianna sniffed. "It was better to let him play tag than to keep arguing with Kadir."

"He has a right to be worried. You still don't know who attacked you at Lehane's place." Tivonté glanced around. "For all we know, they could be tracking your every move to do another extraction."

Shawn joined in Tivonté's paranoia. It was understandable. In the past six months, Tivonté, like Shawn and Draya, had come close to losing his life to protect Abrianna. After a long stretch in the hospital, Tivonté had lost half his body mass and was on the mend, and his restaurant was open for business again.

"Chill out, guys. Nothing is going to happen. T4S is not going to make a move now that I've put them on Front Street. Right now, we're here to talk about this." She jutted out her engagement ring. "Bam!"

Shawn's and Tivonté's jaws dropped.

"You're getting married?" Shawn's jaw looked like it was about to hit the floor.

Tivonté grabbed her hand. "Damn. What's this, about two carats? Niiice."

Abrianna beamed. "You should have seen him. When he got on bended knee, my heart dropped. It was the most romantic thing I've ever experienced."

Tivonté and Shawn snickered.

"What?"

"Nothing." Shawn chuckled. "We've never seen you this glowed up before. You really do love him, don't you?"

Abrianna couldn't stop smiling. "I wouldn't have said yes if I didn't. And even though our worlds are incredibly crazy and topsy-turvy, I wouldn't want to go through any of it with anyone else."

"Aw, he completes you," Shawn cooed.

Tivonté propped his elbows on the table and cradled his face. "No. She's just a girl, standing in front of a boy."

"Enough with the rom-com madness." Abrianna laughed. "I'm . . . happy."

Shawn squeezed her hand. "And it looks good on you. We were just surprised. That's all." He shrugged. *It seems so sudden.*

"It's not sudden," she snapped. "We've known each other for almost a year."

"I didn't say . . ." Shawn's eyes narrowed. "Are you reading my thoughts again?"

"I—I . . ."

Tivonté frowned. "I thought you could only do that when you're . . ." He leaned forward and snatched her shades off so he could see her eyes. He gasped.

"Give me those back!" She snatched her sunglasses and crammed them back onto her face.

Shawn and Tivonté shared disappointed looks.

She made a face. "Don't do that."

"Do what?"

"Don't make that face." She punched his shoulder.

"Ow," Shawn whined, cradling his shoulder. "That hurts."

"Don't judge me. I have to do what I have to do."

The table remained silent.

"Besides, I don't get it." Abrianna changed the subject. "I thought you guys like Kadir?" She searched their faces.

"I do—we do," Shawn said, willing to go along. "It's just . . . don't you think you two are moving a bit fast? You've only known the guy for a few months—though, in some ways, it feels like a lifetime."

"Yeah, but . . ." She shrugged. "When it's right . . . you just know—you know?" Her smile expanded.

Tivonté sipped his tea.

Shawn held out, and then one corner of his mouth crooked up-ward.

"Aren't you happy for me?"

"Are you kidding me?" Shawn stood and moved around the table to throw his arms around Abrianna. "I'm thrilled for you. Kadir is a great guy stacked up next to the drug dealers and gang-sters you used to date."

She shrugged. "He's still an ex-con."

"Well, you do have a type," Tivonté jumped in.

"Bad boys, bad boys. Whatcha gonna do?" Shawn and Tivonté sang, laughing.

"Ha. Ha." Abrianna rolled her eyes.

Tivonté came around the table and hugged her, too. "C'mon,

fish. You know us queens are happy for you. I'm jealous you're beating me to the altar. Your ass never even believed in love."

She shrugged. "I guess it's true what they say. People change." Abrianna squeezed him back. "Now, I'm going to need a caterer for the wedding."

"I got you, girl." Tivonté winked before returning to his chair. "I'm going to hook you up."

"You have a date?" Shawn asked.

"Not yet. But soon, I hope."

"How many people are we talking about?" Tivonté asked.

Abrianna laughed. "You know me. My circle is small. I only have the one brother. Kadir has me beat with one brother *and* a mother—and then there's our clique and—"

"So small." Tivonté held up an okay sign. "Got it."

"How are you getting along with the new family?" Shawn asked. "I rarely hear positive stories about mothers-in-law."

"It's good," Abrianna's voice spiked. "Really good. They seem nice. We're going to get along fine—once we get to know each other better—I hope."

"They hate you," Shawn and Tivonté declared in unison.

Abrianna gave up the ghost. "That's putting it *nicely*. The second Kadir introduced me as his fiancée, his mom looked at me like I'd stabbed her in the heart."

"Yeah, I hear that's their superpower." Shawn laughed. "Good luck with that."

"Thanks, something tells me I'm going to need it. His brother isn't too crazy about me, either, but then again, he doesn't like Kadir, either."

"Cain and Abel?"

"Not quite, but it has potential." She shook her head and glanced out the restaurant's glass front, where she spotted a face and then had to do a double take.

"What? What is it?" Shawn asked, suddenly alert. He attempted to follow her line of vision.

Abrianna squinted to make the man out.

"You'd tell us if you sense danger, right?" Tivonté asked. "I'd like to get a head start out the back if a platoon of militant soldiers is descending on this bitch to snatch your ass."

Abrianna dragged her gaze back to Tivonté as a laughed rumbled from her chest. "Oh, you're running?"

"Damn right, bitch. I've already taken a beating from Zeke's gangster ass for you. I draw the line at well-armed militias."

"Well, damn. Thanks."

"Just so we're clear." Tivonté picked up his cup and saucer and sipped his tea like an old English woman. "Besides, you're the only one who is indestructible. You'll be fine. I, myself, am precious cargo."

"You better preach," Shawn cosigned, holding his hands up.

Abrianna shook her head, laughing.

"How exactly did Kadir's mother and brother get out of Sana'a?" Shawn asked.

"Yeah. I thought the State Department would contact you once they learned anything?" Tivonté questioned.

Abrianna shrugged. "What? You guys still have faith in the government? Really?"

"Hell, naw." Tivonté laughed. "I don't have faith in anybody other than myself."

Abrianna lifted a brow.

"And maybe you guys," he added with a shrug. "I have trust issues."

Abrianna smiled. "You're preaching to the choir."

❧

Baasim arrived at Masjid Muhammad in time for noon prayer. The moment he entered the place, it was like returning home. It had been seven years, but the more things change, the more things stay the same. He grew up at the mosque. Before he kneeled, he'd recognized half the men there.

After Zuhr was over, old friends approached.

"Baasim Kahlifa. I never thought I'd see you again."

"Farooq. Hey, man." Baasim dabbed with his old high-school buddy. "Long time, no see."

"Yeah. The last I heard, you were in Yemen."

"I was, until about five days ago."

Understanding dawned on the small crowd.

"The Sana'a strikes," Farooq commiserated. "America's undeclared war on the Middle East still running amuck." He shook his head. "How is the family? We've seen your brother being hailed as a hero for the last few months. But no matter who they put in the White House, their policies for the Middle East stay the same: arm everyone and spread chaos and dissension."

Baasim nodded, but then lowered his head. "I've definitely experienced some of that." There was another beat of silence before he added, "My father was killed in one of the strikes."

"Muaadh has passed away?" one of the elders said, moving into the group's small circle. "I'm so sorry to hear that."

Word circulated like wildfire, and another wave of men approached Baasim and gave him their condolences and shared personal memories of his father. Until that moment, Baasim had kept his emotions at bay. But now, among so many of his father's old friends, grief overwhelmed him.

"Come," Farooq said. "We should talk."

24

After placing their dessert orders, Shawn turned to Abrianna. "So, what's the story? How did Kadir's people get out of Yemen?"

"Baasim survived a missile strike at a funeral—their father didn't. Hours later, President Washington's other colossal screw-up nearly took out their mother. Baasim said it took about a day for him to locate his mother and get her over to the embassy. But the rebels had seized the embassy, too."

"Damn." Tivonté clutched his imaginary pearls.

"Yeah, tell me about it." Abrianna shook her head. "It sounds like a real mess over there. The civil war has been going for like fifteen years. And then you throw Iran and Saudi Arabia into the mix, and it's chaos."

"Fifteen years? Then why did his parents move back there?"

"Their father believed they were better off in their own land fighting than to fight in a land that only gives lip service about being the land of the free and justice for all."

"Ouch."

"But where is the lie, though?" Abrianna asked.

The table went quiet.

"Exactly." Abrianna played with blueberries on top of her cheesecake. "Anyway, the embassy was evacuated, and the airport had been bombed—"

"Then how did they get out?"

"The state department here was telling us they were working on getting Americans out, but on the ground, the embassy was telling Yemeni Americans that they should find passage out of the country by any means possible. Since al-Qaeda and the Islamic State are so heavy in Yemen, the US couldn't risk a large evacuation. They had no way to screen all the prospective passengers on a plane or ship. They couldn't risk unintentionally bringing a terrorist into the United States. Basically, they were told to shelter in place. Baasim took a chance that the ports were still working."

"The ports?" Tivonté asked.

"Freighters were still shipping livestock and people between two ports I can't remember the names of; even though they were still fighting over control of the ports, they were still running. They didn't get on a freighter, but several bribes later, they boarded some tiny boat that didn't look like it could make it across a pond let alone the Red Sea. But beggars can't be choosy. They took the small boat to some place called Djibouti, I think. I don't know how to pronounce it. But there the US had a functioning embassy. Once they got there, they flew to a place called Addis and from there to the United States."

"Damn. That sound like a complete season of *Homeland*."

"Amen," Shawn agreed.

"The main thing is they made it here safe and sound—at least two of them," Abrianna said.

Shawn and Tivonté nodded.

Abrianna glanced out the restaurant's window, and her gaze snagged on the same guy down the street. "If I'm not mistaken, I think that's Baasim." She leaned forward.

"Where?" Shawn and Tivonté craned their neck to see out the window.

"In front of the Industrial Bank building."

Shawn frowned. "You can see all the way down there?"

She shrugged. "It's not that far."

Shawn and Tivonté looked at each other.

"I wonder who that guy is he's talking to?" Abrianna scanned the man next to Baasim and decided that she didn't like him. It wasn't only because his hair looked oily or his beard was unruly. It was his appearance—way too shifty.

Tivonté snapped his fingers in front of Abrianna's face.

She jumped.

"Welcome back." He smiled. "Do you have a date for when this wedding is going to be?"

"Um, not yet. But I'll get all that information to you soon. I promise."

The guys shared looks again.

"I don't know how many people are coming, and I don't have a date. I get it. But we will get everything together, and you will cater the event."

"Yes, ma'am." Tivonté saluted.

Abrianna reached for her purse. "Before I go, I have one last bit of news to tell you." She removed her copy of her father's will and placed it in the center of the table.

"What's that?" Tivonté asked. "You're not serving me no warrant or no shit like that, are you? 'Cause on the real, I should be suing your ass."

"Chill out." Abrianna rolled her eyes. "It's Cargill's last will and testament."

Shawn grabbed the thick manila envelope and pulled out the papers. "Why do you have it?"

Abrianna smiled. "Because I'm rich, bitches."

⟶•◦•⟵

Baasim felt at home when he and Farooq entered one of their old hangouts, Bezoria's. It was a quaint Mediterranean and Middle Eastern restaurant owned by Farooq's family that served the best beef and lamb meatballs sandwiches in D.C. No sooner had

he and Farooq taken their seats, then more familiar faces entered
the restaurant and joined them.

Cousins Yasser and Awsam Rizq gave Baasim a quick bro-hug
before introducing him to fresh faces, Saoud al-Khyat and Kamel
al-Dhaheri.

"It's nice to meet you." Baasim nodded.

"It's cool to meet you, too," Saoud said. "You and your brother
are legends around here. We were sad when it turned out he
didn't have anything to do with the airport bombing last year,
though. But he made up for it by taking that asshole out of the
White House."

"Hmmph. That remains to be seen. Maybe if Kadir and his girl
had left Walker in there, we would never have had those air
strikes that killed our father," Baasim growled.

The table fell silent while Saoud's gaze seared into Baasim.

"And what side of the war were you on?"

Baasim cocked a half smile. "The right side."

Saoud's gaze grew darker as if looking into Baasim's soul. "I'm
truly sorry for your loss. I've heard many wonderful things about
your father."

Baasim's gaze fell away for a second time. "Thanks, man."

Saoud wasn't finished. "A man like your father deserved justice. A lot of people deserve justice who aren't getting it and
haven't been for a long time. I don't know about you, but it's time
for that to change."

Baasim locked gazes with Saoud. "Change how?"

Saoud glanced at the other men at the table and the same sinis-
ter smile carved on each of their faces—and then across Baasim's
face.

<hr>

Outside of Ghost's warehouse apartment, a black van rolled to
a stop, and six people hopped out dressed in black and armed to

the teeth. Within seconds, plastics were placed on the door and the men took cover. Three seconds later, an explosion blew the door apart. The half dozen military-like men charged inside.

Down the street, Ghost watched the action while a five-alarm panic exploded inside of his chest. His off-the-grid apartment was now compromised. "Fuck, fuck, fuck." He glanced out the passenger side mirror and pulled away from the curb and back into traffic. "Fuck, fuck, fuck."

He rode around for an hour before deciding to head across town to hammer on Kadir's door. The second it opened, Ghost bolted through and launched into a tirade. "I fucked up, man. I fucked up."

"I'm sorry?"

"T4S caught us in their mainframe, and I think they tracked us back to the bunker. I'm not sure. We snatched everything out of the walls and evacuated the place." Ghost paced in a circle. "Then I went back to the warehouse apartment, but before I pull up, a fuckin' commando squad bounded out of nowhere and blew their way inside—in broad muthafuckin' daylight. Like it wasn't shit." He stopped talking and glanced up. "Is that a fucking lace-front? When the fuck did you grow your hair out?"

"Hey, Ghost. Long time, no see."

Ghost's expression fell. "Baasim?"

"The one and only."

Daishan inched into the living room. "Is everything all right in here?"

"You two are alive. Well, hot damn. Get in here." Ghost threw his arms around Baasim before he had a chance to object and squeezed him like he'd found an old childhood toy. "Your brother was so worried about you. When did you guys get stateside?"

"A couple of days ago." Baasim eased awkwardly out of Ghost's bear hug and stepped back. "Now, what's this about commandos and T4S?"

"T4S?" Daishan asked. "Those are the people who put Kadir in prison."

"Um, I-I think you may have misunderstood me." Ghost laughed. "I didn't say anything about T4S."

Baasim's eyebrows rose comically. "Ah. My bad, then." He smiled.

Ghost grinned. "Is Kadir here?"

Daishan shook her head. "He's at work."

Ghost nodded. "And Bree?"

"Bree?" Baasim asked. "Is that the girlfriend's nickname?"

"Frankly, I like to call her 'badass,' but since it's unwise to piss her off, I go with the flow with Bree."

Baasim crossed his arms. "So, you like her?"

"What's not to like?" Ghost joked, but when he saw that neither Baasim nor Daishan cared for it, his laughter petered out before he coughed and cleared his throat. "Anyway, I take it that she's out, too?"

"Yeah. She had some brunch she had to get to with her friends—but that was hours ago, actually." Baasim checked his watch.

"Ah, I see." Ghost backpedaled toward the front door. "Well, I'll go and check a few places and, um, if you see them before I do, tell them I'm looking for them. And for them to stay away from the warehouse apartment."

"You mean *my* warehouse apartment?" Baasim checked.

Ghost shrugged as his smile expanded. "Hey. I told you I would look after it while you were gone. You know that I love you like a play cousin."

Baasim cast a look at his mother and then lowered his voice. "We'll talk later."

"Sho you right." Ghost opened the door and winked. "I'll catch you on the flip side."

25

"Where in the hell is Kadir?" Castillo griped, settling in behind her desk. "Does he still work here or not?"

Julian and Draya, sensing Castillo's bad mood, put their heads down and kept working.

"I mean, it's not asking too much to expect people to show up for work, is it? If you can't make it, call in sick," she fumed. "And for the record, giving national interviews doesn't qualify as an excuse not to show up for work." She slapped a file down on her desk when she really wanted to throw something. She was mad at Dennis, not Kadir, but damn if she could stop herself from bitching.

The door blew open, and Kadir rushed inside. "Sorry I'm late."

"Oh, are you late?" Castillo glanced at her watch. "I hadn't noticed."

Draya and Julian kept their heads down.

Kadir didn't miss the sarcasm, either, "My mother and brother showed up at the apartment last night."

"What?" Draya bounded out of her chair.

"That's great news, man." Julian also rushed over to congratulate him. "I know that has to be a load off of your shoulders." He pounded him on the back.

"You have no idea." He turned his gaze back to his boss, who propped up a smile.

"That is good news, Kadir," she relented with a sigh. "I'm happy for you."

"Thanks." He flashed a smile.

"How did they get out, man?"

Kadir settled behind his desk and then relayed Baasim and his mother's extraordinary escape out of Sana'a, Yemen—and how his father was killed.

Castillo listened, feeling like an ass for barking all morning. The good news was few and far between around there, so she welcomed it. Still, they weren't any closer to finding Tomi Lehane.

"Did you catch Abrianna's interview yesterday?"

"We watched it here at the office. Definitely must-see TV. I'm sure that you've gotten T4S's attention."

"That was the plan, but—"

"But?" Castillo crossed her arms.

"The interview may get T4S to back off Abrianna for the time being. But what does it mean for Tomi? If they have her, they can never let her go to blab to the whole world."

Castillo's heart sank as he gave voice to the very thing she'd been worried about.

The Agency's door flew open again. Everyone looked up as Ghost rushed inside.

A smile spread across Castillo's face. "My eyes *must* be deceiving me, because I know that Douglas Lamar Jenkins isn't risking his freedom and liberty by racing into an *ex*-cop's place of business."

"So, it's like that? You gonna put my whole government name on blast?"

Castillo smiled. "Force of habit."

A smile touched Ghost's lips before he glanced around. "Anyone else here?"

"Why? Are you looking for someone in particular?" Castillo stood from her desk.

"Yes or no?" Ghost asked, agitated.

Castillo finally noticed that Ghost looked nervous, and she dropped the attitude. "Yeah. It's just us."

"Good." Ghost turned back toward the door, and pulled down the shades.

Castillo and her employees shared *what-the-fuck* looks before Ghost addressed them again.

"The Bunker and the warehouse are burnt."

Kadir's head snapped up with alarm in his eyes. "T4S?"

Ghost bobbed his head. "They finally discovered me ghosting around in the mainframe. Couldn't get out fast enough, so we snatched everything out the walls and evacuated."

"Shit." Kadir raked his hand through his hair.

"Yeah, then I went to the warehouse apartment, and I got there in time to see a private commando unit raiding the place—complete with explosions in broad daylight. I came to warn you guys not to go to either place. My guys and I are going to lay low for a while."

"Then Abrianna isn't safe." Kadir made a move toward the door.

"Where are you going?" Castillo asked.

"To find Abrianna. She's out in the open with just Roger guarding her."

Ghost blocked Kadir with his hand. "No offense, bruh. But not everything is about you and Abrianna. *I'm* the target this time. And I haven't told you the most interesting part."

"There's more?"

Ghost nodded. "Someone broke into T4S."

"What? You mean another hacker?"

"No. I mean somebody *physically* invaded that muthafucka. Their entire system went down, and emergency responders were called to the scene and everything."

"But that's impossible." Castillo crossed the office and stopped before Ghost. "That place is crawling with soldiers. It's impenetrable."

"Hey. I thought so, too. But *somebody* got balls of steel out there. My problem . . . is that with them finding us snooping around so soon after and uploading those stolen files—"

"They think that you broke in and invaded the premises."

"Crazy, huh?" He attempted to laugh it off.

"I wonder who is the one with the steel balls," Castillo said aloud.

"I'm wondering about that shit, too." Ghost smirked. "I'd like to shake their hand."

Castillo's mind raced a mile a minute. "They broke in and what?"

"Don't know. The point is they broke in that muthafucka and got away with it."

"Any fatalities?" Kadir asked.

"Don't know. But there were casualties. They were taken to the hospital."

"They were looking for something," Kadir concluded.

"Or looking for *someone*," Castillo amended with hope.

The front door of the Agency swung open again, and everyone in the small office turned. Ghost, unfortunately, swung around with his gun, ready to fire.

"Don't shoot." Dinah Lehane's eyes widened as she dropped her purse and held up her hands. "Please."

"Nobody is going to shoot anybody." Castillo lowered Ghost's arm. "Sorry to alarm you, Ms. Lehane. Please, come in." She picked up the woman's purse and took her by the hand.

Lehane allowed herself to be pulled inside while her gaze scattered around the room again. "If this is a bad time, I can come back later."

"No. No. Please have a seat."

Draya sprang out of her chair. "Can I get you a cup of coffee or tea, Ms. Lehane?"

"Um, no. But I'll take a bottled water if you have one."

"We do. I'll be right back."

"Lehane," Ghost repeated, staring at the petite-size woman. "As in Tomi Lehane's mother?"

Dinah's large brown eyes centered on Ghost. "Do you know my daughter?"

"Indirectly." He glanced at Castillo. "She's a friend of a friend."

Dinah looked confused.

"Here you go, Mrs. Lehane." Draya handed her a bottled water.

"Thank you." She sat down in the vacant chair in front of Castillo's desk. "It's been a long time."

Castillo nodded as she settled into her chair. "Yes. It has."

"Have you been following the news? Do you know what has happened to my baby—again?"

"Yes. I've heard. And I'm so sorry. I can't imagine what you must be going through right now."

"Thank you." Dinah sniffed and then reached for Castillo's hand. "Tomi told me how you kept in touch over the years."

"Yes. Sometimes Tomi hires me for freelance work. We're friends."

"I'd like to hire you," Dinah blurted. "You found my baby once before, and I know that you can do it again. Please. I don't care how much it costs. Her father and I have some money saved up. He's just so devastated about all of this. I'm afraid that he's been drinking again. But please. Find my baby. Bring her back home again. You can do that, right?"

Castillo sandwiched the woman's hand. "Keep your money. This one is on the house."

26

The White House

Kate pulled the phone from her ear. "He hung up."

McMullan shook his head. "What are the fucking chances of Kahlifa losing a family member in those air strikes?"

"The way my luck has been running lately?" Kate stood from behind her desk. "Of course they were. The man fucking hates me. There's no way they'll agree to come here and smile in front of the cameras."

"He did say Parker *might* have a different opinion," McMullan argued.

"He also said she was his *fiancée*. Parker will likely side with him and tell me to kiss her ass. I'm right back where I started: ground zero with Hardy's boot on my neck."

T4S Headquarters . . .

"Governor Hardy, thank you for coming." Pierce Spalding sprang up from behind his desk and approached Governor Hardy with his hand outstretched.

Bo Hardy slapped palms with Pierce Spalding and then performed a hard yank-shake while he reassessed the man before him. "You left me with no choice after I was caught with my fly hanging open on national television." He released Spalding.

"That certainly wasn't our intent," Spalding assured him, shaking the pain out of his hand. "Please, sit down. Can I get you anything?"

Hardy waved him off. "Nah. I see I need to be clearheaded when dealing with you paramilitary nuts."

Spalding laughed off the insult. "It's nothing like that, I assure you. We have been nothing but transparent and leveled with you about what it is that we do here. We are a full-service risk-management consulting firm. We put our men at risk around the world to uphold the same ideology as the American military. We train soldiers, worked with the SEAL and SWAT teams. Hell, we were one of the first private security firms hired following the US invasion of Afghanistan. We have the largest training facility in the country. And—"

"When are you going to get to the part where you guys kidnap teenage girls off the street and experiment on them?" Hardy asked, stretching back in his seat and looking bored.

Spalding closed his mouth and evaluated the man before him.

"And before you get started, let me warn you that you can't bullshit a bullshitter."

Spalding took heed. "We are serious and passionate about what we do here, Governor Hardy. Uncle Sam turns to firms like us to color outside the lines of wartime laws and international treaties—also political culpabilities and public backlash when it comes time to put more troops in hostile territories—something President Washington should have considered to avoid the type of backlash she's experiencing right now over the Yemen air strikes. Had she turned to us, instead of slashing military budgets and private contracts, we would have used a more surgical touch than the billion-ton gorilla that is the US military. Deniability is worth its weight in gold."

Hardy engaged in a stare-down with Spalding before a smile curved his lips. "Deniability, huh?"

"Yes, sir." Spalding returned to his seat. "The vision of an army of elite soldiers may have been the well-worn plot of many science fiction books and movies for decades, but we have brought this vision closer to reality then anyone has dared to hope. What government wouldn't salivate at the possibility of having soldiers who were stronger than the average man or woman, ones who wouldn't rely on expensive robotics that blow holes into budgets and are vulnerable to hacks and wear and tear?"

"And how do you conduct the research for these wonderful sci-fi soldiers?"

"*Discreetly.*"

Laughter rumbled from Hardy's chest as he climbed back to his feet. "*That*, my friend, may be up for debate."

"We can handle the Abrianna Parker situation," Spalding assured him, standing.

Hardy cocked his head and challenged, "Do you really think that's wise—in this political climate?"

"I don't get what you mean."

"Yes, you do. *If* what Ms. Parker is out there squawking about is true, and now I believe that it is, you making a second girl from your experimental lab go missing or turn up dead will only be red meat at a feast for the blue snowflakes on the left. We need confusion, not confirmation, to handle this . . . situation. That's where I come in." Hardy's grin expanded while he puffed up his chest. "You don't need to kill anyone in American politics just destroy their reputation. Leave it to me." He buttoned his suit jacket.

Spalding relaxed as he walked with Hardy toward the door. "Glad to see that you're still on board."

"It's like they say, you can't change horses in midstream." He stopped when he placed his hand on the door. "Are there any more surprises that I need to know about? Are you hiding E.T. or any of his friends at any of your facilities?"

"Do you really want to know?"

Hardy paused. "Forget I asked." He opened the door and waltzed out.

Spalding's phone rang. He closed the door and returned to his desk. Ned Cox's name showed up on the caller ID screen. "Make it quick."

"Dr. Zacher is awake."

27

Castillo entered through the doors of the *Washington Post* building and expanded her smile when she approached the receptionist. "Hello. I was hoping that you could help me. I'm looking for a Jayson Brigham. Is he available?"

The young woman held up a slim finger while she answered the ringing phone. About a dozen calls later, Castillo still stood in front of the receptionist, waiting for her to help her talk to Brigham when she spotted him exiting an elevator and heading straight toward her.

"Okay. Sorry about that. Now, how can I help you?"

"Never mind." Castillo moved away from the receptionist desk to cut off Brigham's path before he exited the building. "Jayson Brigham," she called out.

Brigham's head sprang up from the camera in his hand, and he stopped before he plowed into her. "Oh, hey."

Castillo plastered her fake smile back on. "Hello. We've never officially met before, but I'm Gizella Castillo. A friend of Tomi Lehane's."

"Ah, the cop."

"*Ex*-cop," she corrected.

"Right. You're the one who found Tomi when Craig Avery kidnapped her." He jutted out a hand. "It's nice to finally meet you. Tomi used to talk about you all the time."

"Really?" She shook his hand.

"Well, not *all* the time. But . . . you know what I mean."

Castillo nodded and sized up the photographer. "Um, do you have a few minutes? I'd like to ask you a few questions."

"I, um . . ."

"You were one of the last people to see Tomi before she disappeared, right?"

"Um, yeah. She, um."

"Have you had lunch yet? We could talk over a meal."

Brigham looked like he wanted to refuse.

"Please," Castillo added. "This is important."

He hesitated a second longer and then relented. "I got about thirty minutes."

"Great. My favorite sandwich shop is around the corner." She winked before leading the way.

Five minutes later, Castillo and Brigham sat across from each other in the Colada Shop with two piping-hot ham and roasted pork sandwiches between them.

"Nice jacket," Castillo commented to loosen him up.

"Thanks. It's actually a vintage racer jacket. I inherited it from my dad. The zippers are cool and the wrists have these really nice buttons that . . ." He frowned and did a double take.

Castillo cocked her head. "It looks like you're missing a button."

"Damn it." He looked on the floor around their table.

Castillo looked around, too, until the photographer sighed and gave up.

"Forget it." He picked up his sandwich. "It's not often a beautiful woman buys me a meal. I can get used to this."

"That sounds sad." Castillo whipped out her notepad.

"You have no idea." He chuckled.

"Tell me about the last time you saw Tomi?"

Jayson's gaze dropped to his sandwich. "The night of the fire," he said. "We both worked late that evening. Nothing unusual."

"How did she seem?"

"Seem?"

"Yeah? Did she seem normal? Was she upset—or distracted?" Jayson hesitated.

"What? What is it?" She inched forward in her chair. "You know something. What is it?"

"No. It's nothing. She was . . ."

"What?"

He shrugged. "She was upset. But only because Abrianna Parker refused to return her calls."

Castillo's shoulders slumped. "What?"

"Yeah. Ever since Tomi ran that article on Parker's stepmom, the two hadn't been exactly seeing things eye-to-eye." Castillo collapsed back against her seat. It wasn't the news that she was looking for.

Brigham added, "Tomi blamed herself for what happened to Marion Parker. At the time she ran the article, she just wanted to get the truth out there. I can testify to that. She did try to contact Abrianna before the article ran but was unable to reach her and . . . well, you know we do work on deadlines. She had no idea the woman would hang herself in her cell."

"I see." Castillo sighed. "Well, Abrianna didn't have anything to do with her disappearance."

"Are you sure about that?" Jayson challenged.

Castillo's head snapped up. "Come again?"

Jayson shrugged. "Just because you paid for the meal doesn't mean you're the only one allowed to ask questions."

Castillo eased back in her chair. "What are you saying? You think Abrianna had something to do with her disappearance?"

Jayson hunched his shoulders again. "Anything is possible. She has a motive. And it's a hell of a coincidence that her father Cargill also kicked the bucket the same night of the fire."

"So, now Abrianna is a serial killer?"

He smirked.

"What's so funny?"

"You are. You'd make a lousy journalist. You can't be objective."

"I was a cop."

"My point exactly." He chuckled, but then sobered when Castillo didn't appear amused. "Look, I get it. You probably have some affinity toward Abrianna just like you did with Tomi. After all, you rescued them once. You're too close to the trees to see you're in a forest."

"But, I can see you're barking up the wrong tree."

"Like I said." He shook his head and took another bite of his sandwich.

Castillo drew a patient breath. "Okay. I'll bite. What's your evidence?"

"Nothing solid—yet. But you have to admit that an awful lot of bodies have dropped around this woman: the house speaker, the chief justice, a madam she used to work for, her ex-boyfriend Moses Darrough is MIA, but the streets are saying he's dead, too. Then like I said, her father *and* his lawyer—all dead. But she goes on television and feeds the American people a whole new story that no one had ever heard about regarding her and Tomi's kidnapping when they were teenagers and—"

"*I* heard it before," Castillo pushed back.

"Right. Did Abrianna do a test run with you?"

"No. Tomi did."

Jayson stopped eating.

"Yeah. She showed up at my office one night with all this research material. Apparently, this Dr. Zacher had reached out to her, and it freaked her out. And I'm sorry to blow a hole in your lovely theory, but it was Tomi who outed Dr. Zacher to Abrianna. He'd been posing as some harmless, homeless guy in the park for years. Tomi dug up all this information about T4S. And you know

what? I believe her *and* Abrianna. And I'm going to prove it."
Castillo stood from her chair. "I think I got all I need. Thank you
for your time." She marched off before Brigham responded.

"How did it go?" Kadir asked when Castillo returned to
the SUV.

"It didn't. That guy is a real asshole."

⟶•⟵

"So, how did it go?" Ghost asked when Castillo and Kadir returned from the *Washington Post*. He leaned back in Castillo's
chair and even kicked up his booted feet on the corner of her
desk. "It was a waste of time, wasn't it?"

"Comfortable?" Castillo marched over toward her desk.

"I am, actually." Ghost grinned as he folded his arms behind
his head.

Castillo swiped his feet off the corner of her desk. "Un-ass my
seat."

When his boots hit the floor with a thud, he laughed as he was
forced to sit up straight. "No problem. But you did tell me to
make myself comfortable before you left."

"I said no such thing." She shoved him out of the way.

"No? Huh. Maybe I need to get my hearing checked."

"That's not all you need to get checked out," Castillo mumbled, taking her seat.

Ghost leaned against the desk. "You still haven't answered my
question. Did Brigham know anything?"

"Not a damn thing," Kadir answered for Castillo. "Gigi says
the photographer believes Bree has something to do with Tomi's
disappearance."

"Gigi?" Ghost smirked, turning to Castillo. "Your name is
Gigi?"

"It's Gizella, but I prefer for assholes to call me Castillo."

"And I prefer for hot chicks to call me Daddy. You scratch my
back, and I'll scratch yours." He grinned.

Draya shook her head and folded her arms. "Is there a woman that you *won't* hit on?"

Ghost's grin grew. "Hey, hey. No need to be jealous. There is plenty of me to go around."

Castillo laughed. "Does this routine really work for you?"

Kadir jumped in. "Ladies, don't encourage him. He really can go at this all day."

"And *night*," Ghost added, wiggling his brows.

Both Draya and Castillo groaned.

"My point is," Ghost sighed, "that your little trip was a complete waste of time. We already know who is behind Tomi's disappearance. It was T4S. We need to be figuring out a way how to burst into that place and snatch old girl back."

Kadir smirked as he made it over to his chair. "You're just mad that someone physically broke in a place you said was impenetrable."

"Damn right," Ghost charged. "And if someone else can do it, it means we can do it, too."

"Okay. I hate to break your ego—not. But, nobody is breaking into anything," Castillo said. "There's no need when we can just walk in through the front door."

"The front door?" Ghost and Kadir looked at each other and then burst out laughing.

"What's so funny?"

Kadir informed her, "*I* can't get anywhere near T4S physically—or digitally, for that matter. It violates the terms of my parole. You guys can do what you want."

Castillo's gaze swung toward Ghost.

He threw up his hands. "I'm pretty sure they have orders to shoot my ass on sight if I walked through the front door."

"And you guys want to give me *pointers* on how to do *my* job?"

"Oh, we're going to gloss over the fact that you were kicked off the force, Ms. By-the-book?"

Castillo's expression hardened. "I *quit* the force. I was never kicked off of anything, jackass. And while we're at it, I don't always color inside the lines, either. But there's a science to breaking the rules. That's what you guys haven't figured out yet." She twirled an old-fashioned Rolodex, found a number, and picked up the phone.

"Who are you calling?"

"Dr. Zacher," she answered matter-of-factly.

"Oh, you're a gangster?" Kadir laughed.

Castillo held up a finger for them to be quiet when someone answered the line. "Yes, Dr. Charles Zacher, please. Thank you." She glanced up at her team. "They're patching me through."

"Dr. Zacher's office," a young male's voice answered.

"Yes, this is Gizella Castillo from the Agency. Is Dr. Zacher available?"

"The Agency?" the young man repeated.

"Yes," she answered and allowed silence the line afterward.

"And this is regarding . . ."

She pulled a deep breath. "It's a personal matter," she informed him. "Is he available?"

"Not at the moment. Can I take a message?"

"Who am I leaving it with?"

"Um. Ned Cox."

"Cox?" Castillo repeated. "And you are?"

"I'm Dr. Zacher's personal assistant."

Castillo wrote his name down. "In that case, you can take my number and tell him that it's urgent that he calls me back." She gave him her personal cell number. "Please stress that he should call me as soon as he can."

"Will do."

Castillo hung up the phone, thinking.

Ghost laughed and broke through her reverie. "He's not calling you back. You know this, right?"

"We'll see. Any info on a guy named Ned Cox?"

Ghost and Kadir shook their heads.

"Not off the top of my head. But as soon as I get another place set up, I can dig into it a little more for you. Why?"

Kadir leaned forward in his chair. "Looks like the name may mean something to you. What is it?"

"Ned Cox," she repeated. "I heard that name before." Castillo suddenly wrenched open her bottom drawer and then thumbed through a set of folders.

"Do you want to clue us in on what you're looking for?" Ghost asked, moving to stand over her shoulder.

"Dennis brought me a folder a few months back. Here it is."

"Wait. You already had a folder on Zacher?"

"Yeah. Tomi had me look into him, and Dennis brought this over."

"Is this the boyfriend cop?"

"He's not . . . we're . . . never mind. That's not what's important. Dennis told me that from time to time, he'd get calls to make certain records of T4S employees disappear. Dr. Zacher was one of them recently."

"Oh, shocker. A dirty cop."

"Dennis is *not* a dirty cop."

"No. I'm sure erasing arrest records are by the book these days."

"Dennis was just following orders."

"That's how it always starts off. Ask any Nazi."

"Anyway, Dr. Zacher was at Zeke Jeffreys's last birthday bash and was swept up in the raid."

"Zacher was there?" Draya glanced over at Julian.

"Yeah—and so was his assistant." She held up Ned Cox's arrest photo. "Clearly, he doesn't rank high enough for the company to watch his back."

"Wouldn't that suggest that he's a nobody to us as well?"

"It wouldn't make him a very good personal assistant, now, would it?"

"You're going to waste time on this nobody, too?"

"Unlike you, Mr. Jenkins, I like to know about *all* the players on the board. Ned Cox could prove valuable in case we can't get our hands on the real McCoy."

"Get our hands on?" He cocked a smile. "Like snatching him off the streets?"

"For questioning."

Ghost's smile stretched wider. "If he refuses?"

Castillo smiled. "No one can refuse me when I ask politely."

"If he does?"

Her smile melted off her face. "Then I won't be so polite."

28

At the end of Abrianna's lunch, her friends circled around her and gave congratulatory pats on the back and hugs. "I'm so happy for you," Tivonté said with tears misting his eyes. "I'm going to create the best menu for your reception. Trust me."

"Thanks. I really appreciate that."

"Our little girl is all grown up," he said and then grabbed her for one more hug.

When she turned to Shawn, he beamed from ear to ear. "When are we saying yes to the dress? Oh, and have you thought about where you guys are going to register? I have a million and one ideas. We're about to turn up and spend Daddy Warbucks's long cash."

Abrianna shook her head. "Can you believe this?"

"Hon, these days I'd believe just about anything. And if you're looking to hire a personal assistant, you let me know. I'm ready to put my days of waiting tables behind me."

"You wanna *work* for me?"

"Hell, yeah. I'm looking for a come-up, too."

They shared a laugh until Shawn cocked his head. "Your nose is bleeding."

"Huh?"

Shawn grabbed one of the unused linen napkins from the table. "Here."

Abrianna took the napkin and dabbed her nose. "Oh damn." She rushed from their small circle and made a beeline toward the restrooms. At the long vanity, blood dripped into the sink the moment she removed the napkin from her nose. "Goddamn it." She turned on the water to clean herself up—but the trickle of blood quickly turned into a stream and then a flood. Finally, she pinched her nose and then tilted her head back, but within seconds, she grew lightheaded and swayed on her feet. "Fuck, fuck, fuck." She braced herself on the counter. "C'mon, Bree. Pull yourself together." She repeated that to herself over and over, but it wasn't working. Her head continued to spin higher by the second. But then her panic ebbed away. She was floating, light as a feather.

Abrianna closed her eyes and smiled as the cold air pouring from the vents kissed and caressed her skin. Damn, she felt good.

There was a knock on the bathroom before Shawn poked his head inside. "Bree, are you all right in here?"

"Hmm?"

"Oh my God. Bree." Shawn rushed to her side. "C'mon. Get up."

Get up? She looked around. *What am I doing on the floor?*

Shawn pulled her to her feet, but the sudden rise in elevation made Bree dizzy.

Tivonté entered the bathroom. "What happened?"

She frowned. "I'm sorry, guys. Did I go into the wrong bathroom?"

"No. You're fine. Can you walk?" Shawn asked.

"Of course, I can walk," she chided. "What kind of question is that? I'm not a baby." She chuckled. "I've been walking my whole life."

Shawn and Tivonté shared a look.

"C'mon," Shawn said. "Let's get you out to the car. Roger will take you back home so you can sleep whatever you took off."

Bree frowned. "What? I didn't take anything," she lied defensively.

"You didn't take *anything?*" Shawn asked.

Abrianna heard the judgment in his tone and felt compelled to lie. "Well, I did take some *pain* medication. Maybe I shouldn't have mixed that with the champagne."

"What pain medication?"

"What? You think I'm lying? You think getting shot in the neck is like some walk in the park with me?" She snatched her arm free. "Let go of me. You guys have no idea what I go through. You don't understand what it's like to have this buzzing in your head twenty-four-seven."

Shawn sighed. "We can talk about this later. Right now, you need to rest."

"You don't believe me," Bree accused.

"It doesn't matter. C'mon." He draped her right arm around his shoulder while Tivonté swung her left around his shoulder before leading her toward the door.

"Wait. Where's my purse?"

Shawn spotted it on the counter. "I've got it. Now, let's go." As they exited the ladies' room, a few heads turned their way.

Roger bounded out of his chair and joined them. "What happened? Is she all right?"

"She's fine. She just needs some rest, that's all. Can you just get her home?"

Roger frowned. "Yeah, of course." He went and held open the restaurant's front door and then helped her friends cram Bree into the back of the SUV.

Once they slammed the door shut, Abrianna heard Roger promise to get her home safe and sound. After that, Abrianna leaned her head back and tuned the world out while her mind continued to climb.

Roger climbed in behind the wheel and glanced back at Abrianna.

She didn't even have to open her eyes to feel his gaze centered on her. "What?"

There was a pause before Roger mumbled, "Nothing."

Bree peeled open her eyes and stared at the back of his head. *You have no right to judge me.*

"I'm not judging you," Roger answered, but realized he was lying. "Well, not entirely."

She rolled her eyes and then closed them again.

"I shouldn't have taken you over to that apartment," Roger mumbled. "Kadir is going to kill me."

"Snitches get stitches."

Roger sighed.

Abrianna grinned and then she must have dozed off for a few minutes, because when she peeked through her lashes again, the vehicle was on the move—and her scalp was tingling. *Danger.*

Abrianna sat up with a bolt of adrenaline.

"What is it?" Roger asked, instantly alert.

Bam!

Their SUV was T-boned in the middle of an intersection.

Jolted to the other side of the vehicle, Abrianna slammed her head against the window, shattering it. Glass rained over her like a sparkling waterfall before another car rammed into them from the opposite side before they'd stopped spinning. Abrianna suffered another crack to the head from another window and then dropped onto the floorboard like a rag doll.

"Fuuuck." Bree pulled herself off the floorboard. "Roger, are you all right?"

He didn't answer.

"Goddamn it." She glanced around and saw someone in black lower their hoodie. A nest of blond hair tumbled out and a tiny spark of recognition flared.

A crowd of people rushed toward the accident until the crack of an assault weapon rang out.

What the fuck?

The blonde turned and ran.

Bullets slammed into the body of the SUV. "Roger, drive!"

Roger didn't respond. He couldn't. He was knocked out behind the wheel.

"Shit." Abrianna climbed over the seat. She unbuckled Roger and yanked him over to the passenger seat, all while bullets sprayed all around her.

The SUV's back window exploded.

She slammed on the accelerator. As she whipped around in a donut, more bullets slammed into the body of the vehicle with one sailing past her head. Finally, she peeled off.

HOOOOOONK!

She headed toward a head-on collision.

"Mutha . . ." Abrianna jerked the wheel, pitching into the right lane, but still clipped the side mirror of a red Mercedes.

Rat-at-tat-tat-tat.

The front window shattered but remained in place, making it nearly impossible to see.

A cacophony of horns rose up, but the cars in front of her pulled off to the side of the road. Abrianna blazed through an intersection on a wing and a prayer.

An Escalade in hot pursuit also made it through each light, continuing the one-sided gun battle. Abrianna had no idea what she was doing or where she was going, but as long as the bullets flew, she kept the pedal to the metal.

The next intersection had heavy cross traffic. Hands locked on the steering wheel, her heart rate escalated, but with these devils on her tail, she committed to the suicide trek through the red light.

HOOOOOONK!!! HOOOOOONK!!!

Her entire scalp tingled as she willed the cars to move out of her way. Many of them parted like the Red Sea, but there were just too many of them.

BAM!

The SUV spun like a pinwheel.

BAM!

BAM!

BAM!

One car after another kept plowing into her.

By the time the vehicle stopped spinning, destruction was all around her—but the bullets had stopped firing—and more important, she had survived.

"What the hell is wrong with you, lady?"

Jumping, Abrianna swiveled her head toward a bloated, red-faced man in an Italian suit.

"Look at what the fuck you did to my new car!"

Where are the shooters? She twisted around in her seat, scanning the area. Nothing. Roger groaned as he came around. "What the hell?"

"I saved you," Abrianna said. "You're welcome."

⟶•◦•⟶

Zacher woke with a start, dragging oxygen through his lungs in huge gulps and then choking on it. He glanced around, and for a few alarming seconds, he didn't recognize anything, nor any of the people who were trying to push him back down. With one good shove, he sent them flying backward. When he started to rip the needles out of his arm, Ned shouted, "Boss, please don't!"

Zacher froze.

"It's okay. You're at the lab."

"The lab," Zacher repeated and then took another look around. He calmed and lay back down. "What happened?"

Ned lowered his voice. "Our headquarters were infiltrated three days ago. You were knocked through a wall."

Images flashed in Zacher's head: the power outage, the explosions—the *blonde*. Zacher bolted straight up again, but it was too fast. Pain exploded in the back of his head as his stomach muscles cramped. Rolling to his right, he gagged and dry-heaved until his entire mid-section locked into a charley horse.

"Just rest, boss. You're going to be all right."

Zacher nodded and closed his eyes. He thought it was for a few seconds, but when he opened his eyes, the light in the room had changed.

"He lives!" Pierce Spalding's voice boomed into the lab as he marched inside.

Zacher groaned.

Spalding waved a single finger at Zacher. "But *you* have been a naughty boy."

"Sir?"

"You've been holding out on me." Spalding crossed his arms. "How long have you been experimenting on yourself?"

Zacher blinked.

"And don't bother lying, because technically for the past couple of days, you didn't have a heartbeat. If Ned here hadn't requested we run a brain scan on you, you might've woken up in coffin six feet under."

"I see."

Spalding laughed. "You see? That's it? Don't sound too grateful to me."

Another wave of panic hit him. "Lehane."

"She's gone." Spalding sucked in a breath. "Someone kidnapped our kidnap victim. What the hell is the world coming to, huh?"

"Gone?"

"Yeah. The bastards who breached our headquarters did it like it was nothing. They came strictly for Lehane."

"Government?"

Spalding shook his head. "Are you kidding? Washington would be gloating all over the news had she pulled off the impossible. Nah. Clearly, we have a new player in town. We're still working on how they pulled it off, without letting the whole world know that we were hit. Call me crazy, but it may look bad for a security firm not being able to secure its own damn headquarters. Hell, I just pulled off a miracle myself by wooing Hardy back to the dark side."

Zacher cocked his head. "You're not upset that we lost her?"

"Upset, no." The smile vanished from Spalding's face. "I'm fucking pissed. *But,* it all may be a blessing in disguise—since you didn't take care of Parker like I told you months ago, her interview has been all over the news in a loop, telling the world that we kidnapped and murdered teenage girls to advance science. It's true, but it doesn't play well in the court of public opinion. We've been fending off calls from the media, congressmen, and even the White House. Everyone is demanding to see whether this place is on the up-and-up—and more importantly, the world is waiting to hear from *you.*"

"Me?"

"Your pet project mentioned you by name in her interview. It's only right that you respond to her. So get well fast. You have a media tour to handle." Spalding slapped Zacher on the shoulder. "And when you get through with that, I'm assigning a new team to examine you."

Zacher's gut clenched.

"We need a thorough account of just how far your experiments have gone."

"A new team isn't necessary. I'll be more than happy to share my notes."

"You misunderstood me." Spalding's smile expanded. "This isn't up for debate. With Lehane and Parker out of reach, you are our new lab rat. Every drop of blood in your body now is the sole property of T4S. And I intend to get my money's worth. Do I make myself clear?"

"Crystal."

Spalding winked and slapped his shoulder again. "Good talk." He turned and walked away.

Once they were alone, Ned moved next to Dr. Z. "We have another problem, boss."

Zacher sighed. "Don't we always. Does this trouble have a name?"

"Yep. Her name is private eye Gizella Castillo. She's looking for you."

Dr. Zacher chuckled. "She can get in line."

<hr />

Abrianna refused medical assistance, but with blood pouring from Roger's scalp, he was in no position to refuse help. The SUV was totaled, and she was forced to call Kadir. After she hung up, he made it to the scene of the crime in less than fifteen minutes.

"Bree," he shouted, threading his way through the crowd.

Relieved, she pulled away from the paramedic who was still arguing with her about going to the hospital. "Kadir." Abrianna rushed into his arms. She needed him to ground her when she was most certainly losing her mind.

"What happened?" he asked.

"I don't know." She looked around and then lowered her voice. "I'm still trying to make sense of everything."

"It had to be T4S," Kadir hissed. "Fuck." He looked her over. "Are you all right?" He touched her sunglasses, but she shrugged him off.

"I'm good. Roger was banged up pretty bad, though. He's on his way to the hospital."

"The interview changed nothing. You're not safe," Kadir said. "We need to get you off the grid again. Get you somewhere safe." He paused to think. "Ghost's place has been compromised, so we can't go there."

"What?"

"Our place is too open, too," he said. "If T4S is coming after you—"

"It wasn't T4S," Abrianna blurted and then clamped her mouth shut.

"What?"

"I mean, maybe they were there, but . . . at that point I don't think I was the target."

Kadir frowned and then finally whipped her glasses from her face. "Are you sure you're all right? You're not making any sense."

Abrianna pulled Kadir aside. "I know. I need more time to work it out in my head. I saw . . . and I heard a voice in my head."

"You were reading someone's mind?"

"No. A woman projected her voice to me. She said that she didn't want to hurt me and then suddenly a second team of black SUVs showed up and attacked the first team. Roger and I were caught up in the crossfire"

"Let me get this straight. You don't think you were the target?"

"I might have been the target of the first team—but they weren't shooting at me—I don't think. But the second team was definitely after the first team, and I just got Roger and me out of the way."

Kadir stared at her.

"I know it sounds crazy." She shrugged.

"Your eyes are dilated."

"What?"

Kadir sighed while disappointment drifted across his face. "Never mind. We'll talk about this later. Right now, we need to get you someplace safe."

"No." Abrianna shook her head. "Take me home. I'm not running. We'll hire some additional protection if need be, but I'm not running anywhere."

He started to argue but saw the stubborn set of her jaw and knew that it was futile. "All right. Let's get you out of here."

However, when the paramedic informed the police that she wasn't going straight to the hospital, they didn't want her to leave without taking her statement. While she waited around, she noticed Castillo roaming around, checking over the vehicles, and watching the officers collect shell casings.

"She is good at this, isn't she?" Abrianna said.

"If I were to choose a word for her it would be dogmatic," Kadir said. "Working with her has been an eye-opener. If anyone is going to find Tomi Lehane, it's going to be her."

＊◦＊

The police had their hands full, taking statements from witnesses and requesting cell phone footage to be forwarded for review. Castillo maneuvered around the scene while Kadir checked on Abrianna. She even checked the vehicle over and ear-hustled on what the crowd was saying.

"It was like something out of a movie," one guy told his friend.

"Man, they were spitting bullets out here like it wasn't nothing," someone else said.

"I'm surprised nobody was killed. We need to do something about all these damn guns in these streets. It's getting so that you can't even walk outside."

Castillo waltzed over toward a group of teenagers with a friendly smile. "The whole thing was wild, huh? Did you guys see what happened?"

"See it?" a tall kid in a Howard University T-shirt laughed. "I got the whole thing on my phone."

"Really? Do you mind if I see it?"

He paused as he narrowed his gaze. "Why? Are you a cop?"

She laughed. "Not the last time I checked."

He nodded. "A'ight." He pulled up his video footage and showed it to her. It started with Roger's SUV already T-boned at a different intersection; then it was hit two more times by different cars, coming from opposite directions. Then nothing for a few seconds while the Howard kid commented. "What is she looking for?" He laughed as he first zoomed in on Abrianna, and then panned the camera around. "She must be in shock."

Then came the crack of an automatic weapon.

"Holy shit." The camera was jostled around as the gunfire continued; there was a squeal of tires while the voice instructed the driver, "Go, go, go!"

"Hey, they're going after that other chick, too."

"What?" The camera panned around again, but only for a second before it was directed back to Abrianna while she hightailed it toward the next intersection. "Oh shit. She's not slowing down."

Bam!

"I told you that it was wild," the Howard guy said, reaching for his phone.

"Who was the other girl?"

The guy bounced his shoulders. "Don't know. Didn't really get a good shot of her."

"Can I see it again?" Castillo asked.

Howard shrugged his shoulders. "Sure. Knock yourself out."

29

The White House

"Have you seen the news?" Davidson marched into the Oval Office without knocking.

Kate glanced up from her phone call with Senator Scott Presley bitching in her ear and welcomed the excuse to get off the phone. "I appreciate you talking to me about the party's concerns. I will take it all into consideration. We'll talk again soon." She hung up and expelled a long breath before turning her attention to the television. "Okay. What is it now?"

Her chief of staff, Haverty, and senior advisor, Gohl, breezed into the office next. "Madam President, there is something you need to see—oh." They stopped short at seeing the television already on CNN.

"What am I looking at?"

Davidson rushed to answer first, "There's been a shooting downtown with multiple car pile-up."

"Okay. This is a local matter."

"Abrianna Parker was smack-dab in the middle of it," Haverty informed her.

"What?" She stood from behind the desk just as her phone

rang. Instead of answering the call, she buzzed her secretary. "Diana, hold my calls."

"It's Mr. Washington—"

"HOLD. MY. CALLS."

"Yes, Madam President."

Kate directed Davidson, "Turn it up."

"Witnesses describe the shooting as something straight out of a Hollywood blockbuster. A multicar accident quickly escalated into a wild shoot-out with assault weapons near Logan Circle. So far, there have been no fatalities, but two people were critically injured, according to police. There are others wounded, and as we reported earlier, one of those people who was injured in the chaos is Abrianna Parker. Many know Ms. Parker in recent months with her involvement in solving the late house speaker Kenneth Reynolds's death, and her participation in exposing collusion between the late chief justice Katherine Sanders and President Daniel Walker. In recent days, Ms. Parker gave a bombshell interview claiming the private military company T4S was behind missing reporter Tomi Lehane's disappearance. Back to you, Anderson."

Davidson muted the television while all eyes turned to the president.

"Holy shit." The president crossed her arms. "The bitch might be telling the truth," she concluded.

"A lot of people are going to be thinking that now. A wild shoot-out with assault weapons? They aren't exactly subtle, are they?" Gohl asked.

Kate agreed with her senior advisor.

"What's even better is Hardy sticking with his support for T4S," McMullan added, waltzing into the impromptu meeting late. "Where are we in getting Ms. Parker to visit the White House?"

"No change," the president admitted. "Clearly, she's been too preoccupied to return my message."

"We need to call again. If Abrianna won't come to us, then we'll go to her if need be. We just need reports of your concern," McMullan rattled off while typing notes into his smartphone. "We need to strike while the iron is hot."

* * *

The moment Abrianna returned to the apartment, Daishan rushed to check her over. "Oh, you poor thing. Are you all right?"

Abrianna tensed from the unexpected concern and then recovered with an awkward smile.

Kadir's mother *tsk*ed under her breath. "That's a nasty gash." She attempted to examine Bree's bleeding hairline, but Abrianna stepped back.

"Oh it's nothing. Don't worry about it."

Daishan turned and scolded Kadir. "Why haven't you taken her to the hospital? She probably needs stitches."

"No doctors," Kadir and Bree barked at the same time.

Daishan frowned.

"Trust me. I'm all right," Bree assured her. "I've been through worse."

"You know, I'm pretty handy with a needle. Being in a family of boys, I've had to patch up a number boo-boos." She smiled.

"I'm fine," Abrianna insisted, but when the smile melted off Daishan's face, she added, "But thank you. I appreciate the concern."

Daishan nodded and forced a smile back onto her face. "Well, I'm glad that you're okay. What happened?"

"I don't know," Bree said. "It happened so fast. But, you know. It's a scary world out there."

"No kidding. Did Kadir tell you the news yet?"

Kadir stiffened.

Abrianna noticed. "What news?"

"The president of the United States called here," Daishan said.

"The president of the United States called? Here?" Abrianna double-checked while she swung her gaze between Kadir and his mother. "Is this some kind of joke?"

"If it is, it's being played on the both of us," Kadir said. "And . . . there's more."

"The best part," Daishan boasted with a smile cracking her lips.

Abrianna lifted a brow before crossing her arms. "I'm all ears."

Kadir laid it on her. "We've been invited to the White House."

"The president has offered him a pardon," Daishan blurted and then clapped her hands in excitement. "His whole criminal record will be wiped clean."

"Plot twist," Abrianna joked. "Can't say I saw that one coming."

"That makes two of us." Kadir stared as if he read her mind.

"It could be a trap," she said.

"I was thinking the same thing," he confessed.

Daishan's smile vanished. "A trap?"

Kadir nodded. "We pissed a lot of people off with that last interview and probably embarrassed even more than that. And they spent a whole lot of time scouring the city looking for us the last time; they could be just using a different tactic."

"The good old bait and switch." Abrianna nodded.

"That doesn't make any sense." Daishan puffed up and crossed her arms. "Arrest you on what charge? Kadir hasn't done anything wrong . . . *lately*. Unless there's something he left out this morning."

Abrianna turned her questioning gaze toward Kadir. "Left out?"

"We, um, had a talk this morning." He scratched his head and dodged meeting her gaze.

"Yes." Daishan stood next to her son. "He filled me in on your . . . extraordinary time together this past year."

"I see." Abrianna's fake smile stretched from ear to ear while the room became layered with tension. "I, um . . . you know what? I'm going to go change and then maybe we can order a pizza."

"A pizza?" Daishan blinked in horror.

Abrianna tossed up her hands. "Okay—we can order Chinese. I'm not picky." She marched off to the bedroom.

"Bree." Kadir followed behind her. The second he closed the door behind them, Abrianna rounded on him.

"What did you tell them?"

"What do you mean? I told them the truth."

"No wonder they're looking at me like I'm stuck on the bottom of their shoes."

Kadir sighed. "No, they're not." He pulled her into his arms. "You're not giving them a chance."

"Me?"

"Yes. You. This morning you were bitching about how they didn't like you, and that's before I told them anything."

"You told them my story so they would feel sorry for me?"

"What? I told them your story because they're my family and it was better to hear it from me than on the news—or on the internet—or even the made-for-TV movie that was made years ago about Dr. Avery, the serial killer. More importantly, I told them because they are my *family*—and pretty soon, you're going to be a part of that family." Kadir cocked his head and studied her. "Are you sure that you're all right? You seem . . . off."

"What?" Abrianna backed out of his arms. "No. I'm simply saying that . . . ."

Kadir kept staring.

Abrianna closed her eyes and sighed. "All right. Maybe I am . . . overreacting. I . . . just want them to like me. Now I can feel her, she's constantly comparing me to Malala."

"Babe—"

"It's true," she insisted.

Kadir's smile returned. "Oh, baby. They will *love* you." He stroked the side of her face. "Like I told you this morning, you *have* to give them some time. And yes, my mom can be a tough cookie. But let me let you in on a secret." Kadir leaned closer. "Malala thought my mom hated her, too."

"No, she didn't." Abrianna scanned Kadir's face for the truth. "Did she?"

Kadir nodded. "Relax, be yourself, and the rest will take care of itself."

Abrianna sighed. "You're right. I'm sorry. I'll chill out."

"Thanks, babe." He pecked her on the cheek and sighed. "There has been so much going on today."

"Like what?"

"Like Tomi's mother going into the Agency today and hiring us to look for her daughter."

"What? That's great."

"Yeah. We didn't tell her that we were already looking into the case, but it's official now."

"So, what's the next move?"

Kadir folded his arms. "Well, Gigi wants to make sure we dot every I and cross every T."

"Gigi?" Her eyes narrowed.

He nodded. "Castillo. You knew her first name, right?"

"Yeah. It's *Gizella.*"

"Her friends call her Gigi," he told her off-handedly. "Anyway, we went to the *Washington Post* and talked to one of Tomi's colleagues who might have been the last person to see her."

"And?"

Kadir folded his arms with another sigh.

"It's that bad?"

"His name is Jayson Brigham, and he believes that *you* had something to do with Tomi's disappearance and that your media tour is just to spread propaganda away from yourself."

"Please, tell me you're joking."

"Haters are going to hate."

"That's not helping."

"Sorry, babe. You can't win them all. And you have to remember that you and Tomi weren't exactly on good terms when she disappeared. Maybe that's what's influencing him."

Abrianna conceded. "You're right. I know you're right. It . . . doesn't feel good to know that people out there are thinking the worst of me."

Kadir wrapped an arm around her waist. "You're not so bad. I think you're kind of great."

She blushed and leaned into him. "Yeah?"

"Uh-huh." He kissed the tip of her nose. "If I didn't, I wouldn't have asked you to marry me. I don't mean to brag, but I'm a pretty good judge of character."

At the Agency, Castillo reviewed the video from the Howard kid until her eyes crossed. It was still hard to make sense of what was going on. One thing for sure, she was convinced that nothing was what it seemed. The first accident at the first intersection was anything but. The utility vehicles clearly ran the red lights to slam into Abrianna and Roger intentionally. But there was a clear thirty seconds when Abrianna poked her head up and looked around. She stopped to look at something—or someone. But there were so many people on the street. Then the gunfire started, and Castillo agreed with the voice on the video. There was a second target.

The front door opened, and Castillo's hand went to the weapon holstered on her hip.

Ghost walked in with a smile. "Don't shoot."

Castillo's hand fell away from her weapon. "What are you doing here?"

"Saw the lights on and had a funny feeling that you were still obsessing over your new case and figured you probably hadn't eaten." He held up a pizza box.

"I'm not hungry."

On cue, Castillo's stomach growled, long and loud.

Ghost's smile stretched wider. "Do you want to try again?"

Castillo rolled her eyes while she returned his smile. "Damn pepperoni."

"That's not the pièce de résistance." In his other hand, Ghost held up a six-pack of beer.

"If I didn't know any better, I'd say you were an angel." She stood and headed toward the break room. "I'll get some napkins."

"Cool." He waltzed over to a desk and plopped the pizza box down. "Whatcha looking at?"

"Abrianna was in a car accident today."

"What? When was this? How come nobody told me?"

Castillo laughed. "How were we supposed to do that? You don't believe in cell phones."

"I have a cell phone. I just . . . change the number a lot." He shrugged before folding into one of the vacant chairs. "I have a system."

"Don't worry. Our girl is all right." Castillo returned with a roll of paper towels. "Here you go." She broke off a few sheets and handed them over before she dove into the pizza box."

Ghost popped open two beer bottles and then handed one over. "So, was it an accident-accident or T4S making their move?"

"Not sure. Believe it or not, it looks like a combination of both."

He took a monster bite out of his pizza and then climbed out of his seat. "Mind if I take a look?"

Castillo shrugged. "Knock yourself out."

Ghost sat at Castillo's desk and then tapped her mouse for the video to start playing. "Damn," he muttered, watching Roger and Abrianna get plowed into at the intersection.

"Keep watching."

"Wait. Who is shooting?"

"Exactly. Notice anything else?"

Ghost hit the replay button and watched again. "I'm confused. They are shooting at Abrianna and someone else in the crowd."

"Bingo."

"But who?"

"I can't tell on that video."

"We need to get a better image." He exited out of the program and started tapping.

"What are you doing?"

"Doing what I do."

"You're hacking into something?"

"Just into the city's surveillance system. There are cameras all over downtown. I'm sure that they have better footage than what's on that thing."

"No shit?" Castillo continued munching on her pizza as she went to stand behind him. "You can do that?"

"Piece of cake." Ghost's fingers flew across the keyboard, and within minutes he was in the police's closed-circuit camera network.

"Holy shit."

"What time was the accident?"

"Um, I believe like one-thirty."

More typing.

"Can you get caught doing this?" Castillo asked.

"The risk is what makes it fun," he said. "Okay. Here we go. Let's make a copy of this file and this one here."

"Why a copy?"

"Playing the file on the circuit increases our chances of getting caught. This way, it's just a hack-and-grab. We can play the video on any video app. Of course, after I erase our digital trail."

"I appreciate that."

"Okay. Let's see what we have."

Castillo pulled a second chair up to her desk, so she could watch the video, too. "Oh, this is much better."

"I'll invoice you."

"How are you invoicing me when they're your friends, too?"

Ghost shrugged. "Fine. I'll give you a friend's discount." He hit play, and they watched the video together. "There is a second target."

Castillo nodded and then pointed on the screen. "The blonde. Can you zoom in on her?"

"Let me see what I can do." Ghost pointed and clicked, but when they zoomed in, the picture's pixels became blurry. "Sorry, but this looks like this is as good as it gets. No offense, but your system is pretty shitty."

"Offense taken anyway." She took hold of the mouse and hit replay. "Does it look like Abrianna and this woman are making eye contact to you?"

Ghost leaned forward and frowned. "Bree is looking in her direction, but the chick is hardly the only one on the sidewalk."

"Yeah, but when the shooting starts, it sure does look like she is the second target."

"And in seconds, she's diving into another car and speeding off." Ghost leaned back in Castillo's chair, making the springs creak.

"Don't break my chair, Hoss."

Ghost grinned. "Professional opinion, this whole thing looks suspect. Bree may need to go off the grid again. Only, I can't help her this time. As for the other chick, I don't know what her deal is, but, clearly, T4S thought they could do a two-for-one in broad daylight—again."

Castillo heard Ghost, but she couldn't take her eyes off the blonde. "We need to find this girl and find out why T4S wants her dead, too."

30

Abrianna and the Kahlifas were all smiles throughout dinner, but the tension remained thick. "This is delicious," Abrianna praised. "You must teach me how to make this, Mrs. Kahlifa."

"It's just roasted chicken and sumac flatbread. It can't get any easier than this."

"Mom," Kadir warned with a tilt of his head.

Daishan pushed up a smile. "But, of course, I'll be happy to teach you whatever you'd like to learn. It would be my pleasure." She reached over and squeezed Abrianna's hand.

It was a small peace offering, and Abrianna took what she could get. "Thanks."

Baasim clapped his hands together. "Well, would you look at that? I always knew that world peace would be resolved over roasted chicken."

They shared a laughed before Baasim turned his attention Abrianna. "You had an interesting day."

"Just your normal day that ends with a Y." She smiled.

Baasim nodded. "Really? Getting that nasty gash is normal?"

"What can I say? I've pissed a lot of people off in the past year."

Baasim cocked a half smile while his voice dripped with sarcasm. "No. Not you."

"Baasim," Kadir snapped.

Daishan changed the subject. "How was your brunch, dear? You did get to see your friends before the accident, right?"

"Um, yes." Bree went along with the change of subject. "It went as expected. They were surprised to hear about the engagement."

"Oh, you're just now telling your friends?" Daishan asked.

"I told you, Mom. I just popped the question last week," Kadir reminded her. "I didn't give her a ring until last night."

"I thought you told us that to soften the blow," she admitted.

"No. I had every intention to call you and . . . Baba," Kadir choked over the word. It seemed to surprise him, but he coughed and cleared his throat.

Daishan reached her other hand across the table to clasp Kadir's. "It's okay. I know that your father would be very proud of you right now. I'm happy that you found someone you want to share your life with. You've been through so much. You deserve happiness."

Kadir smiled and kissed his mother's hand. "Thank you."

The table went quiet for a moment before Kadir turned his attention to his brother. "So, what about you? What did you do today?"

"I went to noon prayer and then I spent the rest day down at the DMV. Of course, I stood in line all afternoon just to be told that I didn't have all of the necessary paperwork. But I guess I'll just try again tomorrow."

Abrianna frowned. "You were at the DMV all day?"

"All afternoon," Baasim corrected before he bit into another piece of chicken.

Abrianna stared at him while the buzzing in the back of her head started up again. *You're lying.*

Baasim jerked and dropped his chicken on his plate.

Kadir frowned. "Is something wrong, bro?"

Baasim ignored his brother to stare at Abrianna.

"Is something wrong with the chicken?" Abrianna asked innocently.

"There's nothing wrong with my chicken," Daishan insisted, frowning.

"The chicken is fine." Baasim kept his eyes leveled on Abrianna until she lifted a brow at him.

"Is something wrong? Do I have something on my face?" Abrianna touched her face.

"No. I thought I heard . . . I was just thinking. That's all." He shook his head and went back to eating—occasionally stealing a glance at her.

Abrianna smiled.

After dinner, Abrianna and Daishan cleared the table and washed the dishes while Kadir and his brother huddled together in the living room, laughing and sharing stories. Meanwhile, Abrianna's future mother-in-law needled her about details of a wedding that she hadn't planned yet.

When they finished, Kadir pulled Abrianna aside. "Baasim and I are going to go out for a little while."

"Out?" Did that mean she would be forced to do more wedding planning?

"It'll just be for a couple of hours." Kadir kissed her. "Don't stay up."

The Stallion Gentlemen's Club

"Out of all the bars in D.C., you happened to choose this one?" Kadir joked.

"I don't know what you're talking about. I used to come here all the time." Baasim grinned. "Why, is there a problem?"

Kadir eyed his twin. "You know that Abrianna used to dance here, don't you?"

Baasim's grin exploded into a smile. "I might've read an article or two about your new *fiancée* on the internet. Your taste in women has changed."

"Not really." Kadir climbed out of the car and slammed the door. "Abrianna is beautiful both inside and out—just like Malala."

Baasim slammed his door while maintaining his smile. "Yeah, but I have a hard time picturing Malala sliding down stripper poles—not that I wouldn't have paid a king's ransom to see that."

"I'm not even going to tell you how disturbing it is that you'd try to picture that."

"Why? I was in love with Malala first."

Kadir glanced at his watch. "That didn't take long for you to bring up. We haven't even made it inside the building yet."

"Wait until I get a couple of beers in me." Baasim winked.

They nodded to the club's bouncer and entered the premises.

Inside, Kadir stopped and took it all in.

Baasim folded his arms next to him. "It's like a time capsule, isn't it?"

Kadir grinned. "You read my mind."

"C'mon. The first round is on me."

"This night keeps getting better."

The brothers chuckled as they threaded between customers and cocktail waitresses to a table close to center stage. The second their bottoms hit the chairs, their waitress appeared as if by magic.

"What can I get you two handsome . . . oh my. Twins? It must be my lucky night."

"Indeed it is." Baasim winked. "We've started the night with two scotches on the rocks."

"Actually, I—"

"Ignore him and just bring us the drinks." Baasim held up some folded money.

"You got it, handsome." The waitress plucked the money out

from between his fingers and tucked it between her breasts. "Two scotches on the rocks, coming right up." She sashayed off.

Baasim cocked his head while he enjoyed the view as she went.

Kadir laughed.

"What?"

"Dry spell?"

"You're one to talk. Didn't you meet your future wife here? You never know—maybe I'll get lucky, too."

"Ha. Ha. Go ahead and get all your jokes out. You're like a third grader, you know that?"

Their waitress returned. "Here you go, gentlemen." She set down their drinks and smiled. "Is there anything else I can get you?"

Baasim picked up his drink and tossed back his scotch in two seconds. "Yeah, sweetheart. You can bring us two more." He held up his glass.

"All right. It looks like you really want to party." She winked, took the money, and rushed off again.

Kadir leaned back in his chair and studied his brother. "It's going to be that kind of night, huh?"

Baasim placed his folded arms on the table. "Is that going to be a problem?"

Kadir met his brother's gaze, just as pain flickered in his dark depths. Before he could take a second look, Baasim shifted his attention to the stage where a stripper took center stage.

"Look, bro. I know that you've been through some shit in the last few years. Shit that I can't possibly comprehend, but . . ." Kadir laid his hand on Baasim's arm. "I want you to know that I'm always here if you need someone to talk to—about Dad—or anything."

Baasim smirked. "Is that right?"

Kadir frowned. "Of course. You're more than my brother—you're my best friend." He waited until Baasim's gaze found his.

"All other bullshit aside. I hope you know that. I'm going to always be here for you."

Tension was layered between them before Baasim pushed up a smile. "I appreciate that, bro. And you're right. I may be a bit wound up. I, um, keep seeing Baba on his prayer rug, and refusing to leave that funeral—even when we could hear the missiles whistling in the air. He refused to budge."

"But . . . why?"

"I honestly don't know." Baasim bunched his shoulders. "Maybe he just had enough. He was sure that some ancient honor code would prevent the very thing I warned him that would happen. Every week, he was so sure the fighting was almost over. Peace was always just around the bend, and then the country would work together to restore its former glory. I told him constantly that it would never happen. There are too many countries playing puppeteers. America included." His jaw hardened as he leaned forward. "And that bitch in the White House. She's making things worse. I can't believe you're actually considering going up there for her to drape a damn medal around your neck right after she killed our father."

Their drinks arrived.

"I'll take both of those." Baasim removed the extra glass of scotch from in front of Kadir. "My brother has a low tolerance for the devil juice. Unless that's changed, too?"

Kadir chuckled. "You know me so well."

"Maybe once upon a time." Baasim tossed back his second drink.

"What is that supposed to mean?"

"I'm stating the facts. I'd hope that after you did your stint behind bars, it would harden you up a bit."

"I'm plenty hard. I didn't need to be behind bars to get an edge."

"Oh my bad. You spent all that time fighting for good ole USA to—what was it—to spread democracy? Or was it something about weapons of mass destruction? Or our saving Muslim women from sharia law? Or maybe it was just for the fucking oil, weapons proliferation, and greedy rich bastards getting richer. That's the thing about this country: We'll believe any lie repeated endlessly. No, I didn't expect you to gain enlightenment in the armed military—only how to take orders without ever asking why. But, in prison? That's where you find true enlightenment in this country."

Kadir grinned.

"Something funny?"

"No. I might have changed some, but you're forever the hard militant."

"I'm a soldier of the truth. I see the world for exactly how it is—not how the corporate media programs me to believe. While I'm on this soapbox, you're a fool if you go up there and let the bitch who killed our father decorate you with some bullshit medal in front of the world. Pardon or no pardon. Have some fucking pride."

Kadir jerked. "I have no intentions of going to the White House. I'm surprised you'd think that I would."

"Are you?" Baasim chuckled. "You were the first one to teach me about betrayal. I assure you it was a lesson that I never forgot."

Kadir picked up his drink. "You're never going to forgive me for Malala, are you?"

"What do you think?"

"No, but I wish you would. I miss my best friend." He tossed the liquor down his throat and resisted choking while it burned.

"Look, bro. It is what it is. You're my brother. I love you, but we ain't seen eye-to-eye on a lot of shit for a long time."

Kadir's face twisted while he weighed his next words. "Do you blame me for what happened to Baba?"

Baasim cocked his head. "I'm not going to lie. I feel some type of way about it. Not that you could've prevented his death, but that . . . things would have been different. Maybe I wouldn't have had to shoulder so much on my own with Ummi and Baba. It was Dad's dream to see Yemen restored to its former glory. His fight became my fight. It still is."

Kadir reclaimed his second scotch, to his brother's amusement. "Baasim!"

The Kahlifa brothers looked up.

"Farooq." Baasim stood from his seat and threw one arm around his old friend. "It's good to see you again. You remember my brother, Kadir."

Farooq turned and stretched out a hand. "Of course, Kadir. How you doing, man?"

"Doin' great, man." Kadir shook Farooq's hand. "I haven't seen you in ages."

"You would if you came back to Masjid Muhammad. We miss you around there, man."

Kadir hung his head. "Yeah. Sorry about that. Life has kind of gotten away from me."

"Clearly. You guys mind if I join you?"

"Nah. Not at all." Baasim answered and quickly made room for his old friend on his side of the booth. Their waitress returned and took Farooq's order. No sooner had she left the table than cousins Awsam and Yasser Rizq arrived. Before Kadir knew it, Saoud and Kamel joined them, and a full-fledged reunion had emerged.

It felt good to see so many old friends. While baby-oiled dancers took the stage, the guys reminisced over their high-school days and then the various roads they'd traveled since. Kadir held the table when they interrogated him about his name being in the news in the past year. It took another two rounds of drinks for Kadir to recount the tale of how he, Abrianna, and Tomi Lehane brought down a presidency. However, by the end of the night, they were all upset about the recent US air strikes, which had not only killed Kadir and Baasim's father, but also one of Saoud's uncles.

"These are dark times, and the west is blind to the pain and destruction they're causing throughout the Middle East. They're making just as much on arms sales as they are securing oil fields," Yasser said.

Kadir agreed while he kept nursing his beer. By the time he stumbled out of the club with Baasim, his hatred for President Washington had grown by leaps and bounds.

31

A weakened Dr. Zacher climbed out of bed and, in his open-ass gown, took hold of his IV pole and pushed it out of his lab.

"Can we get you something, doc?"

Dr. Z jumped, surprised to see two soldiers posted outside his lab. At least he recognized Keith. "No. I, um . . ." He glanced around at the destruction of the place. "Wow."

Keith nodded. "You should see the top floor."

"Any idea who pulled this off?"

"I don't have a name, but I heard a team had a line on them earlier today and tried to take them out, but the big man called in a stand-down order at the last minute. We made a big mess in the middle of downtown that's all over the news, but I'm sure they'll figure out a way to cover our asses. But I have to tell you, doc, in all my years here, I've never seen anybody even try to penetrate this place, let alone the speed and precision with which they did it. Trust me, heads have been rolling all over this place."

Dr. Z nodded. "I can imagine. Well, I'm heading to my office. Since I can't get any sleep, I may as well get some work done."

Keith shook his head. "Sorry, doc, but we were given strict orders to watch you."

"You're more than welcome to post outside my office." Dr. Z resumed his march with his pole, daring them to stop him. But as he walked, a pain started on his right side and intensified with every step he took. By the time he reached his office, he was relying on the IV pole to hold him up.

"Are you all right, doc?" Keith asked.

"I'm fine," Zacher lied. "Just a little winded." He pushed on into his office and then closed the door. From there, he hunched over to half his size, praying to make it to his desk before he passed out. He made it, but barely. In his bottom drawer, he found the drug that he needed, but he trembled so badly it took him a while to get the needle into a vein. Once he pushed the plunger through, his euphoria was instant—his shaking stopped.

Relieved, Zacher took a few minutes to gather himself before turning to his computer. With his high clearance level, he accessed the headquarters' closed-circuit security cameras and reviewed the footage of the break-in. The whole thing looked like shock and awe with military-grade weapons, bombs, and something else—or rather someone else.

Zacher followed the invaders' stealth moves through the building, but once they made their way down to his lab, the feed stopped. "What the hell? End of transmission?" He searched the files again, but there was nothing. Either nothing was captured on his floor, or the footage had been erased. But that didn't make any sense. After exhausting every way to find the file, Zacher checked the log list to see who all had seen the footage. Pierce Spalding's name stood out—mainly for the number of times he'd logged into the system.

"He's hiding something," Zacher whispered under his breath. The image of the blonde surfaced in his mind, but just as quickly, he rejected it because what he saw was impossible. There was another answer out there, and he was determined to find it.

⋆•⋆

"What do you mean that you're not going to the White House?" Abrianna asked. "It's the president—and she's offering a *full* pardon if we go, shake her hand, and smile before a few cameras."

"It's not that simple."

"What are you talking about? Yes, it is. We're talking about no more probation—no more pissing in cups and being treated like a second-class citizen."

"What are you talking about? We're minorities. We'll always be treated like second-class citizens no matter what we do."

"Okay." She shook her head. "I still don't get it."

"What's not to get? The woman *killed* my father," Kadir shouted. "I'm not going to go up there so she can prop me up like some trophy to make it appear like I'm okay with this country's chaotic foreign policy. No way. I do have some pride."

"But it's okay for you to tell me to accept Cargill's billions."

Kadir's laugh boomed. "That's not the same thing at all, and you know it. The man made you a multibillionaire."

"So that erases all the horrible things he did to me—to Samuel—to all those hundreds if not thousands of kids?"

"No." Kadir expelled a long breath. "That's not what I'm saying, and you know it. Look. I would love a pardon, but not like this. I can't do it. I won't do it." He folded his arms and stood his ground.

"Oh I see." Abrianna mimicked his stance.

"You do?"

"Absolutely. Baasim has been buzzing in your ear, hasn't he?"

Kadir rolled his eyes. "Bree, don't start."

"Am I right or wrong?"

"There is no right or wrong. Baasim and I happen to agree on this."

"Oh, I bet you do."

"What is that supposed to mean?"

"It means that Baasim and your mother haven't stopped criticizing everything you do and believe since they got here."

Kadir's hands became stop signs. "Leave my mother out of this."

"I wish I could. She's made that impossible. When are you going to tell her that we're not having a five-day traditional Yemeni wedding? She's insisting on buying me something called a qamis."

Kadir sighed. "I'll talk to her."

"But?"

"But—can't you meet her halfway?"

"What is that supposed to mean? What is a halfway Yemeni wedding? Either it is, or it isn't."

"Well—Ummi is having a hard time understanding the whole atheist thing."

"What's so hard to understand about my not believing in God—or Allah?"

"The whole thing," he countered. "The concept just"—he shook his head—"if you *don't* believe—what harm is there?"

Abrianna stepped back. "Are you serious?"

"What's wrong with compromising?"

"That's not compromising—you're asking me to ignore my beliefs."

"What beliefs? You just said that you didn't have any."

"My belief is *not* believing in a fictional God who hovers over everyone with a scorecard. It's *my* wedding day. She should be the one to quote-unquote compromise. Not me."

"Correction. It's *our* wedding day. And the last time I checked, I'm still very much a Muslim."

"Non-practicing."

"For now." He shrugged. "But I've been thinking about going back to Masjid Muhammad."

"Sure you were. Another one of Baasim's ideas?"

"No. *My* idea. I'm capable of processing my own thoughts."

"I didn't mean—"

"Yes, you did." He stopped her. "There's nothing wrong with

my family reminding me who I am, where I'm from—and even reminding me what's right and wrong."

"Your brother is an extremist."

"Based off of what? You've been rummaging around in his
head?"

"No—not exactly."

"Then don't talk about things you don't know and have never
tried to understand," he snapped.

Abrianna's brows shot upward.

Kadir took another deep breath. "The civil war in Yemen is
more complex than the American corporate media makes it out
to be. Baasim and my father were on the front lines of that fight. I
should have been there, too—fighting for my ancestral country.
But now, with so many other countries inserting their will and
arming all sides, it will never be the country we used to visit every
summer. The country I loved." Kadir hung his head. "The country I *still* love."

Abrianna approached and placed a hand against his face. He
cupped it and kissed her palm. "I'm sorry. I—guess I didn't real-
ize—I *should* have realized how much the war meant to you.
We've never really talked about it."

"Yeah. I know. There's so much that we're still learning about
each other."

Fear pricked Abrianna's heart. "Does that mean that we're
going too fast?"

"What?" He searched her face and read her like a book. "No,
no. We're fine." He pulled her into his arms. "We're always going
be learning new things about each other. That's the gig."

"But . . . we're so different," she reasoned soberly.

"Hey." He tipped her chin up. "Haven't you heard that oppo-
sites attract?"

"Yeah, but—"

"I love the fact that we're so different," he insisted.

"You do?"

"It keeps me on my toes and makes life exciting. Not a single day with you has been boring. And I wouldn't have it any other way." He cocked his head. "What about you?"

"Me? Are you kidding? I wake up every morning wondering what I did to deserve you. I'm now one of those corny chicks with my head in the clouds. I love you—I love *us*."

"Okay, then, let's do this—with a few compromises."

Her shoulders dropped. "All right. Deal."

"Yeah?"

She nodded.

"Thank you, baby." He kissed her forehead. "I knew you'd understand."

"So . . . you're asking me to compromise for you and not your mother?" she checked.

"Exactly."

Abrianna studied him to weigh whether he was telling the truth. "Okay."

Kadir climbed into bed, kissed Abrianna, and then tucked her underneath his arm. "I wish you'd ease up on Baasim, too. If you did, I think you'd understand him better. He's a good man—he's like Ghost. He's passionate about the things he believes in. How is that a bad thing?"

Abrianna tossed up her hands and buttoned her lip.

Kadir had a blind spot when it came to his twin brother. "You know that Baasim is full of shit, right?" Abrianna tested.

Kadir burst out laughing as he curled an arm over her hip. "What are you talking about?"

Abrianna brushed off his arm and sat up. "I'm talking about that bullshit story he told us at dinner. He wasn't at the DMV *all* afternoon. I saw him going into a restaurant with some other Middle Eastern guy."

"What?"

"Yeah. If you ask me, they looked suspect."

Kadir's brows sprung up. "Why, because he was *talking* to someone? Did you ever think that it was just an old friend? We did grow up here in D.C., you know."

"I know—but why lie?" She crossed her arms. "Why not just say, I ran into my old buddy John Doe, and we kicked it for a while?"

"Bree, don't." Kadir sat up, shaking his head.

"Don't what?"

"You know what. First, my family hates you, and now they're liars?"

"No. I'm not saying that. I'm just saying . . . that Baasim . . . didn't . . . tell the truth."

Kadir sprang out of bed and grabbed fistfuls of his own hair while he reined in his frustration. "Bree, I love you, but you're being impossible right now."

"Me? Baasim is the one who—"

"Baasim doesn't owe you a detailed account of his day! He doesn't owe you anything. He doesn't even *know* you. Stop it. Please."

Abrianna's arms remained folded while she pressed her lips together.

Kadir sighed. "Can we just . . . go to bed and get some sleep? I'm sure that you'll find loads of things wrong with my mother and brother tomorrow."

"That's not fair."

"*That's* not fair? Are you even listening to yourself? You've known them twenty-four hours, and already you're . . ." He searched for the right words.

"Okay. Okay." Abrianna tossed up her hands. "I see your point. You don't believe me."

"You're paranoid. Maybe if you stop using . . . You know what?" Kadir grabbed his pillow. "I'll sleep on the couch."

"What? Kadir? You don't have to do this. Can't we just talk about this?"

"There is nothing to talk about. Just because your family was fucked up, it doesn't mean that everyone else's is, too. Some of us actually love and trust each other. How about you give that a try for once?"

Abrianna flinched as if he'd sucker punched her, but she didn't have a ready retort.

"Get some sleep." He headed toward the door.

"We shouldn't go to bed angry," she told him.

Kadir stopped. "I'm not angry," he said. "I'm disappointed." He opened the door and walked out.

32

Abrianna didn't sleep a wink. She lay in bed, ignoring the buzz in her head and the tightening of her scalp while the coke hidden in the bathroom called her name. It promised to take the edge off and mellow her out. She needed that. She and Kadir had been through a lot in the past year, but never once had they gone to bed angry. Worried—yes. Scared—yes. But angry? No.

And it's my fault. Abrianna hung her head and raked her fingers through her hair. In the next second, she rejected the blame. *No. He chose his family over me.* Then again, why wouldn't he? Last week, he feared his family had been wiped out in the Sana'a air strikes, and since they'd popped up in their lives, Abrianna had done nothing but complain. What did she expect Kadir to do—choose her over them?

Yes! Goddamn it. Yes! Adrianna threw back the top sheet and climbed out of bed. She had expected her man to have her back. Kadir had proposed for them to become *one*—that meant she came *first.* Baasim was up to something. She had to prove it.

Abrianna entered the adjoining bathroom and locked the door behind her. Beneath the sink's cabinet, Abrianna pulled out a box of tampons and removed the hidden coke inside. The second it was in her hand, her body vibrated with need. One hit wasn't going to hurt anyone. Her body naturally healed itself, so what harm was she doing?

Abrianna hit a winning internal argument, and seconds later, she cut and vacuumed two lines of the pink cocaine. The drug hit and blazed through her system like a locomotive. She sighed and slumped to the floor while her mind floated in another dimension. A smile eased across her face as her heavy eyelids drifted closed. Her senses heightened. The air in the room kissed and caressed her skin while she floated on cloud nine.

Humming to herself, she took her time cleaning and returning the drugs to the tampon box and cleaning up the bathroom counter. When she lay back down and closed her eyes, euphoria washed over her in waves. There was no buzzing—only peace. Images emerged from behind her closed eyes. They were scenes from earlier in the day: the bathroom, the nosebleed, and the accident.

Don't forget the blonde.

Abrianna opened her eyes, and the images vanished. When she struggled to recall it again, the only thing she could remember was the hair. *Didn't I get a good look at her face?* She couldn't remember.

Abrianna grew restless and threw off the top sheet again, but this time, she crept out of the bedroom and tiptoed to the living room.

Kadir lay on the couch with one arm still tucked behind his head. He spotted Abrianna immediately when she waltzed in in her pink satin gown. He was relieved she came to him. He was seconds from giving in himself and returning to the bedroom.

"Hey, baby. You up?" Abrianna hiked up her gown and swung one leg over him to straddle his hips.

He was hard instantly.

"Yeah. You're up." She brushed a kiss against his lips while doing a slow grind against his bulging cock. "Are you still mad at me?"

The way she purred the question had Kadir fighting not to smile.

"Hmmm. What if I told you I'm so, so sorry?" She trailed kisses over his chin and down the column of his neck.

Kadir's resistance crumbled. He grabbed a fistful of her hair and pulled her close to devour her lips in a kiss. His other hand worked its way up her gown. She was wet and ready for him.

Kadir no longer remembered what they'd been fighting about. He only had one mission right now. "We should go back into the bedroom." He went to pick her up.

"No." She pushed him back down. "Let's do it right here."

"What if someone wakes up and sees us?"

"So?" She nibbled on his bottom lip and yanked his pants down over his hips.

Abrianna swallowed his protest in another long kiss that made their blood run hot. Seconds later, they were naked and making love in the center of the living room.

From the hallway, Baasim watched the show.

33

Castillo rose at the crack of dawn, not because she was an early bird but because sleep had eluded her the entire night. After a quick shower and two cups of coffee, she collected her car keys and headed out to work. Her first stop: Abrianna and Kadir's apartment. After Bree's car accident the police cleared her to leave, and Kadir took his fiancée straight home. Now, Castillo wanted Bree to take a look at the video Ghost hacked from the city's surveillance cameras.

After Castillo parked at Kadir and Abrianna's apartment complex, she hopped out of her car with her thermos cup of coffee. As she approached the building, she spotted Kadir getting into a car with a group of Middle Eastern guys. Before she could holler out, the blue sedan peeled off. "That was odd." She glanced back at the building and spotted Abrianna in the window. She also watched the car peel off.

Is there trouble in paradise?

Castillo climbed the outdoor staircase to Bree's apartment. She landed one knock before the door jerked open.

"C'mon in," Abrianna told her and marched off.

"Okay." Castillo stepped into the apartment and sniffed the air. "It smells wonderful in here. Whatcha cooking?"

A smiling, petite woman stepped out of the kitchen. "Good morning," she greeted.

Abrianna parked at the breakfast bar. "Daishan, I'd like for you to meet a friend of mine and Kadir's employer, Gizella Castillo. Castillo, I'd like for you to meet my future mother-in-law, Daishan Kahlifa."

"Oh, hello." Castillo stretched out her hand. "It's nice to meet you."

The woman's smile bloomed. "Ah. You're Kadir's boss. It's nice to meet you. Have you had breakfast? I made plenty of food." She ignored the offered hand and took Gizella by the arm and led her straight toward a banquet of food.

Gizella opened her mouth to refuse the offer, but her stomach growled loud enough for the neighbors to hear.

Daishan chuckled. "Please, sit down. I'll fix you a plate."

"Thank you, ma'am." Castillo glanced over at Bree, who wore a plastic smile until Daishan disappeared back into the kitchen. "Is everything all right?"

"Next question," Bree muttered.

Castillo pulled out her smartphone and scooted closer to Bree. "Take a look at this." She pulled up the video. "Ghost hacked into the city's surveillance on yesterday's shooting."

"Ghost?"

"Yeah. It's scary what the man can do with a computer." Castillo hit play.

Abrianna watched the clip several times. It was like an out-of-body experience.

"What do you see?" Castillo tested.

"I see those T4S assholes trying to kill me. Am I supposed to be seeing something else?"

Castillo pointed to the blonde. "Her."

Abrianna stiffened.

"Do you know her?" Castillo asked.

"No." Abrianna shook her head. "At least, I don't think so."

"We cleaned it up and zoomed in for a better look, but no dice. Whoever she is, the gunmen seemed more interested in her than you yesterday."

Bree frowned. "Wait. You don't believe I was the target?"

"You both were. The question is why."

Bree opened her mouth to say something but was cut off.

"Gizella." Kadir stepped out of the bedroom as Daishan returned to the table with a platter of food.

"What are you doing here this early?" he asked.

Castillo frowned. "Me? What are you doing here?"

He laughed. "I, um, live here." He glanced at Abrianna. "At least I did the last time I checked."

"No, I mean, I thought I saw you leave a few minutes ago with a group of guys."

Kadir and his mother laughed.

"That must have been Baasim."

Bree rolled her eyes. "Yeah. He's Mr. Popular."

"Ah." Castillo laughed. "Twins. Gotcha."

"Come, Kadir. Sit down and eat." Daishan pulled out another chair and patted the seat.

Kadir looked at his platter and grinned like a child on Christmas morning. He was in his seat so fast there should have been track marks on the hardwood floor. "Thanks, Ummi."

Daishan kissed the top of Kadir's head. "It's my pleasure. You know that."

Kadir beamed.

Momma's boy.

Castillo choked on her coffee and cut an amused look over at Abrianna, who smiled back.

"I find it exciting that you're a private detective." Daishan joined them at the table. "You guys are searching for the missing reporter, right?"

Castillo nodded.

"Any leads?"

Castillo glanced at Abrianna.

Bree smiled. "Other than Brigham's bullshit theory."

"Not yet, but we're working on it," Castillo informed them. "I figure this morning we'll head over to Lehane's place and check it out."

Kadir stopped eating. "You want to go back over to Lehane's?"

"I want to survey the place myself. Go over every nook and cranny. Ghost already got me a copy of the unreleased fire report." She glanced at Kadir. "I gotta tell ya, having you and Ghost around has come in handy."

"Yeah. He's one of the best when it comes to tracking and hacking. I'm surprised you're into all that *illegal* stuff."

"I'm into getting results—and time is of the essence if we're going to find Tomi alive."

———⋆———

Baasim climbed out from the back of a cramped Toyota Camry and followed his buddy Saoud into the Denco Air Conditioner & Supplies building. Inside, the place was loud, and there had to be at least a dozen workers on an assembly line. In one open crate, Baasim saw stacks of assault weapons. Another dozen employees loaded and stacked crates into the waiting trucks. Overall, the company ran a tight ship.

"Baasim," Saoud called.

Baasim jerked his attention from the well-oiled machine back to Saoud.

"This way." Saoud waved for him to follow.

Baasim fell in line behind his friend and followed him to the main office while Awsam and Farooq punched in at the time clock. There, Saoud introduced him to his boss, an older Shia Muslim with more salt than pepper in both his hair and beard.

Saoud closed the door.

"Mr. Almasi, this is my friend—"

"Baasim Kahlifa." Almasi stood from behind his desk, unfolding a six-four frame and stretching out his hand. "Or is it Kadir? You boys loved trying to fool people when you were younger."

Baasim smiled. "It's Baasim, Mr. Almasi. Forgive me, but I don't—"

"Ah. It's been a long time," Almasi said. "I knew your parents a long time ago—before life took us down different roads." They shook hands, but Almasi held on longer. "I heard what happened to Muaadh. I'm sorry. He was a good man. I'm not surprised to hear he was fighting on the front line."

"They both were," Saoud interjected, pumping out his chest. "My man here has seen *real* action. The prostitute in the White House almost killed Baasim and his mother in two separate air strikes in Sana'a."

Almasi shook his head in disgust. "This fucking country, huh? They won't be happy until they've destabilized the entire Middle East. The US is clearly at war with Islam. They sell arms to all sides of every conflict and hold up their hands and act like they haven't done a damn thing."

"Exactly," Baasim agreed.

The two men sized each other up. "Saoud informed me you were looking for work."

"Not just any work. I'm also looking for revenge."

Almasi and Baasim engaged in another stare-down before Almasi smiled. "Then you came to the right place."

34

"Where in the hell are you taking me?" Shawn complained, hobbling on his walking cane. "Are we underground? Do you know what could be living down here? We could catch the bubonic plague or something."

Abrianna stopped and turned around. "The bubonic plague?"

"Shit. I don't know. Probably. You never know."

She rolled her eyes and resumed marching. "Quit your bitching and come the hell on. I know where I'm going."

Shawn caught up with her only because he was too scared to find his way back out. "I swear to God if you're dragging me to some new underground drug dealer, you're catching these hands on general principle."

Abrianna rolled her eyes. "Don't start."

"What, I'm not supposed to mention how your nosebleed looked like a damn geyser the other day? I know you do the drugs for the headaches, but what's the side effects?"

"Are you forgetting I self-heal?"

"That didn't look like any healing I've ever seen. You need to see a doctor."

Abrianna laughed. "No offense, but I've had my fill of doctors. Plus, do you believe a normal doctor could help me?"

"Shit, Bree. I don't know. I'm fucking worried about you, okay? Is that so fucking terrible?"

Abrianna sighed and stopped walking. "No. It's not. I appreciate you caring. You know I do. This shit is complicated. I'm doing the best I can to manage this shit. I do what I do out of necessity, not for the high. We've been over this. You don't know what I go through every day. The cravings—and the endless buzzing is driving me insane. You believe somebody can help me in rehab from hearing everyone's thoughts buzzing in the back of my head like a chainsaw twenty-four-seven?"

"Maybe not that part."

"Oh, you *do* want me to go insane—because that's what's happening. I can take the night sweats, pain, and nausea. Barely—but I can handle it. It's the fucked-up shit Avery and fucking Dr. Zacher did to me that can't be fixed. I have to figure out a way to live with it the best way I can. You have to trust me."

"I have a bad feeling something is going to happen to you. I can't shake it. When it does happen, it's going to be my fault 'cause I can't get you clean. I couldn't deal with that. None of us could. You're more than my best friend, Bree. You're my family. We've been through too much shit together. Now, you're inheriting billions and—there are too many forces pulling us apart: T4S, politics, and your engagement."

"Stop it." Abrianna took his hand. "We are family. You're not going to lose me. None of you are. I won't let it happen. I promise."

Shawn looked dubious. "I'm going to hold you to that."

She smiled. "Deal."

They hugged it out and wiped their eyes dry.

"Now, c'mon. We're almost there." She quickened the pace. In no time, they arrived at Ghost's underground bunker.

"So, this is the infamous bunker?" Shawn marveled, looking around. "Where are we?"

"We're nowhere. When we leave, forget you were ever here."

"Got it." Shawn took another nervous look around.

Abrianna hammered on the door like the police and waited. And waited.

She hammered again.

"Maybe no one is here," Shawn suggested,

"But someone is always here," she insisted.

"There's a first time for everything."

Abrianna ignored him and pulled the door, not expecting it to open.

It did.

"What the hell?"

"Maybe we should leave?"

"I got you." Abrianna unholstered her weapon and crept inside.

Accustomed to D.C. street violence, Shawn also went for his weapon while clutching his cane. "What's with you always rushing into danger?"

Abrianna ignored him. She couldn't leave. She had to make sure Ghost and his crew weren't lying inside dead. Ghost was annoying at times, but she still considered him a friend if not a part of her street family. She pulled the metal door open, but its iron hinges made a high-pitched squeak as it opened.

"We may as well wear T-shirts that read 'two dumb asses,'" Shawn hissed.

"You know what? You could have stayed back at the car." She stepped into the bunker.

"And tell Kadir what when you get yourself killed?" Shawn argued.

"And dying *with* me is a solution?" She searched around for a light switch. When she flipped on the switch, she gasped in horror.

"What the—?" Shawn looked around the place. It was wrecked.

Broken chairs, tables, and numerous wire and cable cords were strewn everywhere, but the computers were missing—and so were Ghost and his team.

"Stay here," Abrianna ordered before hopscotching over the mess and rushing toward the back of the bunker. This time, Shawn ignored her order and followed her. "Where are you going?"

"I'm going to check out the rest of the place."

"There's nobody here."

"It won't hurt to double check," she insisted. The entire place was trashed—including the small break room.

"Are you happy now? Can we go?"

Abrianna lowered her weapon. "Yeah. Let's go."

Boom!

Abrianna and Shawn jumped as the lights shut off.

"The fuck?" Shawn swore. "I knew it."

"Shh." Abrianna crept forward, leading Shawn out of the break room, but they were far from silent. There was a lot of junk on the floor.

"Is someone in here?" Shawn asked.

Abrianna's scalp tingled. "Get down." She turned and threw her weight into her best friend, knocking him off his feet. They hit the ground as a series of bullets flew over their heads.

Someone stormed toward them.

Abrianna acted on instinct and returned fire. She fired off four rounds and heard each one hit someone who was repelled backward with a roar. Another spray of bullets flew toward their heads.

Abrianna threw up her hands, and a blistering heat rolled over her like a heat wave and then pulsed off of her like a sonic boom. Her eyes were still squeezed tight when she heard the bullets fall like trinkets in front of her.

"Bree?"

She peeled open her eyes, not at her name, but because of the voice. "Ghost?"

⟶•◦◦•⟵

Ground zero. Castillo ducked underneath the yellow crime scene tape still wrapped around Tomi Lehane's home. The place was nothing but a blackened ruin. She had no clue what she was looking for but remained optimistic she would know it when she saw it. Julian and Kadir combed the site along with her.

Kadir was edgy. "I don't mind telling you I don't like being out here in the open like this."

A smile twitched on Castillo's lips. "We picked up on that the first dozen times you told us."

"Why are we out here?"

"I needed to see the destruction for myself—only the problem is there's not much to see. Though I have read the fire marshals' report to the point I have most of it memorized, but they could've missed something."

Woof! Woof!

The team's heads jerked up as a hundred-pound German shepherd bounded up the townhouse's concrete stairs and made a beeline straight to Castillo. "Whoa." She caught the dog's paws seconds before they landed on her chest. "Now, who are you?"

"Rocky, come back," a teenage girl yelled, racing up the sidewalk behind the dog.

"Oh, you're Rocky?" She scratched behind the dog's ear. "It's nice to finally meet you. I'm a friend of your momma's."

"I'm sorry. Is he bothering you?" The teenager caught up with Rocky and took hold of his leash. "He's big, but he's harmless."

"It's okay . . . Serena," Castillo said, reading her vanity necklace. "He used to live here, right?"

Serena nodded. "He almost died, too. My dad said it was a miracle he made it out of the house alive. Those guys who took Ms. Lehane must've left the door open for Rocky to crawl out."

"Guys?"

"They looked like guys, but I suppose they could've been girls."

Castillo cocked her head. "How do you know someone took Ms. Lehane?"

"Because I saw them."

The bombshell caught Kadir and Julian's ear. "You what?"

Serena sighed. "Don't tell my dad I told you. He doesn't want us to get involved. He's okay with me watching Rocky here until Ms. Lehane comes back, but I had to beg him for a long time."

Castillo dropped to one knee. "Did you get a good look at their faces?"

"No. It was too dark. That's why I said they *could* have been girls—but I doubt it. They looked pretty strong when they put Ms. Lehane in their van."

"Van?"

The girl bobbed her head again.

"Okay. From the beginning, what did you see?"

Kadir and Julian closed in and spooked the girl.

"I gotta get home." Serena backed away. "I'm not supposed to be talking about this. C'mon, Rocky."

"It's okay." Castillo waved her team to back off. "I'm not a cop. You're not going to get into trouble talking to me. I'm concerned about my friend. That's all. I want to know what happened to her. I want to find her and bring her back home. Can you help me do that?"

Rocky barked and jerked away from Serena and pushed Castillo back onto her ass, where he proceeded to slobber all over her face."

Serena chuckled. "He likes you."

"I like him, too." Castillo studied Serena. "Can you tell me more about the van?"

Serena shrugged. "It was dark. I saw a couple of people dressed in black carry out a body and shove it into a van."

"Did you happen to see a license plate?"

She shook her head.

"Did you record it?" Kadir asked.

Serena lowered her head. "Maybe."

Castillo and her team exchanged looks.

"Can I see it?"

"My dad erased it from my phone."

Their hope crashed. "I see."

"But I'd already uploaded it to my laptop," Serena admitted. "If you give me your email, I can send it to you when I get home."

"Great." Castillo dug into her jacket and removed a business card. "My contact information is on here. If you can send me the video as soon as you can, it will help me."

Serena read the card. "You're a private investigator?"

"Yeah. We all are. I used to work for Ms. Lehane from time to time. Now, can you get me the video and send it to the email address on the card?"

Serena smiled. "I'll go home and do it right now. C'mon, Rocky. Let's go." She grabbed the dog's leash again and tugged him away.

Castillo and her team gathered together.

Kadir asked, "Should we go with her?"

"And risk freaking her and her parents out?" Castillo shook her head. "No. We know enough to find her again if she doesn't send the video. C'mon. Let's go. I've seen enough." She headed out of the blackened ruins. As she descended the concrete stairs, she stepped on something and stopped.

"What is it?" Julian asked.

Castillo knelt and picked up a silver button. When she wiped off the soot, she recognized it. "I've seen this before."

Kadir leaned over and took a look. "Yeah? Where?"

"On Jayson Brigham's jacket."

35

Shawn patted himself down. "Am I dead? Are we dead?"

Abrianna rolled her eyes. "We're not dead." She picked herself back off the floor and then helped Shawn. Ghost hit a switch, and the lights flooded the bunker. "What the fuck are you doing here?"

"I came to see you," Abrianna explained.

"Why? I expressly said for no one to come here or the warehouse apartment," he barked. "I could have killed you."

"Well, nobody told me."

Shawn elbowed her. *I said we shouldn't be here.*

"You don't count," she said.

Shawn rolled his eyes and picked up his cane.

Ghost's eyes narrowed. "You're doing that freaky mind-reading shit again, aren't you?"

"Never mind that. What the hell happened here?"

"Security breach," he answered. "Our friends over at T4S."

"Fuck."

"Yeah. But we destroyed and got rid of the servers before we cleared out. And they found the apartment, too. What can I say? When it rains, it pours." He grimaced.

"So, what's the play? Y'all got a new spot?"

"We better head out." Ghost changed the subject. "You never know who's listening. You feel me?"

Abrianna glanced around. *You mean the place could be bugged?*

Ghost jumped at the sound of her voice inside of his head.

"Hey, cut it out with that shit." He waved them toward the front door.

What? It's not like anybody can hear me in this big, empty space between your ears.

"Ha. Ha."

Hello? Hello? She echoed inside of his head. *Is anybody in here?*

Ghost grumbled. "I can't believe this is my life."

Abrianna smiled and followed Ghost back topside. Instead of piling into separate cars, she and Shawn scrambled into Ghost's black van.

"Now what?" Ghost asked.

"I'm glad you asked." Abrianna smiled. "I need your help."

Ghost lifted a brow. "You stopped bullets in midair, and you need *my* help?"

"I need to do some recon on someone—and I need some spy gear to do that."

"Recon?" Ghost grinned. "What, you in the military now?"

"No, but I'm on a mission to prove something to my pigheaded fiancé."

Ghost's brows stretched higher. "Don't tell me you and my man are already about to do an episode of *Cheaters*."

"What? No. I'm not spying on Kadir."

"No?"

Abrianna hesitated. "If I tell you, you can't tell Kadir."

"So, we are at the keeping secrets phase in the relationship?" He held up his hands. "All the same, I'd appreciate not being dragged into any pre-domestic issues. Plus, Kadir is my boy. And—"

"Will you shut up? I'm not spying on Kadir."

Ghost cocked his head. "Then who is it?"

"You promise not to tell?"

"Does it have it anything to do with T4S? Because you two should be working together on this."

Abrianna dropped her head into the palms of her hands and groaned. "You know what? Never mind. You're giving me a headache. I'll figure this shit out on my own. C'mon, Shawn. Let's go." She opened the van's door, but before she could hop out, Ghost grabbed her arm.

"Wait."

She paused.

What am I getting myself into?

"Would you like me to answer that?" Abrianna asked.

"Who are you stalking?"

She cocked her head.

"My lips are sealed," he said. "I hope you don't make me regret this."

"You won't," she assured him, but then added, "I don't think."

He sighed.

"Look, I need some tracking devices that are simple enough for me to use. You don't need to know what's up. That way you don't have to lie to anyone. How's that?"

"Is it dangerous?" he asked.

"Far from it. I need to prove I'm right about something. That's all."

"I don't know. You need to be off the grid, not out here playing Nancy Drew."

"You know I'm going to do this with or without your help, so why don't we cut to the part where you help me?"

He weighed his options before remembering she could hear his thoughts. "Deal."

A smile exploded across Abrianna's face before she leaned over and delivered a peck against his cheek. "Thanks, Ghost."

He grunted. "Yeah, yeah. When are you going to need this stuff?"

"As soon as possible. Like—tomorrow?"

"What's the rush?" He sighed. "Wait. Don't answer that. I'll throw you a package together and get it to you tomorrow."

"You're a sweetheart."

"Yeah, that's what the ladies keep telling me."

Shawn groaned. "Can we go shopping now?"

⊰•⊱

Ghost arrived at the Agency, looking for Kadir. When he walked in the door, Castillo and her team were hunched over one terminal studying something on the screen. "What's going on?"

Castillo looked up. "Gosh. It's like when you feed a stray cat. It keeps coming back for more."

Draya snickered.

Ghost crooked a half smile. "Ha, ha. You have a whole bag of jokes."

"I'm tryna stay two steps ahead of you." Castillo grinned and returned her attention to her screen."

"Hey, man. Can I holler at you for a moment?"

Kadir removed himself from the group. "Sure. What's up?"

Ghost pulled Kadir to the Agency's small break room. "Hey, um, is everything cool with you and your girl?"

Kadir frowned.

"With you and Bree."

"Yeah, I know who my girl is. Why are you asking?"

Ghost put on his blank poker face. "No reason. Just asking."

Kadir kept staring at his friend, but he said nothing else. "Yeah. Bree and I are good."

"We're still . . . heading toward the altar and all that good stuff?"

Kadir cocked his head.

"I mean, sometimes dudes have buyer's remorse or second thoughts."

"Second thoughts?"

Poker face.

"Have you been talking to Bree? Did she say something?"

"What? No." The poker face cracked. "I was curious, you know? With so much going on, people's wires could get crossed. Communication." He snapped his fingers as if he had an epiphany. "People say communication is key—and trust. I hear that's important, too."

"Okay. Thanks for . . . sharing."

"Yeah. Good talk." He whacked Kadir on the back. "I'm rooting for you guys."

"Thanks, man. I appreciate it."

Ghost cracked an awkward smile and exited the break room.

Kadir abandoned a coffee refill and replayed his and Ghost's odd conversation as he followed Ghost back into the office.

"What are you looking at?" Ghost asked.

"Videotape," Kadir said. "A teenager over in Tomi's neighborhood recorded her kidnapping."

"Sweet." Ghost joined the group around Castillo's computer terminal.

"The tape is just as the girl described, though," Castillo said. "It's too dark to make anything out. Four bodies entered the house, and five bodies came out. Plus, it's a horrible angle."

"Why aren't the street lights on?" Ghost asked.

"I was wondering the same thing." Castillo zoomed in, angling for where the license plate should be on the van, but it did no good. It was simply too dark. "Goddamn it."

"It's T4S," Ghost said. "It has to be. Look at the precision these muthafuckas have. I know professionals when I see them."

She agreed and released a long sigh. "Yeah, but this is hardly proof."

"No, but it's proof that she was taken," Kadir said. "And leaked to the right people, it will back up Bree's claim about her being kidnapped."

"Leaked?"

"It would no longer be a conspiracy theory," Kadir pushed. "It's now a fact."

Castillo glanced over at Ghost.

"My man is right." He grinned. "We release this, and Bree is no longer a whack-job compared to the dignified Dr. Zacher."

"Let me guess. You want to be the one to leak the tape?"

"You damn right. Our site has been down for a few days. People are talking. We need to come back online with a bang."

"What about li'l Serena?"

"What about her? Nobody knows the tape came from her. I doubt her or her parents will come forward."

Everyone stared at her as she weighed her options. "Fuck it. Go ahead."

"Yes!" Ghost pumped his fist.

Castillo turned back toward her computer and pressed play again. Then she stopped it, cocked her head, and stared.

"What is it?" Kadir asked.

"That jacket." She grabbed the button she recovered from the scene from her pocket. "Bingo. Brigham was there that night."

———※◆※———

Castillo and her team hauled ass back to the *Washington Post*. This time, she wasn't in a great mood, but Jayson Brigham had some explaining to do. Once she gave her name to the receptionist, she was instructed to wait in the lobby. After ten minutes, she paced around like a caged tiger, clutching her leather satchel.

"Aren't you Lieutenant Castillo?" a man asked.

Castillo pivoted around on her heel and flicked a smile at a familiar face. "Martin Bailey." She stretched out her hand. "Good to see you."

"I could say the same about you." He puffed out his chest. "Talk about a long time, no see. What are you doing here?"

"I'm working a missing person case."

"Oh yeah. I heard you were a private dick now. What's your case?"

"Your reporter: Tomi Lehane."

Bailey's brows jumped up. "Is it?"

"Yeah. I came by the other day to talk to you, but you were busy. I talked to Jayson Brigham, and I'm back for a follow-up."

"Jayson and Tomi paired up a lot. Plus, they were pretty good friends, too."

"Were? You've already written her off?"

Bailey hung his head. "Sorry about that, but, um . . . I've been in this business a long time and unfortunately missing people tend to stay missing or turn up dead."

"Damn. I thought I was a pessimist." She folded her arms. "If I had that attitude, I would never have found Tomi the last time she went missing."

Bailey reddened. "Sorry, again. You're right. If anyone can find her, it's you. Come on up to my office. I'd love to hear what you have so far . . . and we can swing by Brigham's cubicle for those follow-up questions." He winked.

Castillo's smile stretched wider. "Sounds like a plan."

Bailey gestured for her to take the lead. "After you."

Castillo tilted her head and walked out of the lobby. Bailey escorted her past the security guard and toward the elevator bay.

"So, any good leads?" Bailey asked as they rode up a few flights.

"One," she answered.

"Care to elaborate?"

"No."

Bailey smiled. "You know I have a reporter working the case, too."

"Yeah?"

"She has a lead, too."

"Let me guess: Abrianna Parker?"

The elevator doors slid open, and Castillo walked out ahead.

"How did you know that?"

"Because I'm guessing that she talked to the same source who lied to my face," Castillo told him.

"What?"

She glanced around. "Which direction to Brigham's desk?"

Bailey pointed. "Last cubicle on your right."

"Thanks. I'll swing by your office when I'm done."

"I can't wait."

Castillo marched toward Brigham's cubicle and plopped down on his desk while he was turned toward his computer.

Brigham jumped and pulled the EarPods from his ears.

"Busy?" she asked.

Brigham closed his mouth, but his eyes remained as wide as silver dollars.

"Good. This shouldn't take too much of your time—unless you lie to me again: then I'd be forced to kick your ass in front of everyone in this office."

Jayson swallowed.

She leaned forward and whispered, "I know."

Jayson frowned as he leaned back. "Know what?"

"I'm glad you asked." She opened her leather satchel and pulled out the photograph and slapped it on the desk next to her. "This is from the night Lehane was kidnapped. I had a friend clean this image up, and guess what?"

Jayson stared at the picture and grew nervous.

"I believe this guy right here . . . is you."

"What?" He laughed, but it sounded like a misfired muffler. "I can't even see anything."

"No? Look again."

Jayson made a show of examining the photograph before shaking his head again. "Nope. Sorry. You're barking up the wrong tree."

"Really?" She pointed. "This man is wearing a distinctive jacket, would you say? Vintage, even."

Jayson's eyes widened as he shook his head. "That could be anybody."

She removed the plastic bag from her satchel. "I found your missing button at the crime scene."

What little color Jayson had left in his face vanished.

"Like I said. I know. You were there that night, helping your friend and colleague be kidnapped by the same people who had snatched her off the streets seven years ago. The same people who'd tortured and experimented on her. Why would you do that? Hmm?"

Jayson's jawline hardened.

"See. Dr. Zacher was Abrianna's handler after the fact. He watched over her—became her friend so that she would trust him while he studied her. I believe you were Tomi's handler. You're more than what meets the eye. This job is a front for you, isn't it? You *work* for T4S."

Jayson picked up the picture and handed it back to her. "You should leave."

Castillo smiled. "Sure thing." She hopped off the desk. "I'm finished here anyway. But I have to swing by your boss's office before I head out. He has this insane idea about Abrianna being the one behind Tomi's disappearance. I wonder where he got that idea from?" She headed out of the cubicle.

Jayson sprung to his feet. "Wait."

Castillo stopped and did a slow pivot. "Yes? You got something you want to tell me?"

"You can't go in there and tell my boss that . . ." He looked around and lowered his voice. ". . . that I had something to do with Tomi's disappearance."

"It's the truth."

"This is ridiculous. You can't prove any of this."

"Where is Tomi?"

"I—I don't know."

"Then Martin and I are going to have a talk."

Jayson grabbed her arm. "I'll find out. Please. Give me some time."

Castillo smiled. "You have forty-eight hours."

36

The video of Tomi Lehane's kidnapping hit the dark web and went viral within an hour. Cable news played the video under the breaking news banner and then proceeded to replay it in a loop every twenty minutes. Pundits from the left and the right praised and discredited the video while #FreeLehane remained the number one trending topic on Twitter. Beneath that trended #Parkerwasright. In third place #Hardywasright took a spot. Talk radio lit up with conspiracy theories. While the video proved Tomi Lehane was snatched from her home, it didn't prove *who* took her. Every frame of the video was dissected and analyzed. By the end of the day, President Washington extended another invitation to Abrianna Parker to visit the White House via Twitter.

———— ⋅•⋅ ————

"Congratulations, Ms. Parker," Silvo Ricci announced. "Cargill Parker left everything to you."

Even though the reading and announcement had been expected, reality kicked Abrianna in the gut, and guilt slammed down on her shoulder. It had a lot to do with the number of unknown and angry faces that were also in the room. Many of them were attorneys, bankers, and CEOs of various companies her father owned around the world—and they all wanted to talk to her.

Once the reading was over, they circled around her like sharks, jetting out business cards, pressing her about meetings, and asking for decisions on subjects she had no clue about.

Thankfully, Kadir and Shawn came with her and intervened. Shawn collected the cards and scheduled appointments on an app on his phone.

Kadir played bodyguard and navigated her out of Ricci's law office. To her surprise, a few reporters were waiting.

"Ms. Parker, how does it feel to be the sole benefactor to your father's estate?" a reporter asked.

"How does it feel to be a part of the one percent?" another reporter asked. "What about your father's victims?"

Abrianna ignored their shouted questions and ducked into the waiting car parked at the curb. She was still unsettled when Kadir climbed in behind the wheel.

"Are you all right?" Kadir squeezed her hand.

"Yeah," she lied but knew she hadn't sold it. "It's surreal. That's all. I mean, now that it's official. Am I supposed to be running all those companies now? I don't know anything about running a business or anything about those questions everyone was asking me."

"It's okay. We'll figure it all out." Kadir squeezed her hand. "It's going to be all right." He sounded confident, but he didn't erase all doubt.

Shawn made it to the vehicle and climbed into the back seat. "I've found my calling in life."

"What, as a personal assistant?"

"Hey, don't knock a man with a dream," Shawn volleyed back, laughing.

"You're hired," Abrianna said as Kadir pulled away from the curb.

Yasser and Awsam Rizq led Baasim to the back of Bezoria's and then down a dark staircase where a cell of Yemenis clustered in small groups and talked in hushed tones. A couple of smiles broke across a few of the guys' faces when they recognized him. When they reached the bottom of the staircase those friendly faces approached with their hands stretched out.

"Baasim, welcome. We're so glad that you've joined us," Tamer, another friend from the mosque, greeted.

Baasim's smile widened. "Are you kidding? I'm thrilled to be a part of the team. Anything to advance the cause."

Tamer bobbed his head. "I hear you, but, um, where's your brother?"

"Kadir." Baasim laughed. "Nah. My brother doesn't have the stomach for something like this."

Yasser frowned. "Are you sure about that? The other night at the Stallion, he seemed sympathetic to the cause."

"He's more into starting a new family," Baasim countered. "Trust me. Kadir's fiancée has him wrapped around her fingers. He doesn't take a piss without calling and asking her first."

The men's faces collapsed in disappointment.

"I see." Tamer shoved his hands into his pants pockets. "That's too bad. A lot of the guys want to shake his hand for getting rid of that asshole Walker. Some of us still believe he had something to do the with the airport bombing."

"According to Kadir that was a different cell. A pair of brothers, I believe."

Tamer bobbed his head. "Who happened to live in his apartment complex with him and who he drove to the airport."

"As an Uber driver."

"Sure." Tamer winked. "If that's his story."

The door above their heads opened, and another group of men descended the staircase, carrying file boxes. Saoud shouted, "All right, men, gather around. We're working on a tight schedule."

Farooq and Kamel marched over to a line of folding tables and dropped the boxes on them.

Saoud took over the meeting, pairing men together and handing them checklists.

Baasim paid careful attention to who were the soldiers and who were the generals. Right now, he was a soldier. That wasn't good enough. He needed to climb up the chain of command—fast.

———————

Tina Bouchard opened her front door and gasped when Abrianna flashed her engagement ring. "Oh, Bree! How wonderful." She threw arms around Bree, squeezing and rocking her from side to side. When Tina released her, tears shimmered in her eyes. "I wish your mother could be here to see this day. She would have been so happy for you."

Abrianna's smile expanded while tears brimmed her eyes. "Thanks for saying that."

"It's true." She cupped her cheeks as if she was a proud parent before her gaze drifted behind Abrianna's shoulder.

"Let me introduce you to Kadir's mother, Daishan. She just arrived back in the States from Yemen. Daishan, this is . . . an old friend of my mother's, Tina Bouchard."

"It's nice to meet you." Daishan shook Tina's hand before they were invited to enter. Daishan took in the place with a faint smile. "What a lovely home you have."

"Thank you." Tina grinned proudly. "Would you care for something to drink? Coffee, tea, or perhaps some lavender lemonade?"

"Lemonade would be lovely. It's such a warm day."

"Amen," she chuckled. "Bree?"

"Lemonade would be great."

"Coming right up. Why don't you have a seat in the dining room? I made a pie—apple."

Abrianna blinked as she led Daishan to the table.

"You bake?"

"Oh, I live in the kitchen. My problem is finding enough people to cook for." She laughed. "I'm always throwing dinner parties. You and Kadir should come sometime—and you, too, Daishan. You're more than welcome to come."

"Only if I can join you in the kitchen. I love to cook, too. I don't get to do it as often as I used to. My boys are grown now and . . . I believe it's called empty nest syndrome."

Abrianna squeezed Daishan's hand for an awkward moment before Daishan drew it back.

"You're more than welcome to join me at any time," Tina said. "It would be a pleasure."

Abrianna brushed off Daishan's rejection and kept smiling. When Tina returned with the lemonade, they dissolved into wedding planning. Abrianna held her tongue as Daishan took over the conversation, describing a traditional Yemeni wedding.

Compromise, Abrianna reminded herself.

"I'm sorry. Did you say something?" Daishan asked.

"Uh, no." Abrianna shook her head and held up her smile. "You were saying?"

Daishan happily resumed telling her vision. However, everything came to an abrupt halt when Daishan asked, "You *are* planning to convert to our religion, right?"

Abrianna drew a blank for so long Tina had to rescue her. "How about we table that for another time? Let's talk about the other details. Like, um . . . when are you thinking about getting married? Spring? Summer?"

The room remained silent. It was going to be a long afternoon.

———⟶•⟵———

Dr. Zacher walked through Stanton Park with a stubborn cough. He ignored the flood of memories of his daily trips to this park to meet Abrianna for their daily lunches. He'd monitor her progress and test her abilities without her knowledge. He'd long suppressed any guilt for his part of the Avery experiments that had altered Abrianna's life. He was a man of science and believed in the greater good—even if it cost his life.

When he approached his regular bench, Jayson Brigham was already there. Zacher read Brigham like a professional poker player. He was nervous.

Zacher grunted as he sat next to the photographer. "Care to tell me why I'm out here?"

Jayson held up his camera and took random pictures of the park. "We have to let her go."

Zacher almost laughed out loud. "Do we now?"

"It's too much heat around her disappearance. First, it was the police, then it's the FBI and Parker all over the news, and now the president and Hardy dragging T4S in by name." He took a few more pictures.

"And?" Zacher tested.

"And?" Brigham lowered his camera and cut a side look at the doctor. "People are sniffing around my job."

Zacher chuckled. "I hope so. You do work at a newspaper—unless you guys really do sit up there and make up stories."

"You know what I mean," Jayson mumbled before snapping away.

Zacher gave the photographer a long look. "Who is coming around, Jay?"

Brigham shook his head. "This was never supposed to blow back on me, man."

"Give me a name," Zacher said. "I'll look into it."

Brigham hesitated.

Zacher changed tactics. "Jay, look at me." Brigham lowered the camera and then met Zacher's gaze. "Haven't I *always* looked out for you? If you're feeling some heat, tell me who it's from?"

"Can't you let her go?"

"No." *Even if we still had her.* "That was never part of the plan."

Jayson's eyes glazed over. "Tomi was a nice person. I liked her."

"Don't make this personal. You knew the gig when you signed up for it."

Brigham lowered his gaze back to the camera. "Is she dead?"

"No."

"Not that you would tell me, huh?"

Zacher smiled and placed a hand on his shoulder. "Nothing is going to blow back on you. Give me a name, and I will take care of it. Trust me." He squeezed his shoulder. "Give. Me. A. Name."

Brigham drew a deep breath. "Castillo."

Zacher removed his hand. "The detective?"

"Tomi told Castillo everything before we grabbed her. You and T4S. Castillo said Tomi is the one who connected the dots for Parker, too. Plus, Castillo knows that I was there that night. She has video."

"Video?"

"Somebody in the neighborhood must have filmed it, and she got a hold of it. You can't make out any faces, but she was able to make out my vintage leather jacket and . . ."

"And?"

"I lost a button at the crime scene, and she found it."

Zacher processed the information. "Anything else?"

Brigham shook his head. "Castillo is like a dog with a bone. She doesn't believe in letting anything go."

Zacher patted Brigham's back and stood. "Leave everything to me."

37

Castillo woke late morning to the smell of blueberries, and had she not been hung over, she would have enjoyed it. Instead, she bolted from the bed and made a beeline to the bathroom. She prayed and hugged the toilet bowl while she emptied her stomach of alcohol and beer nuts. Once her stomach was emptied, a part of her soul went into the bowl as well. Once she had nothing else to give, Castillo climbed up from the floor and made her way over to the shower. After she cranked the hot water as high as she could stand it, she scrubbed herself clean. When she walked the staircase in one of Dennis's large T-shirts, she noticed a wheelchair mobility unit had been installed. Clearly, Denise was on top of everything.

Castillo steeled herself as she followed the scent of blueberries to the kitchen. To her surprise, Dennis was the only person at the kitchen table, drowning blueberry pancakes in maple syrup.

"Hungry?" he asked.

Castillo looked around. "Where's Denise?"

"Home would be my guess." He glanced up. "The coffee should be ready."

She turned toward the kitchen counter and smiled at the full coffeepot. "You know me so well."

"Well, I didn't know that you'd creep in here in the middle of the night—drunk."

Castillo winced as she poured coffee into her favorite mug. "I had a bit of a rough night."

"Problems with the case?"

"You can say that." She returned to the table. "T4S has more chess pieces on the case than I originally thought." Castillo shook her head. "This case is uniquely designed to drive me crazy."

Dennis chuckled.

She smiled, drinking him in. "You look good."

"I feel good. I'm still getting used to the wheelchair and figuring out my limitations."

"And you sent Denise home?"

He sighed. "Denise meant well . . . but she rode the hell out of my last nerve."

Castillo smirked.

"She never should have told you to stay away." Dennis reached across the table and covered Castillo's hand. "I'm glad you came last night—even if it was just to pass out next to me."

Castillo lowered her wall. "I missed you. Sue me."

"If that's true, then come over here and give me a kiss."

Castillo exchanged her chair for Dennis's lap, where she wrapped her arms around his neck and kissed him thoroughly. "You taste yummy."

"There's more where that came from."

"Oh?"

"Yeah, I prepared you a short stack, too."

She squeezed his neck. "Pancakes. You're talking about pancakes? Well, I oughta . . ."

They laughed . . . and for a few seconds, it felt like old times.

"So, tell me about your case," Dennis asked. "Maybe I can help."

Castillo sighed before returning to her chair and coffee and then laid out everything they'd learned about the case so far.

"That's fucked up."

"Oh? Did I bury the lead?"

Dennis glanced over Castillo's shoulder and frowned.

"What? What is it?"

"What's the photographer's name again?"

"Jayson Brigham. Why?"

"Because he's on the news right now." Dennis reached for the remote in the center of the table and unmuted the television.

Castillo swiveled around in her chair toward the eight-inch TV sitting on the kitchen counter. The local news had a picture of Jayson Brigham in the right-hand corner.

"Washington Post photographer Jayson Brigham was found this morning in his Georgetown apartment, and was pronounced dead at the scene."

Castillo plunked down her coffee. "Goddamn it."

———————

Shawn and Draya talked Abrianna into wedding dress shopping and then immediately pressed her about having either a fall or winter wedding instead of putting it off until next year.

"Why the rush?" Abrianna asked.

Her friends deflected. "Have you thought about having two separate ceremonies?" Draya asked.

"What?"

"It's not like you can't afford it," Shawn added.

"Plus, I've heard of a couple of celebrities who have done it."

"Like who?"

"Um, Kid Rock and Pamela Anderson—and, oh, Katie Perry and Russell Brand."

Draya dropped a hand onto her hip. "Just because white people do some crazy shit doesn't mean we should do it, too."

Abrianna chuckled.

"Besides, both of those couples are no longer together."

"Their status isn't the point," Shawn countered. "The point is that it could be done, especially when we're talking about mixing two different cultures. You can have one for his family and then one that's important to you."

Abrianna stopped drinking her champagne in mid-sip. "You may have a point."

Shawn puffed out his chest. "Of course I do."

Draya rolled her eyes. "Nice going, Bree. Now, his head is going to get bigger."

"Jealous?" Shawn asked, grinning.

"In your dreams."

Two sales ladies returned to their room, pushing a rack of dresses they'd selected for Bree.

"Oh. Goody." Draya hopped up from her chair and made it over to the dresses before Abrianna.

"This is so exciting." She perused the racks. "Have you decided on your wedding colors? Do you and Kadir have a song?"

"What?"

"What about your maid of honor?" Draya shot a look to Shawn. "Have you decided on who that's going to be yet?"

Abrianna stopped rummaging through the rack as the energy in the room changed. "I, uh . . ."

Her gaze darted between her friends.

"Come on, out with it." Tivonté entered the room late. "And speak up."

Shawn leaned against his cane. "I want to go on record and state that Abrianna has known *me* longer."

Draya turned with her hands on her hips. "I'd like to remind you guys that the term is maid of honor for a reason. Tacos before sausages."

Abrianna laughed as she held up her hands. "Is that a real saying?"

Draya shrugged. "Maybe."

"C'mon, guys, no fighting. This is supposed to be a fun outing."

"We are having fun." Shawn settled a hand on his hip. "Now, who's it going to be, bitch?"

"I—I don't know." She laughed. "I haven't thought about it."

"Uh-huh." They echoed each other.

"I haven't," she insisted. "But whoever it is, it won't mean that I love any of you any less."

Shawn frowned. "Why are you looking at me like that? Are you tryna say I'm not getting the gig?"

"What? No."

Draya challenged. "So, you are picking him over me?"

"I—I didn't say anything."

Tivonté stepped in. "All right. That's enough. Let's cut her a break. She looks like she's about to have a heart attack." He chuckled. "Let's find a dress to match that rock on your finger. Bitches are going to see that rock from space."

The gang lightened up as the sales ladies returned with another tray of champagne.

For the next two hours, the friends sat back and selected dresses for Abrianna to wear. In the end, she felt giddy when she handed over the credit card and signed her name on the receipt. "The dress should be back from the seamstress in eight weeks."

Shawn elbowed her. "I see that smile."

"What?"

"Tivonté came up behind her and sniffed her hair. "Y'all smell that?"

"What? Smell what?"

Draya agreed. "I smelled it the minute she showed up."

Concerned, Abrianna smelled herself. "Do I stink?"

"Nah." Draya laughed. "You smell like new money. Let me hold fifty dollars." She held out her hand.

"Ha. Ha." Abrianna slapped her hand away. "Funny."

They left the shop laughing. It was a good day.

In the parking deck, Tivonté kissed Abrianna and headed back to his restaurant.

Abrianna, Shawn, and Draya climbed into Shawn's new car.

"Exactly how much am I paying you to be my assistant?" Abrianna asked.

Shawn flashed a smile. "We're still negotiating."

Abrianna cut Draya a look, but her girl shrugged. "Tacos before sausages, that's all I'm saying."

"Drive."

"You got it, boss." Shawn started the car. During the ride back home, they floated ideas back and forth about the wedding as they passed by Bezoria's.

"Hey, are you guys hungry?" Abrianna asked.

Castillo proved her point. The best way inside of T4S was through the front door. After more than two dozens calls, Ned scheduled her for an appointment. Despite her thorough investigation, she still didn't know what to expect. Getting onto the property was like entering a military base. Two forms of ID, her name had to be on three different lists, and a call to Dr. Zacher's assistant was placed at each checkpoint as she progressed through the building. Hell, the building itself was gigantic—at least fifteen stories high and with two wings connected to two main buildings, forming an open-air, trapezoidal courtyard. The concrete-and-stone building wasn't fancy; in fact, it looked more like a federal building than a billionaire's expensive playground. Then again, it seemed like every American billionaire was dead-set on taking over the world in one form or another these days.

"Ms. Castillo," Ned greeted, standing from his desk and offering his hand. "You're right on time. Dr. Zacher is expecting you."

"Ned, I presume?"

"Yes, ma'am." They shook hands.

"It's nice to finally place a face with a name," she joked.

"Absolutely." He picked up the phone and hit one button. "Dr. Zacher, Ms. Castillo is here to see you."

"Send her in."

"Yes, sir." He disconnected the call and then nodded toward a large door. "You may go in."

"Thank you." Castillo headed toward the door.

"Oh." Ned stopped her. "Could I get you some coffee, tea, or bottled water?"

"No. I'm good." She flashed him a smile and then pushed through the door.

Dr. Zacher's voice boomed across the room. "Ms. Castillo, please come in. Have a seat."

"Thank you for seeing me." Castillo offered her hand. "I know that you're a busy man."

"The pleasure is all mine." They shook hands. "Please, sit."

Castillo took a seat and studied the doctor.

"Is something wrong?" he asked.

"No. It's just . . . you look so young."

Dr. Z smiled. "Aw. Someone told you that flattery will get you everywhere with me."

"Actually, you're quite an enigma, doc." Castillo took out her phone. "Do you mind if I record our conversation?"

He tensed. "As a matter of fact, I do."

"Ah." She tucked the phone back in her pocket, but not before she hit record. She reached into the other side of her jacket and withdrew a notepad. "I guess we'll have to do this the old-fashioned way."

"Thank you." Dr. Z leaned back in his chair and steepled his fingers. "Now, how can I help you, Ms. Castillo?"

"I'm sure that your assistant told you that I'm investigating the disappearance of Tomi Lehane."

"I believe the whole country is. The entire company has been inundated with calls from the crazies to the insane. Everyone has a conspiracy theory."

Castillo nodded. "Well, Ms. Lehane was a public figure. And

I'm sure it doesn't help that Abrianna Parker has dragged your name into the mix."

A muscle twitched along the doctor's temple. "Yeah. That is most unfortunate."

She waited to see if he would say anything else. When he didn't, she continued. "I've seen your interviews on cable news, countering Ms. Parker's claims."

Zacher hitched up a half smile. "Yes. As you said, Ms. Parker dragged me into this mess. I can't let her destroy my good name as well as let what we really do here be destroyed by a . . . *troubled* woman."

"Troubled?"

"From what I've read in the paper, I believe it's a fair summation."

"And you've never met Abrianna Parker?"

"If you've been watching my interviews, you already know the answer to that."

"I like to hear things straight from the horse's mouth," Castillo volleyed, leveling him with a hard stare. When he stared back, she thought of nothing else but her lying on a beach under blue skies and in front of even bluer waters to prevent him from reading her thoughts.

Zacher lifted the other half of his smile. "I do not personally know Abrianna Parker. No."

"And Lehane?"

"Never met her, either."

Liar. Castillo groaned when the thought slipped through her Bahamas dream vacation.

Zacher continued smiling. "Now, if that's all . . ."

"That's *not* all," Castillo said. "Tell me about Shalisa Young." He froze.

"Or are you going to tell me that you never met her, either?"

"Shalisa Young," he repeated, stalling for time.

"You used to visit her quite often over at St. Elizabeth Hospital even though you weren't listed as her physician—or even a staff member at the facility. Care to tell me why that is?"

Zacher stood. "That will be all for today."

Castillo blinked. "But I have more questions."

"I'm sorry I couldn't help, but I have other things to do—more *important* things to do."

"I see." She flipped her notepad closed and stood as well. "I leave you to it, then. Thank you for your time." *Asshole. I'm going to take you down.*

His smiled dropped.

"Have a good day," Castillo added with a wink. "I'll see you around." She walked out of the office and cast a long look over at Ned Cox. "Have a good day."

⇒•⇐

Entering Bezoria's was like walking into Daishan's kitchen. The rich aromas wafting out of the kitchen made Shawn's and Draya's stomachs growl loudly enough for Abrianna to hear.

"Oh, this is a nice little spot," Draya praised, looking around as they took their seats. "Have you guys eaten here before?"

"First time." Shawn turned to Abrianna. "I'd figured you were getting your fill of Middle Eastern food with Kadir's mom at the crib."

Abrianna kept twisting her neck around the restaurant.

Shawn elbowed Abrianna.

"Huh? What?"

He frowned. "Are you looking for someone?"

"Nah. I'm just checking the place out." She flashed them a smile. "It's nice."

Draya and Shawn frowned at her.

"This is your first time here, too?"

"Yeah, I just figured we'd try something new." Abrianna swiveled her neck again.

"Uh-huh." Shawn shot Draya a look. "Are you buying this?"

"Not at all."

Shawn leaned over the table. "You mind telling us why we're here and why you're rubber-necking all over the place?"

"Huh?"

Shawn cocked his head. "You have got to be the worst actress I've ever seen."

Abrianna sucked in a breath as the creepy guy she'd seen huddled up with Baasim headed their way.

Draya and Shawn jumped. "What is it?"

"Shh. Shh. Act normal." Abrianna picked up her dinner menu and pretended to read.

Draya and Shawn followed suit.

"Good evening. Welcome to Bezoria's. I am Farooq. I will be your waiter this evening."

"Farooq," Abrianna repeated. "Nice name."

Farooq's smile expanded, but it didn't reach his eyes. "Thank you. Can I start you off with something to drink?"

"Absolutely," Shawn said. "And whatever it is, make it a double."

"We'll all have some iced tea," Draya contradicted.

Farooq nodded and walked away.

Abrianna's gaze tracked him back to the kitchen. "That's him."

"That's who?" Shawn and Draya asked simultaneously.

Abrianna leaned over the table. "That's the guy I saw with Baasim the other day."

Shawn groaned. "Sweet baby Jesus, not this again."

Draya remained lost. "What am I missing?"

Shawn leaned back and crossed his arms. "Our girl thinks her future brother-in-law is a secret terrorist."

"A terrorist," Draya gasped.

Abrianna slapped a hand across Draya's mouth. "Shh." She glanced around. "You want someone to overhear you?"

Draya removed Abrianna's hand and inched closer. "Are you shitting me? You think Kadir's twin brother is a—"

Abrianna's hand returned to Draya's mouth. "I never said that." She cut a sharp look to Shawn.

He shrugged. "Don't give me that look. You were thinking it."

Was she? "All I know is that something fishy is going on, and I'd like to get to the bottom of it." She looked up and saw Farooq. "Shh. Here he comes again."

Farooq arrived with another fake smile. "Here you go. Three iced teas. Are you guys ready to order?"

"Um . . ." Abrianna picked up her menu again.

"What do you recommend?" Shawn asked. "It's our first time here."

"Ah. First-timers." A real smile finally emerged. "You're in luck. My uncle is in the kitchen today, and he makes a delicious fall-off-the-bone roasted lamb haneeth." He kissed his fingers. "Perfection."

"Your uncle?" Abrianna asked. "So, this is a family restaurant?"

"Yep. Has been for almost forty years."

"Yeah?" Draya leaned forward. "That means you grew up in D.C.—and probably know a lot of the locals?"

Farooq frowned. "Yeah. So?"

Shawn took over. "You wouldn't happen to know the Kahlifas, would you?"

Abrianna kicked him under the table.

"Ow."

Farooq stiffened while his smile flat-lined. "Why do you ask?"

Now, on the spot, Abrianna flashed her ring. "Kadir Kahlifa is my fiancé. I, um, just haven't met too many of his friends."

Farooq lit up. "I thought you looked familiar." He folded his arms in front of him. "You're Abrianna Parker. I've seen you on the news."

Shawn sat up with a smug look.

Now, Abrianna's smile stiffened. "Well, it has been an interesting year."

"You don't say. And, yes. I do know your fiancé—and his entire family. We went to school together. It was good to see him again the other night."

"The other night?" Abrianna frowned. "You saw Kadir recently?"

Farooq froze. "Um, briefly." He cleared his throat. "Have you decided what you'd like?"

The table went quiet.

"Would you like a few more minutes?"

"You know what? I will try that lamb haneeth." Shawn handed over his menu.

"Make that two," Draya said.

"I'll just have the fahsa," Abrianna decided.

"Very good." Farooq's fake smile returned before he waltzed off.

Shawn tossed up his hands. "See? They are old friends. They grew up together. There's nothing fishy about a man returning to his hometown and linking up with his old friends. Hell, he's even cool with Kadir. Are you satisfied now?"

Abrianna's gaze once again tracked Farooq across the restaurant while the bad feeling in her gut grew. "Not in the slightest."

38

Abrianna Parker arrived at the White House—alone. She and Shawn had taken special care in picking out an appropriate outfit to wear to the White House: a navy skirt and jacket and white blouse. Her dark hair was brushed back into a ponytail, and she wore close to no makeup. She wanted to look conservative and humbled by the invitation.

After being rushed through security and paraded before the cameras, Abrianna felt like a puppet on display, but it was worth it to secure Kadir's pardon.

"Ms. Parker, it's a pleasure to finally meet you." Kate stretched out her hand as she approached.

Abrianna hesitated but accepted the president's hand in a firm handshake. President Kate Washington was prettier in person than on camera—taller, too, and with a perfect Colgate smile. "I assure you the pleasure is all mine, Madam President."

Washington glanced at her team. "Give us a few minutes, won't you?"

"Yes, Madam President." A man directed everyone else out of the room.

A bubble of anxiety rose up in the center of Abrianna's chest. She glanced around and took in the whole Oval Office. It was much smaller than she had thought.

"Please, won't you have a seat?" The president gestured to a cream-colored couch.

Abrianna hesitated again, but waltzed over and sat down.

"I'm sorry your fiancé couldn't make it. I had hoped both of you would join me here today."

"Yes, well. Kadir, um, doesn't care for too much attention," Abrianna lied.

"You mean, he doesn't care too much for *me*," the president corrected.

Abrianna clamped her mouth shut.

"We had an interesting conversation on the phone." The smile melted off of Washington's face. "I know he blames me for his father's death in Sana'a. I understand. As president, I'm forced to make a lot of tough calls. The buck stops with me, but I'm terribly sorry for your fiancé's loss. My thoughts and prayers are with him."

"I'm sure he appreciates that."

Kate pulled a deep breath but kept her perfect smile leveled at the right angle. "You'll be happy to know I'm still issuing him a full pardon today. The country appreciates what you and Mr. Kahlifa have done for the country. It may be unprecedented for a president's successor to award the Presidential Citizen's Medal to someone who aided in bringing the previous administration's corruption to light—but it's the right thing to do."

Abrianna buttoned her lips to prevent herself from reminding President Washington that she was a part of the previous administration, too.

Washington continued, "I want the American people to know that no man is above the law and that everyday citizens can make a difference."

Even though Walker had nothing to do with Reynolds's death.

Abrianna blinked at the president's voice inside of her head. "I'm sorry. What?"

The president leaned against her desk. "I was saying how

everyday citizens could make a difference in our nation. You, Mr. Kahlifa, and Tomi Lehane have done just that."

By making me president.

"Anyway, I'm more interested to hear about your experience with T4S," the president segued. "I caught a clip of your interview and saw reports of what happened the other day. Your story has captured my full attention. I'd like to hear the story straight from you about what happened seven years ago."

Abrianna blinked. A one-on-one debriefing with the president? She hadn't expected that. She waited to see if she would hear the president's thoughts again, but there was nothing. Washington appeared genuinely interested in what she had to say.

Kate was losing her one-woman audience and redoubled her efforts to win Abrianna over. "I remember the Avery case—sort of. I had my office pull old clippings of news reports. After reading them, I still can't imagine what kind of nightmare that must have been to live through. Until your interview, I don't believe anyone had linked Dr. Avery's serial killings to T4S before."

"Tomi Lehane pieced it all together," Abrianna admitted. "She'd found an article with Dr. Zacher's picture and she, being the reporter she is, did some digging and connected the dots. When she brought me the information, I recognized Dr. Zacher immediately."

The president shook her head. "Amazing."

"More like it was fucked up. Pardon my French."

"You're right. It was pretty fucked up." Washington chuckled. "I don't mean to be insensitive, but . . . what can you tell me about these experiments? What were they testing on you?"

Abrianna stiffened. "I'm not sure. Different poisons, serums— that's really a question for T4S, don't you think?"

"Poison?"

"Avery killed nearly every girl he dragged down in that basement."

"Except for three."

"That's right."

"And you don't have any idea what they were trying to achieve?"

Abrianna hesitated again. "I had no idea *at the time.*"

"At the time?" Washington questioned. "What about now? What is your theory?"

Abrianna met the president's gaze. "What do you think a private paramilitary conglomerate who is in a global race for super soldiers wants?"

Washington chuckled. "Super soldiers."

"You think it's funny?"

"Hardly. You wouldn't believe half the things I hear about while sitting in this office: super soldiers, space force, and life on other planets. I've heard it all." Washington stared at Abrianna for a long time before announcing, "I believe you."

"You do?"

"Yes. My administration is ready to launch a full investigation into your allegations."

"You will?"

"Absolutely. The American people deserve to know the truth about what's happening at T4S. I promise I *will* get to the bottom of it."

⟶⊶◈⊷⟵

Kadir, Castillo, Ghost, and Julian hung back as they followed Ned Cox's blue Tesla from T4S to his one-bedroom apartment in the heart of Washington, D.C. They'd mulled several options on how to extract Dr. Zacher's assistant and decided the best and most effective place to do it was the young man's home.

"Fear works best when you shatter your target's perceived security," Ghost told her.

She agreed.

Kadir was skittish about the plan.

"It's no different from how you got the confession from Chief Justice Sanders," Castillo told him.

"Yeah, and that was her last night," Kadir reminded them.

"Nobody is dying tonight." She patted him on the shoulder. "Time is of the essence, right?"

He nodded. "Yeah, I get it."

Ned turned into his parking deck while Castillo's team pulled around the apartment building. Julian remained behind the wheel as the rest of them hopped out of the van. They entered the building through the service elevators and separated.

Castillo went straight to the roof while Ghost and Kadir extracted Ned from the comfort of his home. When they joined her on the roof, Ned was out cold, blindfolded, and slung over Ghost's shoulders like a sack of potatoes.

"Dude put up a fight." Ghost grinned. "It was cute."

Castillo smiled and placed the voice modulator device over her mouth. "Wake him up."

"With pleasure." He winked.

Kadir helped place Ned on his feet and smacked him awake.

"Wha . . . what?" Ned's head swiveled around. "Where am I?" He attempted to jerk his hands free, but they were tied securely behind his back. "What's going on? What's happening?"

"Calm down, Mr. Cox," Castillo's robotic voice instructed, but it had the opposite effect.

"I don't have any money. Take what you want. I won't call the police. I promise. I didn't see you guys. I couldn't describe you if I tried."

"Ned—"

"Oh, Jesus. I don't want to die."

Ghost looked down. "Is this li'l fucker peeing?"

"I'm sorry," Ned cried.

Kadir shook his head while Castillo sighed and rolled her eyes.

"Mr. Cox, I'm going to need you to calm down, so we can talk."

Ghost whacked Ned on the back of the head. "Breathe, asshole."

Ned gasped from shock. The lungful of air did settle him.

"Are you all right now?" Castillo asked. Her impatience climbed.

Ned nodded, but he still shook like the last fall leaf on the first day of winter.

"I'm going to ask you this one time"—Castillo stepped forward—"so make sure you listen real good, okay?"

"Okay," Ned agreed shakily.

"Where is Tomi Lehane?"

"Whut?" Confusion twisted Ned's face.

Ghost hauled Ned over to the ledge, and he and Kadir held him over by his feet.

Ned screamed, but the busy nightlife below absorbed the sound. "Okay, okay, okay. Please, don't drop me."

"We made it clear we were only asking one time, li'l man." Castillo grinned.

"All right. All right. I'll tell you whatever you want, just don't kill me."

"Let him up," Castillo ordered.

Kadir and Ghost obliged.

The second Ned's feet touched the roof, his knees folded, and he doubled over as if in prayer.

"You're wasting my time, Mr. Cox."

"I don't know where she is."

"Lies."

Kadir and Ghost each grabbed an arm and lifted Ned back to his feet.

"I'm not lying. It's the truth! I swear!"

"Nice try, Mr. Cox," Kadir growled. "We know a professional team extracted her from her home. We have it on tape. We know you work for those people." They pulled Ned back to the ledge.

"Wait. Wait. I'm not lying. I swear. They took her!"

"Stop," Castillo ordered the guys. "*Who* took her?"

Ned panted to catch his breath. "You're right. T4S did take

Lehane from her home, but we were hit—we don't know by who. They're working to find out, but they came in and took the reporter and nothing else. I swear. It's the truth."

The team all shared a look.

"Please don't kill me. Please." Ned dropped to his knees again and prayed.

Castillo had had enough. "Cut him loose." She turned and walked away.

Minutes later, Julian picked up the team after having circled around the place for the past half hour. "Anything?"

Kadir nodded. "Yeah. We're fucked."

"I need a drink," Castillo said.

Kadir agreed.

⸻✦⸻

"One of the great privileges of being president is being able to recognize and honor some of our finest Americans. That's what I'm doing today by awarding the Presidential Citizen's Medal to Abrianna Parker . . ."

Kadir shook his head while he watched Abrianna stand next to President Kate Washington while she showered his fiancée with praise. He should have been more forceful in expressing how much he didn't want her to go to the White House, but with her abilities, surely she knew.

He drained his beer and signaled for the bartender to bring him another one.

"Is everything all right with you two?" Castillo nodded toward the television.

"Yeah, we're all right," Kadir mumbled into his empty beer bottle.

"Have you guys settled on a date yet?"

He shrugged. "Nah, Bree and my mom are hashing it out. Spring, I think, though." His new bottle arrived. "Thanks."

"Spring is nice." Castillo swung her gaze back to the television.

"Summer is a runner-up. If I can get Bree and my family on the same page."

"Ah, I see."

"Do you?"

"Unfortunately. Melding families together takes a delicate touch. At least that's what I've heard."

Kadir shook his head. "Bree has it in her head my family has it in for her—and she and Baasim mix together about as well as oil and water. Then again, my brother is kind of an acquired taste."

"At least she got you a pardon out of the deal. No more pissing in plastic cups."

Kadir grunted.

"You didn't want her to go?"

"No, I didn't," he admitted before taking a deep chug. "I should've known better than to expect her to listen. Bree does what she wants when she wants."

"I thought that was what you liked about her?"

One side of his lips hitched upward. "It can also be adorable at times."

"Just not right now?"

"Exactly."

They sat mute at the bar for another couple of swigs before Castillo muttered, "Relationships are hard. Trust me."

Kadir cocked his head toward her. "Are things all right with you and Dennis?"

"Peachy keen." She took another swallow.

"Wow." He chuckled. "I thought you'd be a better liar."

She shrugged. "I must be out of practice."

"The rehab not going so well?"

"He doesn't talk about it much."

"How do you feel about his condition?"

Castillo thought it over for a moment. "I feel . . . like if I'd gotten there a minute sooner, he wouldn't be in this condition."

"You blame yourself. That's what you're telling me?"

"Nah, I just wish things would have turned out differently."

"So you could've prevented Dennis from being shot."

Castillo sighed. "Okay. Maybe I blame myself *a little*. It doesn't change anything."

"Did he tell you this, or did the self-righteous sister?"

"The sister, but—"

"Let me stop you there." Kadir held up his hand. "We haven't known each other a long time, but you don't strike me as a person who takes no for an answer. You didn't listen when you were looking for Avery's victims. You didn't listen when Bree was framed for murder. I don't know why you're listening now— unless you agree with her?"

Castillo stopped drinking. "Damn." She looked at him. "You're pretty good at this."

Kadir glanced up at the television as CNN looped Bree and the president's story again. "Now, if I could just fix my life."

Baasim strolled up next to his brother. "Nice little bar you found here, bro."

"Glad you could make it." Kadir beamed as he stood from his chair. "I'd like to introduce you to my boss, Gizella Castillo. Gizella, this is my twin brother, Baasim."

"Nice to meet you."

"Same here."

While they shook hands, Castillo compared the brothers. Baasim had more hair, both on his head and on his face. Other than that, the men were identical.

"I got the next round." Baasim saddled onto a stool.

"You'll have to enjoy it without me." Castillo stood from her stool and tossed money down to cover her tab. "I'm going to go have a long talk with my boyfriend."

Kadir smiled. "It's about time. Good luck."

She slapped a hand on Kadir's shoulder. "Maybe you should have your own talk? See you in the morning."

Kadir nodded. "Night."

"It was nice meeting you, Baasim."

"Likewise." Baasim watched Castillo gather her things and head out of the bar before he turned to Kadir. "*She's* your boss? Nice." He signaled to the bartender. "Bree is more trusting than I thought."

"It's not like that," Kadir said.

Baasim smirked. "If you say so." He ordered a beer.

"So, what kept you?"

"I have a job."

"What? That fast?"

"Saoud got me one." Baasim grinned. "It pays to network."

"Yeah? Who are you working for?"

"It's a warehouse gig. It's not much, but it's a paycheck. So you won't have to worry about me."

"Are you short on cash?"

Baasim side-eyed him. "I'm not your charity case. I'm not going to freeload off of you and your *billionaire* girlfriend for too long."

"I didn't say—"

"I'm fine. I pull my own weight. You know that."

Kadir held up his hands. "My bad. I was only trying to help."

"Well, don't. I got this." He took a swig of his beer and glanced up as Bree and the president's story looped again on the channel. Baasim shook his head but said nothing.

"I'll have another talk with her." Kadir guessed what his brother was thinking.

"Why? What's done is done now. What's one more shame to the family name?"

"Shame?"

"You know what I mean."

"Pretend I don't." Kadir twisted around on his stool to stare at him. "What do you mean by shame?"

Baasim smirked. "For starters, she's not Muslim. Second, she has a hell of a lot of baggage. And third . . ." He shrugged.

"I swear if you say because she's black, I'm taking your head off."

Baasim laughed. "I'm an asshole, Kadir, not a racist. As my twin, you'd think you'd know that."

"No harm in double-checking." Kadir twisted back toward his drink. "What's the third thing?"

"She's officially one of *them*."

"Them?"

Baasim nodded. "A part of the one percent. And if you marry her, you'll be part of the problem, too."

"Oh, you're a classist, not a racist."

"The gap between the haves and the have-nots is expanding around the world. Democracies, even the fake ones, are being overturned for dictatorships for a reason. The root of the chaos here and every damn where else is greed: Saudi Arabia's greed, Iran's greed, and the biggest offender, America's greed."

Kadir shook his head. "Abrianna isn't like that. You don't know her."

"I know enough."

"So you're not going to give her a chance?"

Baasim sighed and chugged his beer.

Kadir hung his head. "Look, I know we have had our differences in the past, especially when it comes to women."

"You mean when it came to Malala," Baasim corrected. "The girl you stole from me."

"Are we going to fight about this *again?*"

"Nope. I want you to keep the facts straight."

"Fine. The past is the past, and I can't change it. But Abrianna is my future, and you're my brother."

"And if I liked her, Mom would go easier on her," Baasim deduced.

Kadir buttoned his lip and counted to ten.

Baasim laughed. "You were always the calculating one."

39

Castillo changed her mind. She was too restless to call it a night. Tomi was still out there somewhere with God knows who doing God knows what to her—and, once again, Castillo felt helpless to do anything to stop whatever the fuck was going on. There were more players on the board—and she had no idea who *they* were. It could be anyone.

She drew in a deep breath and reexamined what she knew. Maybe she was asking herself the wrong question. She'd been too focused on who instead of why. Why would someone want Tomi—and Abrianna? *Because they are the last two living survivors of Craig Avery and Dr. Charles Zacher's plan to create super soldiers.* Surely, they weren't the only organization interested in those experiments.

Castillo's heavy foot eased off the accelerator as puzzle pieces snapped together inside of her head.

Castillo grabbed her cell phone from her car's center console and dialed Kadir. However, her call went straight to voice mail.

"Shit." Castillo waited through the voice mail instructions to leave a message when blue lights flashed in her rearview mirror. "Fuck." She checked her speedometer but couldn't remember what the speed limit was in the area. "Shit." She pulled over to the other side of the road. While she reached into the glove compartment for her insurance card, the cop spoke over his speaker. "Keep your hands on the steering wheel."

Great. I'm about to get one of those cops. Castillo rolled her eyes while the cop climbed out of his patrol car. Castillo watched with waning patience as the officer approached her vehicle with a cowboy swagger and his hand already on his weapon.

Once he made it to her window, she powered it down and forced on a fake smile. "Is there a problem, officer?"

"Driver's license and insurance."

Since she already had it in her hand, Castillo handed it over.

The cop removed his hand from his weapon and took the cards. He flashed his flashlight directly into Castillo's face. "Are you Gizella Castillo?"

"I am."

"As in the former lieutenant of the MPDC?"

"The one and only." She smiled. "Um, do you mind lowering that light? It's a bit bright."

"Sorry about this, lieutenant." The cop dropped her credentials and whipped out his weapon. "It's not personal."

Castillo's eyes widened. "What the fuck?"

"I'm following orders." The cop fired.

Castillo jumped as hot lead slammed into her body. The second bullet missed her by a mile but shattered the passenger-side window. Despite her ears ringing, Castillo heard a loud crack. She glanced up, shaking, only to see the cop's head twisted at an odd angle before he dropped like a stone beside her car.

What the fuck?

She attempted to move, but the pain ricocheted throughout her body and stole what little breath she had left. *Calm down. Breathe.*

Breathing hurt, and it was cold—freezing. *Shit. I'm dying.* Castillo wrapped her head around the notion, when she heard a set of boots rush toward her car. She slumped back against the headrest as darkness encroached on her vision.

Calm down. Breathe.

The boots drew closer. Castillo remained still.

"Is she still alive?" a voice asked.

A cold hand reached into the car and pressed against Castillo's neck. "Her pulse is low."

In Castillo's world, what wasn't dark went blurry. She couldn't tell who her rescuers were—but she did see a wisp of blond hair.

Abrianna paced the floor waiting for Kadir to return home. Him not returning any of her phone calls told her how pissed he must be. Their failure to communicate was another sign they were moving too fast toward the altar. At long last, Abrianna heard a key rattle in the door. She rushed to the sofa, sat, and looked casual.

When Kadir and Baasim strolled through the door together, her hope for at least a civil conversation nosedived.

"You waited up," Kadir said.

"I was worried." She folded her arms. "You didn't return any of my phone calls."

"What, you and the president weren't chumming it up over at the White House?" Baasim asked.

Kadir rolled his head toward his brother. "Good night, Baasim."

"Sure thing." Baasim smirked. "Night, Bree."

Abrianna glowered as she watched her future brother-in-law head off toward the guest bedroom. When she and Kadir were alone, she crossed her arms and leaned back on the sofa.

Kadir removed his jacket. "I already know what you're going to say; let's talk about it in the morning."

"No." She shook her head. "We'll talk about it now. Why didn't you return any of my messages?"

Kadir sighed and headed toward the bedroom.

Abrianna bolted to her feet. "Don't make me stop you."

Kadir stopped. "You would do that, too. Wouldn't you? After I asked you to never use your powers on me?"

"Why not? You never do what I ask."

He laughed. "We're keeping score? How about when I asked you *not* to go to the White House to be the president's patsy?"

"You did *not* ask me not to go. You said *you* weren't going. *Big difference.*"

"You were supposed to back me on this. That woman is responsible for my father's death."

"And she may have been responsible for Tomi's disappearance, too. Remember her? You're supposed to be looking for her. At least, that's the excuse you keep giving me to why you're out at all hours of the night with Castillo."

"What? We've been staking out Ned Cox's place."

"That's right. You guys are so focused on T4S, you're not chasing down any other leads."

"Other leads? You said T4S was behind Tomi's disappearance on national television."

"That doesn't mean we should close ourselves off to other possibilities."

Kadir frowned and cocked his head. "What are you talking about?"

Abrianna pulled a breath and sat back down. "At the White House, there were a couple of times when I heard the president's thoughts."

Kadir sighed. "You mean you were using again."

"Can we stay on topic?" she asked.

"Fine." He tossed up his hands. "Tell me, what did you hear lurking around the president's head?"

"I don't think President Walker killed the former house speaker, Kenneth Reynolds."

"What?"

"She said, and I quote, *Daniel had nothing to do with Reynolds's death.*"

"That doesn't make sense. Sanders confessed that her plan went all the way to the White House."

"She didn't specifically name President Walker, did she?"

Kadir laughed. "What? Now you're siding with the conspiracy theorists on talk radio?"

"I'm telling you what I heard her say. Are you saying you don't believe me?"

Their gazes crashed before Kadir sighed. "Of course I believe you. But damn it, Bree . . . I expected you to have my back on this. I don't give a damn about a pardon. I don't give a damn about the political games the people in this town love to play with each other. I do care about finding Tomi. She had our backs when the whole world was after us."

"And she wrote a hit piece that made my adoptive mother kill herself."

"You mean the mother you turned your back on?"

Abrianna jerked.

Kadir held his hands up. "Let's keep everything one hundred if we're going to have this conversation. You're not mad at Tomi for writing that article. You're mad at yourself for not forgiving your mother when you had the chance. When she was standing in front of you, begging for forgiveness."

Tears sprang into Abrianna's eyes. "That's not fair."

"Neither is blaming Tomi for your mistakes or regrets. Whatever you want to call it."

Abrianna shook off his harsh rebuke. "Tomi and I will deal with our issues *after* we find her. If President Washington pulled an okie-doke once, who is to say she's not doing it again?"

"You're telling me you went to the White House specifically because you believed the president was behind Tomi's disappearance?"

"No. I went because I wanted her administration to investigate T4S for Tomi's disappearance. And that's exactly what she's promised to do; but now, I don't know what to believe."

Kadir hung his head. "The shit is confusing, but we've found some solid evidence we're on the right trail with T4S." He moved over to sit next to Abrianna, and she placed her head on his shoulder.

She smiled when he sighed and looped his arm around her. "What did you find?"

"We got lucky. A kid in the neighborhood captured Tomi's kidnapping on her camera phone. It was a professional job."

"The government is filled with professionals, too."

"Yeah, but Jayson Brigham doesn't work for the government."

"Brigham?" She ran the name through her memory. "He works with Tomi, right?"

"Yeah. Photographer. He took our picture for Tomi's article."

"So what does he have to do with anything?"

"Apparently, he was Tomi's handler—like how Zacher was yours. *Gigi* identified his jacket in the video and found a button he lost there that night."

"No shit?"

"No shit. And tonight, we paid a visit to Ned Cox. Dr. Zacher's personal assistant."

Abrianna's head popped up. "What did he tell you?"

Kadir sighed. "That T4S had kidnapped Tomi."

"Then we have to go get her."

"Not so fast, speedy. T4S doesn't have her anymore."

"What do you mean? Then who does?"

He shrugged. "That's the million-dollar question. It could be anyone."

40

ITCS International CEO Nate Hunter had a face made for TV, Hollywood charm, and a politician's tongue. On Fox News, Hunter ducked and weaved the host's probing questions about the services that paramilitary companies provided around the world and played down the growing hysteria that they were lawless, ungoverned corporate soldiers.

"What do you think about the hoopla surrounding T4S?"

"I view it as unfortunate," Hunter answered with a shake of his head.

"Do you believe the charges of them having something to do with the Craig Avery serial killings?"

"I have no opinions on that—but certainly hope not."

"Do you support the president ordering the FBI to investigate the private company?"

"I'd imagine T4S supports anything that would put this to bed."

"What's your opinion on Abrianna Parker?"

Hunter's brows pinched. "I believe Ms. Parker has been through some horrible experience, and she has my complete sympathy. But these latest charges, I don't know. I hope she's wrong. We'll have to wait and see what the FBI's investigation turns up."

Kadir's heart sounded like a jackhammer inside his chest, giving Abrianna a splitting headache. She stumbled out of bed as quietly as she could, but walking a straight line to the bathroom was problematic. She crossed the threshold on her knees. After kicking the door closed, the lies started. She would only use a little. This would be the last time. She didn't have a choice.

She made her two pink lines and inhaled them as fast as she could. Instead of instant euphoria, her entire nasal passage burned like fire. Abrianna sprung up from the floor and splashed water on her face.

"Shit. Shit. Shit."

For a full minute, Abrianna couldn't tell whether the water was helping or drowning her. Eventually, the fire died down, and she pulled herself together and took a shower. The buzzing in her head mellowed out a few seconds before the hot water cooled. By the time she stepped out of the shower, she was back to normal.

When she returned to bed, a noise outside their bedroom door caught her attention. Curious, she slipped from the bed again and put on her robe before checking it out. In the living room, Baasim threw a duffel bag over his shoulder and headed for the door.

"Going somewhere?" Abrianna crossed her arms.

Baasim stopped and turned his smirking smile toward her. "Yeah. Thanks for the hospitality and all, but it's time for me to find my own place."

"What about . . ."

"Mom?" Baasim chuckled. "She's sticking around to help with the wedding. Didn't Kadir tell you?"

Abrianna drew a deep breath.

"You know, you guys should work on your communication skills. I hear it's kind of important for a marriage to work." He took another step toward the door.

"So . . . where are you staying? Do you already have a place lined up?"

"No. I'm staying with some friends for a while."

"Are they the same guys I saw you palling around with downtown?"

Baasim frowned as he squared up his shoulders. "You've been following me around?"

"You were at a public restaurant." She smirked back. "Paranoid much?"

Baasim sized her up again while Abrianna concentrated and searched around in his head. She heard him speaking but didn't understand the language. "Smooth." She chuckled.

Baasim grinned back.

"What's the matter? You're not up on your Arabic?" He shook his head. "Shame. You should learn it if you're planning to marry into the family." He opened the front door. "I'll catch you later, *sis*." He exited the apartment.

"Damn it." Abrianna marched over to the window. Downstairs, a Toyota Camry waited until Baasim and his duffel bag climbed into the back seat. "This isn't over, asshole. Not by a long shot."

"You're up early," Daishan said. "Would you like for me to put on some coffee?"

"I can do it," Abrianna said.

"No, no. It's no trouble at all." Daishan waved her off. "I'll get breakfast started, too. Is Kadir up?"

"I'll go check." Abrianna sprinted back to the master bedroom and climbed back into bed. She pressed a kiss to Kadir's chest and watched a smile expand across his lips.

"Good morning." Kadir kissed the tip of her nose.

"Morning." She caressed his face. "Are we good?"

"Better than good."

"Yeah?" Surprise and hope mingled in her chest.

He nodded, but she remained dubious.

"Look, I'm not going to lie and say I'm happy you went to the

White House. I'm not. I wish you understood why I didn't want you to go—"

"But I do."

"And you went anyway?" He shook his head. "That makes it worse." He pulled away and broke their cocoon to climb out of bed.

"What about the president killing the House speaker?"

"What about it?" He laughed. "We told the world it was President Walker. You want to go back on TV and tell them 'oops, my bad'? It will do a hell of a lot of damage with our credibility against T4S—then again, they no longer have Tomi, either—so, we're wrong on that one, too. Maybe we're not so good at this detective shit, after all."

Kadir's cell phone rang, interrupting their morning argument.

"Don't," she pleaded. "It can wait."

He answered the phone. "Hello."

Pissed, Abrianna yanked the top sheet off of her body and climbed out of bed. It took everything within her not to think about hurting him for that slap in the face. No one knew better than she did about how dangerous her thoughts were—especially when she was angry.

"What?" Kadir sat on the edge of the bed. "Are you shitting me?"

The note of despair buried within his baritone made Abrianna paused with concern. "What is it?"

Abrianna's cell phone rang.

She glanced over at it while Kadir hung his head.

"This can't be fucking happening," he said.

Abrianna answered her cell. "Hello?"

Draya's tearful voice came over the line. "Bree, thank God. Have you heard?"

"Heard what? Why are you crying?" Abrianna chanced another look over at Kadir.

"It's Castillo."

The room tilted beneath Abrianna's feet and she sat next to Kadir. "What about her?"

"They tried to take her out last night—"

"I'm on my way," Kadir sprang back to his feet and disconnected the call.

"Draya, let me call you back later."

"Sure. I'm here at BridgePoint with Julian and Dennis," Draya said. "If it wasn't for Gigi, we—"

"Yeah. I know." Abrianna wanted out of this conversation. "I'll call you back." She hung up the phone before Draya succeeded in dragging her down memory lane.

"Kadir, I'm coming with you."

He opened his mouth.

"Not up for discussion," she added.

He closed his mouth.

Jacksonville, Florida

Backstage at her latest campaign rally, President Washington handed her campaign manager back his cell phone after watching Nate Hunter's Fox interview. "I want to meet him."

"Great," McMullan said. "He wants a meeting with you, too."

"I love it when the stars align." She patted him on the shoulder. "Set it up."

"I'm already ahead of you on that one, too, Madam President. Nate Hunter has offered to host a fund-raiser for you in Washington."

The president lifted a brow. "Really? Even better."

"Five minutes, Madam President," an intern announced.

"I'll be ready in two," she volleyed with a fake smile before she returned her attention to McMullan. "You know, Mr. Hunter may be another blessing in disguise. His support could help neutralize Hardy's charges about my being weak on foreign policy, *and* we can pit ITCS support against T4S's tarnished reputation."

"I had the same thought as well."

"Good. Let's make it happen." She gave him the thumbs up and allowed Davidson and her Secret Service detail to escort her out to the stage, where an estimated crowd of thirty thousand people greeted her with exuberant cheers.

Abrianna and Kadir made it to the BridgePoint Hospital. Draya, Julian, and Ghost sat gloomily in the lobby but sprang to their feet when Abrianna and Kadir joined them.

"Where is she?" Kadir asked.

"In room 3214," Draya told them. "I'll come with you."

"Did she tell you what happened?" Bree asked.

"No, but she's pissed off about being shot. I can tell you that much."

"Yeah. It does tend to ruin your day."

When they entered her hospital room, Castillo was attempting to slide her arm into her jacket.

"Going somewhere?" Kadir asked.

Castillo glanced over her shoulder and flashed them a smile. "As a matter of fact, I am."

Abrianna cocked a head. "Has the doctor released you?"

"Hell, no, he hasn't." Dennis rolled in behind them in an electric wheelchair. "But my girlfriend is as stubborn as an ox, and she thinks she knows better than everyone else."

"I know better than most, especially when it comes to my own body." Castillo struggled to put her arm back through the sleeve.

Dennis shook his head. "Gigi, please. You lost a lot of blood."

Abrianna rushed over to the bed and sat next to her. "What happened?"

Castillo snickered. "Believe it or not, a cop shot me."

"Why wouldn't we believe that?" Kadir asked.

"You'd think one would hesitate from pulling the trigger on one who used to be one of them. The asshole knew who I was."

Dennis cocked his head. "What? You didn't tell me that."

"I'm telling you now." Castillo gave up putting on the jacket and stood up. "Whoa." She sat back down.

"Dizzy?" Abrianna asked.

"Yeah, a little."

"Maybe Dennis is right. Maybe you should wait for the doctor to release you?"

Castillo lifted a brow. "You have got to be kidding me. If memory serves me right, you never waited to be released by a doctor. You avoid them at all cost."

"That's different."

"Yeah? I'll cut you a deal. I'll stay and let a doctor poke and prod me if you do."

Abrianna didn't have a snappy comeback.

"Yeah. That's what I thought." Castillo stood again. "I'm leaving." She took one step and stopped.

"Baby," Dennis pleaded. "You're not ready."

"I'm fine," she insisted but pulled at her shirt's collar. "Damn. Why is it so hot in here?"

Everyone shared knowing looks under Castillo's radar, but none of them risked saying anything else.

"Maybe I will sit for a few more minutes." Sweat beaded Castillo's forehead and slicked down her hairline.

"Good idea." Abrianna pulled back the sheet and Castillo lay down.

Castillo pulled in deep gulps of air like she'd just completed a marathon. "Just a few minutes."

Dennis wheeled his chair to the bed. "I know what you're going through," he told her. "It's frustrating when your mind and body are out of whack. Take it from me, it's okay to take the S off of your chest and rest every once in a while."

Castillo rolled her head in his direction. "Learn that recently, did you?"

"And the hard way."

Abrianna moved next to Kadir. He draped his arm around her shoulder. "Maybe we should give them a few minutes?"

They turned for the door.

"Where are you going?" Castillo asked.

The gang spun back around.

"We figured we'd give you two some time alone."

"That's not necessary. We're good," she told them.

"Yeah?" Kadir and the gang moved as one toward the bed. "What else can you tell us about last night?"

Castillo shook her head. "Honestly, I'm not sure. It was fuckin' . . . strange."

"A cop shot you. Do you know who it was?"

"No. Never seen him before. But I'll be able to identify him down at the morgue."

"You killed him?"

"No. I was too busy trying not to bleed to death—but somebody snapped his neck."

"What?"

"I know. It was weird as hell. I can still hear the bones in his neck snap like a twig, and he hit the ground like a rock."

Again, the gang shared another look.

"How did you end up here?" Abrianna asked.

She shook her head. "I don't know. I blacked out in the car after I saw . . ." Castillo stopped to review the images in her mind.

"After you saw what?"

Castillo shook her head again. "Nothing. I'm not sure what I saw."

Dennis crossed his arms. "Doctor told me they found you outside of the emergency room. We need to get our hands on the security tapes outside to see if we can identify who brought you to the hospital. I'll put in a call to MPDC and see if we have a missing officer." He glanced at Castillo. "I hate to ask this, but were you drinking last night?"

Castillo's gaze shot to Kadir.

Abrianna caught it.

"I may have had a few." She shrugged. "But I was fine."

"She was," Kadir cosigned.

Abrianna side-eyed Kadir. "You were out drinking with everyone last night, huh?"

"We hit a couple of hard brick walls in our investigation yesterday, and . . . it was nothing."

Abrianna let it go. "I'll be back. Anybody else wants some water or something?" She didn't wait for an answer before she slipped out of the room.

"Bree . . ."

"I'm good," she told Kadir and left the room.

Draya followed her to the vending machine. "Are you sure you're all right?"

"Yeah. I'm cool." She slipped two dollars into the machine and removed a bottled water and took a seat in the waiting room.

"Are you sure?" Julian asked.

"Yeah, I need a minute."

"We'll wait with you," Julian said.

Instead of returning to Castillo's room, Abrianna took a seat in the lobby. Overhead, MSNBC broadcasted President Washington at a campaign rally in battleground Ohio. The crowd looked huge. Campaign placards declaring America Strong were waved enthusiastically while attendees screamed and shouted.

The president smiled and waved before she thanked the local leaders and acknowledged the crowd as the backbone of her campaign. Washington highlighted the minor successes of her administration while limiting comments about the mistakes of President Walker.

"One thing we cannot do now is turn back the clock to Beauregard Hardy's repressive, oppressive, misogynist, and racist America," Washington said.

The crowd cheered. The camera zoomed in for a tight shot,

and she saw a face over the president's right shoulder. Abrianna stood from her chair and walked closer to the television.

"Bree? What's wrong?" Draya asked.

Abrianna gasped. "There he is again."

Now, Draya launched to her feet. "Who?"

Abrianna scanned the screen again. "There." She pointed. "Who does that look like?"

Draya squinted. "Wow. That guy looks like Kadir."

"It's Baasim," Abrianna announced. "Why the hell is he at President Washington's rally? He can't stand her." She turned and faced her friends. "Do you believe me now? Baasim is up to something."

41

For Immediate Release: T4S denies all criminal charges alleged by Abrianna Parker. While we regret our connection to our former employee Dr. Craig Avery, it is important to remind the public that he was not in our employ at the time he went on his crime spree. Any implication otherwise is false. We will look forward to cooperating with any federal investigation to clear our name.

Dr. Zacher made awkward small talk as he walked onto the local Fox News studio set for the Jacobs's Report Show. When he settled into his seat, one assistant miked him up while another powdered his face.

"I don't think I could ever get used to this," Zacher joked.

"You'll be fine," Tim Jacobs assured him.

"We're on in five," the show's producer told everyone in their earpiece.

Matthew Rowland rushed onto the set at the last minute, spewing apologies. "Sorry, guys. Traffic."

"As always," Jacobs said, unfazed.

Rowland turned his expensive smile toward Zacher and jutted out a hand. "Nice to see you again, doc."

"It's always good to be seen." Dr. Z shook the offered hand.

Pierce Spalding stood out of view of the camera along with a pair of overpaid T4S lawyers, a public relations fixer, and even a bodyguard. They watched Dr. Z like a hawk. They were serving him up to the public on a silver platter. From here on out, Charlie would be the public face of T4S.

While the producer counted them down, Rowland elbowed Dr. Z and whispered, "Time to spin. I hope you're ready."

The red light on the camera lit up.

"Good evening," Jacobs greeted at the top of the hour. "Tonight, we have a special guest for you. I'm very much looking forward to this conversation. As most of you know, Abrianna Parker has been back in the news. This time, Parker has an incredible story about her and Tomi Lehane's teenage abduction by serial killer Dr. Craig Avery. It's such a wild story that every media organization worth their salt in the industry is digging into the story. Well, after forty-eight hours, T4S has responded to the uproar. Joining us tonight is Research and Development Director Dr. Charles Zacher. If that name sounds familiar to you, it's because it's the *same* Dr. Zacher Abrianna Parker accused of aiding and abetting Dr. Craig Avery in the kidnapping and torturing of these kids.

"Also joining us is Matthew Rowland, Governor Bo Hardy's campaign manager. Hardy has thrown his hat in the ring, standing with T4S and their mission. So, now let's hear straight from the accused what he has to say to Ms. Parker's charges."

The host turned toward his guests. "Dr. Zacher, welcome to the show." He stretched out his hand.

Dr. Z shook Jacobs's hand. "It's a pleasure to be here."

"Under the circumstances, I find that hard to believe." The host laughed.

"I'll admit it's a bit uncomfortable," Zacher joked. "But I need to make it clear that neither I nor T4S has anything to hide. Ms. Parker's charges are completely unfounded and fabricated. I was blown away when I heard that I'd been cast in Ms. Parker's wild conspiracy theory."

"Why would Ms. Parker make up such a story?"

"Your guess is as good as mine." Dr. Z shrugged. "We live in a world where a lie can travel around the world before the truth can get out of bed."

"Dr. Zacher is right," Rowland cut in. "It's too easy these days to slander anyone at any time. Ms. Parker goes on national TV with outrageous claims and doesn't offer one bit of proof to back any of it up. It's just . . . take my word for it." He laughed. "What's sad is to watch the lame-stream media gobble this nonsense up like Ms. Parker is some kind of truth-sayer. It's ridiculous."

Jacobs jumped back in to wrestle control of the debate. "You're saying, on record, that you and T4S had nothing to do with the teenagers' abductions?"

"That is one hundred percent what I'm saying," Dr. Z said. "It's fake news. And if Ms. Parker continues her unprovoked attack, we're not afraid to hit back. We will not have our reputation dragged through the mud."

Jacobs leaned forward. "I'm still trying to understand. Do you even *know* Abrianna Parker and Tomi Lehane?"

"No. That's what makes this whole thing so bizarre. I've never met Abrianna Parker or Tomi Lehane in my entire life."

Shawn's apartment . . .

"That lying sonofabitch," Abrianna hissed. The plasma screen cracked and spider-webbed before there was another pop, and the picture went black.

Shawn snapped, "Goddamn it, Bree." He yanked the power cord out of the wall. "Not all of us inherited a kajillion dollars. I just bought this TV."

"Sorry." She hung her head and massaged the tension from her temples.

Shawn returned to his vanity mirror to get ready for the night's show. "What did you expect that crazy doctor would do? Confess? Really?" Shawn laughed. "You're going soft."

"I expected him . . . I expected . . ." She sighed. "I don't know. It's weird seeing him so pristine and polished on the news. He doesn't look anything like the broke-down old man I had lunch with in the park for years. The same man I trusted with all my . . . baggage. He knows everything about me—and I thought I knew everything about him. How he came to live on the streets, his probably made-up granddaughter that he claimed to sneak off to see on the weekends. It was all lies. I was a fool."

"Well, the man is a professional at this, and when you met him, you were a kid. Don't beat yourself up about it."

"I can't let this shit go."

"Then don't." Shawn shrugged. "Since he's so comfortable being out in the open, calling you a liar and whatnot, then let's handle it like we would in the streets. Confront him."

"Right. They'll snatch me like they did Tomi. She's probably reduced to a fucking lab rat somewhere."

"I didn't say anything about confronting him on *their* turf." Shawn stopped contouring and twisted around in his chair. "Let's keep it real. So far, your news bombshell has been reduced to some 'she said, he said' shit—even between the president and that clown from Texas. That reporter is lost in the mix. I don't think that anyone is looking for her."

"Castillo and the team are on it."

"You know what I mean. Since you gave that interview, has anyone interviewed you—anyone *official* who is supposed to be looking into her disappearance?"

Abrianna took a deep breath. "Does the president count?"

Shawn frowned. "That shit doesn't pass the smell test, either.

You bring down one administration, and now the backup one is hoping you'll save it?" He shook his head. "Unbelievable. No wonder people hate politics—and politicians."

"Okay, now you sound like Baasim."

"Humph, maybe your future brother-in-law isn't so crazy."

Abrianna's eyes narrowed.

Shawn tossed up his hands. "Just a thought."

Ghost knocked once and then entered the premises without permission.

"Please, come on in," Shawn deadpanned, crossing his arms.

"Don't mind if I do." Ghost flashed him the same flat smile and then dropped a small chest in the center of the floor.

"What is that?" Bree asked.

"What you asked for," Ghost countered. "And you're welcome." He glanced around the room. "Now, what does a guy have to do to get a beer around here?"

Shawn glanced at his best friend and rolled his eyes. "No. Please. Let me. I'll get it." He took hold of his silver cane and waltzed to the kitchen.

Ghost jabbed a thumb in Shawn's direction. "Rainbow boy is pretty funny."

"Can you flip the asshole switch off for about five minutes?" Bree knelt before the chest.

"Only for *five* minutes?" Ghost weighed the request like it was a hard decision.

"I don't want to put you out or anything."

Ghost glanced at his watch. "Time starts right . . . now."

Shawn returned. "Here's your beer, Suge Knight."

Ghost looked at Bree. "What about him? Why isn't he in time-out, too?"

"You two are giving me a headache." Bree shook her head. "How do you open this damn thing?"

"With this." Ghost reached into his jacket and then held up a key.

"Thanks." Shawn snatched the key and handed it over to Bree.

"Again, you're welcome." Ghost chugged half of his beer down in one gulp.

Bree opened the chest and then stared at the electronics inside. "Damn. Is your middle name Go-Go Gadget?"

Ghost took a knee and picked up a couple of items. "What you got here is everything you'd ever need to pull off a spy operation: mikes, listening devices, binoculars—with cameras. I'll go over all of it with you, but I want you to ask yourself—I mean, really, really ask yourself—if you want to do this." He met her gaze. "Once you go down this road, you might not be able to turn back."

"Got it." She turned back toward the chest.

"I mean it," Ghost said. "Sometimes it's best to communicate with one another."

"Ghost, will you please stop stalling, and tell me how to operate these things?"

He sighed. "All right, but don't say that I didn't warn you."

———⊷•⊶———

"It's all bullshit," Bo Hardy boasted. "Pardon my French—but we all know that the little lady in the White House is grasping at straws. Abrianna Parker and her plus-one have been nothing but a thorn in this administration's backside, and *now* suddenly, Washington is parading Parker in the Rose Garden, handing out medals, and handing out pardons like they are BFFs all of a sudden. It's pathetic the lengths the president will go through to detach herself from her predecessor and pass herself off as some kind of *change* agent for the Democratic Party." Hardy turned and looked straight into the camera. "Don't fall for the okey-doke, folks. You can never forget that Washington was President Walker's right-hand gal. And some have said, she was closer to him than the former first lady, if you get my drift."

The host's smug smile expanded. "Are you insinuating that Walker and Washington—?"

"I'm saying what the lame-stream media refuses to report—the truth. And the truth is that President Walker couldn't keep his pants up, and his vice president wore pantsuits to hide her rug-burned knees."

"Governor Hardy—"

"It's a bit harsh, I know. But the American people are fed up with the Democrats using the White House as a whorehouse. No. I won't allow it—and I have faith in the American people to see through this charade. Washington is using this ridiculous conspiracy theory conjured up by Ms. Parker to take the heat off herself in Lehane's disappearance. It's sad, really."

"So, you're still sticking by your support for T4S?"

"You damn right I am. T4S has a spotless, patriotic record defending and protecting this country, and unlike this president, I'm not about to throw them under a bus on the say-so of some unstable call girl—or are we all forgetting that Ms. Parker up until a year ago made her living on her back or sliding down poles?"

The host chuckled.

"You know what? I take it all back. Maybe the president and Ms. Parker *are* two peas in a pod. God help us all."

———◦•◦———

Kate shut off the television. "I can't stand that man."

Davidson laughed. "With good reason. But you can't say that the man isn't entertaining. He's good television."

"Tell me about it. Cable news is obsessed with Hardy. The medal ceremony and pardon were supposed to win me at least *one* news cycle."

"You got half of one."

Kate whipped her head toward Davidson. "You find this funny?"

Davidson held up his hand. "No, but I do think you're overreacting."

"Overreacting? He just called me a whore on national television. We're not debating policies. He's rolling around in the mud and loving every minute of it."

"Well, when they go low—"

"Don't start with that shit," Washington snapped. "This country and its politics love to wallow around in that mud. Now, they've found their king pig, and they love him for it."

Davidson pushed himself up from the couch. "Don't sell yourself short. The last time I checked, you love yourself a good mud bath, too." He marched over to her and stopped short of pulling her into his arms. "Stop playing Hardy's game and play your own. The media may love him, but since you back Abrianna's story, you're leading by an average of four points in every poll."

"I don't trust polls. Plus, they all have a three-point margin of error, so I could only be ahead by *one* point."

"Then fuck the polls and trust your own instincts. Fuck Mc-Mullan and Haverty. You made *yourself* president—with a little help from myself—and you're going to stay president by playing *your* game. Don't chase Hardy. Make him chase you."

———◊———

Nate Hunter blocked off Shalisa's path when she returned to ITCS's lab. "Is there something you want to tell me?"

Shalisa's eyes lit in defiance. "Not particularly."

Hunter cocked his head. "You saved that private detective the other night, didn't you?"

She didn't respond.

Hunter drew a deep breath. "I really wish you would have consulted with me before you did that."

"Castillo is a friend of mine."

"Is she really?" He lifted a dubious brow. "How many times did she visit you while you were in St. Elizabeth's?"

"A couple of times."

Her answer surprised him.

"You never told me that."

"You never asked."

Hunter's smile tightened. "Still. I really don't think that it's a good idea to get too involved with T4S's messes. We took a big risk in rescuing your *other* friend from their clutches."

Shalisa smiled. "You had your own reason for doing that."

"That's true, but . . ."

"Like I said. Castillo is a friend of mine. She saved my life once. I owed her."

Shalisa made sure that Hunter read in her face that this discussion was over, and when he did, he flashed her another strained smile. "Again. Just let me know these things."

"I'll consider it," she told him stubbornly.

He nodded and walked off. When he made it to his office, he made a mental note to correct some mistakes he'd made with Shalisa in Tomi Lehane. He needed soldiers to take orders without argument. Shalisa was too willful for her own good.

42

Dr. Zacher ended his latest interview and handed his mike pack back to the studio assistant. Pierce Spalding approached with a fake smile. "Great job, Charlie." He pounded Zacher's back. "I know how much you hate doing this kind of stuff. Don't worry, we'll get you back to the lab soon enough."

"That would be great." Zacher smiled as Spalding and his security team headed off the local Fox studio floor.

Zacher weighed how to question his boss about the missing time in T4S's security footage when they ran into the head of their company's number-one competitor.

"Nate Hunter," Spalding acknowledged, stopping at the edge the studio. "What are you doing here?"

"Hey, guys." Hunter flashed his perfect teeth. "I caught the tail end of the show. Entertaining segment. Deny, deny, deny." He laughed. "No worries. I'm sure that about a third of the country believes you. That's pretty good—considering."

Spalding squared his shoulders. "Since when are you a day-walker, Nate?"

"Since you've dragged everybody's business into the sunlight."

"Ha. Ha."

"You're not the only private military in town. Your Frankenstein experiments have crammed a microscope up all of our asses. Too many people are asking too many questions. It looks like we all have to pitch in to clean up your mess—as usual."

Spalding's and Zacher's smiles tightened.

Hunter smacked Spalding's shoulder. "Don't worry. We at ITCS International are always happy to lend our services. And in this case, we're here to help you guys muddy the waters."

Dr. Z smirked. "All out of the goodness of your heart, I assume."

Hunter centered his searing green eyes on Dr. Z. "What else?"

Spalding laughed. "There will be a cold day in hell before we'll need any help from you."

"Then your winter coats must be in the car, because it's snowing like a muthafucka." Hunter laughed and stepped closer. "How are things over at headquarters? Heard you guys had a little trouble recently. Man, when it rains, it pours, huh?"

Dr. Z focused on Hunter, but when he attempted to roam around inside his mind, he was hit with a piercing sound inside his head.

"Aargh." Dr. Z doubled over and clutched his head.

Spalding jumped. "Charles, are you all right?"

Hunter *tsk*ed and shook his head. "Don't you know it's rude to search around in someone's head without permission?"

"Aargh." Dr. Z nearly dropped to one knee before his ears stopped ringing.

"What the hell is going on?" Spalding asked.

Hunter reached into his jacket and handed Dr. Z a handkerchief. "Here. That nosebleed can get a little nasty."

Dr. Z took the offered handkerchief. "How?"

"You're not the only private military company with a research and development department." Hunter laughed.

A studio hand rushed toward the small group. "Mr. Hunter, we need to get you miked up."

"Sure thing, love." He flashed the woman a smile before returning his attention to Spalding and Zacher. "It's showtime."

Dr. Z settled into the back of a limousine next to Spalding outside of the News Corp. Building. Almost immediately, Spalding whacked him on the back. "Charles, I have to hand it to you. That was one hell of a performance."

"I'd say," one of the lawyers whose name escaped Dr. Z said, grinning.

"I aim to please." Dr. Z flashed a thin smile.

"Thrilled to hear it. Because the company expects for you to do about a dozen more interviews just like it before the week is out."

Zacher drew a deep breath.

"Is that going to be a problem?" Spalding lifted a brow.

"Pierce, I'm a scientist—not a political media star."

Spalding pushed a button and lowered the partition. "Driver, pull over."

The car pulled over.

Spalding glanced at the two lawyers. "Get out."

"Sir?" the lawyers questioned in sync.

"Get. Out," Spalding said succinctly.

The lawyers cast a final look at Zacher and then followed orders. Once they'd climbed out and the door slammed closed, Spalding directed his cold smile at Zacher. "Let's get one thing straight, Dr. Z. You are whatever I need you to be. And right now I need you to put out the fire that *you* and *your* buddy Craig Avery started."

Dr. Z's jaw hardened.

"This is *your* mess. Clean it up. Had you taken care of Parker when I told you to, *months* ago, she wouldn't be all over the news, telling people about what you and Avery had done to her and

Lehane. And since she mentioned you by name, you have to be the one to answer for it. If you do a good job, then when Hardy gets into the White House, our funding goes back into the black, and you can squirrel away back into the lab and finish getting me my super soldiers; can I make this any more clear to you?"

Zacher shook his head.

"Good." Spalding straightened his jacket.

"What about Lehane?" Zacher said.

"What about her?"

"She's still out there—somewhere. What's the plan if she shows up writing another blockbuster headline or corroborates Bree's story?"

"Bree?" Spalding laughed. "You really are attached to this girl."

"We should prepare for the possibility."

Spalding nodded. "Let's deal with one crisis at a time, shall we? I have a team reviewing the tapes and combing through our system on who was responsible for the security breach. We already have a prime suspect."

"You do?" Dr. Z tested, wondering if Spalding was finally going to confide in him.

"You sound surprised."

"Nah. I'm just . . . impressed. Who is it?"

"Some meddlesome hacktivist, who leads something called the Revolution."

Zacher frowned. "What?"

"Yeah. Apparently, they've been snooping around in our system for a while, stealing files. Now, they're uploading them on the dark web. It's easy enough to declare the files as fakes. The mainstream media won't dare air or publish them until they can confirm them. We both know that will never happen. We're pretty much in the clear on that—at the moment."

"A hacktivist?" Dr. Z repeated.

"Yes. The leader is a Douglas Jenkins aka Ghost. Have you ever heard of him?"

Zacher shook his head.

"Well, he's a slippery bastard. I'll give him that much. But I have no doubt it's a matter of time before we get our hands on him and the girl."

"A *hacker* physically broke into a heavily armed paramilitary base. *That's* your working theory?"

"Do you have a better one?"

An image of blond hair spilling out from a black hoodie flashed in Dr. Z's mind, but he quickly shook the impossible idea out of his head. "No."

"Then we go with my theory," Spalding declared.

"Are we not going to talk about the elephant in the room?" Dr. Z seared a hard look at Spalding.

"You mean Nate Hunter?"

"Of course I mean Nate Hunter. Why the hell do you think he's really entering the stage now?"

"Sharks always come out when they smell blood in the water." A muscle twitched at Spalding's right temple.

Dr. Z pressed, "You think *maybe* ITCS had something to do with the attack at our lab?"

Spalding stiffened in his seat. "I don't put anything past that company. But don't you worry. I'll handle Hunter. You handle the Parker mess."

Dr. Z stared out the window for an hour before they came to an area he recognized. This time, he rolled down the partition. "Let me out here."

Spalding frowned. "Charlie, there's no need. I can give you a lift back to headquarters."

The limousine stopped.

"It's all right. I need to pay a visit to someone." He nodded toward Rosewood Cemetery.

Spalding's brows lifted. "Oh, of course."

Dr. Z opened the door.

"How about I order a car to come back for you? Say, in about an hour?"

"That will be great. Thank you." Dr. Z slammed the door shut and stood there until the limo pulled off and faded from view. Then he turned and glanced at the cemetery's ominous entrance. Once he gathered his courage, he waltzed inside to find answers.

43

Denco Air Conditioning & Supplies warehouse . . .

"What the hell is this place?" Shawn asked.

"Baasim's new place of employment," Abrianna said.

"Please tell me that we're not going to sit out here all night while he works." Shawn groaned.

"You don't have anything better to do."

"Actually, I do," Shawn informed her, sinking down into his seat. "You're not the only one with a love life, you know."

Bree lowered her binoculars. "You're seeing someone?"

"Kind of." He shrugged. "It started as a one-night stand, but you know how it is. Once men take a bite out of this white chocolate, they lose their minds."

Bree laughed. "I'll take your word for it." She glanced back up at the building and caught movement. "Here we go." She lifted her binoculars as the warehouse's back metal door rolled up, and a truck pulled up to the loading dock.

"Small crew," Shawn noted.

"Yeah." She searched for any sign of Baasim.

"Huh." Shawn lowered his binoculars.

"What?"

"Is this like a Middle Eastern company or something? I only see Arabs working the place."

Abrianna shrugged. "It might be. Oh, wait. There he is."

She zoomed in on Baasim huddled near the back of the truck. She pressed a button on the spy binoculars and snapped pictures. "I've seen that guy to his right before," she said. "He was at the restaurant with Baasim."

"Ooh, he made friends." Shawn rolled his eyes. "Toss him in jail and throw away the key."

Bree lowered her binoculars. "Don't do that."

"Sorry, but you're talking like a crazy person."

She shrugged the comment off. "We need to get in there."

Shawn's eyes widened. "You want to run that by me again?"

"We have to see what they're up to in there."

"What?"

"Don't be a wuss." Bree flashed him a smile. "We haven't broken into anyplace in some time. It'll be fun."

In the dead of night, Dr. Z and Ned returned and traipsed through Rosewood Cemetery with a pair of high-powered LED work lights and shovels. While Zacher charged forward, Ned crept behind with his ears perked to every sound emanating around them.

"Um, Dr. Z, are you sure about this?"

"Yes, yes. We've already been over this. Keep up," he snapped.

Ned grumbled but marched farther into the cemetery. After another ten minutes, he asked, "How much further?"

Dr. Z stopped. "We're here." He dropped his gear, sighed, and rolled his shoulders.

Ned dropped his gear and bent over to catch his breath. However, the late-night summer humidity meant he required extra energy to process the oxygen in his lungs—that, or he was out of shape.

Zacher stripped out of his jacket. "We don't have all night, so we better get started."

Ned took another look at the grave and then felt his dinner lurch in his stomach. "I don't mind telling you this, boss, but . . . I'm uneasy about this." He looked around at the other graves. "It doesn't feel right."

Dr. Z cut a sharp look at his assistant. "What's the matter? Are you afraid of cemeteries?"

"Well, um . . ."

"I assure you the dead aren't going to climb out of their caskets and attack us, and there is no such thing as zombies." He rolled up his sleeves and placed the portable LED lights around the grave and plugged them into the portable battery. When he turned them on, their powerful beams blinded them.

Ned folded an arm across his eyes. "Wow. Those are bright."

"Yeah. Maybe we just need one of them." Dr. Z switched two of the lights off and was able to see again. "There, let's get started." He picked up a shovel.

Ned hesitated.

"What's the matter now?"

"If the dead stay dead, then what are we doing here?"

Good question. "Just start digging. The sooner we start, the faster we finish."

Ned sighed and picked up the other shovel.

Snap!

Ned scrambled to Dr. Z's side. "What was that?"

Zacher paused and waited. When the cemetery remained silent, he shook it off. "It was nothing. Now, come on." He jammed the shovel into the earth.

Ned made a sign of the cross and then followed suit. It turned out that digging up a grave was backbreaking work, even for someone as strong as Dr. Z. The hard earth was unforgiving. When Ned was close to weeping, his shovel hit something hard. "I think we reached it." He hit it again to make sure.

Dr. Z hit the casket, too. A relieved smile spread across his face.

With renewed energy, the men quickly shoveled off the last layer of dirt from the casket.

Ned quickly worried about the next problem. "How are we going to get this out of here?" He looked from the six-foot hole. "We need at least two other guys."

"We don't need to lift it, we only need to open it," Zacher said.

"Open it? Here?" Ned repeated. "We're not taking it back to the lab?"

"No, I just need to verify something."

Ned's face turned ashen.

"You can go ahead and pop out if you want."

Dr. Z didn't have to say it twice. Ned grabbed hold of the nylon rope they had connected to a stake on the top level and climbed out within seconds. However, the cemetery was as eerie above ground as it was below.

Meanwhile, Dr. Z maneuvered himself around the coffin and, with a strong deadlift, opened the casket.

It was empty.

Abrianna and Shawn snuck into Denco's warehouse like a pair of ninjas. It only required Abrianna taking out one distracted guard by the east exit wing of the warehouse. With one punch, she'd knocked him out. Since they didn't know how much time they needed, they duct-taped and tied him up before hiding him in a thicket of trees at the side of the building.

Once they entered the warehouse, they crept through a labyrinth of stacked crates. It was ear-piercingly loud inside the place. None of the recording devices Ghost had given them was going be of any use. Abrianna's sensitive hearing had her doubling over in pain. Shawn tugged on her arm and gave her a concerned look. Despite the pain, Abrianna gave him the thumbs-up.

She had to sate her curiosity once and for all. Between the assembly line and the forklifts, Abrianna and Shawn didn't need to concentrate on being quiet—just invisible.

Within seconds, they were able to see that everything in the warehouse ran like a well-oiled machine. The farther they moved into the warehouse, the more adrenaline pumped through Abrianna's veins. She was excited and determined to prove that there was more than what met the eye inside the air-conditioning plant.

Abrianna fished the camera out of her pocket and snapped pictures, but they were of mundane things like the assembly line, air conditioner parts, and crates. After that, she decided to take pictures of the workers while Shawn covered her back.

Then Abrianna came across a face that she recognized. Excited, she spun around and motioned Shawn to take a look.

Confused, Shawn's gaze scanned all over the place until she grabbed the sides of his face and pointed it in the right direction. "Is that . . ."

Abrianna nodded. "Our waiter from Bezoria's." She struggled to recall the name. "Guess he works two jobs," she mumbled under her breath. "C'mon. We need to get closer."

"What?" He doubted she heard him, so he made a grab for her wrist, but he was hardly strong enough to restrain her. "Bree," he hissed.

She stopped only because she felt his weight dragging on her arm.

"Are you crazy?" he barked over the loud machinery; he was sure that she could read his lips. "Just take your damn pictures and let's get out of here."

Abrianna wanted to argue, but the sharpness in Shawn's blue eyes told her that he was over this game of hers and wanted out. "Fine." She sighed and resumed taking pictures—of Farooq.

Shawn tapped her on her shoulder and rolled his hand for her to hurry it up.

When Abrianna lowered her camera, she knew that she didn't

have much of anything and glanced around again. She placed her hand on one of the crates. "You think all of these boxes only have air conditioners and parts inside of them?"

"What? Why wouldn't they?"

"All right, let's go." She rolled her eyes and in her mind planned for a night when she could return alone. They stood from their crouched positions and headed back out the way they had come. After they rounded a few crates away from the noise, they ran straight into a group of three angry-looking Middle Eastern guys. One of them was the guy they'd tied up in the woods.

One guy spoke into a walkie-talkie. "We found them."

The guy they'd tied up launched forward to make a grab for them. Abrianna threw up a hand. Three men flew backward, slamming into and toppling over crates.

"Go! Go! Go!" Abrianna shouted.

Shawn didn't waste time hauling ass. Abrianna stayed close behind him.

The guys behind them weren't down for long. While running, Abrianna took one look over her shoulder and saw two of the guys on her heels. She threw another look at the stack of crates. With a flick of her hands, they tumbled down. The men shouted as the crates crashed and cut off their path.

Abrianna and Shawn bolted for the back door—but Shawn's bad knee gave out. Abrianna didn't have enough room or time to course correct and tumbled over him. They crashed into another stack of crates. One tumbled from the top and headed straight for Shawn's head. Without thinking, Abrianna threw herself over her best friend's body and took the whole force of the falling crate, knocking her out cold.

———※◆※———

Kadir, Julian, and Castillo watched as Dr. Zacher and Ned headed out of Rosewood Cemetery.

"Shouldn't we follow him?" Kadir asked.

"Absolutely, but first I want to get a good look at that grave."
Castillo crouched low and maneuvered around the tombstones.

Julian followed but felt awkward about creeping through a
cemetery—especially in the dead of night. The place was a giant
labyrinth. When they reached the tombstone Zacher had visited,
the color drained out of Castillo's face.

"What is it?" Kadir asked.

When Castillo didn't respond, Kadir placed a hand on her
shoulder, and she jumped.

Kadir's expression crinkled with concern. "Are you all right?"

"I don't know."

Kadir read the headstone. "Shalisa Young." He paused. "Why
does that name sound familiar?"

"Because she was the third teenager I rescued out of Dr.
Avery's basement."

Kadir reread the tombstone. "But—why would Zacher be vis-
iting her grave?"

The truth hit Castillo like a ton of bricks. *The blonde.* "Because
she's *not* dead."

44

Baasim fell asleep exhausted in a cramped bedroom he shared with a new recruit. It seemed as if he'd just closed his eyes when the bedroom's light switched on, and someone shook him as if the place was being raided.

"Baasim, get up!"

He sat up as if he were connected to a spring. "What is it? What's going on?"

"You need to come with us," Saoud barked.

Something is wrong. Baasim scanned the half dozen stern faces surrounding him. "Can you tell me what this is about?"

"You'll see."

Saoud tossed him his clothes. "Get dressed."

With little choice and no privacy, Baasim followed orders. Next, he was shoved to fall in line with the room and then out of the apartment. Baasim's mind raced a mile a minute. What kind of trouble was he in and could he talk his way out of it?

"C'mon, guys. This is crazy. Can't someone tell me what the hell is going on?"

Everyone remained silent.

Baasim's nerves twisted into knots, but he shut down and matched their solemn faces with his own. When they reached the Toyota Camry, the back door was opened. Saoud placed his hand on top of his head and then crammed Baasim into the back. Two other Yemeni brothers flanked his sides and made sure he saw them palm their weapons.

His heart raced, but ice pumped in Baasim's veins.

Saoud climbed behind the wheel, and Awsam claimed the last seat on the passenger side. The car turned into a tomb as they rode across the Potomac and then to Denco's Air Conditioning and Supplies. Since the company shut down at midnight, the place was dark when they pulled up.

Guns remained trained on Baasim as he climbed out of the back seat and marched toward the back door. As hard as it was, he remained quiet as they led him to a back room. However, when he entered, a small gasp left his body before he stiffened with shock.

Crumpled on the ground was Abrianna's lifeless body, and in a chair, a thin white dude was being worked over.

"What the fuck is going on?"

"I take it that you recognize them?" Saoud asked.

Baasim broke ranks and rushed over to check Abrianna's pulse. "What the fuck, Saoud? Why is Kadir's fiancée here?"

Saoud finally smiled. "See? That's what *we* want to know."

Baasim's face twisted with genuine confusion.

Saoud gestured for his men to lower their weapons.

Shawn groaned while blood streamed from his mouth.

"The white boy is a tough son of a bitch. We haven't got so much as his name out of him, let alone why the hell these two knocked out one of my guys and tossed him aside like a bag of garbage before sneaking around the property, putting their noses into places they don't belong."

Baasim shook his head because he didn't have any answers.

A nervous Farooq spoke up. "These two also came to Bezoria's. That's how I knew who she was."

Baasim's hand returned to Abrianna's neck. When he couldn't find a pulse, he had to redouble his efforts to suppress his panic.

She's dead. The room fell silent. Baasim mentally scrambled for how Kadir would react to losing his fiancée. *It would destroy him.*

"We're waiting," Saoud reminded Baasim.

Baasim lifted his head. "I wish I had an answer. Abrianna and I haven't exactly gotten along since we've met, but I have no clue to why she's here." In this situation, it was best to go with the truth.

Farooq nodded and cosigned, "They asked a lot of questions at the restaurant. I didn't think anything about it at the time."

"What sort of questions?" Saoud asked.

"How long I lived in D.C. Did I know the Kahlifas." Farooq shrugged his shoulders. "She did mention she hadn't met many of Kadir's friends."

A smile spread across Saoud's face. "I see."

The room fell quiet again while Saoud thought the situation over. "I guess it doesn't matter *why* she's here anymore. We need to get rid of her—and the white dude, too. We're on a tight schedule to take out President Washington. We can't afford for your domestic issues to fuck everything up."

Baasim nodded. "I understand."

"Good. *You* and Farooq clean this mess up," Saoud ordered. "And will any more family members come snooping around?"

"No, sir."

"Good." Saoud's eyes darkened. "I'm going to hold you to that."

———※———

Dr. Z and Ned had returned to their vehicle. They were sweaty, dirty, and exhausted. Dr. Z's mind raced. What did this mean? Why was the casket empty? How was it empty? Had the hospital made a mistake?

This discovery changed everything. He just didn't know what to *do* about it.

What are we going to do now?

"That, my boy, is a good question," Dr. Z answered his assistant's thoughts.

Ned swallowed and pulled away from the cemetery.

Dr. Z felt Ned's gaze stare a hole through him from the rearview mirror.

"Eyes on the road, please."

"Yes, sir," Ned said in time to brake to stop from ramming into the back of a car.

Dr. Z flew into the back of the front seat.

"Sorry about that, sir," Ned apologized.

"Just . . . watch where you're going." Dr. Z settled back into his seat and searched for the seat belt.

A phone trilled.

Dr. Z shot a gaze back up to Ned, who shrugged. "It's not my phone, sir."

Zacher searched around for his jacket and found it on the floorboard. He pulled out his smartphone and read the screen. Unknown caller. He relaxed and was about to let the call go to voice mail when instinct told him to answer it. "Hello."

"Hello, Dr. Zacher."

The voice chilled him to the bone.

"It was awfully nice of you to come by my grave and pay me a visit."

The air in Zacher's lungs thinned. "Shalisa?"

"The one and only."

45

Zacher gripped the phone. "I don't understand."

"Oh come on now. You're a smart guy."

Zacher's grip on his cell phone tightened. He glanced back toward Ned, who was still steadily watching him through the rearview mirror.

"Have I blown your mind, doc?" Shalisa asked. "I hope you're not disappointed about my being alive."

"No. It's not that. It's just that . . ."

"It's just that you miss poking and prodding me like I was your personal lab rat? You and your cronies at T4S ruined my life. You and your lackey Craig Avery tortured me and put me through hell. When that wasn't enough, all those experimental drugs turned me into a murderer."

"That was an unfortunate side effect."

"You made me kill my own mother!"

"That's not how that went—"

"Then you had the audacity to declare me insane so you could transfer me to a hospital where you could go right back to poking and prodding until I was out of my mind. All those drugs you jammed into my system turned me into a freak."

"Shalisa, listen to me."

She laughed. "I have been listening to you. You've been all over the news lying about what you and that evil company have been doing behind closed doors. You had years to come clean. I had to do what I had to do to end it all. Stepping off that roof was the best thing I ever did. I see things so much clearer now. I can't describe the feeling. I had to die to be born again. You should try it sometime."

"Dying?"

"Don't worry. There's nothing to be afraid of. I'll make sure that it won't hurt—much."

Zacher took a deep breath and shook off his shock. "We need to talk."

"Oh, we're going to do a lot more than just talk when the time is right, and at the place of my choosing. Who knows, I might even bring my old friend Tomi Lehane along." She laughed and then disconnected the call.

"Wait. Shalisa? Are you there? Hello." Zacher pulled the phone away from his face and saw that the call had indeed disconnected. "Shit." He tossed the phone aside and muttered another curse.

"Is everything all right, sir?" Ned asked again.

Dr. Z ruminated for a few seconds. "You know, Ned. I take back what I said earlier. There is such a thing as the walking dead."

Back at the cemetery . . .

"What do you mean that she's not dead?" Kadir asked. "Bree said Shalisa jumped off a hospital building last year."

"She did." Castillo marched back to their vehicle. "But maybe you haven't noticed, Avery's survivors have a habit of rising from the dead." She climbed in behind the wheel.

Kadir and Julian got into the car.

However, once everyone was in the vehicle, Castillo didn't start the car. She had a hard time wrapping her head around this new revelation.

"Gigi, are you all right?" Kadir asked.

"Shalisa is the blonde."

"I'm sorry. What?"

"I've seen her twice now."

"The walking dead girl?" Julian clarified.

Castillo nodded. "She was at Abrianna's car accident and . . . I think she saved my life that night with the cop."

Kadir shook his head. "I'm confused. Is she a hostile or a friendly?"

She shrugged. "Maybe both."

"I wish that was more comforting," he said.

"Yeah." Castillo started the vehicle. "Me, too."

46

Castillo followed Kadir's directions to Ghost's new off-the-grid bunker in Arlington, Virginia. However, they were surprised to catch Ghost chilling in a pair of Superman pajamas. Once Castillo and Kadir finished looking him up and down, Ghost crossed his meaty arms.

"Are you guys alone?"

"Are we interrupting anything?" Kadir asked.

"Just the revolution." Ghost stepped back. "C'mon in."

The bunker was almost an exact replica of the one Ghost had been forced to evacuate. "Wow. You didn't waste much time," Kadir said.

"In a war, it pays to have a plan B, C, *and* D." Ghost closed the door behind them. "If you guys are here, it means you're bringing me more bad news. Go ahead and spit it out."

Kadir took a stab at it. "In short, we have a zombie roaming the streets of D.C."

Ghost shrugged. "Sure. Why not?"

Castillo smirked. "Just like that?"

"It's D.C. What do you want from me?"

"How about help in finding her?" she asked.

"Ah, it's a chick. Cool. Do you have a name?"

"Shalisa Young."

Ghost cocked his head. "Oh, *that* type of zombie."

Castillo quickly caught Ghost up on her team's stalking Zacher to Rosewood Cemetery.

"The dignified doctor has been reduced to digging up graves?" He laughed. "I would have paid good money to have seen that. I'm surprised that he even has the strength to pull it off based on what I read in his medical records."

"He had help," Julian said.

"Yeah. That assistant that's always glued to his hip."

"Figures." Ghost shuffled over to his computer terminal.

Castillo and her team waved to both Roger, whose arm was still in a sling, and Wendell.

"So, what do you have for me? If Ms. Young is legally dead, it's going to be a little difficult to find her."

"We just have the video you cleaned up."

Ghost stopped click-clacking on the keyboard to look up Castillo. "*That* was Shalisa Young?"

"I believe so."

"Then she is the same chick I'm looking for," Ghost told them. "I got lucky and found another backdoor into T4S's servers. I piggy-backed off Dr. Zacher's username and password into their surveillance system. It appears the doctor has some questions, too."

"What did you find?" Kadir asked.

"Turns out that Zacher is a bit of a hacker, too. When he couldn't get the full video, he used his superior's access code and found what we were looking for." He hit play.

They crowded around and watched a storm troop of military-type personnel invade T4S; but when Dr. Zacher flew into a wall with no one laying a hand on him, it caught everyone's undivided attention. Then, seconds later, the leader removed her hood to reveal she was a woman with a mass of blond hair.

"Well, I'll be damned," Kadir and Castillo said at the same time.

Ghost nodded. "Wait. There's more. Watch."

Everyone's gaze remained locked on the screen as they then watched the storm troop and their blond leader enter a lab and then exit with an unconscious Tomi Lehane."

"So, Ned told the truth. T4S no longer has Tomi," Julian said.

"Yep. The new questions are who does Shalisa Young work for, and what the hell do they want with Lehane?"

Kadir shook his head. "It's got to be for the same reason T4S wanted her. T4S aren't the only ones who are interested in producing super soldiers. It's got to be a competing company."

Ghost and Kadir locked gazes as light bulbs went off inside their heads. "ITCS International."

Castillo nodded. "What can you get me on them?"

"I can prepare you some reading material," Kadir told her.

"Great. Another player on the board." She thought for a second. "If ITCS has Tomi *and* Shalisa, T4S is going to need another guinea pig—and ITCS may be looking for a trifecta as well."

"Shit." Kadir spun for the door.

Castillo and Julian rushed behind him, seeing that Castillo was the one with the car keys.

Ghost shook his head. "Y'all come back now. Y'all hear?"

ITCS International Headquarters . . .

Tomi was in hell.

In her head, she remained trapped in her apartment with flames licking up the walls. The insufferable heat baked her from the inside out while black smoke clawed at her throat. She'd been clinging to life for forever. Exhausted, she wanted to give up—but couldn't. Curled in a fetal position in her burning apartment, Tomi heard voices—like they came from the great beyond. She didn't hear them all the time, but they were there, whispering.

"Are you sure that this is going to work?" a woman asked.

"It should," a man said.

What are they talking about? Tomi strained her ears to listen, but then suddenly the woman's voice surrounded her.

It's okay, Tomi. We're going to get you out of here.

Tomi uncurled herself from the floor. *Who are you?*

"I can hear her," the woman said, but back in the great beyond again.

Hello?

Hello, Tomi. I'm an old friend. Hang on. Is there any way you can get yourself to take a deep breath?

Tomi glanced around and started choking again. *There's too much smoke. I could die.* She coughed harder and curled up on the floor again.

You're not going to die, Tomi. The fire isn't real. You have to trust me and breathe.

What was the woman talking about? Of course the fire was real.

Tomi, can you still hear me? Breathe.

No, no, no. I can't.

Okay, Tomi. You're in a cocoon. You know how like sometimes people think you're dead because your pulse is so low? That's happening right now. Your townhouse fire was months ago.

Tomi's ears perked up. *What?*

I'm using telepathy to talk to you. We need you to take one big breath—just one. We have an aerosol that will help you wake the rest of the way up. Okay? Do you believe me?

Tomi shook her head, but she did trust the voice. She sounded familiar. *Who are you?*

Wake up and see for yourself.

Tomi weighed her options while staring at the fire around her. It looked real—too real.

Trust me.

Tomi closed her eyes and then sucked in a deep breath. She woke with a prolonged, hacking cough. In between the hacking, she struggled to get enough air into her lungs. A mask over her nose wasn't pumping in pure air. She went to yank it off, but someone restrained her hand.

"Leave it on," the woman said. "Try to take another deep breath."

Easier said than done. Tomi tried and then tried again. At last, the burning in her throat and chest eased, and she could settle down in the bed. *Where am I?* Panicked, Tomi glanced around, but it was like looking up from underwater. The world was a blur.

"What's wrong with me?"

"Nothing. You need to give your body time to adjust."

Tomi shifted her gaze to the woman standing over her, but after blinking several times, she still couldn't make out her facial features. However, the woman had an awful lot of blond hair. "Who are you?"

"I know it's been a few years, but we'll always share a bond."

Tomi pieced the hair and the voice together in the back of her mind, but the conclusion didn't make sense. "It can't be. You're dead."

"According to some people, so are you."

47

"She's not dead," Shawn wheezed at Baasim and Farooq. Now that his beating had stopped and he was alone with the last two remaining Middle Eastern men, Shawn appealed to their humanity. "I know she appears dead, but you gotta trust me on this. She's not."

Baasim's temper exploded. "What the hell were you two doing here?"

Shawn crooked a lazy smile. "She had a bad feeling about you, man. From the moment she met you. I should've listened to her."

"We still have to get rid of them, Baasim," Farooq said. "You heard Saoud."

"Yeah, I heard him." Baasim expelled a long breath. He needed more time to think.

Farooq slapped him on the back. "I understand. She was about to become part of your family. If you want, I can take care of her for you. You can take care of the kid."

Baasim hesitated. "No, I can do it. Let's load her up in the back of one of the company vans."

"No! She's not dead," Shawn insisted, jerking around in his chair.

Farooq removed his weapon from his waist and pointed it at

Shawn's head. A millisecond before Farooq tapped the trigger, Baasim knocked down his arm, and the gunshot went wild.

"What—?"

"What are you doing?" Baasim hissed.

"What else are we supposed to do?"

"We drive them out to a isolated area—away from D.C."

Farooq hesitated.

"Trust me." Baasim held out his hand. "Give me the gun."

Farooq looked at his weapon and then back at Baasim. Sighing, he handed over the gun.

"Thanks." Baasim took the gun and walked over to Shawn. "Sorry about this, buddy. But this is going to hurt."

Shawn lifted his chin and leveled his gaze on Baasim. "Fuck you."

"Thanks for making this easier." Holding the barrel of the gun, Baasim swung the barrel like a golf club at the back of Shawn's head and knocked him out.

Baasim and Farooq loaded up Abrianna's and Shawn's limp bodies into the back of a Denco Air Conditioning & Supplies van and then climbed behind the wheel.

"Do you know a spot?" Farooq asked.

"Yeah. I have a place in mind." Baasim started the van and headed out.

Kadir stormed through the front door of his apartment shouting, "Bree! Are you home?" He blazed through the living room, casting a cursory look toward the kitchen before rushing down the hallway. His mother came out of her bedroom, clutching at her robe.

"What's going on?"

"Nothing, Mom. Go back to bed." He rushed into his bedroom. "Abrianna?"

"She's not here," his mother told him.

Panic reached Kadir's eyes. "Where is she?"

"How should I know? Nobody tells me anything around here," she snapped, affronted.

"I'm sorry, Mom. I'm not upset with you." He forced a smile and braced her shoulder. "I swear. Now, I've been calling Bree's cell phone all the way over here. She's not answering. I'm worried, that's all."

Castillo and Julian finally entered the apartment.

"Is she here?" Castillo asked.

"No." Kadir raked his hands through his hair and coached himself to calm down.

Julian dug his cell phone out of his pocket. "Maybe she's with Draya or Shawn. Those two are competing for the maid-of-honor title."

"Good idea." Kadir scooped his phone out, too. "I'll call Tina, too." Within minutes, they were able to eliminate Tina and Draya. Shawn was the only other person not answering his phone."

"Okay. Maybe they are together." Kadir breathed easier. "They could be at a movie or something." He glanced at his watch. "At two in the morning?"

"They could be at a club," Julian offered. "Shawn and Tivonté are constantly performing somewhere." He shrugged. "At two a.m., the party could just be getting started."

It was a plausible explanation, but it didn't feel right. The only thing Kadir could do was sit and wait.

48

At sunrise, Kadir was in full panic mode. The team stayed with him and his mother as they waited for Abrianna to walk through the door. Kadir lost count of the number of messages he'd left on Abrianna's phone. The problem was that she wasn't returning any of them.

"She's in trouble," Kadir said. "I just know it. I can feel it."

Daishan placed a hand on her son's shoulder. "Please, Kadir. Don't get yourself so worked up. I'm sure there's a reasonable explanation for all of this. Maybe Abrianna is . . . having second thoughts?"

"What?"

His mother shrugged. "It's a possibility. You have to admit that you guys are moving rather fast. Who could blame her if she wanted to take a breather?"

Kadir's brows dipped together as the scales fell from his eyes. "You would like that, wouldn't you, Mom?"

"What do you mean?" She carefully removed her hand from his shoulder.

Castillo interrupted. "I'm going to step outside and give you two some privacy."

Julian climbed up from the couch. "I'll join you, Gigi."

Kadir pressed his lips together until the door closed behind his colleagues. Then his gaze returned to his mother.

"Don't look at me like that." Daishan lifted her chin.

"Enough with the games, Ummi. You never gave her a chance. Not really."

Daishan looked aghast. "You're going to pin this on me? I've been nothing but nice to the girl."

Kadir's gaze hardened.

"*But* if you're asking me whether I'm happy that you're all set to marry an *atheist,* then the answer is no. I preferred you marry a nice *Muslim* girl."

"Malala was Muslim, and you never cared for her, either."

"A *Shia* Muslim," she clarified.

"Mom, just face it. You're not going to like any woman I choose to marry."

"Which is why *I* should be the one doing the choosing! That is how it is done. Your father and I knew plenty of families who would have loved to be attached to our family, too. But you and your brother are pigheaded. Traditions are traditions for a reason."

Kadir shook his head. "I can't do this with you right now. Bree didn't leave me. She's in real trouble. I have to find her."

"Fine." Daishan tossed up her hands. "But you're going to feel silly when you find out I'm right."

"I gotta get out here." Kadir turned and grabbed his jacket.

"Where are you going?"

"Out. I can't stay cooped up in here while Bree is going through God knows what out there—alone. Plus, I really can't be in the same room with you right now."

Daishan stepped forward. "Kadir."

"I have to go. If Abrianna does show up while I'm gone, call me, and you tell her to stay put until I get back. You think you can handle that?"

"Kadir—"

"Thanks." He left the apartment and slammed the door.

———⊷•⊶———

Baasim rushed inside Bruce's Boxing Club and then headed straight to the manager's office to meet up with his lead agent, William Dean, on the CIA and FBI special task force. "Good. You're here." He slammed the office door and then closed all the shades.

"Of course, I am here, Agent Kahlifa. You said it was an emergency."

"We have a problem."

"Has your cover been blown?"

"Not exactly," Baasim admitted, moving toward the desk.

"Then what?"

"My sister-in-law and a friend of hers have been out playing detective and were caught snooping around Denco's warehouse."

"That's not good."

"No. Saoud ordered me and Farooq to get rid of their bodies."

Dean settled back in his seat. "And did you?"

"We had to do something or risk our own lives. I have no doubt that I wouldn't have made it out of that room alive had I not agreed to get rid of the bodies."

"So they're dead?"

Baasim hesitated. *Trust me. She's not dead.* "No."

"Where are they? We should bring them in."

Baasim remembered the stories Kadir had told him about his future sister-in-law and knew that handing her over to the government might not be such a good idea. "They're safe."

"You're worried that they don't trust you now?"

"I can't see how they could. We're going to have to move up the timetable," Baasim insisted.

"Whoa." Dean held up his hands. "Let's slow down. We have a

lot at stake and only one shot to get all the players involved in this plot."

"We know enough. They are going to make their move on the president in less than forty-eight hours."

"Exactly. We need to play this out."

When Farooq reached out to Baasim, it was a major break for the CIA; but with the threat being inside the United States, the CIA teamed up with the FBI, and a special task force was created. Saoud's whole operation could have gone under the radar until it was too late, and the administration would have had another national crisis on their hands.

"We need to know *all* the players and the details of their plans."

"I've given you all I know. There isn't enough time. They are going to hit one of the president's campaign rallies. They've been sending us in to survey the ins and outs of how the campaign handles security, but as far as *which* rally they're going to hit, they're keeping that information close to their vest until the time is right. I probably won't know until the last minute."

"Try harder," Dean pressed. For a few seconds, the decades-long rivalry between the CIA and FBI pulsed between them. "If you haven't been made, we stick to the original plan. I will take your concerns to the higher-ups and get word to you if we do make any changes; but for right now, stay the course."

⚜

Another day, another talk show interview.

Zacher smiled into the camera and quoted the talking points T4S's public relations department had written for him. While he spun the company's bullshit, he remained mentally preoccupied with Shalisa's return to the living. After a twenty-minute segment on Fox's popular morning news show, Dr. Z removed his mike and shook the hosts' hands before making his exit. Off camera, he received another round of back swatting and praises for a job well done. It all went in one ear and out the other as a two-man security team fell in line behind him as he headed toward the elevator bay.

When the elevator's door opened, Dr. Z and his men stepped inside. After he pressed the button for the lobby and the door closed, the air seemed charged with a bolt of electricity. The hair on the back of his neck stood at attention a second before the elevator stopped—but not at the lobby.

The door slid open again, and a woman stepped inside.

"Shalisa."

She smiled. "Guys, why don't you give us some privacy?"

Dr. Z's security men looked confused, but with a flick of her wrists, the men flew out of the elevator and smashed into a wall.

Dr. Z stepped back as the elevator's door slid closed behind Shalisa.

"Alone at last," she said.

Dr. Z noticed the elevator hadn't moved. "What do you want?"

"Revenge." She stalked forward. "You helped Avery kidnap and torture me. I didn't kill my mother. *You* did. You turned me into a freak and then crammed me into a mental hospital where you continued to torture me for *years*."

Zacher slammed back against the wall, and an invisible force lifted him by the throat and choked him. "What kind of sick fuck does something like that?"

Dr. Zacher waved his arm and broke Shalisa's telekinetic hold. Once back on his feet, he gasped, "I don't expect you to understand."

"I have no interest in understanding. I want you dead." Shalisa moved toward the doctor. "First, I want to hear you scream."

Zacher waved his hand, lifting Shalisa off her feet and throwing her in the opposite direction. When she hit her head, stars danced behind her eyes, but rage boiled her blood.

Zacher opened the elevator door.

Shalisa telekinetically slammed it closed again, damn near taking off Zacher's arm before she threw him upward—several times, knocking out the lights. Then her rage sent him bouncing around like a rag doll. His being off balance made it impossible for him to protect himself.

"I should snap you in half."

A commotion started outside of the door.

"Dr. Zacher, are you all right in there?" someone shouted. "Hang in there. We're going to get you out of there."

Shalisa stepped back and looked down at Dr. Zacher's limp and unconscious body. She removed a syringe from her pocket and uncapped the needle. "Fuck you." She stabbed him in the side of his neck and emptied the syringe into his blood. His veins bulged and turned an ugly eggplant color on one side of his face. "You feel that? You're going to die, muthafucka. No more self-healing for you."

Shalisa snatched the needle back out of Dr. Z's neck. More veins swelled and spider-webbed across his face. His breathing thinned and sounded raspy. Shalisa stood and got hold of herself. "My job is done here." She glanced at the elevator's paneling, and the elevator moved again. She took it to the ground floor, but before exiting, she looked back down at Dr. Zacher. "Rot in hell."

<hr />

Kadir, Castillo, and Julian watched as Dr. Zacher stumbled out of the local Fox studio with the help of his assistant, Ned, and into a waiting car.

"What the hell happened to him?" Castillo asked.

"Trust. It pales compared to what I'm going to do to him," Kadir promised. "Stay with him, Julian."

"I'm on it." Julian sped up to keep up with Ned drifting in and out of lanes like he was in a Smokey and the Bandit movie.

"Don't lose them," Castillo ordered.

"We know where he's going," Kadir said. "Back to T4S. The man practically lives there."

Julian shook his head. "He's heading in the wrong direction for that. Something must be wrong. They are driving like a bat out of hell."

Kadir's nerves jumbled into knots and then rolled around in his gut. "Just don't lose them."

Ten minutes later, they were off the main roads and coasting into a residential area.

"Zacher must live out here," Kadir concluded.

"I was thinking the same thing," Castillo said.

"You don't think he stashed Abrianna at his place, do you?" Julian asked.

"Anything is possible," Castillo asked.

Zacher's car pulled up to a gated property. To avoid looking suspicious, Julian rolled past Zacher's car as the driver punched in a code to open the gates. When they circled back around, the gates were closing behind Zacher's car.

"Well, fuck. What are we going to do now?" Julian asked.

"We have to get onto that property," Kadir said.

"Agreed," Castillo cosigned.

"But how?" Julian asked.

Kadir and Castillo glanced at each other. "Ghost."

49

Baasim punched in for his shift at Denco on time. As he anticipated, most of his new coworkers eyeballed him with suspicion. He kept it cool as best he could and relied on his poker face. No one spoke to him as he worked the first half of his eight-hour shift, but when he punched out for lunch, Saoud materialized out of thin air and popped a squat next to him at a table in the break room.

"We good?" Saoud's gaze seared into Baasim.

"Why wouldn't we be?"

Saoud's face remained as still as marble. "Farooq said you were a real tough son of a bitch. I'm glad to see that he was right."

Baasim unwrapped his sub sandwich. "We all have to do what we have to do."

Saoud bobbed his head. "I like your focus—and dedication to the mission. You really want revenge for your dad, huh?"

"I thought I made that clear."

"Are you willing to risk your life for it?"

Baasim didn't miss a beat. "Absolutely."

"What about your brother?" Saoud asked. "What are you going to tell Kadir about his missing fiancée?"

"Nothing." Baasim cocked his head. "Why would Kadir tie her disappearance to me?"

Saoud's smile expanded. "You know what? I'm going to give

you that chance. I'm taking you and Farooq off grunt work and putting you on the team."

Baasim lifted a single brow. "Yeah?"

"Yeah." Saoud reached across the table and swatted Baasim on the shoulder. "You two more than proved yourselves last night. On this job, we can use the extra eyes and hands."

"Count us in."

———≫•≪———

Ned and the driver helped Dr. Zacher into his house. Zacher attempted to walk, but every bone and tendon hurt. His face looked like a crime scene. Blood gushed from his face while his mind spun like a pinwheel.

"Don't worry, sir. We got you."

Zacher barely recognized his own home.

"We should have taken him to the hospital," the driver worried.

"No. He's going to be all right," Ned assured him. "Help me get him up to the master bathroom."

Zacher wanted to hug Ned. His assistant knew how to handle this, and Zacher had never appreciated him more. He blacked out for a couple of minutes. When he came to, Ned barked at the driver to help him strip Zacher out of his bloody clothes.

"Man, this isn't in my job description," the driver complained.

"There's a big tip in it for you," Ned told him.

That satisfied the man. They quickly undressed Dr. Z and carried him into the marbled shower. When the cold water slapped Zacher in the face, it was like a thousand pins and needles stabbing him repeatedly.

"I'm going to get you cleaned up, sir," Ned kept saying.

However, the pain proved to be too much. Zacher passed out again.

———≫•≪———

Kadir and Castillo stalked Zacher's estate, looking for an entrance point to get onto the property. Ghost still had to be a few miles out, but Kadir couldn't sit and wait. Abrianna could be hurt. Sure, she was freakishly strong, had certain powers, and healed quickly, but Kadir wasn't convinced she was indestructible. As her man, *he* was supposed to be her protector—and he had failed.

"A car is coming," Julian hissed.

Everyone hunched down and watched the car that had brought Zacher home approach the gate.

"Julian, you stay out here and wait for Ghost," Kadir ordered. "Gigi and I are going to make a run for it."

"You got it."

The gate opened.

Kadir and Castillo raced to the gate. The driver stopped and rolled down the window.

Castillo smiled and waved like a suburban soccer mom. "Hey, is the doctor in?"

"Yeah, but—"

"Great! Thanks." She and Kadir jogged off toward the house. They felt the driver's gaze follow their progress toward Zacher's house. They waited with bated breath to see whether the driver would back up or call in reinforcement, but apparently the driver decided Kadir and Castillo were not his concern and went ahead and drove off the property.

———◦———

Ned poured his boss into his king-size bed after dragging him from the shower stall. The driver had wasted no time hightailing it out of there. It was clear he was uncomfortable with the doctor's situation. Ned was nervous, too. He'd never seen the doctor this weak, but at least he'd finally got the bleeding to stop. Desperate, Ned reconsidered calling for an ambulance.

"Let me rest for a few minutes," Zacher groaned, hugging the pillow. "I'll be all right."

Ned nodded, but doubt crept around the back of his head. He backed out of the bedroom and scooped his cell phone from his pocket and placed a call. "I need to speak with Pierce Spalding."

"May I ask who is calling?"

"This is Ned Cox."

"Please hold."

Someone hammered on the front door. Curious, Ned peered over the upstairs railing. The hammering continued as if a whole police squad stood on the other side.

"Mr. Spalding is in a business meeting at the moment. Can I take a message?"

Ned started down the staircase when the front door opened. He recognized Kadir and Castillo. "I'll call him back." He disconnected the call.

Kadir's neck swiveled in Ned's direction. "Where is he?"

Ned stopped in the middle of the staircase. "You guys can't be here."

"Answer the muthafuckin' question." Kadir charged the staircase.

Ned climbed the stairs backward. "Wait. You don't understand. Dr. Zacher can't see anyone right now."

"He's going to see me." Kadir swatted Ned out of his way and bypassed him on the staircase.

"I'm calling the police," Ned shouted.

"Do what you have to do."

When Ned punched numbers into the phone, Castillo snatched the phone out of his hand.

"Why don't we hold off on that until after we ask the doctor a few questions, huh?"

"You don't understand. The doctor isn't well right now."

"Found him," Kadir shouted.

Castillo ignored Ned's sputtering and rushed to join Kadir.

Kadir didn't process the scene before he dragged Dr. Zacher from his bed. "Where is she?"

Confused, Dr. Z lifted his swollen face. "Where is who?"

"Abrianna! I know you monsters took her. Where are you keeping her?"

Zacher shook his head. "I don't know what you're talking about."

It was the wrong answer.

Kadir crashed his fist against the doctor's chin.

Zacher crashed to the floor. Before he could clear the stars circling behind his eyelids, Kadir pounded Zacher's jaw until his mouth filled with blood.

"Enough," he choked out, lifting a hand.

Kadir tumbled backward.

Dr. Z was too weak to keep him back. "Please. I don't know what you're talking about. I don't have Abrianna."

"Bullshit."

"No," Ned interjected. "He's telling the truth."

Kadir's and Castillo's heads swiveled toward the assistant.

Ned stepped back again. "Don't hurt me."

Castillo grabbed Ned by his shirt. "Then start talking."

"About what? We don't have her."

"Why should we believe you? You guys attempted to grab her before for more of your freak experiments."

Ned stuttered. "We've been issued a stand-down order."

"Ned," Zacher croaked.

"He's lying," Kadir growled and took another threatening step toward the doctor.

"I'm not lying. The orders came from the top. There's too much heat on the company since the Lehane debacle," Ned said. "If Parker is missing, it has nothing to do with us."

"Bullshit." Kadir took another step.

Dr. Z pulled himself into sitting position and leaned back

against his bed. "Look, son. I'm dying." He choked over another gulp of blood. "I can feel it."

"Am I supposed to give a shit?" Kadir barked.

A rueful grin curved Zacher's face. "No. I suppose not." He slumped down. "I've done some . . . misguided things in my time. Things that I regret."

"Misguided?" Kadir squatted down so he could be eye level with the doctor. "Is that how you see murdering children?"

"Of course you would see it that way." Zacher shook his head.

"Is there another way to see it?"

"I understand objecting to our methods. But, in the pursuit of science, it was for a great cause."

"The cause of creating super soldiers to *die* in more manufactured wars? Please, tell me that you can do much better than that."

"Manufactured wars?" Zacher shook his head. "Liberal talk. Haven't you ever heard that freedom isn't free? Would you rather we have the technology and science we do than the enemy? Because that's what's happening. You think we're the only country going down this road?"

"I'm not here to argue morality with you," Kadir growled. "Where is Abrianna?"

"We told you. We don't have her."

"Like you would tell me if you did," Kadir countered.

Dr. Z chuckled. "Probably not, but in this instance, we happen to be telling the truth. But if she's missing, then maybe the same people who broke Lehane out my lab have her."

Kadir shot Castillo a look.

"And who was that?" Kadir asked.

"You're not going to believe me if I told you."

"Try us," Castillo challenged.

Zacher dragged in a ragged breath. "Another Avery survivor." He swung his gaze from Kadir to Castillo.

"Shalisa Young," she said.

"You guys don't look surprised," Dr. Z noted.

Kadir smirked. "We had a clue after watching you and your sidekick here dig up her grave."

Ned asked. "You followed us?"

"We tend to be thorough in our investigation."

"I don't know why I didn't put it all together before. I knew about the self-healing, but a fall like that?" He shook his head. "Then we saw her body at the morgue. She looked like she'd died in her sleep. I should have known then. I ordered her body to our lab, but then a family member popped up from nowhere and took possession of the body and buried her. End of story, I thought. But now . . ."

Kadir didn't care for the backstory. "How do we find a legally dead person?"

Dr. Z coughed. Once he started, he couldn't stop.

Ned broke away from Castillo's grip and rushed to the bathroom to prep a wet towel and returned to his boss. The coughing died down. Dr. Z wiped his mouth and painted the cloth with blood.

"Shalisa had no problem with finding me this afternoon."

Kadir frowned. "She worked you over?"

"It's safe to say that she's not a fan of my work." Dr. Z coughed again.

"Who is?" Kadir asked. "How do we find her?"

"By finding who backs her," Dr. Z smirked. "She didn't rescue Lehane by herself."

"ITCS International," Kadir and Castillo said together.

Dr. Z smiled. "You *are* thorough. But if they do have her, good luck getting her out."

50

On the drive back to the outskirts of D.C., Baasim placed a call to his special task force leader, William Dean, and updated him on his and Farooq's promotion with the sleeper cell.

"Do we know who Saoud gets his orders from?"

"Still no intel on that, but they are getting ready to move."

"Copy that, but it sure would be nice to get that final piece to the puzzle. Someone is funding this operation. According to our research, Mr. Almasi isn't liquid enough to pull something of this size off. Denco is a front and nothing more. We're going to need you to keep digging before we make a move."

Baasim sighed. "We're cutting it close, don't you think?"

"We need to get this right. After the airport bombing last year, we can't afford to fuck this up."

"I hear you."

"Where are Parker and her sidekick?"

Baasim parked in front of an old decaying building and shut off the engine. "They're safe . . . for now."

"We need to bring them in."

Baasim thought over Abrianna's condition. "Nah, I have it under control right now."

Dean sighed. "All right. Keep me posted."

"Will do."

Inside the looted and mildew-smelling three-story building, Farooq paced like a nervous wreck.

"How are they doing?" Baasim asked.

"Exactly how you think they're doing. The girl is still dead, and the guy is still a pain in the ass." Farooq raked both hands through his oily hair and kept pacing. "I don't feel comfortable about this. What did Dean say? Why can't we turn these two over to them? The longer we hold them, the more we're at risk to be exposed."

"Calm down, Farooq."

"Calm down? Do you have any idea what Saoud and his guys will do to me if they find out that I vouched for a fucking CIA agent to join the group?"

"That's not going to happen," Baasim assured him. "We need to act normal. Saoud already approached me at work."

"What did he say?"

Baasim smiled. "We've been promoted."

The tension in Farooq's face was replaced by shock. "What?"

"What can I say? Saoud was so impressed with how we didn't bat an eye to get rid of my future sister-in-law that we've been promoted from grunt work to being actual players in the game."

Farooq's entire body slumped with relief. "So this may be coming to an end soon?"

"All you have to do is keep calm and play your role." Baasim glanced at his watch. "That means you reporting to work like normal."

Farooq nodded and then glanced at the door. "Are you staying here?"

"For a few minutes. If I don't show up at the apartment tonight, I'm sure it'll raise a few eyebrows."

Farooq nodded. "Okay. Yeah. All right." He backpedaled toward the door.

"Remember to stay calm," Baasim told him. "We're almost at the finish line."

"Got it. Right." Farooq flashed a smile and then rushed out of the abandoned building.

Baasim twisted the key that rested in the lock and opened the door to the room holding Abrianna and Shawn. When he entered the room, Shawn's angry blue eyes speared and tracked him as he walked over to Abrianna.

"You stay away from her, asshole."

Baasim sighed and then felt around Abrianna's neck to check for a pulse. There wasn't one. "Are you sure she's not dead?" he asked gravely.

"Like you care," Shawn spat.

Baasim glanced over his shoulder. "If I didn't care, you wouldn't be breathing right now."

Shawn squirmed in his seat while he reevaluated Baasim. "Then what? You're casting yourself as some kind of hero?"

Baasim smirked "Something like that."

"Then let us go."

"Sorry. I'm afraid I can't do that." Baasim stood. "It would cause a problem for me and my friend if you were seen alive right now."

"By those other criminals you work with?"

"Let's make one thing clear. You have no idea what's going on here—or what you stumbled into."

Shawn's cold gaze never wavered. "Why don't you enlighten me?"

"After you tell me why I shouldn't bury Abrianna."

"Because like I told you and your idiot friend, she's not dead."

"She looks dead."

"Really?" Shawn licked his dry lips. "Then where is the rigor mortis?"

Baasim frowned.

Shawn sighed. "Abrianna is . . . different."

"This has something to do with all those wild experiments she went through as a kid?"

"She's . . . healing," Shawn said. "It usually takes three days.

Probably not bad for a crushed skull." A tear streaked down his face. "She's going to be just fine."

Baasim lowered his gaze. The guy's torment tugged at him. "Look, I can't tell you exactly what's going on, but I need you to trust me on this."

"Trust you?" Shawn barked. "Why the hell would I do something like that?"

Baasim glanced back at the door and then lowered his voice. "Because I'm not who you think I am."

"I think you're the guy who knocked me out with the back of a gun."

"Well, it was either that or blow my cover."

Enlightenment dawned in Shawn's eyes. "Cop?"

"CIA."

* * *

After Kadir and Castillo left Zacher's place, they weren't sure the doctor would live to see another twenty-four hours. Ned looked shattered. When they walked out of the gate, Ghost climbed out of a van behind their vehicle.

"Everything copacetic?" he asked.

"Far from it." Kadir engaged in a one-shoulder hug. "Thanks for coming to the rescue . . . again."

Ghost smirked. "It's what I do. Of course, it doesn't look like you guys needed my help this time."

"We will. Abrianna is missing."

Ghost nodded. "Yeah, Julian filled me in that she never returned home last night."

Kadir nodded. "Zacher and T4S don't have her, so we think ITCS may. How do you feel about going in guns blazing?"

Ghost hesitated.

"Is there a problem?"

"Um." Ghost winced.

"What?"

"Are we sure that ITCS is at the top of the list?" he asked dubiously.

"What do you mean?"

Ghost hesitated again.

"You know something," Kadir concluded. "What aren't you telling me?" He stepped forward and grabbed Ghost by his shirt. "What the fuck are you not telling me?"

"See? This is exactly the scenario I wanted to avoid. The last place I want to be, in the middle of you and the future missus."

Castillo approached with her arms crossed and her head cocked.

"Look, I'm offering up another possibility. I don't *know* anything. Just . . ."

"Just what?" Kadir barked.

Ghost sighed. "When was the last time you've seen your *brother*?"

51

"CIA?" Shawn questioned. "You've got to be kidding me."

Baasim grinned. "I'm afraid not."

"You're undercover?"

"Bingo." Baasim crossed his arms. "Now you see why I can't just let you leave and risk you being seen? It'll blow my cover."

"So, you're *not* going to kill us?"

"No." He shook his head. "Despite you two almost getting *me* killed."

Shawn relaxed. "Oh thank God for plot twists."

Rat-tat-tat-tat!

Rat-tat-tat-tat!

Shawn hung his head. "And here comes another one."

Baasim grabbed his weapon from the back of his waist and rushed toward the room's door.

"Whoa. Hold up! You can't just leave me tied here," Shawn shouted as Baasim raced out of the room.

Baasim made it to the nearest window and stole a peek outside. Up the small dirt road, he made out the taillights of Farooq's car. The problem was the two sets of headlights in front of the vehicle. Then he saw men moving around Farooq's car.

"Shit." He must have been followed.

"Hey, what's going on out there?" Shawn shouted.

Baasim heard Shawn bouncing around in his chair.

"Those were gunshots. Who is out there shooting?"

Baasim glanced down at his lone weapon, a .45, and then counted four men approaching the building who were undoubtedly armed to the teeth.

"Hey, man. You can't keep me tied up in here." The chair bounced around again. "C'mon, man. You gotta cut me loose. Give me a fighting chance."

Baasim had two seconds to think it over before he ran back to the room. "We're outgunned, so we're going to have to make a run for it." He untied Shawn from the chair.

"We better head out the back."

Shawn sprang up, but immediately raced over to Abrianna's unconscious body. "We have to take her with us."

"What?"

"We can't leave her."

Baasim stared at Shawn like he had sprouted a second head. "We don't have time for that. She's safer here. She already appears dead."

"We're not leaving her," Shawn insisted. "Help me."

The front door of the abandoned building squeaked open.

"Fuck," Baasim swore. "We're out of time."

Panic seized the men.

Again, Shawn turned to Abrianna. "Bree, I know you're in there. If you can hear me, we could really use your help!"

Baasim frowned as he gathered Abrianna off the floor and slung her over his shoulder. "Let's go." He headed out the door and hung a left. Shawn limped close behind them.

Immediately, they were almost picked off. A bullet whizzed by Shawn's head. After rounding a corner, Baasim picked up speed but knew there was no way they were getting out alive.

"Bree, if you don't wake up, we're going to die. Please," Shawn pled.

Rat-at-tat-tat!

Rat-at-tat-tat!

A hundred feet from the back door, Baasim experienced a spark of hope. However, it was dashed when the door bolted open and two men charged inside. Baasim slowed to a stop.

Shawn crashed into him.

A smile curved on Yasser's face as he raised his weapon at Baasim. "Going somewhere, Baasim?"

Baasim lifted his chin and weighed whether he should attempt to shoot his way out.

Behind him, Awsam and another goon caught up with them. They were surrounded.

Yasser smiled. "I knew there was something fishy about you when you returned stateside so quickly," Yasser continued. "You would've had to have some major connections to get out of Sana'a that fast. And I've always had my suspicions about Farooq, but Saoud was too blinded by his friendship to see the obvious. But nothing gets past me." His grinned looked menacing. "Farooq never had the stomach for this kind of life, so it was odd for him to be bringing someone new into the group."

Baasim said nothing.

"I have to give it to you, you're a hell of an actor. I like how you used your father's death to your advantage with Saoud."

"Does Saoud know you're here?"

"Nah, me and my boys were just following a hunch. This shit is going to break his heart. But this will prove my point to the other guys that we're way past time for new leadership." Yasser moved forward. "But first, I need to know: Who do you work for? And how much do they know about our plans for President Washington?"

Baasim clenched his jaw and lifted his chin.

"Just shoot him," Awsam huffed. "If Farooq didn't talk, neither will he. All we have to do is prove that they didn't get rid of the gay guy and the bitch like they were ordered."

Baasim saw the wheels spinning in Yasser's head. Behind, Shawn continued to talk to Abrianna.

"What the fuck is he saying?" Awsam barked. "Who is he talking to?"

Baasim groaned. "You wouldn't believe me if I told you."

"Try me."

Baasim shrugged. "He's talking to Abrianna."

Yasser frowned. "The dead girl?"

"What can I say? He doesn't know how to let go."

"Search them," Yasser barked. "Make sure they're not wired."

Awsam and his guy rushed Shawn and Baasim.

"Ah, ah, ah." Baasim moved against the wall and warded off Awsam by swinging his aim between the men as if indecisive on whom to shoot first. As a result, everyone's gun came back up aiming at Baasim's head.

Yasser's grin spread wider. "C'mon, Baasim. We all know how this is going to end. But I promise you if you tell me what I need to know that we will make it quick."

Baasim struggled to keep his aim straight while Abrianna's dead weight weighed down his left shoulder.

"Who do you work for?" Yasser asked. "Are you a cop—a federal agent? Who is going to come looking for you when you turn up missing?"

Baasim refused to answer.

Shawn kept mumbling to Abrianna.

"All right. Have it your way," Yasser said. "Awsam, shoot him in the leg."

"Which one?"

Baasim's left shoulder grew warm—then hot.

"I don't give a fuck. Just pick one."

Awsam shrugged and then took aim, but instead of firing, he dropped the weapon. A shot went wild. "Aah. Goddamn." He waved his hand around. "Fuck!"

Yasser looked at him. "What the hell is wrong with you?"

"I don't know. The shit just got hot as hell." Awsam knelt to pick up the weapon again, but couldn't. "Ouch."

Yasser rolled his eyes. "*Somebody* shoot this muthafucka!"

But the other two men hissed and also dropped their weapons. One wild shot missed Baasim by inches.

"What the fuck is wrong with you, *ahbil*?"

They looked flummoxed themselves.

"Fuck it. If you want something done, you have to do it yourself." Yasser aimed and fired.

But the bullet didn't hit Baasim. It fell to the ground in front of him. However, Baasim fired back and nailed Yasser between the eyes.

Everyone was stunned. A second later, the other three men charged Baasim, but before Baasim could fire off another shot, the three men were propelled backward and slammed against the opposing brick wall, knocking them out cold.

Baasim stood dumbfounded. "What the fuck just happened?"

"Yasser! Is everything all right in there?"

Baasim's gaze shot to the phone lying inches from Yasser's dead body.

"Yasser!"

"There are more guys outside," Baasim concluded. He eased Abrianna's body down to the ground and stared at her. "Did she . . ."

Shawn nodded. "She may be out, but on some level, she's conscious of the things around her, especially if she's in danger."

Baasim heard what Shawn was saying, but had trouble wrapping his head around it.

"Yasser! Talk to me. Do you need backup?"

Baasim walked over to the phone and picked it up.

"We're coming in," the voice announced.

Baasim hung up the call and looked to Shawn. "Any way she could help us out one more time?"

The second he got the question out, two more men came through the back door. The moment they made eye contact with Baasim, they started firing.

Baasim took a bullet to the shoulder but returned fire on his way down to the ground. From the corner of his eye, he saw Shawn feverishly whispering into Abrianna's ear.

Before more bullets sprayed Baasim's way, the last guys' weapons flew out of their hands. There was a sickening crunch that filled the empty building when their heads twisted a hundred and eighty degrees. They fell dead where they stood.

Baasim shot a look over at Shawn. "Holy shit."

Shawn smiled. "How do you like my girl now?"

52

ITCS International . . .

"Mr. Hunter, Pierce Spalding is here to see you."

Nate smiled at the announcement. "Thanks, Sally. Send him on in." He stood from his desk and buttoned his business jacket. "Showtime." When the office door opened, Nate turned on his thousand-watt smile and approached his number-one competitor with a gleam in his eye. "Pierce, what a surprise to see you."

Pierce's face barely cracked a smile as they shook hands. "I hope I'm not interrupting anything."

"Of course you are, but I will allow it." Nate pounded Spalding on the shoulder and then gestured to a vacant chair. "Please, have a seat."

Spalding humbly sat down while Hunter leaned against the front of his desk so that he dominated the meeting.

"So what can I do for you, my old friend?"

Spalding got straight to the point. "How about you hand Tomi Lehane back over?"

Nate laughed. "You want to run that back by me?"

"C'mon. I know it was you and your guys who attacked our compound and stole our test subject."

"Test subject?" Nate repeated with a smile.

"Let's not play games. I know you have her."

"Frankly, I adore games—but in this case, I have no idea which one we're playing. I don't know anything about your missing test subject who, apparently, you kidnapped from her home." He reached across his desk and picked up the phone. "But, if you'd like, I could place a call to the FBI and let them know about your stolen test subject."

Spalding rose from his seat and took the phone out of Hunter's hand. "Very funny."

"I'm just trying to help."

"That's why I'm here," Spalding confessed.

"Come again?"

"Maybe it's way past time we worked together."

"Really?"

Spalding nodded. "We have more common interests than not, especially in the coming election. President Washington is a threat to our industry, and you damn well know it. It's dangerous to let her pit our companies against each other."

Hunter considered him.

"You know I'm right."

"I'm listening."

Spalding flashed a genuine smile. "We have a plan."

"You always do."

Spalding returned to his seat and laid out what T4S had planned to solve their President Washington problem. However, twenty minutes into the spiel, they were interrupted.

"Mr. Hunter, there is a Ms. Gizella Castillo here to see you."

Spalding groaned.

Hunter's smile expanded. "A friend of yours?"

"Hardly, but it's definitely my cue to leave." Spalding stood. "You'd be wise to stay out of Castillo's path, too. She's much too nosy for her own good."

"Oh, I don't know. I love a challenge." Hunter pushed off from his desk.

"Sally, send Ms. Castillo on in."

"Yes, sir."

"We'll continue this later," Nate promised and walked Spalding to the door. "Your proposal is . . . interesting."

When Hunter's door opened, Castillo entered and came face-to-face with Spalding.

Castillo lifted an inquisitive brow. "My, today is turning up a whole lot of surprises." She crossed her arms. "You two wouldn't happen to be teaming up together, would you?"

"Sorry to disappoint you, Ms. Castillo." Spalding gave the private detective a stiff nod. "Maybe you should reel in that active imagination?"

Castillo dismissed him to stare at the television screen over his left shoulder.

Breaking News: *Washington Post* Reporter Found Alive

"Turn that up," Castillo ordered.

Smiling, Hunter picked up the remote control from his desk and turned up the television's volume.

> "Pulitzer Prize–nominated reporter Tomi Lehane was found wandering along a roadside on the outskirts of D.C. The Arlington County Sheriff's Office said late Thursday that Tomi Lehane was taken to Sibley Memorial Hospital for evaluation. WJLA reports the celebrated reporter is conscious and recovering but no word as to where she has been for these past few months . . ."

"I have to go," Castillo announced and then hightailed it out of Nate Hunter's office. Minutes later, Castillo was in her car, racing to the hospital. A million questions swirled inside her head. Was Tomi all right? Who had her? Was she released or had she escaped her captors? Just moments ago, she was sure Nate Hunter was her guy. Now, everything was back up in the air.

Or it was all over.

———⊰•⊱———

At the hospital, Castillo shoved her way through the ring of reporters outside of the hospital and then darted to the nearest nurse's station. However, she received pushback until Dinah Lehane spotted her.

"Ms. Castillo, you're here." Dinah grabbed Gigi's hand and led her up to Tomi's room.

The moment they stepped into the room and looked into Tomi's blank stare, Castillo knew she wouldn't be getting answers to any of her questions.

"Hey, baby, look who came to see you."

A smile hooked the corner of Tomi's lips, but it didn't reach her eyes. Castillo couldn't say whether her friend recognized her or not, but Tomi picked up clues from her mother's inflection.

Castillo played along. Smiling, she walked over to the bed and gingerly took Tomi's hand. "How are you feeling?"

"Like shit," Tomi replied flatly. "I'm ready to get out of here."

"I'm sure when they finish making sure that you're all right, you'll be free to go."

"No more tests." Tomi shook her head. "I'm not a damn lab rat." She moved her hand away.

Dinah stepped forward and brushed her hair back. "Don't worry. I already told them. We're just waiting for the doctor now to release you."

Tomi lowered her gaze and nodded.

Castillo cast a concerned gaze at Tomi's mother and received a confused shrug. "Tomi, um, do you mind answering a few questions?"

A muscle twitched along the side of Tomi's right temple. "What kind of questions?"

"For starters, where have you been? Who took you and how did you get away?"

Tomi shook her head. "I don't know what you're talking about."

"I have footage of you being kidnapped out of your own home. Serena, your neighbor, captured it all on her cell phone the night your townhouse went up in flames." Castillo studied Tomi's face. "She's taking care of Rocky while you're gone."

"Rocky," Tomi repeated. Finally, a genuine smile blossomed. "He's alive?"

Castillo nodded. "Yes. I'm sure that he's going to be really happy to see you again."

"I can't wait to see him, too." Tomi fell silent again.

Castillo waited and then pressed. "Well? What can you tell me about the people who took you?"

Tomi shrugged one shoulder. "Nothing. I . . . don't remember anything."

Castillo frowned. "What *do* you remember?"

During the ensuing silence, Castillo shot Dinah another worried look and received the same helpless expression in return.

"I remember . . ." Tomi struggled. "I remember arriving home from work . . . and Rocky greeting me. Then . . . there was someone in the house, I think. I went to check it out and then . . . everything happened so fast. Someone was shooting, and then . . . someone grabbed me. I . . ." Tomi shook her head. "I don't know . . . suddenly the place was on fire. I went down, and I saw Rocky. I thought he was dead."

Castillo waited for Tomi to continue, but she appeared to be finished. "What happened after that?"

Tomi shook her head. "I don't know. It's all a blank."

Speeding across town, Kadir kept calling his brother's cell phone only to be transferred to Baasim's voice mail. Having already left several messages for a call back, Kadir didn't know what else to say and hung up—again. He attempted to find his brother's apartment complex but decided that he must have remembered the information wrong and had to call his mother. But to his surprise, she also had the same wrong information. *What the hell? Why would Baasim give me bogus information?*

Kadir stopped circling the area of the fictitious apartment complex and wondered at his next move. "Farooq." He snapped his fingers. If there were anyone who knew where his brother was, it would be Baasim's best friend. Within minutes, Kadir sped over to Bezoria's.

When Kadir rushed inside the restaurant, he saw that it was a slow evening.

"Good evening, sir. How many are your party?"

"Actually, I'm here to speak with Farooq. Is he in?"

The hostess looked him over. "I haven't seen him this evening, but let me go check whether he's in the kitchen. What's your name?"

"Kadir . . . Kadir Kahlifa. I'm an old friend of the family."

"Just a second."

With a smile, she deserted her post to head back to the kitchen.

Kadir slid his hands into his jacket and glanced around the restaurant again. This time, his gaze flitted to Saoud huddled in the far corner with a small group around him. A second later, Saoud lifted his head and met Kadir's gaze. Instinctively, Kadir smiled and gave a brief head nod in greeting.

Kadir's cell phone vibrated against his leg as Saoud stood from the table. He scooped the phone out of his pocket. It was Ghost. "Hello."

"Kadir, I know where Abrianna is."

"What?" He plugged a finger in his other ear so he could hear Ghost better.

"Remember when I told you I gave Bree and Shawn a bunch of spy equipment?"

"No. You did *not* tell me that."

"Oh well. It might have slipped my mind," Ghost said. "Anyway, I gave Shawn a locator watch—a sort of bat signal to use if they ran into trouble. It just went off."

Kadir's heart lodged in his throat as he spun around to head back out of the restaurant. "Where are they?"

"I'll text you the coordinates," Ghost promised. "We're locked and loaded and will meet you there."

"Got it." Kadir disconnected the call, but before he could exit the restaurant, three men blocked the door.

Kadir stepped back. "Excuse me, guys."

"The boss wants to talk to you."

Kadir frowned. "The boss?"

The tallest of the men nodded his head to indicate for Kadir to look over his right shoulder.

Perplexed, Kadir turned toward a smiling Saoud.

"Kadir, my man. Let me holler at you for a few minutes."

53

The unmistakable sound of car engines and tires kicking up dirt made Baasim peek out the bottom floor windows, and he felt his heart plunge into his gut. "Fuck!"

Shawn looked up. "Do I even want to know?"

"We got more company."

"No. I didn't want to know that."

Baasim bent down and struggled to pick Abrianna up. "We have to get out of here."

"We're going to make a run for it?"

Baasim's mind scrambled for a possible plan. There was no way they were going to get far on foot and no way they would even make it to his car out front without getting pumped full of lead. "We hide."

"Hide?"

"There are three floors. It will buy us some time while I call in reinforcements—unless you got a better plan?"

Shawn swallowed. "I already called in reinforcements."

"What?"

"The watch." Shawn indicated Abrianna's wrist. "It has an emergency locator signal. Ghost gave it to us."

"Ghost?" Baasim sighed. "Even better. C'mon. Let's go." This time when he hung Abrianna over his shoulder, his shoulder ached, and his knees threatened to drop him on the spot. But Baasim pushed through the pain and hauled Abrianna to the staircase. The moment they pushed through the door, they were assaulted by awful smells of rotten dead animals and fecal matter.

Shawn slapped a hand over his mouth to prevent himself from gagging but kept going.

When they reached the second floor, Baasim's back and thighs screamed for him to put Abrianna down. Still, he pushed on. At the third floor, they heard the staircase's bottom-floor door burst open.

Saoud's men greet the awful smell by gagging and swearing. Still, they charged up the stairs. On the third floor, Baasim and Shawn exited the staircase but almost fell through a large hole in the rotten wood floor.

Shawn looked around the large, deserted floor, trying to figure out where to go next.

Baasim signaled for Shawn to follow him while he took off down a long hallway, but before they could duck into a room, gunfire erupted.

Baasim spun to return fire, but lost his footing from the added weight and fell, sending the three of them straight through the floor.

Shawn yelled out when he landed on his bad leg.

Baasim couldn't even breathe. Abrianna had landed across his chest, knocking the wind out of him. But the hard landing also forced Abrianna to gasp and wake up.

When she groaned, it shocked the shit out of Baasim, while Shawn started to praise Jesus. But there was no time to talk. Abrianna's scalp was on fire. On instinct, she threw up her hands just as a pair of AK-47s cracked and sprayed bullets from above.

Baasim's mouth fell open as bullets slammed into what appeared to be an invisible shield and rolled harmlessly to the floor. More artillery went off, and Saoud's men redirected their fire.

"C'mon, we got to get out of here." Baasim struggled to get to his feet, but Shawn's twisted leg wasn't having it.

"Go ahead," Shawn panted. "Leave me here."

Abrianna turned to her friend and with one hand picked him up from the floor and tossed him over her shoulder.

Baasim stared. "How are you—?"

Abrianna left Baasim standing and marched over and opened a window.

"What are you doing?" Baasim and Shawn barked.

Abrianna hunched low to climb out the window.

"Are you crazy? That's a two-story—"

She jumped.

Baasim raced to the window and looked down. Abrianna landed on her feet. "The fuck?" He glanced around and knew damn well that there was no way he was going to make that jump without breaking something.

Baasim's gaze swung to the large bush climbing up the building and made a calculation—one he wasn't pleased with. "Fuck it." He tucked his gun into his waist and ducked out onto the window ledge. "You can do this," Baasim repeated until he made a leap of faith.

Abrianna set Shawn on his feet as more bullets whizzed by her. She turned toward her attackers and with a flick of her wrist snapped their necks.

Bam!

Abrianna turned around.

Baasim groaned and spilled out of the bushes.

Ghost leaned out of the third-story window. "Is everybody all right?"

Baasim waved his hand and struggled to his feet. "I'm all right."

Shawn hobbled to his side. "Are you sure, man?"

Baasim nodded as he swiped shrubbery from his clothes. "I think so." He looked at Abrianna. "How about you?"

Her gaze narrowed. "You're a fucking terrorist."

"Wait. Whoa." Shawn held up both hands to stop Abrianna from coming closer. "He's not a terrorist," he informed Abrianna. "He's an undercover agent. He works for the CIA."

Abrianna's face twisted. "What?"

"Yeah. Thanks for helping blow my cover."

The information wasn't computing. There had to be some sort of joke, but they looked serious. "A CIA agent?" she repeated.

"Afraid so." Baasim flashed her a smile. "And you . . . are amazing." He glanced up at the second-story window and then back to Abrianna. "You're like a superhuman."

Ghost, Roger, and Wendell raced out of the building. "Is that all of them?"

Baasim glanced around. "It appears so. Thank you for coming and saving our necks. Though I have a feeling we would have made it out either way with our one-woman army."

"You're welcome." Ghost grimaced at the backhanded compliment.

"Now, you guys got to get out of here so I can call in my real backup. If you're here when the feds show up—"

"Say no more," Ghost told him and then looked at his watch. "I wonder what's keeping Kadir."

"Kadir?" Abrianna asked.

"Oh yeah." Ghost chuckled. "You got a lot of explaining to do."

————⋙•⋘————

In the basement of Bezoria's, Saoud stood back as his men worked Kadir over while he was tied to a chair.

"C'mon, Kadir," Saoud said, bored. "Don't make me remove a finger or two. Who do you and your brother work for, um? How much do they know about our organization?"

Kadir spat out a mouthful of blood. "I don't know what you're talking about. I came here looking for Farooq."

"Why?"

Kadir shook his head. "I told you. I thought that he might know where Baasim was. I'm looking for my fiancée. She's missing."

"She's not missing," Saoud informed Kadir. "She got caught putting her nose where it doesn't belong."

Kadir's one unswollen eye widened while he worked the ropes behind his back.

"She's dead," Saoud told him with a shrug. "You can thank me later. It would have never worked out between you two."

Kadir surged forward, surprising Saoud that he'd managed to get free from his bondage. "Where is she!" He managed to get a few blows across Saoud's jaw before his goons pulled him off. After which Kadir endured another series of punches that made him see stars. More blood poured into his mouth, and he was sure a broken tooth floated around in there.

"Fuck this shit." Saoud whipped out his piece and aimed at Kadir's head.

The basement door burst open, and an army of men in FBI jackets poured inside.

"Don't move! Everybody down!"

Saoud snarled with the barrel still pointed at Kadir.

"Put the weapon down," an agent barked.

Saoud took too long to comply and received a bullet to the head.

Brain matter splattered everywhere.

Kadir sighed. He'd never in his life been happier to see federal agents.

D.C. Terrorist Cell Infiltrated

Washington—Terrorists were in their "final stages" of a plot to assassinate the president of the United States, US Homeland Security Secretary Jonathan Nielsen said Thursday. The CIA and FBI teamed up to thwart the attacks. Twenty-four

Yemen-American men were arrested in three targeted raids across a tri-state area, authorities said, including Arab-owned Denco Air Conditioning & Supplies warehouse and the popular Middle Eastern restaurant Bezoria's.
An undercover CIA agent infiltrated the group, giving the authorities intelligence on the alleged plans, several US government officials said. It is believed that the attacks were organized as revenge attacks for the botched Yemen air strikes carried out by the United States in recent months. The suspects were planning to stage a test run within a couple of days, said a US Intelligence official.

President Kate Washington sat mute as she listened to the director of the CIA and the director of the FBI fill her in on how one of their special task forces infiltrated and raided a sleeper terrorist cell in their backyard.

"Kahlifa?" she stopped Martha Rigaud, the director of the CIA, while she rambled through the list of agents involved in infiltrating the cell. "He wouldn't happen to be related to Kadir Kahlifa, would he?"

Rigaud exchanged looks with her FBI counterpart before shifting uncomfortably in her chair. "Actually, Madame President, Agent Baasim Kahlifa is Kadir Kahlifa's twin brother."

"Twin?" She barked out a laugh. "Well, what do you know? It really is a small world." A smile monopolized the president's face. "All in all, this is shaping up to be a pretty good day."

Her cabinet members exchanged confused looks. "C'mon. First, Tomi Lehane reappears with apparently no memory of what the hell happened to her. That takes one weapon out of Hardy's propaganda bag. Now, we shut down a terrorist attack, saving the

American people from yet another tragedy. How is this *not* a win-win?"

The group of stiff shirts cracked smiles and bobbed their heads in agreement.

Kate ended the meeting and returned to the Oval Office. Seconds later, her campaign team joined her. All of them grinned from ear to ear.

"It's good to see you're finally in a good mood," McMullan said, sliding his hands into his pants pockets and rocking on his heels.

"Damn right. My campaign was well overdue for a few home runs, don't you think?"

"Yes, ma'am, Madam President. And just in time for the next Republican debates, too, I may add."

Kate eased back in her chair behind her desk. "I can't wait to see that smug son of a bitch's face spin this shit. And you want to know the kicker? Kadir Kahlifa's *twin* brother is the hero in this damn story. Can you fuckin' believe it? Of course, I can't spread that part all over the news, but damn. What are the chances?" She snapped her fingers. "I want to meet him. Oh, and the reporter, too. Someone arrange for Lehane to be invited to next week's fund-raiser. I'll need some photos with her, too."

McMullan hesitated. "Do you think that's wise?"

"Why the hell not?"

"At the moment, she doesn't have any memory of what happened to her—but that could still change. What if—?"

"What if what? We didn't have anything to do with her disappearance." Kate paused and then speared her. "Did we?"

"No—no."

Relieved, she nodded again, but she knew that she could never be too sure. The Pentagon had an annoying habit of only briefing the president on a need-to-know basis and they had an alarming amount of information that they deemed that the president didn't need to know much of. "Good. Then it's settled."

Her campaign team nodded like good bobble-heads.

"There's one more thing," McMullan said. "Are you any closer to settling on a vice president?"

The president sighed and weighed her options again inside of her head. With this latest win, she calculated she had some breathing room from the national security alarmists that threaded through the independent voters, but political victories were extremely temporary. She still needed to shore up those votes. "I have. I think Joseph Chase will be the right fit for my administration."

A genuine smile exploded across McMullan's face. "I'll get all the necessary preparations ready for the announcement."

Everyone filed out of the office, except for Davidson. Given all that had been going on, she realized that they had spent very little time together—and she missed him.

"Lock the door," she told him, already unbuttoning her blouse. Davidson lifted a brow.

"I'm not finished celebrating just yet," she told him.

Davidson rushed to do as he was told before turning back toward his president. "It's about damn time."

<hr/>

Nate Hunter chuckled as he shut off CNN's reporting of a terrorist cell discovered in D.C. Shalisa, settling on the office's couch, glanced at him. "You're not thinking what I'm thinking, are you?"

"You know I am." He shook his head as he picked up the phone and dialed Pierce Spalding's direct line.

"Hello, Nate," Spalding greeted flatly.

"Please tell me this was your grand plan to get rid of President Washington."

After a pause, Spalding said, "It's a temporary setback."

Hunter's laughter rumbled over the line. "Maybe you guys should go back to the minor leagues with your batting average."

"I'll handle it," Spalding promised.

"No. You had your turn. Why don't you sit back and let the new guys on the block take care of it."

"What do you have in mind?"

"Leave it to me." Hunter disconnected the call. He glanced to Shalisa. "Our girl is up."

Shalisa hesitated. "Maybe I should—"

"I can't risk your being recognized, plus, if I know the president, she's going to want to parade our girl around like a trophy. She's perfect."

54

Kadir woke up in his bedroom with a pounding headache. After blinking several times, he rolled his head against an incredibly soft pillow and then smiled at a familiar face. "Hey, you."

Abrianna lifted her head and smiled. "Hey, baby." She moved over and sat down on a corner of the bed. "Welcome back." She leaned over and pressed a kiss against his forehead.

His forehead wrinkled. "What did I miss?"

"A lot, I'm afraid. For starters, your brother is a CIA agent." She brushed locks of his hair back with her fingertips. "And apparently, Shawn and I disrupted a secret terrorist cell by accident."

"Accident?"

She flashed a smile. "That's my story and I'm sticking to it."

"It's all right, though," Baasim spoke up from the doorway. "I believe we rounded up most of the major players."

Abrianna's gaze sliced toward her future brother-in-law. She lifted a brow at seeing his clean-shaven face. "I'm so sorry. I didn't know."

"Clearly." He smirked. "But don't worry, you made up for it when you saved my ass. I still don't understand how you do what you do. You abilities are remarkable."

"Abilities," she sneered. "They're more like a curse."

"Or a blessing," Baasim countered. "It's all in how you view things, so why not look on the positive side?"

"That's what I keep telling her." Kadir squeezed her hand.

Abrianna studied Baasim like it was the first time she saw him. Maybe he wasn't so bad after all. "I'll take that into consideration."

Baasim winked. "I'll give you guys some privacy." He pushed himself from the doorframe and walked away.

Abrianna's gaze returned to Kadir. "Are you mad?"

"Not in the slightest. I'm just happy you're safe." Kadir cupped her face. "You're precious to me. We're going to have to work harder on communicating. And I promise that I'm going to listen to you from now on—even when it involves my own family members."

"But I was wrong."

Kadir sat up and pulled the covers back. "Doesn't matter. I'm going to be wrong sometimes, too. The point is to *listen.*"

"Does that mean that you still want to marry me?"

Kadir leaned over again and kissed her solidly on the lips. "You damn right."

At the knock on the door, Kadir's and Abrianna's lips pulled apart.

Daishan smiled sheepishly. "Sorry to interrupt," she said. "Baasim told me that you were awake."

Abrianna smiled through her discomfort.

"Bree, can I speak with you . . . alone?"

Kadir hesitated.

Abrianna squeezed his hand to let him know that it was all right. "Sure."

"I'll be right here if either of you needs anything." Kadir gave his mother a pleading look for her to be on her best behavior.

Abrianna followed Daishan to the next bedroom.

Daishan's smile expanded. "I owe you an apology," she started.

Abrianna's brows jumped. "You do?"

She nodded as she walked over to the bed. "If it's possible. I'd like it if we could start over. I didn't really give you a real chance—and I want to change that."

Abrianna's lips curved into a smile. "Yeah? I would like that, too."

"Oh thank you." Daishan threw her arms around Abrianna and squeezed her tight. "You won't regret it. I promise. And . . . you can have what kind of wedding you want. I'm just happy to be gaining a wonderful daughter."

Abrianna felt as if she'd been sucked into the Twilight Zone, but she loved it. "Thank you. I can't tell you how much that means to me."

There was another knock on the door.

Abrianna looked up to see Shawn, Draya, Julian, and Tivonté peeking into the room.

"C'mon in, guys."

Her friends rushed inside and threw their arms around Abrianna. It was officially a celebration. The original team was back together again.

⤙⬥⤚

Castillo led Abrianna up the steps to Dinah Lehane's townhouse. "Now, I'm warning you, Tomi . . . isn't exactly herself."

Abrianna frowned. "You keep saying that. What do you mean?"

"I'm not sure what I mean, but you'll see." Castillo rang the doorbell.

A few seconds later, Dinah answered the door lit up, smiling. "Ah, more guests. Please, come in." She stepped back and allowed the two women to enter.

Abrianna leaped back when a large German shepherd trotted toward her. "Whoa."

"Oh, don't worry. He doesn't bite," Dinah assured them.

Abrianna kept her distance.

"Tomi is in the living room. Can I get you ladies something to drink?"

"No, I'm good," Abrianna answered.

Castillo requested some water before they were led to the next room. Both she and Abrianna stopped in their tracks when they saw Tomi's other guest.

"Shalisa."

Standing tall and composed, Shalisa calmly turned toward the ladies. "Lieutenant Castillo . . . Abrianna."

"I don't understand," Abrianna said, swinging her gaze between Shalisa and Tomi.

"Don't you?" Shalisa questioned.

"But you're dead."

Shalisa laughed. "I've heard that you've died a few times yourself. An interesting gift that Dr. Avery has blessed us with, wouldn't you say?"

"Who are you working for?" Castillo cut to the chase.

Tomi finally spoke up. "C'mon, ladies. Let's not fight."

"Who's fighting?" Castillo challenged. "I think it's a fair question."

Shalisa's smile tightened. "Well, I'm certainly not working for the people who tried to kill you that night on the side of the road."

"So, that was you."

"I just happened to be at the right place at the right time," Shalisa said. "You're welcome."

"But you do work for someone?" Abrianna pressed.

"I do," Shalisa acknowledged. "You can come and work for them, too, if you'd like."

"Is it ITCS?" Castillo asked.

Dinah returned to the living room with Castillo's bottled water and Shalisa's iced tea. "Can I get you ladies anything else?"

"No, we're good, Mom," Tomi told her.

Dinah gave everyone a final smile and then left the women alone to talk.

Castillo folded her arms. "Well?"

"Yes," Shalisa answered boldly. "I work for ITCS. They've been good to me."

"What exactly do you do for them?"

"I help them with their research and development for their enhanced soldiers. They've helped me manage the many bad side-effects of Dr. Avery's sloppy research."

"Like what?" Abrianna asked.

Shalisa reached into her jacket and removed an inhaler. "Like how to control the buzzing in my head without drugs." She handed the inhaler to Abrianna. "One spritz last approximately thirty-six hours."

"You're shitting me."

"I wouldn't do that," Shalisa said. "Try it."

Abrianna looked at the inhaler.

"Go ahead. It's a new can."

"What the hell?" Abrianna took a quick spritz, and immediately, the world became a lot quieter. "Wow."

"Awesome, huh? Plus, that also speeds up the healing process. You're usually knocked out, what—three days on average? One hit of that and you'll wake up in anywhere from twenty minutes to an hour."

"And I have to work for them to get this stuff?"

"Probably." Then Shalisa's grin expanded. "But I'd imagine that with the kind of money you just inherited, you could get what's in that can reproduced."

Abrianna smiled. "I like your thinking."

Shalisa sighed. "Look, we're not going to kidnap you or make you do anything you don't want to do. ITCS isn't T4S. They aren't evil."

"Well, that's good to know," Abrianna said. "But I think it's a firm no for me."

Shalisa nodded. "Well, if you ever change your mind, you now know where to find me."

Abrianna glanced at Tomi. "Are you thinking about working for them?"

Tomi laughed. "I already have a job—that's if the *Washington Post* still wants me. Maybe I can pitch covering the president's campaign fund-raiser since the White House called this morning."

Abrianna smirked. "I guess it's your turn to be paraded in front of the cameras."

"Excuse me?" Tomi asked.

"You'll see what I mean when you get there," Abrianna assured her. She and Castillo stayed at the Lehanes' place a while longer. When the conversation finally died out, Abrianna requested to speak with Tomi privately about the unfinished business between them.

"I'm sorry," Tomi said before Abrianna could bring it up. "About Marion. I know you blame me for what happened to her, and I want you to know that it was never my intention to cause any harm to her. I was . . . just doing my job. And I *did* try to give you a heads-up."

Abrianna nodded. "I know. Kadir made me see that. I was mad at myself for a whole lot of things that went on between Marion and me. I redirected it at you—because I wasn't ready to hold up a mirror. I'm sorry, too."

"Yeah?" Tomi smiled. "Does that mean we're friends?"

Abrianna allowed her wall to come down. "We're . . . getting there."

"That's good enough for me."

The women exchanged hugs.

Later, Castillo and Abrianna left the Lehanes' home. As they walked to the car, Castillo asked, "So what did you think?"

Abrianna shrugged. "She seems fine to me."

Castillo frowned. "Did you happen to, um, you know . . . read her mind?"

Abrianna blinked. "I couldn't—I used that inhaler."

Castillo glanced back up at the townhouse. "I wonder if that was deliberate."

"I thought I had trust issues." Abrianna shook her head and opened the car door. "C'mon. Let's go."

55

On the day of her D.C. fund-raiser, President Kate Washington enjoyed a six-point lead in six out of eight respected political polls. She arrived at a waterfront Hamptons estate with the first gentleman on her arm. Despite his hatred of the political scene, he played his role to the hilt, smiling and laughing at stale jokes while likely counting down the minutes until he could return to his male lover's arms when it was over.

The moment Kate entered the ballroom, McMullan extracted her from her husband and pulled her across the room so that she could shake the right hands and kiss all the right asses. As a result, the donations headed toward a new record. With Washington and Hardy headed toward their first head-to-head debate in the coming week, Washington constantly reminded herself to mix some caution in with her confidence. After all, Governor Hardy may not have had the polls on his side, but he certainly had a grass-roots movement that had a palpable energy that was hard for the political elite to ignore.

Before Kate knew it, it was showtime, and she took the podium while her guests started their evening meals. Her speech wasn't much different from her daily rally speeches, but she made it clear that she was a Wall Street–friendly democrat who wasn't married to prison reform or strengthening unions. Her speech ended to thunderous applause, and then once again, she worked the room.

"Madam President, I'd like to introduce you to Ms. Tomi Lehane," McMullan said, ushering the reporter closer.

The president's face lit up. "Ah, Ms. Lehane, a pleasure to finally meet you." She extended her hand and then turned toward her good side so that her photographer would capture a great picture of the two of them.

"The pleasure is all mine," Tomi greeted in a polite monotone.

A shiver raced up Kate's spine as she immediately noted that something seemed a bit off about the woman; but just as quickly, Kate remembered what the woman had likely gone through these past few months.

"Well, we're all excited to have you back at the *Washington Post*, speaking truth to power."

"It's definitely great to be back," Tomi assured her.

Before the moment turned awkward, the women parted, and the president went off to shake someone else's hand.

Nate Hunter found his way over to Tomi and whispered a code word. In an instant, the light in Tomi's eyes died and programmed orders downloaded. She drifted away from Hunter and tracked the president across the room.

President Washington was in the middle of laughing at a bad joke from the president of Chase Bank when suddenly she couldn't find her breath.

"Madam President, are you all right?" Mr. Diamond asked.

The small circle looked at the president oddly until she dropped her champagne and clawed at her neck.

"She can't breathe," someone announced.

Chaos ensued, involving the Secret Service. The president's doctor tried everything he could to get Kate to draw a breath, but nothing worked.

Across the room, Tomi kept her focus on the president's neck until her eyes rolled to the back of her head and she went completely limp and she hit the floor.

"Oh my God. The president is dead. She's dead!"

Nate Hunter returned to Tomi's side and whispered, "Nice job. It's time for you to leave."

Without a word, Tomi turned and left the private fund-raiser without saying another word to anyone. After she climbed into the back of a private car, she rode to her mother's home.

"Oh, you're home so early," Dinah said, surprised.

Rocky barked, breaking Tomi's trance.

"When I heard the news, I thought you'd be out late covering the story."

Confused, Tomi blinked. "Covering what story?"

"Why the president. It's all over the news. She's dead."

"What?" Tomi rushed into the living room, where CNN blasted from the television. She couldn't believe her eyes.

Dinah shook her head. "Oh dear. You must have left before it happened."

Tomi stared and couldn't shake a bad feeling. "What have I done?"

Epilogue

President Beauregard Hardy took to the podium before the Capitol, placed left hand on the Bible, and raised his right hand. After he was sworn in, an exuberant cheer went up. Smiling, Hardy turned to deliver his inaugural address.

"We, the citizens of America, are now joined in a great national effort to rebuild our country and restore its promise for all of our people . . ."

———※◆※———

Abrianna and Kadir watched the new president of the United States from halfway around the world in Nice, France. Neither one could believe this man was the choice of the American people—but what choice did they have? When President Washington died unexpectedly at a campaign fund-raiser, the Democrats ran her recently announced vice president on the ticket. But the party took a major hit when Ghost dropped his operation research, linking President Washington to Chief Justice Katherine Sanders's death.

Governor Hardy seized on the information and used it to indict the entire Democratic Party—and won. Hardy's inaugural speech echoed the tone and tenor of his divisive campaign that swept him into office. He was a blunt populist, and it was clear that he intended to govern that way.

Abrianna cuddled underneath Kadir's arm in their honeymoon suite. "What do you think about living here for the next four years?"

Kadir weighed the question.

"Eight years if he's re-elected."

Kadir chuckled and kissed the top of her head. "It's tempting—but you know what? I think I'd miss the action."

Abrianna thought it over, too. "Yeah. Me too."

Don't miss a minute of
The Parker Crime series
CONSPIRACY
COLLUSION
COLLATERAL
Available now from
De'nesha Diamond
And
Dafina Books
Wherever books are sold